MUSIC
AND SOME
HIGHLY MUSICAL PEOPLE:

CONTAINING BRIEF CHAPTERS ON

I. A DESCRIPTION OF MUSIC.   II. THE MUSIC OF NATURE.
III. A GLANCE AT THE HISTORY OF MUSIC.
IV. THE POWER, BEAUTY, AND USES OF MUSIC.

FOLLOWING WHICH ARE GIVEN SKETCHES OF THE LIVES OF

REMARKABLE MUSICIANS OF THE COLORED RACE.

With Portraits,

AND AN APPENDIX CONTAINING COPIES OF MUSIC COMPOSED BY COLORED MEN.

BY

JAMES M. TROTTER.

" A man should hear a little music, read a little poetry, and see a fine picture, every day of his life, in order that worldly cares may not obliterate the sense of the beautiful which God has implanted in the human soul." — GOETHE.

" 'Tis thine to merit, mine to record." — HOMER.

FIFTH THOUSAND.

BOSTON:
LEE AND SHEPARD, PUBLISHERS.
NEW YORK:
CHARLES T. DILLINGHAM.
1881.

JOHNSON REPRINT CORPORATION   JOHNSON REPRINT COMPANY LTD.
111 Fifth Avenue, New York, N.Y. 10003   Berkeley Square House, London, W. 1

THE BASIC AFRO-AMERICAN REPRINT LIBRARY
Books on the history, culture, and
social environment of Afro-Americans
Selected by Clarence L. Holte

COPYRIGHT, 1878,
BY JAMES M. TROTTER.

First reprinting, 1968, Johnson Reprint Corporation

Printed in the United States of America

PREFACE.

The purposes of this volume will be so very apparent to even the most casual observer, as to render an extended explanation here unnecessary. The author will therefore only say, that he has endeavored faithfully to perform what he was convinced was a much-needed service, not so much, perhaps, to the cause of music itself, as to some of its noblest devotees and the race to which the latter belong.

The inseparable relationship existing between music and its worthy exponents gives, it is believed, full showing of propriety to the course hereinafter pursued, — that of mingling the praises of both. But, in truth, there was little need to speak in praise of music. Its tones of melody and harmony require only to be heard in order to awaken in the breast emotions the most delightful. And yet who can speak at all of an agency so charming in other than words of warmest praise? Again : if music be a thing of such consummate beauty, what else can be done but to tender an offering of praise, and even of gratitude, to those, who, by the invention of most pleasing combinations of tones, melodies, and harmonies, or by great skill in vocal or instrumental performance, so signally help us to the fullest understanding and enjoyment of it?

As will be seen by a reference to the introductory chapters, in which the subject of music is separately considered, an attempt has been made not only to form by them a proper setting for the personal sketches that follow, but also to render the book entertaining to lovers of the art in general.

While grouping, as has here been done, the musical celebrities of a single race; while gathering from near and far these many fragments of musical history, and recording them in one book, — the writer yet earnestly disavows all motives of a distinctively clannish nature. But the haze of complexional prejudice has so much obscured the vision of many persons, that they cannot see (at least, there are many who affect not to see) that musical faculties, and power for their *artistic* development, are not in the exclusive possession of the fairer-skinned race, but are alike the beneficent gifts of the Creator to all his children. Besides, there are some well-meaning persons who have formed, for lack of the information which is here afforded, erroneous and unfavorable estimates of the art-capabilities of the colored race. In the hope, then, of contributing to the formation of a more just opinion, of inducing a cheerful admission of its existence, and of aiding to establish between both races relations of mutual respect and good feeling; of inspiring the people most concerned (if that be necessary) with a greater pride in their own achievements, and confidence in their own resources, as a basis for other and even greater acquirements, as a landmark, a partial guide, for a future and better chronicler; and, finally, as a sincere tribute to the winning power, the noble beauty, of music, a contemplation of whose own divine harmony should ever serve to promote harmony between man and man, — with these purposes in view, this humble volume is hopefully issued.

THE AUTHOR.

CONTENTS.

	PAGE
A Description of Music	7–11
The Music of Nature	12–21
A Glance at the History of Music	22–50
The Beauty, Power, and Uses of Music	51–65
Elizabeth Taylor Greenfield (the "Black Swan")	66–87
The Luca Family	88–105
Henry F. Williams	106–113
Justin Holland	114–130
Thomas J. Bowers (the "American Mario")	131–137
James Gloucester Demarest	138–140
Thomas Greene Bethune ("Blind Tom")	141–159
The Hyers Sisters	160–179
Frederick Elliot Lewis	180–191
Nellie E. Brown	192–208
Samuel W. Jamieson	209–218
Joseph White (preceded by a brief account of the Violin, pp. 219–223)	224–240
The Colored American Opera Company	241–252
The Jubilee Singers of Fisk University	253–269
The Georgia Minstrels	270–282

PART SECOND.

Introduction	285–288
Rachel M. Washington	288–290
James Caseras	300
John T. Douglass	301
Walter F. Craig	301
W'lliam Appo	302
William Brady	302–303
Peter P. O'Fake	304–306
Frank Johnson, and his Famous Military Band and Orchestra	306–309
Joseph G. Anderson	308–309
Madam Brown	309
Sarah Sedgewick Bowers	309–310
John Moore	310–311

Contents.

	PAGE
SAMUEL LUCAS	312–313
WILLIAM H. STARR	314
G. H. W. STEWART	330
THE LAMBERT FAMILY	338–340
EDMUND DÉDÉ	340–341
BASILE BARÉS	341
SAMUEL SNAER	341–343
PROF. A. P. WILLIAMS	343
E. V. MACARTY	343–344
MAURICE J. B. DOUBLET	344–345
DENNIS AUGUSTE	345
THE DUPRÉ FAMILY	347–348
CHARLES MARTINEZ	348
THOMAS MARTIN	349

OTHER MUSICAL PEOPLE OF —

PORTLAND (ME.)	300
BOSTON	288–298
WORCESTER	300
NEW YORK	301–304
NEWARK	306
PHILADELPHIA	306–311
PITTSBURGH	311
CLEVELAND	311–312
WASHINGTON (O.)	312–313
CHILLICOTHE (O.)	313–316
CINCINNATI	316–321
CHICAGO	321–323
THE MUSIC OF THE SOUTH	324–329
BALTIMORE	329–330
LOUISVILLE	330
ST. LOUIS	330
HELENA	330
MEMPHIS	331
NASHVILLE	331
NEW ORLEANS	333–353

ILLUSTRATIONS.

1. ELIZABETH TAYLOR GREENFIELD.
2. THE LUCA FAMILY.
3. HENRY F. WILLIAMS.
4. JUSTIN HOLLAND.
5. THOMAS J. BOWERS.
6. THOMAS GREENE BETHUNE.
7. THE HYERS SISTERS.
8. FREDERICK ELLIOT LEWIS.
9. NELLIE E. BROWN.
10. SAMUEL W. JAMIESON.
11. JOSEPH WHITE.
12. FISK UNIVERSITY.

MUSIC AND SOME HIGHLY MUSICAL PEOPLE.

I.

A DESCRIPTION OF MUSIC.

"In the storm, in the smoke, in the fight, I come
To help thee, dear, with my fife and my drum.
My name is Music: and, when the bell
Rings for the dead men, I rule the knell;
And, whenever the mariner wrecked through the **blast**
Hears the fog-bell sound, it was I who passed.
The poet hath told you how I, a young maid,
Came fresh from the gods to the myrtle shade;
And thence, by a power divine, I stole
To where the waters of the Mincius roll;
Then down by Clitumnus and Arno's vale
I wandered, passionate and pale,
Until I found me at sacred Rome,
Where one of the Medici gave me a home.
Leo — great Leo! — he worshipped me,
And the Vatican stairs for my feet were free.
And, now I am come to your glorious land,
Give me good greeting with open hand.
Remember Beethoven, — I gave him his art, —
And Sebastian Bach, and superb Mozart:
Join *those* in my worship; and, when you go
Wherever their mighty organs blow,
Hear in them heaven's trumpets to men below."

T. W. PARSONS.

WHAT is music? Quite easy is it to answer after the manner of the dictionaries, and say, " Music is (1) a number of sounds following each other in a natural, pleasing manner; (2) the science of harmonious sounds; and (3) the art of so combining them as to please the ear." These are, however, only brief, cold, and arbitrary definitions: music is far more than as thus defined. Indeed, to go no farther in the description of this really sublime manifestation of the beautiful would be to very inadequately express its manifold meanings, its helpful, delightful uses. And yet the impressions made upon the mind and the depth of feeling awakened in the heart by music are such as to render only a partial (a far from satisfying one) description of the same possible, even to those most skilful and eloquent in the use of language; for, in fact, ordinary language, after exhausting all of its many resources in portraying the mind's conceptions, in depicting the heart's finer, deeper feelings, reveals, after all, its poverty, when sought to describe effects so entrancing, and emotions so deep-reaching, as those produced by music. No: the latter must be heard, it must be felt, its sweetly thrilling symphonies must touch the heart and fill the senses, in order that it may be, in its fulness, appreciated; for then it is that music is expressed in a language of most subtle power, — a language all its own, and universal, bearing with it ever an exquisitely touching pathos and sweetness that all mankind may feel.

And so I may not hope to bring here to the reader's mind more than a slight conception of what music is. Nor does he stand in need of any labored effort to teach him the nature and power, the beneficent attributes, of this beautiful art. With his own soul attuned to all the delightful sounds of melody and harmony that everywhere about him, in nature and in art, he constantly hears, the reader requires no great length of words in explanation of that which he so deeply feels, and therefore already understands. Nevertheless, a due regard for the laws of unity, as well as a sincere wish to make this volume, in all its departments, speak the befitting words of tribute to the love-inspiring art of which it aims to treat, — words which, although they may not have the merit of affording great instruction, may at least have that of furnishing to the reader some degree of pleasure, — these are the motives that must serve as an excuse for the little that follows.

I have sometimes thought that only the elevated and elegant language of poetry should be employed in describing music : for music is poetry, and poetry is music ; that is, in many of their characteristics they are one and the same. But, to put this idea in another form, let us say that Music is the beautiful sister of Poetry, that other soul-expressing medium ; and who would create the latter must commune with the former, and be able to bring to his uses the sweet and finishing graces of her rhythmic forms. In early times, the qualities of the poet and musician were generally actually united in the same person. The poet usually set to music, and in most instances sang, his effusions. Nor to this day have the

> "Poets, who on earth have made us heirs
> Of truth and pure delight by heavenly lays,"

ceased to sing, in bewitching verse, the noble qualities of music.

I have said that music speaks a language all its own, and one that is universal. Bring together a representa tion of all the nations of the earth, in which body there shall be a very Babel of tongues. All will be confusion until the all-penetrating, the all-thrilling voice of music is heard. At once, silence reigns; each ear quickly catches and recognizes the delicious sounds. The language of each one in the concourse may be different: but with "music's golden tongue" all are alike innately acquainted; each heart beats in sympathy with the delightful, absorbing tones of melody; and all seem members of one nation.

Again: music may be called that strangely peculiar form of the beautiful, whose presence seems, indeed is, appropriate on occasions the most diverse in character. Its aid is sought alike to add to the joys of festive scenes, to soothe and elevate the heart on occasions of mourning, and to enhance the solemnity, the excellence, of divine worship.

The poet Collins, aptly associating music with the good and beautiful, calls it the "heavenly maid."

Martin Luther, himself a musical composer and performer of merit, paused in his great work of religious reform to declare, "I verily think, and am not ashamed to say, that, next to divinity, no art is comparable to music." And Disraeli utters this noble thought: "Were it not for music, we might in these days say the beautiful is dead."

"Touching musical harmony, whether by instrument or by voice, it being but of high and low in sounds a proportionable disposition, such, notwithstanding, is the force thereof, and so pleasing effects it hath in that part of man which is most divine, that some have thereby been induced to think that the soul itself is or hath in it harmony: a thing which delighteth all ages, and beseemeth all states; a thing as seasonable in grief as in joy; as decent being added unto actions of greatest weight and solemnity as being used when men most sequester themselves from action. The reason hereof is an admirable facility which music hath to express and represent to the mind, more inwardly than any other sensible means, the very steps and inflections of every way, the turns and varieties of all passion whereunto the mind is subject."[1]

"I would fain know what music is. I seek it as a man seeks eternal wisdom. Yesterday evening I walked, late in the moonlight, in the beautiful avenue of lime-trees on the bank of the Rhine; and I heard a tapping noise and soft singing. At the door of a cottage, under the blooming lime-tree, sat a mother and her twin-babies: the one lay at her breast, the other in a cradle, which she rocked with her foot, keeping time to her singing. In the very germ, then, when the first trace of life begins to stir, music is the nurse of the soul: it murmurs in the ear, and the child sleeps; the tones are the companions of his dreams; they are the world in which he lives. He has nothing; the babe, although cradled in his mother's arms, is alone in the spirit: but tones find entrance into the half-conscious soul, and nourish it as earth nourishes the life of plants."[2]

[1] Hooker.   [2] Bertini.

II.

THE MUSIC OF NATURE.

> "The lark sings loud, and the throstle's song
> Is heard from the depths of the hawthorn dale;
> And the rush of the streamlet the vales among
> Doth blend with the sighs of the whispering gale."
>
> MATIN AND EVENING SONGS.

TO the inventive genius of man must, of course, be attributed the present developments, and the beautiful, diversified forms, existing in musical art. But, before man was, the great Author of harmony had created what may be called the music of Nature.

Afterwards, the human ear, penetrated by sounds of melody issuing from wind, wave, or bird, the rapt mind in strange and pleasing wonder contemplating the new and charming harmonies, — then it was that man received his first impressions, and took his first lessons in delightful symphony.

Take from man all creative and performing power in music, leaving him only the ear to catch and the mind to comprehend the sounds, and there would still be left to him God's own music, — the music of Nature, which, springing as it did from eternity, shall last throughout eternity.

Passing what must appear to human comprehension as vague (an attempt at the contemplation of which would be without profit in this connection), and what has been called the "music of the spheres,"[1] we may proceed to briefly touch upon those forms of natural music which are ever within our hearing, and which constantly afford us pleasure.

First let us go forth into the summer woods. The eye takes in the charming prospect,— the trees dressed in beautiful green; the "grassy carpet," parted ever and anon by a gliding, gurgling brooklet; the wild flower peeping up near the feet; a landscape of even surface, or at times pleasingly undulated. The atmosphere is freighted with a delightful fragrance; and from rustling bough, from warbling bird, from rippling brook, and from the joyous hum of insects almost innumerable,

> "The air is full of noises, sounds, and sweet airs,
> That give delight, and hurt not."

All these, the beauties of animate and inanimate Nature, pleasantly affect the senses. But the chief influence there— the crowning glory of the groves — is the songs, the charming music of the birds, as they warble from tree to tree, untrammelled by the forms of art, their sweetest melodies. How often do their lightsome, inspiring carollings ring out upon the morning air, persuasively calling us from our couches to listen in delight to Nature's minstrelsy! "After man," says a writer, "the birds occupy the highest rank in Nature's concerts. They make the woods, the gardens, and the fields resound with their merry warbles. Their warbled 'shake' has never been equalled by human gifts of voice, nor by art."

[1] Reference is supposed to be made to this in the Book of Job, in these words: "When the morning stars sang together, and all the sons of God shouted for joy."

Indeed, it has been found that many of the songs of birds are sung in certain of the keys; while a learned musical writer has produced a book in which are printed many samples of the music often sung by birds. In very recent times it is stated, too, that birds have been taught to sing some of the popular tunes of the day; this being accomplished by placing a bird in a room for a while, allowing it to hear no other bird, and only the tune to be learned. Professor Brown of Aiken, S.C., has mocking-birds which he has taught to sing such songs as "The Star-spangled Banner" and "Yankee Doodle." These birds were to be taken to the Centennial Exhibition, to there exhibit their marvellous skill.

A writer in "The Monthly Reader" thus speaks of that pretty singer the bullfinch: —

"I heard a lady cry out to a little bird in a cage, 'Come, Bully, Bully, sweet little Bully Bullfinch, please give us just one more tune.'

"And then, to my surprise, the little bird whistled the tune of 'Yankee Doodle' as well as I could have done it myself.

"The lady then told me about the bird. It was a bullfinch. She had bought it in the little town of Fulda, in Germany, where there are schools for teaching these birds to sing.

"When a bullfinch has learned to sing two or three tunes, he is worth from forty to sixty dollars; for he will bring that price in London or Boston or New York.

"To teach them, the birds are put in classes of about six each, and kept for a time in a dark room. Here, when their food is given them, they are made to hear music. And so, when they have had their food, or when they want more food, they will sing, and try to sing a tune like that they have just heard; for perhaps they think it has something to do with what they eat."

But as, in presenting these examples of the musical teachableness of the "feathered songsters," I am entering the domain of music as an art, I will not further digress. Certain it is, too, that these delightful musicians of Nature do not require the aid of the skill of man; nor is it desirable, for the sake of musical effect at least, that their own wild, free, and glad-hearted warblings should be changed. They are better as they are, affording as they do a pleasing contrast, and adding freshness and variety to the many other forms of music. Some one, dwelling upon the charming beauty of bird-music, has expressed in words of very excusable rapture the following unique wish: —

> "Oh! had I but the power
> To set the proper words
> To all your glorious melodies,
> My sweet-voiced birds,
>
> When words and dainty music
> Would each to each belong,
> Together we might give the world
> A *perfect* song."

But I need not refer at greater length to these sweet harmonists of Nature, since scarce an ear is so dull, and few hearts are so cold, as not to be charmed and cheered by their unceasing, joyous melodies.

It might well be thought that flowers, those "fairy ministers of grace," with their delicately tinted, variegated, perfect hues, that emit, in their sweet, delicious perfumes, what may be called the "breath of heaven," possess in these delightful qualities full enough to instruct and charm mankind. But there is a flower, it seems, that, inviting the aid of the evening zephyr, adds sweet music to its other fascinating beauties. Let the poet Twombly sing of the music-giving —

BLUE HAREBELL.

Have ye ever heard in the twilight dim
    A low, soft strain
That ye fancied a distant vesper-hymn,
    Borne o'er the plain
By the zephyrs that rise on perfumed wing,
When the sun's last glances are glimmering?

Have ye heard that music, with cadence sweet
    And merry peal,
Ring out like the echoes of fairy feet
    O'er flowers that steal?

The source of that whispering strain I'll tell;
    For I have listened oft
To the music faint of the blue harebell
    In the gloaming soft:
'Tis the gay fairy-folk the peal who ring,
At even-time, for their banqueting.

And gayly the trembling bells peal out
    With gentle tongue;
While elves and fairies career about
    'Mid dance and song.

It would be tedious to enumerate and dwell upon all the very numerous music-making agencies of the natural world; and I shall therefore allude only to a few of those not already mentioned.

Many have heard the sounds of waterfalls, and know that from them issues a kind of majestic music, which, to be appreciated, must be heard. Musicians of finely-cultivated ears have studied the tones of waterfalls; and two of them, Messrs. A. and E. Heim, say that a mass of falling water gives

" The chord of C sharp, and also the non-accordant F. When C and D sound louder than the middle note F is heard very fully, as a deep, dull, humming, far-resounding tone, with a strength proportionate to the mass of the falling water. It easily penetrates to a distance at which the other notes are inaudible. The notes C, E, G, F, belong to all rushing water, and in great falls are sometimes in different octaves. Small falls give the same notes one or two octaves higher. In the stronger falls, F is heard the most easily; in the weak ones, C. At the first attempt, C is most readily detected. Persons with musical cultivation, on attempting to sing near rapidly-moving water, naturally use the key of C sharp, or of F sharp if near a great fall."

Somewhat similar to waterfalls in the character of the tunes they produce (being distinguished, however, generally, by a greater softness and more gentle flow) are the waves, that, handsome in form, roll majestically shoreward, greeting the ear with a strange, dirge-like, yet, as it seems to the writer, pleasing harmony.

Here is given a duet between the waves and zephyrs: —

"We sit beneath the dreaming moon,
   And gaze upon the sea:
Our hearts with Nature are in tune;
   List to her minstrelsy.
The waves chant low and soft their song,
   And kiss the rocks in glee;
While zephyrs their sweet lay prolong, —
   Their love-song to the sea."

There is a pretty, delicate music made by the rippling, gurgling brooklet, as its transparent waters glide over its pebbly bottom. And there's the musical seashell. Place it to the ear, and you shall catch, as if in the far distance, the reverberating roll of the billowy ocean as it sings a mighty song. To this the poet Wordsworth very gracefully refers in the following lines: —

> "I have seen
> A curious child, who dwelt upon a tract
> Of inland ground, applying to his ear
> The convolutions of a smooth-lipped shell:
> To which, in silence hushed, his very soul
> Listened intensely, and his countenance soon
> Brightened with joy; for from within were heard
> Murmurings whereby the monitor expressed
> Mysterious union with its native sea."

And an anonymous writer (it does not seem that he had good cause for hiding his name) thus discourses on the music of the sea: —

> "The gray, unresting sea,
>   Adown the bright and belting shore
> Breaking in untold melody,
>   Makes music evermore.
>
> Centuries of vanished time,
>   Since this glad earth's primeval morn,
> Have heard the grand, unpausing chime,
>   Momently new born.
>
> Like as in cloistered piles
>   Rich bursts of massive sounds upswell,
> Ringing along dim-lighted aisles
>   With spirit-trancing spell;
>
> So on the surf-white strand
>   Chants of deep peal the sea-waves raise,
> Like voices from a viewless land
>   Hymning a hymn of praise.
>
> By times, in thunder-notes,
>   The booming billows shoreward surge;
> By times a silver laugh it floats;
>   By times a low, soft dirge.

>   Souls more ennobled grow
>   Listing the worldly anthem rise;
>   Discords are drowned in the great flow
>   Of Nature's harmonies.
>
>   Men change and 'cease to be,'
>   And empires rise and grow and fall;
>   But the weird music of the sea
>   Lives, and outlives them all.
>
>   The mystic song shall last
>   Till time itself no more shall be;
>   Till seas and shores have passed,
>   Lost in eternity."

But the wind is one of Nature's chief musicians. Sometimes singing his own songs, or lending his aid in awaking to musical life the leaves and boughs of the trees; whistling melodies among the reeds; entering the recesses of a hollow column, and causing to issue from thence a pleasing, flute-like sound; blowing his quiet, soothing lays in zephyrs; or rushing around our dwellings, singing his tuneful yet minor refrain, — in these, and in even other ways, does this mighty element of the Creator contribute to the production of melody in the world of nature. A writer in "The Youth's Companion" speaks very entertainingly of "voices in trees." He says, —

"Trees, when played upon by the wind, yield forth a variety of tones. Mrs. Hemans once asked Sir Walter Scott if he had noticed that every tree gives out its peculiar sound. 'Yes,' said he, 'I have; and I think something might be done by the union of poetry and music to imitate those voices, giving a different measure to the oak, the pine, the willow, &c.' The same journal from which we take this anecdote mentions, that in Henry Taylor's drama, 'Edwin the Fair,' there are some pleasing lines, where the wind is feigned to feel the want of a voice, and to woo the trees to give him one.

"He applied to several: but the wanderer rested with the pine, because her voice was constant, soft, and lowly deep; and he welcomed in her a wild memorial of the ocean-cave, his birthplace. There is a fine description of a storm in 'Coningsby,' where a sylvan language is made to swell the diapason of the tempest. 'The wind howled, the branches of the forest stirred, and sent forth sounds like an incantation. Soon might be distinguished the various voices of the mighty trees, as they expressed their terror or their agony. The oak roared, the beech shrieked, the elm sent forth its long, deep groan; while ever and anon, amid a momentary pause, the passion of the ash was heard in moans of thrilling anguish.'"

I shall close this chapter on the music of Nature by appending a beautiful reference to what has been called "the music of the spheres." The lines form, as well, an elegant and elevated description of and tribute to music in general. I regret that the author's name cannot be given.

> "The Father spake: in grand reverberations
> Through space rolled on the mighty music-tide;
> While to its low, majestic modulations
> The clouds of chaos slowly swept aside.
>
> The Father spake: a dream, that had been lying
> Hushed from eternity in silence there,
> Heard the pure melody, and, low replying,
> Grew to that music in the wondering air, —
>
> Grew to that music, slowly, grandly waking,
> Till, bathed in beauty, it became a world;
> Led by his voice, its spheric pathway taking,
> While glorious clouds their wings around it furled.

Not yet has ceased that sound, his love revealing;
   Though, in response, a universe moves by:
Throughout eternity its echo pealing,
   World after world awakes in glad reply.

And wheresoever in his rich creation
   Sweet music breathes, — in wave, in bird, or soul, —
'Tis but the faint and far reverberation
   Of that great tune to which the planets roll."

III.

A GLANCE AT THE HISTORY OF MUSIC.

> "Thespis, the first professor of our art,
> At country wakes sang ballads from a cart."
> DRYDEN.

MUSIC is as old as the world itself. In some form or other, it has always existed. Ere man learned to give vent to his emotions in tuneful voice, Nature, animate and inanimate, under the hand of the Great Master, sang his praises. Of this we learn in the sacred writings; while all about us, in the songs of birds, the musical sighing of the winds, the fall of waters, and the many forms of the music of Nature, we have palpable evidence of its present existence, and assurances of its most remote antiquity.

It would seem that not long after "God breathed into the nostrils of man the breath of life, and he became a living soul," he learned to express the joys and yearnings of his soul in song first, and then with some sort of musical instrument. And to man it was given, commencing with the early ages, to develop the simple ejaculations or melodies of a praise-giving soul into a beautiful, a noble art, replete at times with harmonic intricacies, and again with melodies grand in their very simplicity; into a beneficent science, divine from its inception, which has ever had as votaries many of earth's greatest minds, and has become a fountain of delight to all mankind.

The history of the music of antiquity — that is, in an art-form — is nearly, if indeed not quite, enveloped in mystery; and it were futile to profess to give an historical presentation of an art from its birth, when documentary evidence of the same is lost.

We may, however, very reasonably suppose of music generally, that it must have been gradually developed, having had its infancy, childhood, and youth; and that it grew slowly into present scientific form with the advance of the centuries.

From all we can gather in regard to the early history of music as a system, it would appear that it had its infancy in ancient Greece; although it is supposed by some that the Grecian method was founded upon that of the still more ancient one of the Egyptians. Dr. Burgh, a learned musical writer states that, of "the time before Christ, music was most cultivated and was most progressive in Greece." The verses of the Greek poet Homer, who was himself a musician, abound in beautiful allusions to and descriptions of this charming science; while in mythology are recounted the wonderful musical achievements of the god Orpheus, who is said to have been so skilled in music that the very rocks and trees followed in his wake of harmony.

The first artificial music of which the Bible speaks was that which was sung or played in praise of the Creator, — sacred music. In fact, this noble quality of the soul was very rarely called into exercise, save in the worship of the Deity, until many centuries had passed. Of music before the Christian era, both vocal and instrumental, the books of the Old Testament often speak.

As to its exact character, we are left to conjecture, being, as before intimated, without materials from which to form a judgment; but, in some form or other, there was, during that period, abundance of what was called music.

The first mention of music, either vocal or instrumental, in the Scriptures, is made in Gen. iv. 21: "Jubal was the father of all such as handle the harp and organ." Jubal was only seventh in descent from Adam; and from this passage it is thought by some that he was the inventor of instrumental music. In the year B.C. 1739, in Gen. xxxi. 27, Laban says to Jacob, "Wherefore didst thou flee away from me, and didst not tell me, that I might have sent thee away with mirth and with songs, with tabret and with harp?" This is the first mention in the Bible of vocal music. King David, who has been called "the sweet singer of Israel," is said to have been a skilful performer on the harp. By his magical touch upon its strings at a certain time, he produced sounds so sweetly soothing as to drive away the "evil spirit" from Saul.

The poet Byron pays an elevated, glowing tribute to this "monarch minstrel" in the following lines:—

> "The harp the monarch minstrel swept,
>   The king of men, the loved of Heaven,
> Which Music hallowed while she wept
>   O'er tones her heart of hearts had given,—
>   Redoubled be her tears; its chords are riven.
>
> It softened men of iron mould;
>   It gave them virtues not their own:
> No ear so dull, no soul so cold,
>   That felt not, fired not, to the tone;
>   Till David's lyre grew mightier than his throne.

It told the triumphs of our King;
  It wafted glory to our God;
It made our gladdened valleys ring,
  The cedars bow, the mountains nod:
  Its sound aspired to heaven, and there abode.

Since then, though heard on earth no more,
  Devotion, and her daughter Love,
Still bid the bursting spirit soar
  To sounds that seem as from above,
  In dreams that day's broad light cannot remove."

And here I append from the First of Chronicles, xiii. 8, a description of the music of the "house of Israel:" "And David and all Israel played before God with all their might, and with singing, and with harps, and with psalteries, and with timbrels, and with cymbals, and with trumpets."

Josephus, the learned Jewish historian, states that the Egyptians had two hundred thousand musicians playing at the dedication of the Temple of Solomon. This structure was of most wonderfully immense dimensions: and it may have been that this enormous body of performers played in *detachments* about the building; otherwise the statement would seem apocryphal.

The Egyptian musical instruments, it appears, were mostly of very rude construction: performance upon them would not now, probably, be tolerated even in circles of the least musical culture.

Of these ancient instruments the Boston "Folio' thus speaks:—

"The Egyptian flute was only a cow's-horn, with three or four holes in it; and their harp, or lyre, had only three strings. The Grecian lyre had only seven strings, and was very small, being held in one hand. The Jewish trumpets that made the walls of

Jericho fall down were only rams'-horns: their flute was the same as the Egyptian. They had no other instrumental music but by percussion, of which the greatest boast was made of the psaltery, — a small triangular harp, or lyre, with wire strings, and struck with an iron needle or stick. Their sackbut was something like a bagpipe; the timbrel was a tambourine; and the dulcimer, a horizontal harp with wire strings, and struck with a stick like the psaltery."

The following interesting and able summary of the history of ancient Roman music is taken from a recent number of "The Vox Humana:"—

"Art love was not a distinguished characteristic of the ancient Romans; and we are not astonished, therefore, to find them borrowing music from Etruria, Greece, and Egypt; originating nothing, and (although the study was pursued by the emperors) never finding any thing higher in its practice than a sensuous gratification.

"In the earliest days of Rome, the inhabitants were exclusively farmers or warriors; and their first temples were raised to Ceres or to Mars.

"The priests of Ceres came originally from Asia Minor, and were called the Arval Brotherhood. Flute-playing was a prominent feature in their rites, and they were all proficient upon that instrument. Their number was limited to twelve.

"The worship of Mars was conducted by the Salian priests, whom Numa summoned to Rome from Etruria. These also used the flute as an accessory to their sacrificial rites. In these primitive days of Rome, much was borrowed from the Etruscans in style and instruments of music.

"The earliest songs of Rome were in praise of Romulus, and told the story of the twin-brothers and the divine origin of the city. They were sung by choruses of boys. Similar songs were sung during meals by the elders, with an accompaniment of flutes; these latter songs being especially directed to the young men, and inciting them to be worthy of the deeds of their ancestors.

"Under the rule of the emperors, all these worthy compositions went to decay, and were replaced by a much more degrading school of music. At no time, however, was music considered a necessary part of the education of Roman youth.

"There existed in the latter days of ancient Rome some music-schools; but the study was far less universally pursued than in Greece at the same epoch. The musical course has been given by Quintilian as follows:—

"Theoretical: first, arithmetic, physics; second, harmony, rhythm, metrics.

"Practical: composition, rhythm, melody, poetry.

"Execution: playing instruments, singing, dramatic action; which makes a rather formidable array, even to modern eyes.

"Among the Roman musical instruments, the flute was the most popular, and essentially national. We have already stated that it was used in the worship of their two chief deities: it was in secular use to a yet greater extent.

"This flute (*tibia*) was hooped with brass bands, and had an immense resonance. It was used by both sexes; but, on public and on most religious occasions, was played by men.

"The frequency with which it was used made the art of playing it a most remunerative one; and the flute-players soon formed themselves into a guild, or protective society. This guild had many privileges accorded to it, and existed for a period of some centuries. The 'Guild of Dionysian Artists' was a society of later date, and was a musical conservatory, academy, and agency, all in one. It flourished greatly under the patronage of various Roman emperors, and for a long time supplied singers and actors to the Roman world.

"Valerius Maximus has given an anecdote which shows how powerful and exacting the guild of flute-players could afford to be.

"They were one day excluded from the Temple of Jupiter, where they had been allowed, by ancient custom, to take their meals; upon which the entire guild left Rome, and went to the village of Tibur near by. This caused great embarrassment: no religious services could be held, and scarce any state ceremony properly conducted. The senate thereupon sent an embassy to induce them to return,—in vain: the angry musicians were inflexible. The wily ambassadors then called the inhabitants of Tibur to their aid, and these pretended to give a great feast to welcome the flute-players. At this feast the musicians were all made very drunk;

and, while asleep from the effects of their liquor, they were bundled into chariots, and driven back to Rome, where all their old privileges were restored, and newer and greater ones added.

"They received the right to give public representations and spectacles in Rome; but at these they were all masked, the reason being their shame at the manner of their inglorious return to the city.

"Flutes were used at funerals; and it appears, at one time, the luxury and pomp of Roman obsequies grew so excessive, that a law was passed limiting the number of flute-players on such occasions to ten.

"Only at one time did the flute disappear from any public worship, and that was when the worship of Bacchus was introduced into Rome. To this rite the kithara was used; but this worship, which was somewhat refined, though jovial, among the Greeks, became among the Romans so debauched and uxorious, that it was soon prohibited by law.

"The flute was used in combination with other instruments at times. Apuleius speaks of a concert of flutes, kitharas, and chorus, and mentions its deliciously sweet effect. It was also used as a pitch-pipe, to give orators a guide in modulating their voices when addressing an assembly: thus Caius Gracchus always on such occasions had a slave behind him, whose duty it was to aid him to commence his orations in a proper pitch, and when his voice sank too low, or became too shrill, to call him to a better intonation by the sounds of the flute.

"Although the flute was the favorite Roman instrument, it was by no means the only one. Trumpets were used to a great extent. A one-toned trumpet, of very loud voice, was used for battle-signals. These were of very large size, usually of brass; and their sound is described as 'terrible.' There was also a smaller (shepherd's) trumpet of mellower tone.

"Another much-used instrument, of different character, was the *sumphonium*, which did not differ materially from the modern bagpipe.

"Instruments of percussion were few, and not indigenous to the Romans: such as were used came from the East, and were chiefly used in the worship of Eastern deities at Rome. When the worship of Bacchus was prohibited, they passed away with that licentious rite. The most complicated instrument of the ancient world appeared in Rome during the first century of our era. It was an *organ*, not, as in the scriptural days, a mere syrinx, or Pan's pipes, but an undoubted organ, somewhat similar in effect to our modern instrument.

"The instrument is said to have been invented by Ctesbius of Alexandria in Egypt, who lived about 250 B. C. It did not appear extensively in Rome, however, until nearly three hundred years later. This organ has given rise to much fruitless discussion. In the field of musical history especially, 'a little' knowledge has proved 'a dangerous thing;' for, where slight descriptions exist of instruments of music, latitude is left for every writer to form his own theory, to fight for it, and denunciate those who differ from it.

"We have seen what a battle was fought over the three little manuscripts of Greek music; what a host of differing opinions were held about the scriptural word 'Selah:' and now, about this hydraulic organ, each writer mounts his hobby-horse, and careers over the field of conjecture. Vitruvius has given a full description of the instrument from personal inspection; but as his technical terms have lost all significance to modern readers, and have been translated in various ways, and as his work contained no diagrams or illustrations of the various parts, it is useless.

"Some writers imagine the organ to have had seven or eight stops, — that is, so many different *kinds* of tones, — which would place them nearly on a par with our own. Others think that they possessed seven or eight *keys;* that is, so many *tones* only. It has been a point of dispute as to what function the water performed in working it. Vitruvius is rather hazy on this point, saying only that it is 'suspended' in the instrument. The water, when the organ was played, was in a state of agitation, as if boiling.

"There are medals still in existence which were awarded to victors in organ contests, on which this instrument is represented with two boys blowing or pumping; but the representation is too small to clear up any doubtful points."

But, without devoting further space to the music that was in vogue prior to the Christian era, I proceed to notice that our first reliable account of it, as a system, commences with the fourth century; at which time St. Ambrose, Bishop of Milan, arranged the sacred chants that bear his name, and which were to be sung in the cathedrals.

In the year 600 St. Gregory improved upon these chants, inventing the scale of eight notes. His system is the basis of our modern music.

From the close of the eleventh to the commencement of the fourteenth century, minstrels, *jongleurs*, or troubadours, were the principal devotees of music. They seem to have been its custodians, so to speak; and to their guild many of the knights belonged. Some of the kings and nobles of the time were also, in a sense, troubadours; such as, for instance, Thibault of Navarre, and William the Ninth of Poitou.

These roving musicians, who generally united the qualities of the poet, the musical composer, and performer, were treated with much favor by princes and all the nobility, and were everywhere warmly welcomed for a long period. It is, however, far from pleasant to have to say that this for a long time noble class of musicians, to whom we owe so much for the preservation unbroken for three hundred years of the chain of musical life, as well indeed, also, as that of general literature, spoiled perhaps by the excessive praises and indulgences accorded them, became at last quite dissolute, and fell from their high position. All royal favors were finally withdrawn from them, and orders for their restriction were issued from the throne.

Mr. B. W. Ball (in that faithful exponent of art, "The Boston Commonwealth") thus expressively sings the story of the ancient troubadour, styling him —

"THE POET OF OLD."

Once the poet wandered,
   With his lyre in hand, —
Wandered, singing, harping,
   On from land to land.

Like a bird he hovered;
   And, where'er he came,
Kindled he each bosom
   With his song to flame.

Careless of the morrow,
   Journeyed he along;
Opened every portal
   To the sound of song.

Suâ sponte heart's-ease
   In his bosom grew:
Happiness as birthright,
   Like the gods, he knew.

All life's haps and changes
   On his chords he rung:
Every thought, emotion,
   In him found a tongue.

Voiced he for the lover
   Passion of his breast;
Feigned he, death to lighten,
   Islands of the Blest.

Up in ether throned he
   Gods, the world to sway, —
Gods to bend and listen
   While their votaries pray.

Soul and sense, enchanted,
   Drank his accents in:
E'en to marble bosoms
   He his way could win.

> From her casement Beauty
> Leaned his song to hear:
> E'en the haughty conqueror
> Bent a willing ear;
>
> For without the poet
> And his epic lay
> Passed his vast existence,
> Whirlwind-like, away, —
>
> Trace nor vestige leaving
> Where his legions trod,
> Which the year effaced not
> From the vernal sod.
>
> Thus the poet wandered
> In a nobler time, —
> Wandered, singing, harping,
> Free of every clime.

During the fourteenth century, music was most cultivated by the people of the Netherlands, who carried the art towards much perfection, producing several fine composers, and furnishing the leading musical instructors for the other parts of Europe. Among some of the ablest musicians of the Netherlands may be mentioned Dufay, Jan of Okenheim, and Josquin Desprès, the latter being the most celebrated of contrapuntists. The Netherland musical supremacy lasted until 1563.

In the year 1400 the claims of music received the recognition of the crown in England, a charter being granted to a regularly formed musical society.

Commencing with the invention of movable type in 1502 (which invention so vastly facilitated the publication and spreading of the thoughts of the composer), and with the Reformation in the sixteenth century, the noble art of music began a new, unimpeded, and brilliant career among the civilized nations of the world. Dating from thence, the steps in the progress of this delightful science can be plainly traced. Unvexed and unfettered by the obscurities that attach to its antique history, we can contemplate with pleasure and profit the wonderful creations and achievements of its devotees.

This I need not attempt here, save in the briefest form; my purpose in preparing this chapter being only to give, as indicated in the title, a glance at the history of music.

To Palestrina, a learned Italian of the sixteenth century, and whose musical genius and industry were most remarkable, is due the greatest homage and gratitude of a music-loving world. Of him an eminent musical writer says, "It is difficult to over-estimate his talent and influence over the art of music in his day. He was regarded as the great reformer of church music. His knowledge of counterpoint, and the elevation and nobility of his style, made his masses and other compositions, of which he wrote a great number, examples for all time of what music should be."

In this century lived many notable composers, nearly all of whom distinguished themselves in the production of madrigal music. To the latter the English people were much devoted. Reading at sight was at that day, even more than now, a common accomplishment among the educated. The English queen Elizabeth was quite fond of music, and was somewhat accomplished in the art, performing upon the lute, virginals, and viol. She often charmed the *attachés* of and visitors to her court by her skilful performances. During her reign, and by her encouragement, the cultivation of this noble art received a new and strong impulse in England, and several composers and performers of high merit lived.

In the year 1540 oratorio was first composed, followed by opera in 1594. During this period, instrumental music began to be used in the churches; and the violin was brought by the celebrated Amati family to a beauty of form, and sweetness of tone, not since excelled.

During the seventeenth century such great composers as Stradella, Scarlatti, Caldara, and Claudio lived; and the different forms of opera were developed in England, France, and Italy.

During the seventeenth and eighteenth centuries the art of music, in its new, rich, and deep developments, as shown in the masterly, wonderful creations of several of the great composers of those periods, and in the scientific performances of many fine instrumentalists, attained a height of surpassing grandeur. Many men of brilliant musical genius and of remarkable industry and perseverance were born; and, with new conceptions of the scope and capabilities of the divine art, they penetrated its innermost depths, and brought to the ears of the music-loving world new and enrapturing forms of harmony. Among these great masters, leaving out those already mentioned, were Handel, Henry Purcell, Bach, Gluck, Haydn, Mozart, Beethoven, and Spontini.

But, before proceeding farther, the writer considers it proper to remark, that to give a extended description of the progress of music during the three last centuries, mentioning in detail the many creations and achievements of those who have become great, nay, in some instances he might say almost immortal, in its sacred domain, would require a volume far beyond the pretensions and intended limits of this one.

Besides, the author confesses that he pauses with feelings of reverence while contemplating the mighty genius and divinely approximating achievements of Haydn, Mozart, Beethoven, Spohr, and Mendelssohn, fearing that his unskilful pen might fail in an attempt at description. Nor does he feel much less embarrassed when he contemplates the accomplishments of those wonderful interpreters of the works of the noble masters, who have, either through the enchanting modulations of their voices or with skilful touch upon instruments, evolved their magic strains. Let an abler pen than mine portray the sublime triumphs of Hasse, Mario, Wachtel, Santley, Whitney; of Albani, Malibran, Lind, Parepa Rosa, Nilsson; of Haupt, Paganini, Vieuxtemps, Ole Bull, Rubinstein, Liszt, and Von Bulow.[1]

The eighteenth century was a most remarkable period for achievements in the composition of orchestral, oratorio, and operatic music, — the same being finely interpreted by vocal and instrumental artists of most wonderful skill.

In referring to some among that galaxy of bright stars, I use, in regard to Mozart, the clear and beautiful language of another:[2] "The great musical composer Mozart was a wonderful instance of precocity, as well as of surpassing genius. He died at the early age of thirty-five, after a career of unrivalled splendor, and

---

[1] For an able criticism of the composers and some of the performers mentioned, the reader is referred to Professor Ritter's very valuable History of Music, in two volumes.

[2] In the Library of Entertaining Knowledge, vol. iii. p. 76.

the production of a succession of works which have left him almost, if not entirely, without an equal among either his predecessors or those who have come after him. Mozart's devotion to his art, and the indefatigable industry with which, notwithstanding his extraordinary powers, he gave himself to its cultivation, may read an instructive lesson, even to far inferior minds, in illustration of the true and only method for the attainment of excellence. From his childhood to the last moment of his life, Mozart was wholly a musician. Even in his earliest years, no pastime had any interest for him in which music was not introduced. His voluminous productions, to enumerate even the titles of which would occupy no little space, are the best attestation of the unceasing diligence of his maturer years. He used, indeed, to compose with surprising rapidity: but he had none of the carelessness of a rapid composer; for so delicate was his sense of the beautiful, that he was never satisfied with any one of his productions until it had received all the perfection he could give it by the most minute and elaborate correction. Ever striving after higher and higher degrees of excellence, and existing only for his art, he scarcely suffered even the visible approach of death to withdraw him for a moment from his beloved studies. During the last moments of his life, though weak in body, he was 'full of the god;' and his application, though indefatigable, could not keep pace with his invention. 'Il Flauta Magico,' 'La Clemenza di Tito,' and a 'Requiem' which he had hardly time to finish, were among his last efforts. The composition of the 'Requiem,' in the decline of his bodily powers, and under great mental excitement, hastened his dissolution. He was seized with repeated fainting·

fits, brought on by his extreme assiduity in writing, in one of which he expired. A few hours before his death took place, he is reported to have said, 'Now I begin to see what might be done in music.'"

Mozart's compositions number over six hundred, and two hundred of them had not until quite recently been printed. He composed fifty-three works for the church, a hundred and eighteen for orchestra, twenty-six operas and cantatas, a hundred and fifty-four songs, forty-nine concertos, sixty-two piano-forte pieces, and seventeen pieces for the organ.

Of Beethoven, Professor F. L. Ritter, in one of his excellent lectures on music, says, "Beethoven's compositions appeal to the whole being of the listener. They captivate the whole soul, and, for the time being, subdue it to an intense, powerful, poetical influence, impressing it with melancholy, sorrow, and sadness, elevating it heavenwards in hopeful joy and inspired happiness."

The following description[1] of Beethoven's last hours on earth, as he was nearing the time

"When all of genius which can perish dies,"

although replete with sadness, is yet a tribute so touchingly beautiful and eloquent as to make it well worthy of insertion here.

"THE LAST MOMENTS OF BEETHOVEN.

"He had but one happy moment in his life, and that moment killed him.

"He lived in poverty, driven into solitude by the contempt of the world, and by the natural bent of a disposition rendered harsh, almost savage, by the injustice of his contemporaries. But he

[1] Anonymously contributed to the Boston Folio for May, 1877.

wrote the sublimest music that ever man or angel dreamed. He spoke to mankind in his divine language, and they disdained to listen to him. He spoke to them as Nature speaks in the celestial harmony of the winds, the waves, the singing of the birds amid the woods. Beethoven was a prophet, and his utterance was from God.

"And yet was his talent so disregarded, that he was destined more than once to suffer the bitterest agony of the poet, the artist, the musician. He doubted his own genius.

"Haydn himself could find for him no better praise than in saying, 'He was a clever pianist.'

"Thus was it said of Géricault, 'He blends his colors well;' and thus of Goethe, 'He has a tolerable style, and he commits no faults in orthography.'

"Beethoven had but one friend, and that friend was Hummel. But poverty and injustice had irritated him, and he was sometimes unjust himself. He quarrelled with Hummel, and for a long time they ceased to meet. To crown his misfortunes, he became completely deaf.

"Then Beethoven retired to Baden, where he lived, isolated and sad, in a small house that scarcely sufficed for his necessities. There his only pleasure was in wandering amid the green alleys of a beautiful forest in the neighborhood of the town. Alone with the birds and the wild flowers, he would then suffer himself to give scope to his genius, to compose his marvellous symphonies, to approach the gates of heaven with melodious accents, and to speak aloud to angels that language which was too beautiful for human ears, and which human ears had failed to comprehend.

"But in the midst of his solitary dreaming a letter arrived, which brought him back, despite himself, to the affairs of the world, where new griefs awaited him.

"A nephew whom he had brought up, and to whom he was attached by the good offices which he had himself performed for the youth, wrote to implore his uncle's presence at Vienna. He had become implicated in some disastrous business, from which his elder relative alone could release him.

"Beethoven set off upon his journey, and, compelled by the necessity of economy, accomplished part of the distance on foot. One evening he stopped before the gate of a small, mean-looking house, and solicited shelter. He had already several leagues to traverse before reaching Vienna, and his strength would not enable him to continue any longer on the road.

"They received him with hospitality: he partook of their supper, and then was installed in the master's chair by the fireside.

"When the table was cleared, the father of the family arose, and opened an old clavecin. The three sons took each a violin, and the mother and daughter occupied themselves in some domestic work.

"The father gave the key-note, and all four began playing with that unity and precision, that innate genius, which is peculiar only to the people of Germany. It seemed that they were deeply interested in what they played; for their whole souls were in the instruments. The two women desisted from their occupation to listen, and their gentle countenances expressed the emotions of their hearts.

"To observe all this was the only share that Beethoven could take in what was passing; for he did not hear a single note. He could only judge of their performance from the movements of the executants, and the fire that animated their features.

"When they had finished they shook each other's hands warmly, as if to congratulate themselves on a community of happiness; and the young girl threw herself weeping into her mother's arms. Then they appeared to consult together: they resumed their instruments; they commenced again. This time their enthusiasm reached its height; their eyes were filled with tears, and the color mounted to their cheeks.

"'My friends,' said Beethoven, 'I am very unhappy that I can take no part in the delight which you experience; for I also love music: but, as you see, I am so deaf that I cannot hear any sound. Let me read this music which produces in you such sweet and lively emotions.'

"He took the paper in his hand: his eyes grew dim, his breath came short and fast; then he dropped the music, and burst into tears.

"These peasants had been playing the allegretto of Beethoven's Symphony in A.

"The whole family surrounded him with signs of curiosity and surprise.

"For some moments his convulsive sobs impeded his utterance; then he raised his head, and said, 'I am Beethoven.'

"And they uncovered their heads, and bent before him in respectful silence. Beethoven extended his hands to them, and they pressed them, kissed, wept over them; for they knew that they had amongst them a man who was greater than a king.

"Beethoven held out his arms, and embraced them all, — the father, the mother, the young girl, and her three brothers.

"All at once he rose up, and, sitting down to the clavecin, signed to the young men to take up their violins, and himself performed the piano part of his *chef-d'œuvre*. The performers were alike inspired: never was music more divine or better executed. Half the night passed away thus, and the peasants listened. Those were the last accents of the swan.

"The father compelled him to accept his own bed; but, during the night, Beethoven was restless and fevered. He rose: he needed air: he went forth with naked feet into the country. All nature was exhaling a majestic harmony; the winds sighing through the branches of the trees, and moaning along the avenues and glades of the wood. He remained some hours wandering thus amid the cool dews of the early morning; but, when he returned to the house, he was seized with an icy chill. They sent to Vienna for a physician. Dropsy on the chest was found to have declared itself; and in two days, despite every care and skill, the doctor said Beethoven must die.

"And, in truth, life was every instant ebbing fast from him.

"As he lay upon his bed, pale and suffering, a man entered. It was Hummel, — Hummel, his old and only friend. He had heard of the illness of Beethoven, and he came to him with succor and money. But it was too late: Beethoven was speechless; and a grateful smile was all that he had to bestow upon his friend.

"Hummel bent towards him, and, by the air of an acoustic instrument, enabled Beethoven to hear a few words of his compassion and regret.

"Beethoven seemed re-animated; his eyes shone: he struggled for utterance, and gasped, 'Is it not true, Hummel, that I have some talent, after all?'

"These were his last words. His eyes grew fixed, his mouth fell open, and his spirit passed away.

"They buried him in the little cemetery of Dobling."

Among the most eminent composers of the present century may be mentioned Auber, Schubert, Rossini Meyerbeer, Mendelssohn, Weber, Verdi, and Wagner.

In "The Contemporary Review" there lately appeared the following beautifully worded tribute to the noble qualities of Mendelssohn:—

"Mendelssohn reigns forever in a sweet wayside temple of his own, full of bright dreams and visions, incense, and ringing songs, and partly is he so sweet, because, unburthened with any sense of a message to utter, a mission to develop, he sings like a child in the valleys of asphodel, weaving bright chaplets of spring flowers for the whole world, looking upon the mystery of grief and pain with wide eyes of sympathy, and at last succumbing to it himself, but not understanding it, with a song of tender surprise upon his lips."

Since the times of the great writers of the eighteenth century, and of the first half of the present one, no new developments or advancements have been made in musical creations.[1] Indeed, it would seem that the time has not yet come for attempts to be made to improve upon the works of those great musical luminaries; for they have left too much that is deep, classical, charmingly beautiful, and soul-satisfying. The musical world has paused, not caring to go farther, to conscientiously study their noble creations, so fruitful in the delights, the soul-elevating influences, which they afford.

But, although no great genius has of late years appeared with newer and greater creations to claim our attention from those of the past, it is gratifying to know that great advancement is being made in a more general musical culture among the people; while the

[1] It would, perhaps, be better at present to except those of Wagner, upon the *surpassing* merits of which the best critics are as yet divided.

number of really great instrumentalists and vocalists is quite large, and is constantly increasing. In these latter respects the present far exceeds the past.[1] In fact, the study of the art of music has begun to be considered a necessity; and ability in its comprehension and performance is now far from being considered as merely an ornamental accomplishment. All this springs from the very nature of this divine art, the mission, so to speak, of which is, to constantly open new fountains of pleasure in the human heart; to cheer, to soothe, and to bless mankind throughout all time.

But, after all, we know not how soon another great musical genius may startle us from our complacent studies of the masters of the past; for we are even now somewhat threatened in this respect by Richard Wagner, the eminent composer of Germany. He is not satisfied with the music of the past nor the present, and points to his own present and prospective creations as samples of what the "music of the future" will be. Just now, musical critics, while generally conceding to him much power as a composer, are divided in opinion as to whether his ideas are to be accepted in their entirety.

Still, who can now tell what the "music of the future" *may* be?

Before closing this chapter on the history of music, I think it highly proper, as a matter of record and of appropriate interest, to refer briefly to the almost wonderful achievements of that brilliant impressario, P. S.

---

[1] It should also be here remarked, that there has been, too, a remarkable improvement made in the construction of most all musical instruments; they having been brought to a nicety and beauty of form and tone probably not dreamed of by the makers of the past.

Gilmore of Boston, who in the year 1869 conceived the idea of having a grand musical festival, the noble objects of which were to celebrate the restoration of peace in the United States, and to quicken and increase the interest felt in music throughout this country, and also the world, by bringing together in a single performance a larger body of most skilful musicians than was ever before attempted. An immense building called "The Coliseum" was constructed for the purposes of the festival, which was to continue five days. On the 15th of June, in the city of Boston, "The National Jubilee and Great Musical Festival" was begun. The number of instruments and performers composing the great orchestra was 1,011; and an organ of immense proportions and power, built expressly for the occasion, was employed. The grand chorus and solo vocalists numbered 1,040. Besides, one hundred anvils (used in the rendering of Verdi's "Anvil Chorus") were played upon by a hundred of the city's firemen in full uniform; while to all this was added a group of cannon, the same being used in the performance of the "Star-spangled Banner." The vast chorus, the orchestra, and all the leading performers (among the latter were Ole Bull, Parepa, and Carl Rosa), were selected from the finest musical people of the country, being accepted only after strict testing by skilful judges. At this great gathering many of the works of the great composers were performed, and only works of real merit had a place on the programme. These were all performed by this vast *ensemble* with a precision and an excellence that were really grand and wonderful. This achievement of Gilmore was considered the most brilliant entertainment of modern times. Of it, it has been truly said, —

"This great event, by the sublimity of its music, held the nation spell-bound. The great volume of song swept through the land like a flood of melody, filling every Christian heart with 'glad tidings of great joy.' It came like a sunburst upon a musical world, shedding light where had been darkness before, and revealing a new sphere of harmony, a fairy-land of promise, and triumphantly realizing greater achievements in the divine art than were hitherto thought possible. It will ever be a memorable epoch in the history of music, a glorious event; and thousands upon thousands are happier for that week of glorious music. The boom of the cannon, the stroke of the bells,[1] the clang of the anvils, the peal of the organ, the harmony of the thousand instruments, the melody of the thousands of voices, the inspiring works of the great masters, the song of the 'Star-spangled Banner,' the cheers of the multitude, the splendor of the spectacle, — the memory of all this is the rich possession of many, and will be ever recalled as the happiest experiences of a lifetime."

The success of the "National Peace Jubilee" was so perfect, and had produced a musical enthusiasm and revival so great, that, in the year 1872, Gilmore, still prolific in startling musical conceptions, projected and carried into execution another festival of the same general character as the first, only that it was far vaster and more daring in its proportions. This one he styled "The World's Peace Jubilee and International Festival." Several times during the week that this great musical festival was held, not less than fifty thousand people were present in the immense Coliseum building. This time the orchestra consisted of two thousand instruments, and the chorus numbered over seventeen hundred voices; while a mighty organ and cannon and anvils were used as before. The great soloists engaged were Mme. Leutner, Johann Strauss, Franz Abt, and

[1] The church-bells of the city were also employed in rendering some of the music.

Bendel. Foreign governments being invited to send representatives from among their best musicians, England sent the Band of the Grenadier Guards; Germany, its great Prussian Band; France, the brilliant French Republic Band. King William of Prussia sent also, as a special compliment, his classical Court Cornet Quartet; and Ireland sent its best band. To this galaxy of star military bands, perhaps the greatest ever assembled, the United States added its own favorite Marine Band of Washington. At this second great and vast assemblage of artists the almost marvellous achievements of the first " Jubilee " were repeated to the utmost delight of many thousands of people, and Gilmore became at once the most brilliant and daring impressario genius of the world.

As before intimated, Wagner is not at all satisfied with pausing where Mozart, Beethoven, and other great composers, left off. He believes that their music can be improved upon. According to his theory, the music of the opera, in the most highly-developed form of the latter, is but an incidental element, the dramatic part being principal. He lately composed a triology — three operas connected as one — with a prologue, the subjects of the dramas being taken from mythology, and forming beautiful fairy tales. To carry to the greatest perfection his views and firmly-held ideas as to what music should be, and as to what he stoutly avers it will be in the future, ne selected from far and near only the best artists for the performance of his opera (these weie subjected to long and careful rehearsals under his own conductorship), and erected at Bayreuth, in Bavaria, a large and beautiful theatre, which, in its minutest details even, was built under his own supervision, and after his own peculiar ideas. It being calculated to show to the highest advantage his conception, that, in the expression of sentiment, music is only secondary, his orchestra of one hundred and ten performers was placed out of sight of the audience during the acting of the opera.

The great "Musical Festival," as it was called, continued three days, the performance of each part of the triology occupying — exclusive of a wait of one hour after each act — from four to five hours.

At these performances the nobility of Germany and other countries, together with the Abbé Liszt, and many others in the higher walks of music, were present. The audiences were immense, brilliant, and exceedingly demonstrative in applause. At the close of the opera, Wagner was called before the curtain, receiving quite an ovation: and in his speech he said, "Now we see what can be done: at last we have a German art."

It is perhaps too early, as yet, to decide that Richard Wagner's ideal will be adopted by the musical world; nor should we be in too much haste to conclude that it will not be. Certainly he has succeeded, at least, in dividing the highest critics of the glorious art; and the history of music shows, as does also that of all art, that what is rejected to-day may be warmly and even rapturously accepted to-morrow.

Of the festival at Bayreuth, Mr. Hazard, musical critic of "The New-York Tribune," writes, "The effect of the music was magnificent beyond all description. It far surpassed all expectation; and the general verdict is that it is a triumph of the new school of music, final and complete."

Of the impression created by one of the parts of the opera, "Rheingold" (Mr. F. A. Schwabe), of "The New·

York Times," says, " Musically considered, it is not significant. It is hopeless, therefore, to look for popularity for the work; at present, at least."

" The agony is over; and the grandest of all operatic conceptions, the musical drama over which Richard Wagner toiled and dreamed for twenty years, has been given to the world in its complete form." [1]

Very recently, Mr. Moncure D. Conway thus expresses his high admiration for the work of Wagner: —

" I am satisfied that the English-speaking world is little aware at present of the immensity and importance of the work Wagner has done for art. Plato declared that the true musician must have poetry and music harmonized in himself; and the world has waited twenty-five hundred years for that combination to appear. Having carefully read the poems all written by himself which Wagner has set to music, or rather which incarnated themselves in music, and costumed themselves in scenery as he wrote them, I venture to affirm that none can so read them without the conviction that their author is a true poet. In the first place, the general conception of his chief operas, taken together, is in the largest sense poetic, and I might even say Homeric. This man has transmitted an entire religion to poetry, and then set it to music. And it is one of the greatest of religions, — what Nature engraved on the heart of our own Teutonic ancestors. It is all there, — its thousand phantasmal years, from the first cowering cry of the Norse savage before the chariot of his storm-god to the last gentle hymn that rose to Freya under her new name of Mary, — all. It is interpreted as a purely human expression; and, I repeat, no man has done so vast and worthy an artistic work in our time."

While America has perhaps produced as yet no *great* composers, it has several of very high merit, such as J. K. Paine, Dudley Buck, and others. In the United States there are many remarkable vocal and instrumental artists, a large number of classical musical clubs and

[1] From a writer in the New-York Herald.

societies; while several of its great vocalists, male and female, accept and decline engagements in Europe. Perhaps no finer orchestra exists anywhere than that of Theodore Thomas of New York; while nearly as high praise may be given to the Mendelssohn and Beethoven Quintette Clubs of Boston, and to others in different parts of the country.

Music is quite generally cultivated in this country; and there are many excellent critics, musical writers, and periodicals devoted to this beautiful and elevating science.

A very startling late American musical invention is the "telephone," a description of the working of which is given below: —

"MUSIC BY TELEGRAPH.

" A most interesting field for the musical student is the progress that is being made in *telegraphing musical sounds*.

" This is done by means of the telephone, which transmits simultaneously several different tones through one wire by means of steel forks made to vibrate at one end of the line, the pulsations passing through the wire independently of each other, and reappearing at the distant station on vibrating reeds.

" Some very interesting tests were made in the Centennial Main Building a few days ago in the presence of about fifty invited guests, among whom were noticed the Emperor and Empress of Brazil, Sir William Thompson, and quite a number of eminent electricians.

" The experiments were of a very interesting and successful character.

" The inventor, Mr. Gray of Chicago, asked his assistant, Mr. Goodridge, to transmit musical sounds, which were received very distinctly amid hearty applause from those present.

"It was the first time that many present had heard 'Home, Sweet Home,' 'My Country, 'tis of Thee,' or 'Old Hundred,' rendered so beautifully by telegraph; and they evidently enjoyed the treat."

By this invention, music played upon a piano-forte or melodeon is reproduced upon a violin attached to the receiving end of the wire at a distance of twenty-four hundred miles.

Another important musical invention (English) is that of the "voice harmonium." Of this Mr. Theo. T. Seward writes, —

> "To all such the invention of which I speak is a matter of deep interest, because in it is practically solved the problem of perfect intonation. It is called the 'voice harmonium,' because the securing of perfect intonation brings the tones much nearer to the quality of the human voice. The instrument has been invented and patented by Mr. Colin Brown of Glasgow, Ewing lecturer on music. By the use of additional reeds and a most ingenious keyboard, he has succeeded in giving each key in *perfect* tune. The 'wolf' is banished altogether, without the privilege of a single growl. I do not need to say that the effect upon the ear is rich, and extremely satisfactory. After listening to it a little while, the tones of a tempered organ sound coarse and harsh. I wish very much that some of our ingenious American instrument-makers could have the opportunity of examining it. It has been publicly exhibited at the South-Kensington Exhibition, before the recent meeting of the British Association, and elsewhere. The highest scientific authorities have pronounced most thoroughly in favor of its 'perfectness, beauty, and simplicity.' Whether the greater complication of the keyboard will interfere seriously with its popular use, remains to be seen."

Mr. Theodore Thomas recently gave an excellent performance of the works of American composers. Among those rendered were compositions by Dudley Buck, A. H. Pease, and William Mason. One of the gems of the evening was a symphonic poem by William H. Foy, entitled "A Day in the Country."

Mr. Thomas's orchestra, noted for placing upon its programmes only works of the highest merit, has recently also presented with much success a new symphony by the talented composer of oratorios, &c., J. K. Paine.

In alluding to the progress of music in the United States, "The Music Trade Review" says, "If the centennial year could disclose all its triumphs, music would shine among its garlands. A hundred years ago was a voiceless void for us compared with the native voices and native workers who now know a sonnet from a saraband."

IV.

THE BEAUTY, POWER, AND USES OF MUSIC.

"The soul lives its best hours when surrounded by melody, and is drawn towards its home, Paradise, dreaming of its hymning seraphs who adore with ecstasies that can find utterance only in song."

"And how can happiness be better expressed than by song or music? And, if the body and mind are both attuned to a true enjoyment of their resources, how much more will the moral nature be refined and educated!"

THE cultivation of the art of music has ever followed closely the progress of civilization; and those nations that have attained to the highest state of the latter have most encouraged the growth, and have been most skilled in the creation and performance, of music. Montesquieu avers that "music is the only one of all the arts that does not corrupt the mind." Confucius said, "Wouldst thou know if a people be well governed, if its laws be good or bad? examine the music it practises." Again: another has quite aptly said that

"Music is one of the greatest educators in the world; and the study of it in its higher departments, such as composition, harmony, and counterpoint, develops the mind as much as the study of mathematics or the languages. It teaches us love, kindness, charity, perseverance, patience, diligence, promptness, and punctuality."

And a writer in "Chambers's Journal" remarks, that

"In society, where education requires a submission to rule, singing belongs to the domain of art; but, in a primitive state, all nations have their songs. Musical rhythm drives away weariness, lessens fatigue, detaches the mind from the painful realities of life, and braces up the courage to meet danger. Soldiers march to their war-songs; the laborer rests, listening to a joyous carol; in the solitary chamber, the needlewoman accompanies her work with some love-ditty; and in divine worship the heart is raised above earthly things by the solemn chant."

Happily for the world, this beautiful art is one, the delightful forms of which nearly all may enjoy, the inspiring, soul-elevating influences of which nearly all may feel. I say, nearly all; because it is a sad truth that there are some persons who have no ear whatever for music, and to whom the harsh, rattling noise of the cart on the stony street affords just as much melody as do the sweetest tones that may issue from a musical instrument. Again: there are those, who, although possessing to some extent a faculty for musical discernment, are yet so much governed by what is called a sense of the "practical" in life as to avoid all opportunity for the enjoyment of melody, considering such indulgence as a waste of precious time. It is, however, pleasant to know that the number of all such persons — who must, I think, be regarded as really unfortunate — is but a small one, and that almost every one has a born capacity for musical appreciation and enjoyment.

It is true that the mighty genius of Mozart and Beethoven soared far above common musical minds. With a love for the noble art of music almost sacred in its intensity, these great composers penetrated far, far into its depths, finding their greatest enjoyment in so doing. Starting with the simpler forms of the art left by their predecessors, they deepened, they broadened and varied those forms; while, with every intricacy created, they experienced the sweetest of pleasure. And one of the most fitting tributes that can be paid to these and others of the noble masters of harmony is beautifully embodied in the lines of Rogers:—

> " The *soul* of music slumbers in the shell
> Till waked and kindled by the master's spell."

But this far-reaching art, with all its difficult forms to awaken and enchain the interest, and to inspire the love of the man of genius or the ambitious student of æsthetics, has also those more simple ones for the delight of the humbler mind. Even the babe that lies in its mother's arms has within the yet narrow confines of its new-born soul the germ of musical sympathy. Often, when it is in a state of disquiet, its mother sings to it a simple, pretty song. Soon the crying ceases; the little eyes brighten with a delighted interest; the charm of music is working. The mother continues the touching "lullaby," and anon finds that her tender charge, with the pleasing sounds of melody gently ringing in its ears to the last, has been soothed into dreamland. Indeed, the power of music to touch the heart, to fill the soul, lies oftenest in those tones that are comprised in its least difficult melodies. Nothing is truer than that music, so beneficent in its influence, is *meant* for the comprehension, enjoyment, and improvement of *all ;* and that it should never be regarded as an all-mysterious art, the charming domain of which only the gifted few are to enter. Whoever can distinguish musical sounds from their reverse, is, in degree at least, a musician; and whether such a one may enlarge his faculty for musical discernment and enjoyment depends only upon the extent of his observations, or rather upon the amount and kind of his study.

As elsewhere remarked, some time has elapsed since the music-loving world has been called to the contemplation of any great, new revelation in harmony. Meanwhile devotees of the divine art have generally been so much employed in endeavors to properly interpret the sublime works left for their study and enjoyment by the great composers of the past, that they have had neither time nor desire to seek for newer creations. For nearly all seem convinced that what is most needed now is, not new music, but that the masses of the people should possess an intelligent appreciation of, and warm love for, the best of that which is already at hand; and as an intelligent, heartfelt religious faith is needed to carry light and happiness alike into the homes of the highly-favored and the lowly, so is the beauty-shedding art of music — a close ally of that faith — needed to cheer, to soothe their hearts, and to develop in the minds of all God's children a love for that which may be fitly called the " true, beautiful, and good." Associating music with the very highest form of happiness, one of the older poets imagines this beautiful scene in heaven: —

> " Their golden harps they took,
> Harps ever tuned, that glittering by their side
> Like quivers hung, and with preamble sweet
> Of charming symphony they introduce
> Their sacred song, and waken raptures high
> No voice exempt, no voice but well could join
> Melodious part, such concord is in heaven."

But I shall now more particularly invite the reader to a consideration of a few among the many forms in which the beauty, the power, and good uses of music are exemplified, and of the advantages to be derived from its conscientious study.

It may be noticed, that, in those towns and cities containing a preponderance of cultivated people, theatres do not flourish to the same extent as in neighborhoods where the reverse is true. The reason is obvious: cultured people have attractive and generally musical homes, and are thus made, to a great extent, independent of the amusements afforded in public places. This I mention, not to decry the theatre, which, I hold, has its appropriate, and, under proper conditions, educational and refining uses. In fact, the theatre (in which is performed the legitimate drama) would seem to be in certain respects a necessity, affording as it does occasional change of scene, and ministering to that desire for relaxation and amusement so naturally, so invariably felt by those persons who have not, in a true sense, homes. Nevertheless, our firesides should be made to compete with, nay, to far surpass in attractiveness, all places of public amusement; for it is very much better that the employments and *entertainments* of our homes should charm and retain their members, than that these should be sought for outside their, in some respects, sacred confines. The reasons for this are so apparent to the thoughtful, that they need not be greatly enlarged upon. Briefly, then, in the home is *safety:* over its members are extended the protecting wings of guardian angels; while without are often snares and danger, either in palpable forms, or in those hidden by the glittering, the alluring disguises which are so often thrown over vice. On this very subject with what truth and directness Cotton speaks, when he says,—

> "If solid happiness we prize,
>   Within our breasts this jewel lies;
>   And they are fools that roam.
>   The world has nothing to bestow:
> From our own selves our joys must flow,
>   *And that dear hut, our home*"!

Nor need I dwell at great length upon the delights and benefits afforded the members of families whose leisure is given to the study and practice of an art so ennobling as music. How charming are those homes in which it is, in its purest style, cultivated! what refinement reigns therein! and what a gentle yet potent aid it is in parental government! The allurements to outside and often harmful pleasures lose their power over the children of that household in which music's engaging, magic influence holds delightful, elevating sway. And then at times, when instruments and voices mingle in a "concord of sweet sounds," how delightful is the effect, how serenely beautiful is the scene! Often have I, when passing in the evening a dwelling from which floated out upon the air the notes of tuneful voices, accompanied by the piano-forte or some other instrument, paused to listen, lingering long, the ear so ravished by the sweet sounds as to cause me to stand almost spell-bound, and to remain under music's magic influence even after its charming sounds had died away.

> "The music in my heart I bore
>   Long after it was heard no more."

To the great aid afforded them by music in government, the teachers in our common schools can testify. Often a turbulent school, swayed by youthful passions, or wearied by monotonous study into a state of painful unrest, has been stilled, calmed, and refreshed by the singing of a song, — an indulgence in the enjoyment of its melody affording delightful relaxation, and also awaking to life that better, that poetic sentiment that abides in every soul. The writer readily recalls his own experience as a teacher in gently enforcing lessons in polite deportment among his pupils by the aid of music. The exercises of each session of his school were always begun and ended with song; while sometimes, for reasons previously mentioned, books were laid aside, and all joined in singing, even during a part of the time usually devoted to study. By such procedure (the songs were of the simplest kind, and without the adding charm of instrumental accompaniment), even the most unruly pupils were generally induced to yield to the softening influences of "magic numbers and persuasive sound." In regard to the influence wielded over the mind and heart by songs, an eminent writer thus speaks: "Songs have at all times, and in all places, afforded amusement and consolation to mankind: every passion in the human breast has been vented in song; and the most savage as well as the most civilized inhabitants of the earth have encouraged these effusions." The following description of the effects of music at a reform-school is quite interesting in this connection. It is clipped from a recent number of "The Boston Transcript."

"A reporter of 'The San Francisco Chronicle,' who recently visited the industrial school, was very much impressed by what he saw and learned there concerning not only the taming, but the reforming and refining influence of a 'concord of sweet sounds.' Attached to the institution is a music-teacher, who has at all times in active training a number of boys, who perform on the various instruments that make up a brass band. This teacher, who is an intelligent German, and to all appearances an able instructor, testifies to the wonderful efficacy of music in softening the rugged nature of the boys, who are sent to school usually because they are uncontrollable by their parents or guardians. He says he has noticed the singular fact, that boys whose aversion to learning was so great that they could not or would not acquire even a knowledge of their 'a, b, abs,' took hold with evident relish of the comparatively difficult study of theoretical music, and in a very short space of time mastered the notes sufficiently to be able to read a tolerably hard score or piece of music. This seemed to him like a phenomenal phase, and he can only account for it on the ground that a love of music is inherent in the average bad boy. He has usually in training a band of twenty pieces: but he says that this number he could easily augment at any time to two, three, or even four times as many; for he very rarely finds a boy that has not a taste for some musical instrument. The greatest trouble he has yet encountered in the formation of his bands is the fact, that, as soon as his pupils become really proficient, they are ready for a discharge for good conduct, the music possessing such an influence for good over them as to completely reform dispositions that would otherwise be incorrigibly bad. Since he has held the position of music-teacher at the institution, several boys have been discharged for good and promising conduct, who have turned their knowledge of music, acquired within the walls of the industrial school, to profitable account."

We know that music, either vocal or instrumental, and in many cases the two combined, has for many centuries been considered necessary for the proper worship of God. The harmony that issues in grand and melting tones from the noble organ subdues the heart, and fills it with solemnity, sweetness, and hope: the sacred chant, the prayer or thanksgiving, uttered in melodious song by the choir or by all the congregation, — these cause the sordid world with all its cares and wild passions to be for the while forgotten, and the soul, charged with the influences of divine harmony and most holy aspiration, is lifted to heaven. And so music, with its gentle, its ever-winning power, has constantly been used by the churches to secure the attendance of those who without it had been indifferent. This has been especially the practice of the Roman-Catholic Church for inducing the attendance of Protestants, and is after the custom of olden times, when the Gentiles were thus drawn into the Christian churches, coming at first through motives of curiosity. They were, however, often so captivated by the music as to submit to baptism before departing. In most of our large cities, a considerable number of wealthy Protestants are induced, by the superior musical attractions of Catholic churches, to attend for a while, renting pews, and finally, in some cases, to become members; and Protestant churches, to sustain the interest in their services, and to insure the attendance of members and others, have been obliged to recognize this love among the people for the divine art.

The German race is remarkable for the intelligence, steadiness, and industry of its members, and their love for and cultivation of the art of music, — these latter characteristics prevailing to a most pleasing degree among all classes of the race. Indeed, it is rare to find a German not, in some sense at least, a musician. And in what beneficent uses do they employ the art, especially in their social relations! Their children are inducted into its charming beauties and helpful uses from their very earliest years. Of a steady-going, rather practical life, the Teutonic race yet seeks relief from care, and finds delightful rest and recreation, in united song, or in some other form of pleasing harmony;

thus wisely uniting the practical with the poetical in life. How in keeping is a musical love so warm, and a musical proficiency so general, with a nation which has given to the world a Mozart, a Haydn, and a Beethoven!

Most persons have remarked the superior affability, the polish of manners, that distinguishes the people of France. It is also observable that this nation is much devoted to music; that which is produced by their own composers, and most in use by the people, being usually of the graceful, brilliant style. An eminent French writer states, that, for the possession of these pleasing characteristics, this nation is indebted to that ancient order of musicians, the troubadours, whose musical qualities, politeness, and other winning graces, laid the foundation of the same.

It is said that the ancient Egyptians held music in such high esteem that they employed it as a remedial agent, believing it a sure cure for certain kinds of disease. While such a belief — that is, in its entirety — may not be held in modern times, yet this notion of the curative qualities of music does not seem so very fanciful or mysterious after a little reflection. We know that nothing so generally conduces to recovery from sickness as those influences that inspire feelings of cheerfulness, and that serve to divert the mind of the patient from a contemplation of his bodily sufferings, — it being almost a proverb, that " a pain forgot is a pain cured," — and that one of the chief of such agencies is the soothing, inspiriting charm of music. It is not meant by this, of course, that music is of itself and specifically a cure, but that it may be often employed as a powerful aid in effecting the same. We know, more over, that this delight-affording art may be profitably used to "minister to a mind diseased," and that its aid is often invoked by those physicians who are most skilful, if not in curing, at least in ameliorating the condition of, persons afflicted with that terrible malady, insanity. Perhaps Saul of olden times, who is said to have been once possessed with an "evil spirit," was then simply insane; and, taking this view of his condition, — which is, after all, the one that seems the more correct, — the statement in the Bible, that David drove away this evil spirit by his skilful playing upon the harp, becomes easy to understand, since the occurrence is thus divested of its miraculous character.

But I must not fail to notice here the remark sometimes made, that the study and practice of music do not always give to those engaged in the same the graces of a true refinement; that even persons highly skilled in the art are sometimes unamiable in manners, and coarse in habits. To this I reply, that no art nor human agency is capable of elevating every character to perfection; and that the exceptions above mentioned become very noticeable, and cause surprise, because of the known good influence upon the heart and mind generally exerted by the study and practice of good music. Besides, all great musical "*stars*" must not be classed with the conscientious, loving student of the art. Some among the former, gifted with phenomenal voices or with rare powers for instrumental performance, having reached, perhaps, with a few easy strides, their high positions, and caring but little for music save as it ministers to their vanity, conceit, or cupidity, — these have missed that gradually unfolding *culture* of the mind and heart that belongs to the progress of one who conscientiously seeks to know music's manifold beauties, and who with real appreciation for the beautiful in art, *loving music for music's sake,* feels and exhibits in his deportment towards his fellow-men its delightful and elevating power.

And here I cannot forbear to remark, that the musical education of the youth of our country is not being pushed towards that state of *thoroughness* so necessary to a real comprehension and enjoyment of the art. Nearly all intelligent parents are frequent, and even fulsome, in their praises of music; and, when they speak or write of it, the laudatory exclamation is often brought into use. And yet they seem to be satisfied, generally, when their children obtain, by a mere skimming over its surface, but a peep into the realities and refining beauties of the science; when the favorite daughter in the use of the piano-forte, for instance, becomes only the most wearisome of "thrummers."

"The London World" is none too severe on the "accomplished" young lady of the period, when it says, —

"The ordinary young lady can only play set pieces on the piano that she has learned at the price of Heaven knows how many valuable hours' practising. She never remembers any thing by heart; could not compose two notes to save her life; and cannot repeat by ear the simplest melody out of an opera, though she has heard it a hundred times. She is perfectly ignorant of the history of music; hates classical works; knows few of the masters' names save Verdi, Donizetti, Offenbach, and Mozart, the latter only as the composer of 'Don Giovanni.' Gregorian or Latin chants convey no especial meaning to her mind: all she can tell you about them is that they are used in church. As for orchestration, scoring, and such like, they are only fit matters for professionals. She will call Wagner horrid, Gounod lovely, Mendelssohn dull, and Beethoven pretty, without knowing why she likes or dislikes any thing. She yawns at an oratorio, is bored at a concert, and only enjoys opera because she knows everybody that sits in the boxes."

Besides, I think a mistake is made in compelling girls to learn to play only the piano-forte. There are other instruments, for performance upon which many of them have talents. Nor need such performance detract from a graceful, lady-like appearance. I mention, for example, the harp, the violin, and, indeed, all the stringed instruments, and even others. But on this point another says, —

"A recent number of the London 'Queen' contains an article recommending the violin as an instrument peculiarly appropriate for the use of ladies. It protests against the custom of teaching girls to play the piano-forte only, arguing that they should have a larger field in music. There is certainly no reason why girls may not gracefully handle the bow; and it is stated in the article referred to, that they 'can learn the violin in half the time that boys can,' — a statement which indicates that a goodly number of girls somewhere have had the opportunity of learning. In this age of progress, girls may certainly have a choice of instruments, and an opportunity to pursue the delightful art of music in whatever way they choose. If taste or fancy incline them to wind-instruments, why should they not try them?'"

Mr. Dwight, in his "Journal of Music," very justly and considerately discourses of the utillty of violin accomplishment, and the adaptability of the instrument to womanly practice. He says,

"We have always wondered, that in a community where so mucn attention is paid to music, and where almost every girl and boy is taught to thrum the piano, so few acquire, or even seek to acquire, the art of playing on the violin. The piano, to be sure, is a more representative instrument, enabling one pair of hands to grasp the whole harmony of a composition, or a compendium thereof; but the violin, with the other members of its family, viola, 'cello,

&c., is the more social instrument, bringing together groups of kindred spirits who can play in parts, and read together the quartets, &c., of the greatest masters, or play sonata duos, trios, &c., with the piano-forte. And the string-instruments are infinitely the most expressive: their tones lie nearer to the soul, spring more directly from the human breast. They are the heart of the whole orchestra, the most essential part of music, next to the human voice. It is a graceful, manly, healthy exercise, to play the violin. If it be very difficult to play it like an artist, so much the worthier of a manly aspiration. If it is often only vulgar *fiddling*, it is, on the other hand, with those truly schooled, the most gentlemanly of instruments. And we maintain that it is equally the most womanly. We have many times expressed our interest in female violinists. Who that has seen and heard Camilla Urso, or Teresa Liebe, or Mr. Eichberg's accomplished pupil, Persis Bell, could fail to feel that the violin seemed peculiarly fitted to the female constitution and capacity? How graceful the attitude and motions of a young woman skilfully handling the bow! Her finer sense of touch, her delicate tact, her instinctive feeling-out of the pure truth of tone, give woman a great advantage in this art; and the several examples we have had from time to time in the concerts of the Boston Conservatory of Music have shown that this was no mere dream."

But the limits of this book will not permit me to go much farther into this alluring subject. I shall therefore close this chapter by a brief reference to those who occupy the really noble positions of teachers of the sublime art of music.

He whose own mind has been illumined and whose own soul has been especially cheered and enlarged by the various contemplations, the studies and conceptions, of art, will not, in fact can not, hide his light for his own selfish enjoyment, but will seek to brighten the way of such as wish to learn its beauty, power, and uses. And how honorable, how enviable, is the mission of such a one as he who imparts to his fellows a knowledge of the beautiful science of music, leading them, through all the delighting, soul-filling forms of melody, into the region of a very fairy-land!

And finally, as giving fitting expression to the estimation in which the true musician is held by all intelligent people, I append this elegant tribute by Dr. Burgh: —

"The physician who heals diseases, and alleviates the anguish of the body, certainly merits a more conspicuous and honorable place; but the musician who eminently soothes our sorrows, and innocently diverts the mind in health, renders his memory deservedly dear to the grateful and refined part of mankind in every civilized nation."

V.

ELIZABETH TAYLOR GREENFIELD,

THE FAMOUS SONGSTRESS;

OFTEN CALLED

THE "BLACK SWAN."

> "A damsel with a dulcimer
> In a vision once I saw:
> It was an Abyssinian maid;
> And on her dulcimer she played,
> Singing of Mount Abora."
> COLERIDGE.

> "Hovering swans
> . . . . . .
> Carol sounds harmonious."
> <div align="right">CALLIMACHUS' <i>Hymn to Apollo</i>.</div>

IN giving a brief sketch of the life of the celebrated cantatrice, Miss Greenfield, the writer is somewhat embarrassed by the amount and richness of the materials at his command. For it would require far too much space to give all, or even a considerable portion, of the many press notices, criticisms, incidents, and the various items of interest, that are connected with her remarkable career; while to judiciously select from among the same a few, so that, while justice is done the subject, the

ELIZABETH TAYLOR GREENFIELD.

interest of the reader may not be lessened, is far from being an easy task, albeit it is a pleasant one. I find, indeed, that the pages of the public journals fairly teemed with praises of the great prima donna, as she was frequently called by them. The musical world was startled, intensely delighted, electrified, by her notes of sweetest melody. Her magnificent voice, in its great range in both the upper and lower registers, was regarded as nothing short of wonderful. Those who at first were incredulous soon became convinced of this, and were fairly taken captive; while the always friendly ones, especially those with whom Miss Greenfield was most closely identified, felt the keenest pleasure and most unbounded pride in her great triumphs.

All this was chronicled by the press, and formed the theme of constant conversation and correspondence. Many testimonials from persons in this country skilled in music and of fine general culture, as well as others from the Queen of England and several of the English nobility, were among her rich possessions, and were so great in number and so flattering in character as to have made hers almost, if indeed not altogether, an exceptional case.

These strong evidences of approval did not, however, make Miss Greenfield vain. The natural simplicity of her character remained unchanged. All the many exhibitions of great public and private admiration, and the praises that her performances constantly evoked, while of course affording her much pleasure, served mainly as impulses to newer and higher efforts in her chosen and beloved profession. Nor was her disposition less tried by the many difficulties that often formed in her pathway. Of these I need not speak here. But amidst them all this noble lady and artist was ever brave, patient, hopeful, ambitious in a certain sense, yet modest.

Fully aware of the magnificent quality of her voice, and of its phenomenal character; singing a higher and a lower note than either of her great contemporaries, — Parodi, Kate Hayes, and Jenny Lind, — she yet did not rest content, as most persons under the same circumstances would have done, with the enthusiastic plaudits elicited by her performances, but diligently applied herself to a scientific cultivation of a voice in natural power well-nigh marvellous, as well as to acquiring a scholarly knowledge of the principles of general music. In this commendable course she met with remarkable success, considering the circumstances by which she was surrounded.

And now, quoting at times largely from her "Biography," I proceed to give the following sketch of the career of this remarkable queen of song.

Elizabeth Taylor Greenfield, better known perhaps by her musical sobriquet, the "Black Swan," was born in Natchez, Miss., in the year 1809. When but a year old she was brought to Philadelphia by an exemplary Quaker lady, by whom she was carefully reared. Between these two persons there ever existed the warm affection that is felt by mother and daughter. In the year 1844 this good lady died. In her will the subject of this sketch was remembered by a substantial legacy. The will, however, formed the subject of a long legal contest; and I believe Miss Greenfield never received the bequest.

Her family name was Taylor; but, in honor of her guardian, she took the latter's name, — Greenfield.

"Previous to the death of this lady, Elizabeth had become distinguished in the limited circle in which she was known for her remarkable powers of voice. Its tender, thrilling tones often lightened the weight of age in one who was by her beloved as a mother.

"By indomitable perseverance she surmounted difficulties almost invincible. At first she taught herself crude accompaniments to her songs, and, intuitively perceiving the agreement or disagreement of them, improvised and repeated, until there was heard floating upon the air a very 'lovely song of one that had a pleasant voice, and could play well upon a guitar.'

"There dwelt in the neighborhood of Mrs. Greenfield a physician, humane and courteous; capable, too, of distinguishing and appreciating merit and genius, under whatever prejudices and disadvantages they were presented. His daughter, herself an amateur in the science of harmonious sounds, heard of Elizabeth's peculiar structure of mind. Miss Price invited her to her house. She listened with delighted surprise to her songs. She offered to accompany her upon the guitar. This was a concurrence of circumstances which formed the era of her life. Her pulses quickened as she stood and watched the fair Anglo-Saxon fingers of her young patroness run over the key-board of a full-toned pianoforte, eliciting sweet, sad, sacred, solemn sounds. Emotion well-nigh overcame her; but the gentle encouragement of her fair young friend dissipated her fears, and increased her confidence. She sang; and before she had finished she was surrounded by the astonished inmates of the house, who, attracted by the remarkable compass and sweetness of her voice, stealthily entered the room, and now unperceived stood gathered behind her. The applause which followed the first trial before this small but intelligent audience gratified as much as it embarrassed her, from the unexpected and sudden surprise. She not only received an invitation to repeat her visit, but Miss Price, for a reasonable compensation, undertook her instruction in the first rudiments of music. The progress of genius is not like that of common minds. It is needless to say that her improvement was very rapid."

But the lessons above mentioned were taken quite privately, and without, at first, the knowledge of her guardian. Elizabeth was rapidly acquiring an acquaintance with music, when some one maliciously informed Mrs. Greenfield, with the expectation of seeing an injunction laid upon the pupil's efforts. The old lady sent for Elizabeth, who came tremblingly into her presence, expecting to be reprimanded for her pursuit of an art forbidden by the Friends' discipline. "Elizabeth," said she, "is it true that thee is learning music, and can play upon the guitar?"—"It is true," was her reply. "Go get thy guitar, and let me hear thee sing." Elizabeth did so; and, when she had concluded her song, she was astonished to hear the kind lady say, "Elizabeth, whatever thee wants thee shall have." From that time her guardian was the patroness of her earnest efforts for skill and knowledge in musical science.

She began to receive invitations to entertain private parties by the exhibition of the gift which the God of nature had bestowed.

"Upon the death of her patroness, in consequence of the contested will she found herself thrown upon her own resources for a maintenance. Remembering some friends in the western part of New York, she resolved to visit them. While crossing Lake Seneca, *en route* to Buffalo, there came sweetly stealing upon the senses of the passengers of the steamer her rich, full, round, clear voice, unmarred by any flaw. The lady passengers, especially the noble Mrs. Gen. P., feeling that the power and sweetness of her voice deserved attention, urged her to sing again, and were not satisfied until five or six more songs were given to them. Before reaching their destined port she had made many friends. The philanthropic Mrs. Gen. P. became her friend and patroness. She at once invited Elizabeth to her splendid mansion in Buffalo, and, learning her simple story, promptly advised her to devote herself entirely to the science of music. During her visit a private party was given by this lady, to which all the *élite* of the city were invited. Elizabeth acquitted herself so admirably, that, two days ter, a card of invitation came to her through the public press, signed by the prominent gentlemen of Buffalo, requesting her to give a series of concerts.

"In October, 1851, she sang before the Buffalo Musical Association; and her performances were received with marks of approbation from the best musical talent in the city, that established her reputation as a songstress. 'Give the "Black Swan,"' said they, 'the cultivation and experience of the fair Swede or Mlle. Parodi, and she will rank favorably with those popular singers who have carried the nation into captivity by their rare musical abilities. Her voice has a full, round sound, and is of immense compass and depth. She strikes every note in a clear and well-defined manner, and reaches the highest capacity of the human voice with wonderful ease, and apparently an entire want of exertion. Beginning with G in the *bass clef*, she runs up the scale to E in the *treble clef*, and gives each note its full power and tone. She commences at the highest note, and runs down the scale with the same ease that she strikes any other lower note. The fact that she accomplishes this with no apparent exertion is surprising, and fixes at once the marvellous strength of her vocal organs. Her voice is wholly natural, and, as might be expected, lacks the training and exquisite cultivation that belong to the skilful Italian singer. But the *voice* is there; and, as a famous maestro once said, "it takes a hundred things to make a complete singer, of which a good voice is ninety-nine." If this be so, Miss Greenfield is on the verge of excellence; and it remains for the public to decide whether she shall have the means to pursue her studies.'"

To several gentlemen in Buffalo belongs the credit of having first brought out Miss Greenfield in the concert-room. The Buffalo papers took the matter in hand, and assured the public they had much to expect from a concert from this vocalist. The deep interest her first public efforts elicited from them gave occasion to the following certificate: —

Mr. H. E. HOWARD. BUFFALO, Oct. 30, 1851.

Dear Sir, — At your suggestion, for the purpose of enabling Miss Elizabeth T. Greenfield to show to her Philadelphia friends the popularity she has acquired in this city, I cheerfully certify as follows:—

The concert got up for her was unsolicited on her part, and entirely the result of admiration of her vocal powers by a number of our most respectable citizens, who had heard her at the residence of Gen. Potter, with whose family she had become somewhat familiar. The concert was attended by an audience not second in point of numbers to any given here before, except by Jenny Lind; and not second to any in point of respectability and fashion. The performance of Miss Greenfield was received with great applause; and the expression since, among our citizens generally, is a strong desire to hear her again.

Respectfully yours, &c.,

G. REED WILSON.

Rochester next extended an invitation for her to visit that city. We copy the invitation:—

"The undersigned, having heard of the musical ability of Miss Elizabeth T. Greenfield of the city of Buffalo, and being desirous of having her sing in Rochester, request that she will give a public concert in this city at an early day, and feel confident that it will afford a satisfactory entertainment to our citizens." (Signed by a large number of the most respected citizens of Rochester.)

ROCHESTER, Dec. 6, 1851.

This evening, in Corinthian Hall, the anticipated entertainment is to be presented to our music-loving citizens. Curiosity will lead many to attend, to whom the performance of a colored prima donna is a phenomenon at once wonderful and rare. Miss Greenfield has received from all who have heard her the name of being a vocalist of extraordinary power.

Speaking of her concert in Buffalo, "The Express" says,—

"On Monday, Parodi in all her splendor, sustained by Patti and Strakosch, sang at Corinthian Hall to half a house. Last night

Miss Greenfield sang at the same place to a crowded house of the respectable, cultivated, and fashionable people of the city. Jenny Lind has never drawn a better house, as to character, than that which listened with evident satisfaction to this unheralded and almost unknown African nightingale. Curiosity did something for her, but not all. She has merit, very great merit; and with cultivation (instruction) she will rank among the very first vocalists of the age. She has a voice of great sweetness and power, with a wider range from the lowest to the highest notes than we have ever listened to: flexibility is not wanting, and her control of it is beyond example for a new and untaught vocalist. Her performance was received with marked approbation and applause from those who knew what to applaud."

Another city paper says, —

"Much has been said and written of this personage since she was introduced to the public as a musical prodigy. All sorts of surmises and conjectures have been indulged in respecting the claim put forth of her merit; and generally the impression seemed to prevail, that the novelty of 'color' and idle curiosity accounted more for the excitement raised than her musical powers. Well, she has visited our place, and given our citizens an opportunity of judging for themselves. We are ignorant of music, and unqualified to criticise. But a large audience was in attendance at Ringueberg Hall last evening: among those present were our musical amateurs; and we heard but one expression in regard to the new vocalist, and that was wonder and astonishment at the extraordinary power and compass of her voice; and the ease with which she passed from the highest to the lowest notes seemed without an effort. Her first notes of 'Where are now the hopes?' startled the whole audience; and the interchange of glances, succeeded by thunders of applause at the end of the first verse, showed that her success was complete. She was loudly encored, and in response sang the baritone, 'When stars are in the quiet sky,' which took down the whole house.

"We have neither time nor space to follow her through her different pieces. Suffice it to say, that there never was a concert given in this town which appeared to give more general satisfac tion; and every person we met on leaving the hall expressed their entire approbation of her performance. No higher compliment could be paid to the 'Swan' than the enthusiastic applause which successfully greeted her appearance, and the encore which followed her several pieces.

"There was a very general expression among the audience that the sable vocalist should give another concert; and, at the earnest solicitation of several of our citizens, Col. Wood, her gentlemanly manager, has consented to give another entertainment to-morrow evening, when the 'Black Swan' will give a new programme, consisting of some of Jenny Lind's most popular songs.

"The concert on Thursday evening was what in other cases would have been called a triumph. The house was full, the audience a fashionable one, the applause decided, and the impression made by the singer highly favorable.

"We can safely say that Miss Greenfield possesses a voice of remarkable qualities; singular for its power, softness, and depth. She has applied herself with praiseworthy perseverance and assiduity to the cultivation of her extraordinary powers, and has attained great proficiency in the art which is evidently the bent of her genius. By her own energy, and unassisted, she has made herself mistress of the harp, guitar, and piano. We are informed that the proceeds of the entertainment this evening are to be wholly appropriated to the completion of her musical education in Paris under the world-famed Garcia. We predict for Miss Greenfield a successful and brilliant future."

"The Rochester American" says, —

"Corinthian Hall contained a large and fashionable audience on the occasion of the concert by this new candidate for popular favor on Thursday evening. We have never seen an audience more curiously expectant than this was for the *début* of this new vocalist. Hardly had her first note fallen upon their ears, however, before their wonder and astonishment were manifest in an interchange of glances and words of approval; and the hearty applause that responded to the first verse she sang was good evidence of the satisfaction she afforded. The aria, 'O native scenes!' was loudly encored; and in response she gave the pretty ballad, 'When stars are in the quiet sky.'"

The Buffalo "Commercial Advertiser" says, —

"Miss Greenfield is about twenty-five years of age, and has received what musical education she has in the city of Philadelphia: she is, however, eminently self-taught, possessing fine taste and a nice appreciation, with a voice of wonderful compass, clearness, and flexibility. She renders the compositions of some of the best masters in a style which would be perfectly satisfactory to the authors themselves. Her low, or properly *bass* notes, are wonderful, especially for a female voice; and in these she far excels any singing we have ever heard.

"We learn that this singer (soon to become celebrated, we opine) will give a concert in this city on Thursday next. There is no doubt that the novelty of hearing a colored woman perform the most difficult music with extraordinary ability will give *éclat* to the concert. All representations unite in ascribing to Miss Greenfield the most extraordinary talents, and a power and sweetness of vocalization that are really unsurpassed."

"The Daily State Register," Albany, Jan. 19, 1852, said, —

"THE 'BLACK SWAN'S' CONCERT. — Miss Greenfield made her *début* in this city on Saturday evening, before a large and brilliant audience, in the lecture-room of the Young Men's Association. The concert was a complete triumph for her; won, too, from a discriminating auditory not likely to be caught with chaff, and none too willing to suffer admiration to get the better of prejudice. Her singing more than met the expectations of her hearers, and elicited the heartiest applause and frequent encores. She possesses a truly wonderful voice; and, considering the poverty of her advantages, she uses it with surprising taste and effect. In sweetness, power, compass, and flexibility, it nearly equals any of the foreign vocalists who have visited our country; and it needs only the training and education theirs have received to outstrip them all.

"The compass of her marvellous voice embraces twenty-seven notes, reaching from the sonorous bass of a baritone to a few notes above even Jenny Lind's highest. The defects which the critic cannot fail to detect in her singing are not from want of voice, or power of lung, but want of training alone. If her present tour proves successful, as it now bids fair to, she will put herself under the charge of the best masters of singing in Europe; and with her enthusiasm and perseverance, which belong to genius, she cannot fail to ultimately triumph over all obstacles, and even conquer the prejudice of color, — perhaps the most formidable one in her path.

"She plays with ability upon the piano, harp, and guitar. In her deportment she bears herself well, and, we are told, converses with much intelligence. We noticed among the audience Gov. Hunt and his family, both Houses of the Legislature, State officers, and a large number of our leading citizens. All came away astonished and delighted."

A New-York paper says, —

"MISS GREENFIELD'S SINGING. — We yesterday had the pleasure of hearing the singer who is advertised in our columns as the 'Black Swan.' She is a person of ladylike manners, elegant form, and not unpleasing, though decidedly African features. Of her marvellous powers, she owes none to any tincture of European blood. Her voice is truly wonderful, both in its compass and truth. A more correct intonation, so far as our ear can decide, there could not be. She strikes every note on the exact centre, with unhesitating decision. . . . She is a nondescript, an original. We cannot think any common destiny awaits her."

"The Evening Transcript," Boston, Feb. 4, 1852, said, —

"Miss Greenfield, the 'Black Swan,' made her *début* before a Boston audience last evening at the Melodeon. In consequence of the price of the tickets being put at a dollar, the house was not over two-thirds full. She was well received, and most vociferously applauded and encored in every piece. She sings with great ease, and apparently without any effort. Her pronunciation is very correct, and her intonation excellent. Her voice has a wonderful compass, and in many notes is remarkably sweet in tone."

From "The Daily Capital City Fact," Columbus, O., March 3, 1852: —

"Last evening proved that the 'Black Swan' was all that the journals say of her; and Miss Greenfield stands confessedly before the Columbus world a swan of excellence. She is indeed a remarkable swan. Although colored as dark as Ethiopia, she utters notes as pure as if uttered in the words of the Adriatic."

From "The Milwaukee Sentinel," April, 1852: —

"What shall we say? That we were delighted and surprised? All who were present know that, from their own feelings. We can only say, that we have never heard a voice like hers, — one that with such ease, and with such absence of all effort, could range from the highest to the lowest notes."

Said a Rochester (N.Y.) paper of May 6, 1852, —

... "The magnificent quality of her voice, its great power, flexibility, and compass, her self-taught genius, energy, and perseverance, combine to render Miss Greenfield an object of uncommon interest to musicians.

"We have been spell-bound by the ravishing tones of Patti, Sontag, Malibran, and Grisi; we have heard the wondrous warblings of '*the Nightingale;*' and we have listened with delight to the sweet melodies of the fair daughter of Erin: but we hesitate not to assert, that, with one year's tuition from the world-famed Emanuel Garcia, Miss Greenfield would not only compare favorably with any of the distinguished artists above named, but incomparably excel them all."

"The Globe," Toronto, May 12–15, 1852, said, —

"Any one who went to the concert of Miss Greenfield on Thursday last, expecting to find that he had been deceived by the puffs of the American newspapers, must have found himself most agreeably disappointed. . . .

"After he [the pianist] had retired, there was a general hush of expectation to see the entrance of the vocalist of the evening; and presently there appeared a lady of a decidedly dark color, rather inclined to an *embonpoint*, and with African formation of face.

She advanced calmly to the front of the platform, and courtesied very gracefully to the audience. There was a moment of pause, and the assembly anxiously listened for the first notes. They were quite sufficient. The amazing power of the voice, the flexibility, and the ease of execution, took the hearers by surprise; and the singer was hardly allowed to finish the verse, ere she was greeted with the most enthusiastic plaudits, which continued for some time. The higher passages of the air were given with clearness and fulness, indicating a soprano voice of great power. The song was encored; and Miss Greenfield came back, took her seat at the piano, and began, to the astonishment of the audience, a different air in a deep and very clear bass or baritone voice, which she maintained throughout, without any very great appearance of effort, or without any breaking. She can, in fact, go as low as Lablache, and as high as Jenny Lind, — a power of voice perfectly astonishing. It is said she can strike thirty-one full, clear notes; and we could readily believe it."

From a Brattleborough (Vt.) paper, June 23, 1852: —

"The 'Black Swan,' or Miss Elizabeth Greenfield, sang in Mr. Fisk's beautiful new hall on Wednesday evening last to a large and intelligent audience.

"We had seen frequent notices in our exchanges, and were already prepossessed in favor of the abilities and life purposes of our sable sister; but, after all, we must say that our expectations of her success are greater than before we had heard her sing, and conversed with her in her own private room. She is not pretty, but plain: . . . still she is gifted with a beauty of soul which makes her countenance agreeable in conversation; and in singing, especially when her social nature is called into activity, there is a grace and beauty in her manner which soon make those unaccustomed to her race forget all but the melody. . . .

"Nature has done more for Miss Greenfield than any musical prodigy we have met, and art has marred her execution less."

But the limits of this book are such as to preclude my giving all or even a hundredth part of the testimonials and criticisms touching the singing of this remarkable performer, that filled the public journals during her career in the United States. I believe, however, that I have given quite enough to show that her noble gifts of voice, and beauty of execution, were of the rarest excellence, while in some notable respects they had never been equalled. Let it suffice to say also, in regard to the excerpts given, that they are but fair samples and reflections of the opinions entertained and expressed by the press, and by music-loving, cultured people, everywhere Miss Greenfield appeared.

After singing in nearly all the free States, she resolved to carry out her long-entertained purpose of visiting Europe, in order to perfect herself in the *technique* of her art. Learning of her intentions, the citizens of Buffalo, N.Y., united in tendering her a grand testimonial and benefit concert. The invitation was couched in terms most flattering, and signed by many of the most distinguished residents.

The concert took place on March 7, 1853, and was in all respects a grand success.

Leaving Buffalo, she went to New York, where, after singing before an audience of four thousand persons, she received the following complimentary note:—

NEW YORK, April 2, 1853.
Miss ELIZABETH T. GREENFIELD.

Madam,— By the suggestion of many enthusiastic admirers of your talents, I have been induced to address you on the subject of another and second concert, prior to your departure for Europe.

Your advent musical in "Gotham" has not been idly heralded among the true lovers of song, and admirers of exalted genius, of which your unprecedented success on Wednesday evening must have sufficiently convinced you; while all are eloquent in the commendation of your superior powers and engaging method.

Confiding, madam, in your reported magnanimity and generosity to oblige, I will divest myself of tedious circumlocution, and fervently exhort you to make a second exhibition of your skill; which, there can be no doubt, will be highly successful to you, and as interesting to your admirers. THE PUBLIC.

"Miss Greenfield embarked from New York in a British steamer for England, April 6, 1853; and arrived in Liverpool the 16th of April, 1853; rested over the sabbath, and proceeded Monday morning to London, in which metropolis she became safely domiciled on the evening of the same day.

"But painful trials awaited her from a quarter the most unexpected. The individual with whom she had drawn up the contract for this musical tour was unfaithful to his promises; and she found herself abandoned, without money and without friends, in a strange country.

"She had been told Lord Shaftesbury was one of the great good men of England; and she resolved to call upon him in person, and entreat an interview. His lordship immediately granted her request, listened patiently to her history, and directly gave her a letter of introduction to his lawyer.

"It may perhaps be considered a providential concurrence that Mrs. Harriet Beecher Stowe was in London this same time with Miss Greenfield. We notice in her 'Sunny Memories,' under the date of May 6, the following remarks : ' A good many calls this morning. Among others came Miss Greenfield, the (so-called) "Black Swan." She appears to be a gentle, amiable, and interesting young person. She has a most astonishing voice. C. sat down to the piano, and played while she sang. Her voice runs through a compass of three octaves and a fourth. This is four notes more than Malibran's. She sings a most magnificent tenor, with such a breadth and volume of sound, that, with your back turned, you could not imagine it to be a woman. While she was there, Mrs. S. C. Hall, of the "Irish Sketches," was announced. I told her of Miss Greenfield; and she took great interest in her, and requested her to sing something for her. C. played the accompaniment, and she sang " Old Folks at Home," first in a soprano voice, and then in a tenor, or baritone. Mrs. Hall was amazed and delighted, and entered at once into her cause. She said she would call with me, and present her to Sir George Smart, who is at the head of the

Queen's musical establishment, and, of course, the acknowledged leader of London musical judgment.

"'In the course of the day I had a note from Mrs. Hall, saying, that, as Sir George Smart was about leaving town, she had not waited for me, but had taken Miss Greenfield to him herself. She writes that he was really astonished and charmed at the wonderful weight, compass, and power of her voice. He was also as well pleased with the mind in her singing, and her quickness in doing and catching all that he told her. Should she have a public opportunity to perform, he offered to hear her rehearse beforehand. Mrs. Hall says, "This is a great deal for him, whose hours are all marked with gold."'

"Again Mrs. Stowe says, 'To-day the Duchess of Sutherland called with the Duchess of Argyle. Miss Greenfield happened to be present; and I begged leave to present her, giving a slight sketch of her history. I was pleased with the kind and easy affability with which the Duchess of Sutherland conversed with her, betraying by no inflection of voice, and nothing in her air or manner, the great lady talking with the poor girl. She asked all her questions with as much delicacy, and made her request to hear her sing with as much consideration and politeness, as if she had been addressing any one in her own circle. She seemed much pleased with her singing, and remarked that she should be happy to give her an opportunity of performing in Stafford House, as soon as she should be a little relieved of a heavy cold which seemed to oppress her at present. This, of course, will be decisive of her favor in London. The duchess is to let us know when the arrangement is completed.

"'I never so fully realized,' continues Mrs. Stowe, 'that there really is no natural prejudice against color in the human mind. Miss Greenfield is a dark mulattress, of a pleasing and gentle face, though by no means handsome. She is short and thick-set, with a chest of great amplitude, as one would think on hearing her tenor. I have never seen, in any of the persons to whom I have presented her, the least indications of suppressed surprise or disgust, any more than we should exhibit on the reception of a dark-complexioned Spaniard or Portuguese.

"'Miss Greenfield bears her success with much quietness and good sense.'

"Her Grace the Duchess of Sutherland afterward became her ever-unfailing supporter and adviser.

"The piano-forte which previously had been furnished Miss Greenfield to practise upon was taken from her. The Duchess of Sutherland, upon learning the fact, immediately directed her to select one from Broadwood's.

"We cannot refrain from quoting Mrs. Stowe's description of the concert after dinner at the Stafford House: —

"'The concert-room was the brilliant and picturesque hall I have before described to you. It looked more picture-like and dreamy than ever. The piano was on the flat stairway just below the broad central landing. It was a grand piano, standing end outward, and perfectly banked up among hot-house flowers, so that only its gilded top was visible. Sir George Smart presided. The choicest of the *élite* were there, — ladies in demi-toilet and bonneted. Miss Greenfield stood among the singers on the staircase, and excited a pathetic murmur among the audience. She is not handsome, but looked very well. She has a pleasing dark face, wore a black velvet head-dress and white carnelian ear-rings, a black moire-antique silk made high in the neck, with white lace falling sleeves and white gloves. A certain gentleness of manner and self-possession, the result of the universal kindness shown her, sat well upon her. Chevalier Bunsen, the Prussian ambassador, sat by me. He looked at her with much interest. "Are the race often as good-looking?" he said. I said, "She is not handsome compared with many, though I confess she looks uncommonly well to-day." The singing was beautiful. Six of the most cultivated glee-singers of London sang, among other things, " Spring's Delights are now returning," and " Where the Bee sucks, there lurk I." The duchess said, "These glees are peculiarly English." Miss Greenfield's turn for singing now came, and there was profound attention. Her voice, with its keen, searching fire, its penetrating vibrant quality, its *timbre* as the French have it, cut its way like a Damascus blade to the heart. She sang the ballad, "Old Folks at Home," giving one verse in the soprano, and another in the tenor voice. As she stood partially concealed by the piano, Chevalier Bunsen thought that the tenor part was performed by one of the gentlemen. He was perfectly astonished when he discovered that it was by her. This was rapturously encored. Between the parts, Sir George took her to the piano, and tried her voice by skips, striking notes here and there at random, without connection, from D in alto to A first space in bass clef. She followed with unerring precision, striking the sound nearly at the same instant his finger touched the key. This brought out a burst of applause.

"'Lord Shaftesbury was there. He came and spoke to us after the concert. Speaking of Miss Greenfield, he said, "I consider the use of these halls for the encouragement of an outcast race a consecration. This is the true use of wealth and splendor, when they are employed to raise up and encourage the despised and forgotten."'

"Tuesday, May 31, 1853.

"Miss Greenfield's first public morning concert took place at the Queen's Concert Rooms, Hanover Square. She came out under the immediate patronage of her Grace the Duchess of Sutherland, her Grace the Duchess of Norfolk, and the Earl and Countess of Shaftesbury. It commenced at three o'clock, and terminated at five."

"The London Morning Post" says, —

"A large assemblage of fashionable and distinguished personages assembled by invitation at Stafford House to hear and decide upon the merits of a phenomenon in the musical world, — Miss Elizabeth Greenfield, better known in America as the 'Black Swan;' under which sobriquet she is also about to be presented to the British public. This lady is said to possess a voice embracing the extraordinary compass of nearly three octaves; and her performances on this occasion elicited the unmistakable evidence of gratification."

"The London Times" said, —

"Miss Greenfield sings 'I know that my Redeemer liveth' with as much pathos, power, and effect as does the 'Swedish Nightingale,' Jenny Lind."

Again : "The London Observer" remarks, —

"Her voice was at once declared to be one of extraordinary compass. Both her high and low notes were heard with wonder by the assembled amateurs, and her ear was pronounced to be excellent."

"The London Advertiser" of June 16 contained the following comments: —

"A concert was given at Exeter Hall last evening by Miss Greenfield, the American vocalist, better known in this country under the sobriquet of the 'Black Swan.' Apart from the natural gifts with which this lady is endowed, the great musical skill which she has acquired, both as a singer and an instrumentalist, is a convincing argument against the assertion so often made, that the negro race is incapable of intellectual culture of a high standard. . . . Her voice is a contralto, of great clearness and mellow tone in the upper register, and full, resonant, and powerful in the lower, though slightly masculine in its *timbre*. It is peculiarly effective in ballad-songs of the pathetic cast, several of which Miss Greenfield sang last night in a very expressive manner. She was encored in two, — ' The Cradle-Song,' a simple melody by Wallace, and ' Home, Sweet Home,' which she gave in an exceedingly pleasing manner. The programme of the concert was bountifully drawn up ; for, in addition to the attractions of the ' Black Swan,' there was a host of first-rate artists. Herr Brandt, a German artist with a remarkably sweet voice, sang Professor Longfellow's ' Slave's Dream,' set to very beautiful music by Hatton, in a way that elicited warm applause. Miss Rosina Bentley played a fantasia by Lutz very brilliantly, and afterward, assisted by Miss Kate Loder (who, however, must now be known as Mrs. Henry Thompson), in a grand duet for two piano-fortes by Osborne. M. Valadares executed a curious Indian air, ' Hilli Milli Puniah,' on the violin ; and Mr. Henry Distin a solo on the sax tuba. The band was admirable, and performed a couple of overtures in the best manner. Altogether, the concert, which we understand was made under the distinguished patronage of the Duchess of Sutherland, was highly successful, and went off to the perfect gratification of a numerous and fashionable audience."

"In July she gave two grand concerts in the Town Hall in Brighton, under the patronage of her Grace the Duchess of Sutherland, her Grace the Duchess of Norfolk, her Grace the Duchess of Beaufort, her Grace the Duchess of Argyle, the Most Noble the Marchioness of Ailesbury, the Most Noble the Marchioness of Kil dare, the Most Noble the Marquis of Lansdowne, the Earl and Countess of Shaftesbury, the Earl of Carlisle, the Countess of Jersey, the Countess of Granville, the Countess of Wilton, the Viscountess Palmerston, the Lady Constance Grosvenor, and Mrs. Harriet Beecher Stowe.

"*Vocalists.* — Miss E. T. Greenfield (the 'Black Swan'), Madame Taccani, Countess Tasca, Mr. Emanuel Roberts (Queen's concerts).

"*Instrumentalists.* — Piano-forte soloist, Miss Rosina Bently (pupil of Miss Kate Loder); violin, M. de Valadares (pupil of the Conservatoire, Paris); accompanist, Mons. Edouard Henri; conductor, Mr. F. Theseus Stevens.

"She gave a series of concerts at the Rotunda in Dublin, Ireland."

"Extract from programme of Miss Greenfield's benefit concert, Aug. 17, 1853 : —

"*Vocalists.* — Miss Louisa Pyne, Miss Pyne, and Mr. W. Harrison; pianist, Miss Rosina Bently; violinist, M. de Valadares from the East Indies; accompanist, Mr. R. Thomas."

"In October, 1853, we find her again at the Beaumont Institution, Beaumont Square, Mile End, London, at Mr. Cotton's concert, supported by Miss Poole, the Misses M'Alpine, Miss Alleyne, Mr. Augustus Braham, Mr. Suchet Champion, Mr. Charles Cotton, the German Glee Union, and the East-Indian violinist M. de Valadares; conductor, Herr Ganz."

"Nov. 3, 1853, at Albion Hall, Hammersmith, she made her appearance under the patronage of her Grace the Duchess of Sutherland, her Grace the Duchess of Norfolk, her Grace the Duchess of Beaufort, her Grace the Duchess of Argyll, the Most Noble the Marchioness of Aylesbury, the Most Noble the Marchioness of Kildare, the Most Noble the Marquis of Lansdowne, Earl and Countess of Shaftesbury, Earl of Carlisle, Countess of Jersey, Countess of Granville, Countess of Wilton, Viscountess Palmerston, the Lady Constance Grosvenor, and Mrs. Harriet Beecher Stowe.

"*Artists.* — Miss E. T. Greenfield, Miss J. Brougham, Miss E. Brougham, Mr. Charles Cotton, Mr. Augustus Braham the eminent tenor; piano-forte, Miss Eliza Ward."

"At the Theatre Royal, Lincoln, Dec. 23, 1853, under the same distinguished patronage as at Hammersmith.

"*Artists.* — Mrs. Alexander Newton (of her Majesty's Grand National Concerts), Miss Ward, Miss E. T. Greenfield, Mr. Augustus Braham, Mr. Charles Cotton (from Milan), Mr. Distin."

"Again: to verify the fact of her having received the attention of very distinguished personages, the following certificates are laid before the reader: —

"'Sir George Smart has the pleasure to state that her Majesty Queen Victoria commanded Miss Greenfield to attend at Buckingham Palace on May the 10th, 1854, when she had the honor of singing several songs, which he accompanied on the piano-forte.

"'To Miss GREENFIELD, from Sir GEORGE SMART, Kt.,
"'Organist and Composer to her Majesty's Chapel Royal.
"'June 24, 1854. No. 91, GR. PORTLAND ST., LONDON.'

"'This is to certify that Miss Greenfield had the honor of singing before her Majesty the Queen at Buckingham Palace. By her Majesty's command, "'C. B. PHIPPS.
"'BUCKINGHAM PALACE, July 22, 1854, LONDON.'"

"In May, 1854, she received an invitation through the Rev. Mr. Geary to sing at a concert, but declined, being advised not to sing at public concerts until her return to the United States. She therefore sang only at private parties until July, 1854, when that same noble benefactress, the Duchess of Sutherland, secured for her two places in 'The Indiana' steam-packet for New York.

"With a warm invitation to revisit England at some future period, she embarked at Southampton to return to America."

The trip to London and its attendant circumstances resulted in much benefit to Miss Greenfield in an intrinsic, artistic sense, adding decided *éclat* to her professional reputation. "The New-York Herald," a journal which in those days was generally quite averse to bestowing even well-merited praise upon persons of her race, was, however, so much moved upon by her exhibition of an increased technical knowledge of the lyric art as to speak of Miss Greenfield as follows: "'The Swan' sings now in true artistic style, and the wonderful powers of her voice have been developed by good training." This was but echoing the general verdict.

During the years that intervened between Miss Greenfield's return from England and her death, — the latter event occurring at Philadelphia in the month of April, 1876, — she was engaged in singing occasionally at concerts, and in giving lessons in vocal music.

Remembering her own hard contests as she ascended the hill of fame, Miss Greenfield ever held out a helping hand to all whom she found struggling to obtain a knowledge of the noble art of music. Possessing, on account of her great vocal abilities, the high esteem of the general public, from a rare amiability of disposition enjoying the warm love of many friends in those private circles where she was always an ornament and a blessing, this wonderfully gifted lady at the age of sixty-eight years died, deeply mourned by all. Of her brilliant career, of her life, which, in many important respects, was so grandly useful, as well as of her peaceful death, nothing, more need here be added, further than to place her name in the honorable list of those of whom Milton so eloquently says, —

> "Nothing is here for tears; nothing to wail,
> Or knock the breast; no weakness, no contempt,
> Dispraise, or blame; *nothing but well and fair*,
> And what may quiet us in a death so noble."

VI.

THE "LUCA FAMILY,"

VOCALISTS AND INSTRUMENTALISTS.

> "God sent his singers upon earth
> With songs of sadness and of mirth,
> That they might touch the hearts of men,
> And bring them back to heaven again.
> . . . .
> But the great Master said, 'I see
> No best in kind, but in degree:
> I gave a various gift to each, —
> To charm, to strengthen, and to teach.'"
>
> *From* LONGFELLOW'S *The Singers.*

WHILE nearly all persons have to a greater or lesser degree musical sympathy and capability, or, to speak generally, capacity for the enjoyment or production, in one way or another, of harmony; and while, too, a goodly number there are who possess what may be called musical aptitude, — it is yet only once in a great while that we find those who are thus endowed in a degree which may be considered extraordinary. For the Muses, however often and earnestly invoked, are never lavish in the bestowment of their favors. This is especially true as applied to the goddess who presides over the art of music. Only here and there is some one selected to whom is given great

1. ALEXANDER C. LUCA, SEN.
2. CLEVELAND O. LUCA.
3. ALEXANDER C. LUCA, JUN.
4. JOHN W. LUCA.

musical inspiration; into whose keeping is placed the divine harp, which, when swept by his hands, the people shall hear entranced.

Occasionally we may observe in families one member who appears particularly favored by nature in the possession of rich and varied musical talents, the same being improved by careful cultivation. Such a one readily attracts attention: his native endowments and his extensive acquirements often form the theme of conversation, of warmest praise; while everywhere he is a most welcome guest. But, if in a family a single instance of this kind produces the effects just described, the latter can but be greatly enhanced when is found a family composed of a number of persons in no wise small, each one of which is a highly-talented and finely-educated musician. It is, however, — for the reasons already mentioned, — so rare a thing to see the musical faculty thus possessed, and its advantages thus fully embraced, by an entire household of nearest relatives, as to render the circumstance a cause of much surprise; while a family so greatly skilled in the most beautiful, the most charming, of all arts, easily attains to high distinction, its members becoming objects of such general private and public interest as to render their careers quite worthy of the best efforts of those who would make the same a matter of history.

The foregoing remarks, although made in a somewhat general way, may be particularly applied to that excellent troupe of artists, the "Luca family," a brief account of whose remarkable natural endowments, superior acquirements, and interesting musical life, is here appended.

The family, as at first professionally organized, consisted of six persons,—the father, mother, and four sons. Some changes that occurred afterwards will appear as the narrative progresses.

Alexander C. Luca, the father, whose history shows most pointedly how much may be accomplished by devoted study, deserves especial mention. He was born in Milford, Conn., in the year 1805. He is, in the most proper sense, a "self-made" man. Possessing but few opportunities for acquiring an education, he yet made the most of those he had, and is to-day a man of varied culture, an excellent example of the Christian gentleman.
At the age of twenty-one years he apprenticed himself to a shoemaker, having previously spent his life upon a farm; and, while thus engaged, he showed a decided taste for music. In the shop where he worked were several boys who were learning the trade, and who were also members of the village singing-school. Going occasionally into their school, listening eagerly to all they sang and talked about both there and in the shop, he soon learned their songs, and was induced by the surprised teacher to join the school. In a short time, by the aid of a naturally musical ear and a good voice, and by diligent study of the rudiments, he became quite a proficient scholar; surpassing, in fact, most of the other pupils of the school.

After learning his trade he removed to New Haven, Conn., where after a while he was married to a lady of fine musical qualities (she being especially remarked as a singer), and who was also of a musical family. Soon after his arrival at New Haven, Mr. Luca, having acquired by this time quite a fine knowledge of music, and being an excellent vocalist, was chosen chorister of a Congregationalist church. In a short time his choir was considered the equal of any in the city; which was high but well-deserved praise. Some time previously to the formation of what was called professionally the "Luca family," the subject of this sketch organized a quartet consisting of Miss Dianah Lewis,[1] a sister of his wife, his two older sons, and himself, and gave in New Haven and vicinity a number of fine concerts. Mr. Luca trained all his children in music at an early age, and taught them to sing in his choir at the church.

Mrs. Luca heartily sympathized with, and aided her husband in, the musical and general culture of the family. One of the sons thus speaks of her: "Our earlier taste for music was especially encouraged by our mother, who thought that the study of it would claim us from the bad influences which idle hours and mischievous associations engendered."

With such parents it is not strange that the Luca children became so worthy and eminent as exponents of the art of music.

John W. Luca, the oldest son, when quite young, was remarkable, mostly, as a comic singer. He sang frequently at school exhibitions, and often created much sensation in singing a temperance song called "The Old Toper."

Alexander C., jun., who in after-years became so noticeable as a tenor-singer and violinist, was at first the dullest of the boys.

Simeon G. possessed a tenor voice of extraordinary compass, singing high C with the greatest ease. He sang the choicest music from the various operas to

---

[1] She was a vocalist of rare powers, and was considered the equal of the celebrated Miss Greenfield, or, as the latter was frequently called, the "Black Swan."

astonished and delighted audiences. He was also a solo violinist of rare powers; often thrilling his audiences by the smooth, sweet, and expressive strains evolved from his instrument.

Cleveland O. Luca, the justly celebrated, the wonderful pianist, began to exhibit extraordinary talent at the early age of seven years. It was not, however, the intention of his parents to have him begin to study so early. Indeed, little did they think that the fire of musical genius burned so brightly in the soul of their young boy. But Cleveland, or "Cleve" as he was then called, was not to be restrained. Going often into the room where his aunt was playing on the piano-forte, he listened eagerly and delightedly, his little soul stirred and filled by the sweet sounds of harmony; and, after she had left the instrument, he would go and play the selections even better than his aunt. Of course such striking evidences of genius filled the breasts of his parents with delightful surprise; and it was soon decided to place the gifted boy under the care of a competent instructor. He rapidly developed those remarkable powers for ready reading, facility and brilliancy in execution, that afterwards made him so wonderful and so noted.

When but ten years old, he had become a performer of such excellence as to attract the notice and to receive the unequivocal praise of such good judges as Strakosch, Dodworth, W. V. Wallace, and other noted musicians of New York.

When it was resolved to form as public performers the "Luca family," the decided musical powers possessed by young Cleveland made his services indispensable, and he was of course taken as a member. As the "wonderful boy pianist," he everywhere created quite a *furore*. The ladies in the audiences were especially delighted with him; and forgetting often, in their enthusiasm, that he was black, it seemed that they would certainly carry him away.

Never satisfied to rest alone upon his fine natural endowments, our young artist pushed his studies, entering the classical, the technical domain of the great master-composers, and playing with easy, graceful, magnetic touch, and delightfully winning expression, any of their works. As a reader at sight of compositions the most difficult, it is doubtful whether he had an equal in this country.

The prejudiced or incredulous, before having observed his rare powers for reading and playing, often as a test, and sometimes with a hope to embarrass him, placed before him some technical and very difficult work. But the readiness with which he played the piece changed one who had come to doubt or to scorn into a silent, deeply surprised, and interested listener; and it was most always the case, too, that such a one, yielding to the exquisite charm of the music, as well as to the gentlemanly, graceful manners of the young virtuoso, became from that time forth his warm admirer and friend.

But this brilliant artist did not confine himself to the interpretation of the more difficult compositions for the piano. At the time of which I am writing, — twenty years ago, — his success as a performer before miscellaneous audiences could not have been so great, had he not possessed, in a most pleasing degree, a versatility of talent. His *repertoire* was an extensive one, and decidedly "taking" in the varied character of its excellent pieces. Many of the latter were simple, yet always purely musical, and of course highly pleasing.

Before the public, Mr. Luca was, in the best sense, a successful performer; while, in those smaller and finer artistic circles where the more delicate and higher musical forms were appreciated, he delighted and even instructed his listeners, receiving their warmest praise.

True art is ever noble and ennobling: in its domain its devotees are known and valued, not by the color of their faces, but by the depth of artistic love that they feel, and by the measure of success to which they attain. And so the subject of this sketch, although of a complexion quite dark, and often suffering from the coldness, if not the insults, of those afflicted with "color-phobia," was yet ever sought after and cordially received upon terms of equality by all the *great* musicians wherever he journeyed. Nor did the press of the country, nor people of culture generally, fail to pass upon him the highest encomiums. A few of these are elsewhere given.

Besides his ability as a pianist, Cleveland Luca was also a vocalist of fair powers. No especial pains being taken, however, to develop this faculty, he attracted, as a singer, no great attention.

On the 27th of March, 1872, in far-away Africa, whither he had nobly gone to carry the bright, cheering, and refining light of his musical genius, his frail constitution yielding to a fever, he died at the age of forty-five.

It is hard to over-estimate the great good this remarkable artist accomplished for his much-abused race in dissipating, by his wonderful musical qualities, the unjust and cruel prejudice that so generally prevailed against the former at the beginning of his career; for in him was fully and splendidly illustrated the capacity of the dark-hued race for reaching the highest positions in the walks of the art melodious. The example, moreover, of his intelligent parents, who, when they discovered his talents, — avoiding the mistake often made by some, who, alas! but too frequently rest content merely with observing the signs of genius in their children, allowing the at first bright spark to go untended, to burn "with fitful glare," and to finally become, from this neglect, extinguished, — devoted themselves at once to their fullest and most artistic development, — this example, I say, is one to be highly commended, and ever to be followed.

Having thus described the family individually, I now proceed to speak of their combined efforts. Formed as a vocal quartet, the parts were distributed in this wise: Simeon Luca sang first tenor, Alexander second tenor, Cleveland soprano, and John sang bass (or baritone if desired).

Instrumentally they performed as follows: Simeon on first violin, Alexander second violin, John violoncello (or double bass if required), and Cleveland on the piano-forte. The father fulfilled the duties of musical director and business manager; and occasionally he took part in the performances as a vocalist.

Thus excellently equipped musically, each member of the troupe possessed of general intelligence, and being of genteel appearance, they went forth on their mission of music into fields hitherto untrodden by members of their race; and their fine performances everywhere gave delight, refinement, and a new and high impulse, to the many thousands who heard them.

Their services were at first called into requisition at anniversaries and festivals, and they soon acquired an excellent local reputation. The event that most prominently heralded their names before the public was their first appearance at the May anniversary of the Antislavery Society, held in the old Tabernacle on Broadway, New York, in 1853. Over five thousand persons were present. The sensation produced by the performances of this gifted family on this occasion is said to have been indescribable. The wildest enthusiasm was manifested; and many persons in the audience, overcome by the emotions awakened, shed tears. This is, however, not so strange. Gathered as was this immense concourse of people to advance the cause of human freedom, and entertaining and asserting, as they did, a belief of man's equality, we may well imagine the measure of their delight when in witnessing the display of genius by the wonderful pianist, and listening to the sweet strains of classical harmony formed by the tuneful voices and skilfully-played instruments of this troupe of colored artists, they found their claims for the race so fully sustained.

After the performances just mentioned, letters full of praise and congratulation from many sources poured in upon the "Lucas," as they were familiarly called; and Professor Allen, then editing a paper at Troy, N.Y., induced the parents to intrust the children, now so rapidly acquiring fame, to his charge, to make a musical trip through the New-England States in the interest of his paper. This tour resulted in adding to their fame, and confirming them in a belief of their ultimate general success; but, owing to poor management on the part of their business agent, the trip was not a financial success.

I should have mentioned ere this that John and Alexander Luca had been taught by their father the shoemaking trade, and that for some time they applied themselves to this kind of work; using their leisure time, nevertheless, in pushing their musical studies. Occasionally they would drop the awl and hammer, and make excursions into the country towns of Connecticut; sometimes returning with a full exchequer, and sometimes in debt even, but never without having added to their reputations as musicians.

During these times, the family received many valuable testimonials touching their musical abilities; but to none of these do they owe so much as to a highly commendatory letter from the late Rev. Horace Bushnell of Hartford, Conn. Such testimony from one so eminent, and of critical abilities so great, could not fail to arrest public attention in their behalf.

While travelling, the Luca family suffered greatly from the effects of a cruel caste spirit then so much prevailing, — being often debarred from hotels, and often denied decent accommodation in public conveyances. But this barbarous treatment of those whose fine musical qualities and genteel appearance and deportment — albeit they were of dark complexions — gave them title to enter the very best places aroused the sympathy and indignation of many persons. And so, amidst all their disadvantages, the success and reputation of our artists steadily increased, and the critics accorded them high rank as musicians; Mason, Gottschalk, and others among the finest pianists of the country, receiving Cleveland Luca, the pianist, as an equal.

In the year 1854 the family experienced a sad shock in the death of Simeon G. Luca.

As before intimated, he was a vocalist and violinist of remarkable powers; and professionally, as well as otherwise, his loss to the troupe was a great one.

The vacancy occasioned by his death was filled by the engagement of Miss Jennie Allen of New York. She proved to be a very valuable acquisition to the troupe; for she possessed a rich contralto voice, sang with excellent method, had a graceful, winning stage appearance, and was well known in New York as a very fine pianist.

The quartet thus arranged then (in 1857) began to travel more extensively, giving performances in the States of New York, Pennsylvania, and Ohio, where their success artistically and financially exceeded any thing before within their experience. Had they so chosen, they might have visited all the free States with assurance of good fortune. Wherever they went, the bitter color-prejudice, the chilling doubtings, or the cold indifference, displayed by those who had not heard these talented musicians, were rapidly dispelled when on the stage they beheld their easy, graceful appearance, and heard the delightful sounds of harmony that proceeded from the voices and instruments of this accomplished quartet. The writer well remembers the emotions of delight and pride that filled his own breast when at this period, in Ohio, he witnessed for the first time their performances. After their first concert, the town became the scene of a most pleasant commotion. No such music had ever before been heard there, and praises of the "Lucas" were on the lips of all. The family were entertained at the residences of the first citizens, who vied with each other in extending to them the most complimentary attentions. In these homes of wealth and culture, where the study and practice of choice music formed a portion of each day's employment, these talented artists, surrounded by a selected company of educated persons, shone even more brightly than when upon the public stage; for here they could confine themselves to a rendition of that higher class of music so suitable to their own tastes and powers, as well as most welcome to their cultivated audience. But what befell the Luca family in this town — the writer has mentioned somewhat particularly this instance, because he happened to be a witness of the same — is but a sample of the treatment they often received in other places while travelling over the country.

As representing the estimate of the musical abilities of the Luca family, held by the general press of the country during their concert tours, and in order that it may be seen that my own praises of the family are none too great, I give the following notice from a fair and disinterested source; viz., "The Niagara Courier" of Lockport, N.Y., of Sept. 2, 1857 : —

"THE LUCA FAMILY.

"This company of singers, consisting of four [three] brothers and their mother, gave a concert at Ringueberg Hall last (Monday) evening; and their performance was such as to elicit the enthusiastic approval of all present. Coming among us as strangers, their merits were not generally understood; and we presume that the entire audience were agreeably disappointed in the entertainment presented. We hazard nothing in saying that we have not had in our place for years a concert which combined all the elements that please the musical ear, and satisfy the cultivated taste, as did this. The introductory piece, 'Fantasia, from Lucia, evinced the highest order of musical culture, the most excellent taste, with that superior power of execution which long practice only gives. The two brothers John and Alexander have superb voices, guided by a correct knowledge of music, and enriched by cultivation. Madame Luca was laboring under indisposition; but she sang well, and gave abundant assurance of superior vocal powers. But the great feature of the entertainment was the performance of C. O. Luca on the piano. With the exception of the celebrated Mason, we have never had his superior as a pianist in Lockport; and even he could not execute the pieces presented with greater effect. There is music in his playing which we seldom hear from the piano. It is not simply the striking of the keys in order, emitting a succession of musical sounds; but it is one continual flow of melody without interruption. From the moment he first strikes the keys, the harmonious melody gushes forth, note melts into note imperceptibly, wave after wave of melody goes forth and mingles into one as do the waves of the sea; and there is no breaking of the majesty of its harmony until the last note is touched.

"The family, as has been before announced, are colored, and consequently labor under some disadvantages; but we predict for them a successful future. Such superior musical powers must win for them a reputation that will bring its recompense. The pieces they sing are selected with good taste, and evince a determination to deserve public favor. And we may here say, that we believe the Luca family, in the quiet and unostentatious display of their musical powers, are doing more to secure position for the colored man than all the theorists and speculators about the right of man have yet accomplished in America. The possession of such talent, and its cultivation, show genius and industry which any man might emulate; and, when the colored men shall be represented in all the arts and sciences by those who are able to occupy front ranks, they will need no moralist to assert their rights: they can then maintain their own position. The human mind is so constituted, that it will always pay homage to genius, let it be exhibited under a white or black surface.

"A large number of the audience joined in a request that the Luca family repeat their concert; and they have consented to do so on Friday evening next, when we hope to see an audience out worthy of their superior merits. In the mean time we commend the Luca family to the press wherever they shall go, as every way worthy of their aid and indorsement."

During their second tour of Ohio, in 1859, the "Lucas" met and joined the famous Hutchinson family, giving many entertainments in conjunction with them. The Hutchinsons thus proved the entire sincerity of their professions that they loved their brother man "for a' that." The press of the country was much excited over this novel union, and the expressions emanating from the former were various. Without, however, minding the pros or cons, these two troupes travelled more than a month together, experiencing a pleasurable and profitable season.

I append below two advertisements of concerts given by these troupes at the time mentioned: —

(I.)

THE HUTCHINSON FAMILY,

ASA B., LIZZIE C., AND LITTLE FREDDY;

with the

LUCA BROTHERS,

JOHN AND ALEXANDER, AND CLEVELAND,

THE WONDERFUL PIANIST!

———◆———

Humor, Sentiment, and Opera!

———◆———

From the established reputation of both these companies, a rare treat may be expected.

(II.)

> By SPECIAL ARRANGEMENTS,
> THE HUTCHINSONS
> will be assisted at their
> CONCERT
> in this place by the
> LUCA FAMILY,
> with their
> Wonderful Pianist!

As a reflection of the terrible, the foul spirit of caste, then so largely prevailing, I regret that it is my duty to append the following elegant (?) extract from a paper published at Fremont, O., Feb. 25, 1859: —

"The Hutchinsons, — Asa B., Lizzie C., and little Freddy, — accompanied by the Luca family, gave a concert at Birchard Hall on last Wednesday evening. The house was not more than a paying one. When we went to the concert, we anticipated a rare treat; but, alas! how wofully were we disappointed! . . . We have, perhaps, a stronger feeling of prejudice than we should have felt under other circumstances, had their abolition proclivities been less startling; but to see respectable white persons (we presume they are such) travelling hand in hand with a party of negroes, and eating at the same table with them, is rather too strong a pill to be gulped down by a democratic community."

No doubt the writer of the above, if now living, would be ashamed to utter sentiments so uncharitable and so vile.

But as an evidence of honest criticism, and in pleasing contrast with the foregoing, I give the following.

"The Norwalk (O.) Reflector," March 1, 1859, says, —

"The concert given in this place on Saturday night last by the Hutchinsons and Lucas was among the best musical entertainments ever given here. The audience was large, and the artists sang with spirit.

"Where all sang so well, it is difficult to select the best. . . . The Lucas are charming musicians, both instrumental and vocal; and, when two such companies unite, there will be superior concerts."

A Sandusky (O.) paper, March 1, 1859, says, —

"The Hutchinsons and Lucas sang to quite a full audience at West's Hall last evening. The performance could not, coming from troupes possessing talent varied and of the higher order, be otherwise than good. These bands, when they united, made a palpable hit. Their combined concerts are almost invariably successes."

A Wooster (O.) paper, February, 1859, says, —

"The Hutchinsons and Lucas — these two celebrated troupes — will give together one of their unrivalled entertainments at Arcadame Hall on Saturday evening next. They are spoken of in the highest terms by the press in different directions. Both troupes have been in Wooster before; so that it is unnecessary for us to speak of them favorably. The hall will undoubtedly be filled."

A Cleveland (O.) paper, Feb. 28, 1859, says, —

"The well-known Luca family are now giving concerts in connection with Asa B., Lizzie C., and little Freddy Hutchinson, of the Hutchinson family; and their performances are highly spoken of by Western exchanges. They perform in Elyria on Tuesday evening; and will soon appear in this city, we understand."

Shortly after the return of the Luca family from the tour with the Hutchinsons, Cleveland the pianist, with a noble aim, resolved to go to Africa. This circumstance caused the disbandment of the troupe.

Their father has resided for a long time at Zanesville, O., where, although quite advanced in years, he is still esteemed as a vocalist, singing in a church choir, and where he enjoys the respect of all for his many good qualities of heart and mind.

His two sons, John and Alexander, are now, as ever, devoted to the art of music; the former being a valuable member of the celebrated Hyer sisters concert and dramatic troupe, while the latter is vocal director of another company.

As a fitting close to this sketch, as a corroboration of my own testimony, and as an evidence of the noble qualities possessed by that rare musician and Christian gentleman, Asa B. Hutchinson, I add the following beautiful tribute from his pen: —

GENEVA, O., Dec. 15, 1875.

In regard to our dear friends the Lucas, I am glad to state that it was our pleasure to associate with them in public concerts "in the cruel days of the prejudiced past;" and this is our testimony: that, in all our concertizing for thirty-five years, we never formed an alliance with any musical people with whom we fraternized so pleasantly, and loved so well, and who evinced so much real genuine talent in their profession, and such courtesy and Christian culture "in their daily walk and conversation." Our dear lamented Cleveland was a thoroughly educated pianist, and won the enthusiastic admiration of the scientific musicians in every city and town we visited. He executed most rapidly, at sight, any and all of the difficult and new compositions that were presented to him by his friends, to their astonishment and our mutual joy; and when the three brothers, "Alex.," John, and Cleveland, united their respective instruments and voices in one grand choral, the effect was intensely thrilling and electrical. In some of our concerted pieces, where they united with us, we carried our reformatory sentiments and songs to a successful termination; and, notwithstanding the then great and bitter prejudice of our audiences against us all for daring thus publicly to associate together, they cheered our combined efforts with loud applause and frequent encores.

And now that each of our bands are broken by death, still believing that the freed spirits of the departed loved ones are re-united in "singing the songs of the redeemed" in that realm of light, liberty, and love beyond, it is a great satisfaction to me, a poor lingering pilgrim, to revert to one of the sweetest experiences of our entire concert-life, — the acquaintance and fellowship of the Luca family.

ASA B. HUTCHINSON.

VII.

HENRY F. WILLIAMS,

COMPOSER, BAND-INSTRUCTOR, ETC.

"Thy purpose firm is equal to the deed."
"His lyre well tuned to rapturous sounds."

A WRITER in "The Progressive American" for July 17, 1872, said, —

"Having occasion to visit Boston, I attended one of the unrivalled concerts at the Coliseum, where, to my great astonishment, I saw undoubtedly the greatest assemblage of human beings ever congregated under one roof, and heard a chorus of nearly or quite twenty thousand voices, accompanied by the powerful organ and an orchestra of two thousand musicians. I was highly delighted. But what gave me the most pleasure was to see among some of the most eminent artists of the world two colored artists performing their parts in common with the others ; viz., Henry F. Williams and F. E. Lewis. Each of these was competent to play his part, or he could not have occupied a place in the orchestra. I was informed by the superintendent of the orchestra that both these men were subjected to a very rigid examination prior to the commencement of the concerts."

The pleasure afforded this writer, by witnessing our subject's appearance on the memorable occasion referred

HENRY F. WILLIAMS.

to, was shared by many other persons who were able to distinguish him in that vast concourse of fine musicians. It was not so easy to distinguish him from the others by his complexion as it was by his dignified, graceful appearance. Of this, as well as of Mr. Williams's musical skill, the organizer of the great orchestra, Mr. Baldwin, has, since the event, spoken to me in terms the most complimentary. He said it was not more Mr. Williams's good playing, than his handsome, manly appearance in the orchestra, that afforded him pleasure; and that in both of these particulars Mr. Williams stood in favorable contrast with many other members of the orchestra. This was high praise indeed, but no higher than its recipient deserved, as all will testify who know him.

As stated in the extract just quoted, Mr. Williams, before being accepted as a member of the Jubilee orchestra, was subjected to a severe test; being required to execute on the double-bass the parts written for that instrument in the celebrated overture from "William Tell," and also in Wagner's difficult "Tannhäuser." In regard to this test Mr. Baldwin has since said to the writer, "I myself had no doubts as to Mr. Williams's ability as a musician. My object in arranging the test performance was, that I might afterwards point to its successful result, and thus silence many of the instrumentalists that came from other parts of the country, in case they should object (I knew that many of them would do so), on the weak ground of *color*, to playing with Mr. Williams. Neither Mr. Gilmore nor myself knew any man by the color of his face. What we wanted for the grand orchestra was *good musicians*, and, when any one objected to our two colored per formers, we triumphantly referred to the exacting and satisfactory test they had undergone as sufficient answer to the foolish clamors of all those afflicted with 'colorphobia.' Seeing the managers of the Jubilee thus resolved, and convinced that the two colored men were artistic performers, — superior in ability to many with whom they were to be associated, — no one declined to play; and all was harmony thereafter.

And here I may be permitted to record the thanks of all well-meaning people for the noble action of Messrs. Gilmore and Baldwin. The two artists mentioned were not the only members of their race who took a part in the memorable Jubilee concerts. Several others in a vocal way occupied even prominent positions at these concerts. Some sang as artists on the stage, and several were members of that great chorus of nearly twenty thousand voices. In all these places they did their share in making the occasion a grand success, while they justified fully the wisdom of those by whom they were invited to participate. The action of the latter was no more than what was due and right, it is true; but it is well to remember (for we must take things as we find them) that Messrs. Gilmore and Baldwin were not obliged to engage these persons. Had the former not been men of pure principles and firmness, they might have yielded to the mean and by far too popular prejudice entertained against colored people, and have refused to allow them to take part in the performances. That they did not thus yield is much to their credit as musicians and gentlemen; and they are to be thanked, I say, for their manly action.

The little ripple of excitement caused by Mr. Williams's appearance among the musicians of the Jubilee might well have provoked from that gentleman a smile of contempt; for he was a far older and much more skilful performer than many who at first objected to playing with him. He had, indeed, more than thirty years of musical experience behind him, — years which were full of manly, persevering struggle against great odds, and years during which he had many times triumphed over opposition far greater than that met by him at the Coliseum. Born in Boston Aug. 13, 1813, beginning his studies when but seven years of age, he had, mainly by his own efforts (he is in the truest sense a "self-made man"), become a thorough musician; was a superior performer on the violin, double-bass, and the cornet; a fair performer on the viola, violoncello, baritone, trombone, tuba, and piano-forte; having been besides for years an esteemed teacher of most of these instruments. Nor did his musical powers stop here; for in addition to being a skilful arranger of music for the instruments just mentioned, and others, he was a composer, many of whose works bore the imprint of several of the most eminent music publishers of the day. Learning these facts, no wonder that those who at first opposed Mr. Williams's entrance into the grand orchestra (these persons, by the way, were not residents of Boston, but came from the West and South) afterwards were ashamed of their foolish prejudices, and became his warm admirers.

Mr. Williams, as an instrumentalist, devotes himself especially to the violin and the cornet. Upon these he executes in a superior manner the finest music of the day. Possessing fine natural talents, of great versatility, and of long study and experience, he is enabled to play any kind of music; passing with the utmost ease from the "light fantastic" of the dance to the grave and profound of the old masters: in either kind he is always noticeable for the finish and tastefulness of his performance. He has given much of his time to the formation and instruction of military bands, frequently arranging and composing music for them. In the former capacity — that of arranging music — he has often been employed by P. S. Gilmore, director of the celebrated Gilmore's Band, and projector of the two great Peace Jubilees. He was at one time connected with the famous "Frank Johnson's band" of Philadelphia, and of several others in the West, travelling extensively, and giving instruction in music. A short while ago, the manager of the Boston Cadet Band — successors of Gilmore's — showed me a quickstep in manuscript, of the merits of which he spoke very highly, composed by Mr. Williams for the first-mentioned band.

The following is only a partial list of the many songs (words as well as the music his own) of which our subject is the author: —

"Lauriette," published by Firth & Pond, New York, 1840; "Come, Love, and list awhile," published by Pond & Hall, New York, 1842; "It was by Chance we met," published by O. Ditson & Co., Boston, 1866; "I would I'd never met Thee," published by O. Ditson & Co., Boston, 1876.

Of the above, "Lauriette" had a large sale, the *publishers* realizing a considerable profit from the same. In 1854 O. Ditson & Co. published his "Parisien Waltzes." These are a set in five numbers, with a fine introduction, and containing some very bright and sweetly-flowing melodies. These waltzes had a good sale, and added much to the composer's reputation.

Besides the above, Mr. Williams has composed eight or ten polka-redowas, and several mazurkas and quadrilles (some of these have been published); and he is the author of several overtures.

Early in his career he composed an anthem which was much praised by persons of musical judgment. At that time so greatly was the judgment of people affected by color-prejudice, that many persons doubted the ability of one of his race to create a work so meritorious as the one just mentioned. They were, however, soon compelled to admit that Mr. Williams was the talented author of it.

Lowell Mason, the eminent composer of sacred music, was one of those who at first entertained doubts as to the authorship of the anthem; and he, like the others, finally yielded to stubborn facts. Moreover, becoming acquainted with our subject, and learning more of his fine abilities as a musician, Mr. Mason remarked that it was a pity one so talented should be kept down merely on account of the color of his face. I am sorry to say, nevertheless, that this gentleman could rise no higher above the common level of that day than to advise Mr. Williams to go to Liberia. Had Mr. Mason, who was so original and bold in music, been only half as bold in creating a sensible, a humane public sentiment; had he, as he looked with pity upon this gifted and devoted young musician struggling against the ignoble spirit of caste to gain a place in art, thrown his great influence on the side of what he confessed was right; and had he, instead of advising Mr. Williams to *bury* himself in Africa, declared that the latter should have an equal chance with others in *this* country in developing his musical powers, — had Mr. Mason done this, I say, I feel sure that such encouragement, coming in the very "nick of time," would have resulted in placing the subject of this sketch far above even his present excellent position as a musician, while such noble action on the part of Mr. Mason might to-day be considered as an additional gem in the latter's confessedly bright crown. I hope I do not seem too harsh. I love music and those who create it, and I greatly dislike to speak aught that is ill of such persons. And yet I love too, even more ardently, reform and its promoters; and therefore cannot regard with complacency the acts of those, who, possessing great talents and influence, yet fail to use them in furthering the cause of right. I have said that Mr. Williams has written several overtures: one of these was for the orchestra of the famous Park Theatre. At present he is constantly engaged in arranging and composing music.

In concluding this brief sketch, which I fear falls short of doing its subject justice, I will only add, that in the remarkably fine achievements he has made under circumstances and against difficulties that would have caused many to falter, indeed, to yield in despair, — chief among these difficulties being the hateful, terrible spirit of *color-prejudice*, that foul spirit, the full measure of whose influence in crushing out the genius often born in children of his race it is difficult to estimate, — in Mr. Williams's triumphs in a great degree against all these, I say, is presented an instance of art-love, and of manly, persevering devotion, that is truly heroic. Falling short, as he does, of an eminence, that, had he been born with a fairer complexion, would ere this have been his, his life is yet a grand example to those younger members of his race who are beginning their careers in the world of music when fairer skies light their pathway; when the American people, regretting the depressing, blighting cruelties of the dark past, now seek to atone for the same by offering encouragement to *all* who exhibit musical talents, and evince a conscientious desire to improve the same. Mr. Williams may remember with pride that to this gratifying result he has in a very marked degree contributed; and that therefore, in spite of some disappointments, his musical life has really been a noble success.

VIII.

JUSTIN HOLLAND,

THE EMINENT AUTHOR AND ARRANGER,

AND PERFORMER ON THE GUITAR, FLUTE, AND PIANO-FORTE.

> "Gayly the troubadour
> Touched his guitar."
> OLD SONG.

> "Untwisting all the chains that tie
> The hidden soul of harmony."
> MILTON.

NO life can be called a truly great one that has not been a truly good one: a very simple saying, and one which, however trite, yet requires frequent repeating, since its importance is but too seldom considered. And the noble fame that sooner or later surely attaches to the author of such a life belongs chiefly, but not entirely, to him; it being in part, in a certain sense, the property of all who would follow in his footsteps, becoming for them an inspiring example; its history, with all its experiences of hope and fear, its occasional failures but frequent successes, its struggles when environed by poverty or other untoward circumstances, and its final triumph over all obstacles, serving as a guide,

JUSTIN HOLLAND

a beacon indeed, to illumine their pathway as they climb the same difficult but glorious hills of honor.

But such renown comes oftenest to those who seek it not, — to those who perform the right for the sake of right. These are they who

"Do good by stealth, and blush to find it fame."

Thoughts very similar to those just expressed are such as will naturally enter the minds of all who contemplate the history of Justin Holland, the distinguished musician. A mere outline of that interesting history is all that can here be given.

But first let me say, that if a little while ago, when arranging the title for this sketch, the writer had been quite sure that in placing after the name of the person to be treated a certain single word, — which really is one of very extensive meaning, although not always so used or understood, — had he been sure that from that word the general reader would have formed a complete idea of this artist's very varied accomplishments, then the heading would have been simply, "Justin Holland, musician." But judging that such brevity, however desirable in some respects, might yet fail in doing justice to one whose great native talents, joined to remarkable attainments made during a life of most industrious endeavor, entitle him to very particular mention from first to last, I have thought it best to state in detail the several departments of the musical art in which he has won the rarest of laurels.

I am not quite certain, though, that such minute mention will be pleasant to Mr. Holland; for I learn that he is as modest as he is learned, and that he has always had a sort of aversion to having his name appear in print at all, albeit during his long career in music it has thus appeared many times, in spite of said aversion, and always most honorably. But when he shall read these pages, on which nought shall be set down save with a regard for truth, and shall perceive by them, that while he steadily, quietly, and effectively worked for many years, with no attempts at ostentatious display, scarcely looking up the while to observe the outer results of his work, and to catch for inspiration the praises of men; when he shall see in his now mature years that all he so noiselessly invented, and fashioned into practical, useful form, is regarded by a well-meaning chronicler as of vast importance in serving as a noble example for the study and imitation of the youth of the land, and therefore to be faithfully recorded, — then it is hoped he will pardon the somewhat free but well-intentioned use that is here made of his name and deeds.

Mr. Holland was born in 1819 amidst the then "solitudes" of Norfolk County, Va. His father, Exum Holland, was a farmer. When quite a young child, Justin evinced a very decided fondness for music. But, nearly sixty years ago, a farm-life in Virginia, ten miles from any town, as may be imagined, afforded but poor opportunities for either hearing or learning music. Such opportunities, however, as were within reach, our subject very eagerly embraced. It is related of him, that, when less than fourteen years of age, he was in the habit of walking on Sundays to a log meeting-house five miles away, and there listening to and joining in such music (?) as was at that time discoursed in such places. But previously to this, when only a boy of eight years, he accidentally came into possession of an old song-book with words only. Being much delighted with this, he often perched himself upon a rail-fence, quite removed from the farm-house and all chance of interruption, where he sang and heartily enjoyed the songs, the music for which this would-be musician extemporized. Years afterward it was found that some of the tunes he thus early invented, and which he retained in his memory, were equal if not superior in merit to those that really belonged to the songs in the book mentioned. Thus was Holland almost born with the composer's art.

When about fourteen years old, Justin left Virginia, and went to Boston; from whence he shortly afterwards removed, going to Chelsea, Mass. Here he spent his youth and several years of his manhood. A short while after becoming a resident of Chelsea, he determined to study in earnest the science of music. At this time he happened to become acquainted with Señor Mariano Perez, a Spanish musician, and one of a troupe that was performing at the old Lion Theatre on Washington Street in Boston. He had many opportunities for hearing Perez play upon the guitar. The richness and beauty of melody and harmony, and the unsurpassed variety and fineness of expression, that were evolved from this beautiful instrument by this master-performer, so charmed Holland, that he decided to give his chief attention to the study of the guitar. Not that he then dreamed of ever becoming a teacher or professor of the instrument: he wished to learn music simply for his own amusement. His first music-teacher was Mr. Simon Knaebel, who was a member of "Ned" Kendall's famous brass band, and who enjoyed a high reputation as an arranger of music. After a while he began lessons with Mr. William Schubert, also a member of Kendall's band,

and a correct and brilliant performer on the guitar Under this teacher our subject soon made rapid progress, becoming a favorite pupil from his ability to play duets with his instructor; the latter being very fond of that kind of music. He afterwards made fine progress with the eight-keyed flute, taking lessons on this instrument from a Scotch gentleman by the name of Pollock. During all this time, it must be borne in mind that our zealous young student was unaided by any one in defraying the great expense incurred in pursuing his studies. He had to depend upon his own hard earnings. Besides, he had no time for practice save that taken from the hours usually devoted to sleep.

In 1841 (his age was then twenty-two years), desiring more education than his hitherto limited opportunities had allowed him to obtain, he went to that noble institution, Oberlin College, where, feeling anxious to make up for all time lost, he diligently pursued his studies, and made rapid advancement. In 1844 his progress had been so good, that we find him one of the authors of a book of three hundred and twenty-four pages on certain subjects of moral reform. In 1845 Mr. Holland went to Cleveland, O., then only a small city of less than nine thousand inhabitants. While prospecting in Cleveland for something to do, it was found that he was an amateur performer on the guitar, playing the best music with a fine degree of proficiency. This brought him applications to give lessons to members of some of the first families in the city, and caused him to make Cleveland his permanent home. His character had now become finely formed, he being quite noticeable for his gentlemanly, scholarly qualities, and for the close attention he gave to the subject of music and to all that concerned true advancement in the profession in which he had now resolved to remain for life. As illustrating the principles by which he was guided, I give the following extract from a letter of his to a friend, describing his life at the time just mentioned. He says, —

"I adopted as a rule of guidance for myself, that I would do full justice to the learner in my efforts to impart to him a good knowledge of the elementary principles of music, and a correct system of fingering [on the guitar], as practised by, and taught in the works of, the best masters in Europe. I also decided that in my intercourse as teacher I would preserve the most cautious and circumspect demeanor, considering the relation a mere business one that gave me no claims upon my pupils' attention or hospitality beyond what any ordinary business matter would give. I am not aware, therefore, that any one has ever had cause to complain of my demeanor, or that I have been in any case presumptive."

He had now become firmly established as a teacher, and was soon at the head of the profession in Cleveland as a guitar-instructor. This, however, did not satisfy him; and he determined to attain to still greater proficiency. Finding that the best systems for guitar-playing were such as were taught in the works (foreign) of Sor, Carulli, D'Aguado, Giuliani, Ferranti, and Mertz, Mr. Holland entered upon a course of study of the French, Italian, and Spanish languages, in order that he might read in the original the systems of those great masters, and thus be the better able to understand and apply the same. He soon by diligent study acquired a knowledge of the languages mentioned; and, as will hereafter appear, this knowledge became of great use to him.

The secret of our subject's great success as a guitar-virtuoso may be readily gathered from the statement I have just made about the foreign languages. *He was always thorough, enterprising, singularly industrious.* Loving deeply his chosen profession and instrument, he could never be satisfied with a position of mere mediocrity, either as a performer or teacher; but with most studious care he sought both near and far all sources of theoretical information, in order that he might thus secure skill in elucidation; while as a performer he reached to the innermost depths, so to say, of all forms of great musical expression, that he might bring from thence such sweets of melody and harmony as would charm his pupils, and rivet their attention on that beautiful instrument, the guitar. He ever aimed, in fine, to carry guitar-playing in this country to a state that comported with the highest laws of science, — to elevate it to the high level whence it had been taken by the great masters of Europe. His success in these aims will be more fully seen as this account progresses.

Mr. Holland, it seems, has not aspired to distinction as an original composer of music, although he has done something in that line. Of modest pretensions, and rather practical character, he has considered that he could do more for music and the guitar in seeking to make the meritorious compositions of others for other instruments available for guitar practice by skilful arrangements; and in this, his special field of musical labor, — speaking with respect either to the quantity or quality of his works, — he is without an equal in this country: indeed, in certain particulars which will be mentioned hereafter, it will be seen that he has surpassed even the guitar-virtuosos of Europe. His published arrangements for the guitar of the best music composed number more than three hundred pieces, all of them ranking as standard; while with guitar-students, and the principal music-publishers of the day, the name of Holland has been since 1848 as familiar as a household word. It is remarkable, too, that nearly all of this large number of arrangements were made from music sent to Mr. Holland by publishers, with a request that he adapt the same to the guitar. He did not need to sound his own praises. While he quietly worked with his pupils in Cleveland, his fame as a skilful musician was spreading over the country. Soon publishers began to send him orders for arrangements. Such pieces as he had written merely for diversion, or for use with his classes, when it became known that he had them, were eagerly solicited for publication. If the reader will examine the catalogues of the larger music-publishing houses of the country, he will find, that, under the head of Guitar-Music, the name of Holland appears far oftener than that of any other writer. A partial list of his works I have thought of transferring from the publishers' catalogues to the pages of this book; but this, perhaps, is not necessary, nor will space allow it. I will state that his arrangements, with variations, three in number, of "Home, Sweet Home," are considered by competent judges the best adaptations of this immortal air ever made for the guitar. The same opinion is also expressed cf his arrangement, with variations, of "The Carnival of Venice." It is a five-page concert-piece, equal to ten or twelve pages of piano-music. Those who love the guitar, or who are desirous of testing the abilities of the author and the correctness of the judgment just given, would do well to procure these two selections: this they can do from any of the music-publishers. Nor is a guitar library complete unless it contains many more of this writer's works; such, for instance, as the following: "Winter Evenings," a collection of fifteen pieces, eight of them with variations; "Flowers of Melody," twenty-three pieces, among which is to be found the charming "Flower-Song" from the opera of "Faust," arranged as a solo; "Gems for the Guitar," twenty pieces; "Summer Evenings," containing an extensive list of songs; and "Bouquet of Melodies," a series of twenty-four arrangements from the most popular operas, all instrumental.

Most of Mr. Holland's writing has been for the eminent firm of S. Brainard's Sons of Cleveland, O., the most extensive music-publishing house in the country, with one exception; next to them, for J. L. Peters & Co. of New York; G. W. Brainard and D. P. Fauld, Louisville, Ky.; John Church of Cincinnati; and for a house in Michigan.

But our talented author has not confined himself to that department of guitar-writing just under consideration. Equal to his fame as an arranger is his fame as a writer of instruction-books for the guitar. These works are distinguished for comprehensiveness of study, general simplicity of arrangement, and for boldness of attack, and clearness of elucidation, of *all* guitar difficulties. His chief work is "Holland's Comprehensive Method for the Guitar," written for and published by J. L. Peters & Co., New York, in 1874. This book, while in manuscript, was by Messrs. Peters & Co. submitted to the judgment of some of the finest critics in New York, by whom it was pronounced the best ever prepared either in this country or Europe.

On this point I append the following from the Cleveland "Plain-Dealer" of Dec. 24, 1868: —

"AN IMPORTANT MUSICAL WORK IN PREPARATION.

" For several months, Mr. Justin Holland, who has long enjoyed an honorable fame as a teacher of the guitar, a performer upon that instrument, and a successful musical author, has been engaged upon a book of instruction for the guitar. The work was undertaken at the suggestion of Mr. J. L. Peters, the widely-known music-publisher of New-York City, who has purchased the book, and will publish it at once; Mr. Holland having so nearly finished it, that the first portion can be put to press immediately. The work was sent on to New York some time since for Mr. Peters's inspection; and he submitted it to several other prominent musical critics and guitarists, all of whom expressed themselves highly pleased with it. Mr. Dressler, of 'The United-States Musical Review,' published at New York, says, 'I have carefully and thoroughly examined this new method for the guitar, and must confess that it is already, in its present state, the best in this country,—the most thorough, explicit, progressive, agreeable, and satisfactory work ever written in this country or in Europe.' Higher praise than this a book could not receive. The method is very elaborate, and contains many points not heretofore touched on in works of the kind. Mr. Holland's abilities as a composer of music, and his skill as a performer upon the guitar, render him pre-eminently qualified to write such a work; and supplying, as it will, a want long felt, it will achieve popularity at once, we firmly believe."

Some time after the publication of the method just mentioned, the Messrs. Brainard engaged Mr. Holland to write a somewhat similar one, but smaller in size, for them. This they issued in 1876, it being styled "Holland's Modern Method for the Guitar." Although smaller in size than the first one, it is regarded as the best method for beginners that has as yet been produced.

It may perhaps be interesting to those possessing a scientific acquaintance with the guitar, as well, indeed, as to the general student of music, to learn how this accomplished author acquired the power to so clearly — more clearly than it was ever before done in guitar books — explain the method of producing on the guitar the *harmonic tones.* Writing a friend, Mr. Holland thus speaks of this: —

"When, in writing my first book, I came to the subject 'Harmonics,' I found myself at a loss as to how to explain these tones; not as to how to produce them myself, but to give a correct *theory* of their production. I searched in vain through a multitude of musical works, not knowing or thinking of anywhere else to look. I stopped for several weeks, and began a series of observations on the vibrations on the strings of my guitar; having nothing to aid me but my eyes, fingers, and ears, and a knowledge of the fact that the vibrations of a string were doubled in number for every octave of ascent in pitch of tone. I thus discovered the true theory of the harmonic tones to be the vibrations of a single string in a number of equal sections, more or less, and all at the same time; and that their production was at the pleasure of the operator as he desired higher or lower tones. Having fully verified my discoveries, I then corrected the erroneous theory on this subject of the great guitarist, F. Sor. I learned afterwards that the subject was discussed and explained in some scientific works that treated on acoustics."

I have before referred to the pecuniary disadvantages under which Mr. Holland had to labor in the beginning of his career. These followed him for a long period. It seems that much time must nearly always elapse ere even genius becomes acknowledged, and its possessor receives that pecuniary reward so necessary to his support. This acknowledgment, and, to an encouraging extent, this substantial reward, came to Mr. Holland after a while, but not until after he had passed through many very trying scenes. One of the latter has been thus described: —

"He always had a horror of asking any one for credit or a loan. At a certain time he found himself out of ready money. It was Sunday, and he had not the 'wherewith' to get his breakfast on Monday morning. He had always lived retired, forcing intimacy with none, and generally mingling only where business called him. He therefore did not feel intimate enough with any one to offer to borrow, nor did he feel like asking anywhere for credit. He had, however, a small job of writing that had been sent in, for which, when done, he was to receive about twenty-five dollars. Here was Mr. Holland's resource. He began his work about seven o'clock on Sunday evening. He wrote till late. Becoming weary, and his eyelids being heavy, he lighted a spirit-lamp; and with a very diminutive French coffee-pot he prepared, and soon was sipping, a cup of coffee that no doubt would have pleased the Arabian prophet, had he been present to partake. Refreshed by this, he continued his labors until the darkness grew to gray dawn, and the dawn to full light of day. At seven in the morning the last note was written. At eight o'clock he took the work to his patron, and before nine returned with a light heart and good material for breakfast."

A touching incident this, surely, but one that has had either a near or perfect counterpart in the lives of many music writers and teachers, who have often been obliged to labor in season and out of season for the bare necessaries of life. And yet how seldom it is that we are aware of the painful vigils that are kept by these gifted but toiling ones when creating the works that so much contribute to the pleasure of our leisure moments!

Of all the music-publishing firms for whom Mr. Holland has written, I believe the only ones that know him personally, and know that he is a colored man, are the Messrs. Brainard and Mr. John Church. On this point of color, a little incident in his life is well worth recording. One day, in 1864, Mr. Holland went into a large music-store (not in Cleveland) to purchase an instrument. The salesmen present seeming disposed — no doubt on account of his color — to give him no attention whatever, he quietly left, and made his purchase elsewhere. He has since been employed by, and has received large sums of money from, that very firm, as a writer of music for them. He does not even now personally know any one of the firm; nor is it supposed that the latter know him otherwise than by his reputation, and through correspondence with him. It is almost certain, that had it been generally known, as it was not outside of Cleveland, that this gifted and accomplished musician was a member of the colored race, his success would have been much curtailed, so greatly has the senseless, the ignoble feeling of color-phobia prevailed in this country. To the Messrs. Brainard and Mr. Church, who proved themselves superior to the low prejudices of the times, all honor be given! To them the brightness of the artist's genius was not obscured by the color of his face.

As another evidence of the esteem in which Mr. Holland is held by one of the firms just mentioned, I append the following extract from a letter which I received a few months ago: —

S. BRAINARD'S SONS' MUSIC-PUBLISHING HOUSE,
CLEVELAND, O., April 2, 1877.

Dear Sir, — . . . Mr. Justin Holland is one of our finest practical and theoretical musicians. He has written two large methods for the guitar, besides being the composer and arranger of a large amount of guitar-music, both vocal and instrumental. He is a refined and educated gentleman of very modest and unpretending character, but is a thorough musician and student.

Yours,

S. BRAINARD'S SONS.

A few years ago, on his return from a visit to New Orleans, he stopped at Leavenworth, Kan. The editor of the leading paper in Leavenworth, supposing that Mr. Holland intended to remain there, thus spoke of him editorially: —

"PROFESSOR HOLLAND.

"We had the pleasure of a visit yesterday from Professor J. Holland of Louisiana, who is an eminent music teacher and writer of thirty years' practical experience. He purposes locating in Leavenworth, and giving instructions on the guitar, flute, and piano. He has made an especial study of the guitar, and has written a work on it which is pronounced the best in print by competent critics. We need just such a man as the professor in this city, and are glad he has come among us, and hope he may receive a liberal patronage."

And the editor of "The Musical World," Professor Carl Merz, thus mentioned Mr. Holland in the number of that journal for October, 1877: —

. . . " Again we would mention Mr. Justin Holland, teacher of the guitar, and composer of music for this instrument. Mr. Holland is a great lover of art, a gentleman of culture, who reads fluently several languages, and whose labors are highly esteemed by publishers as well as by lovers of the guitar. From 'Der Freimaurer,' a monthly published in Vienna, Austria, we learn that Mr. Holland is now in his fifty-seventh year. He lives in Cleveland, where he enjoys the patronage of the lovers of music, irrespective of color."

As before intimated, Mr. Holland's pupils have been in many cases members of the richest and most highly cultivated families of Cleveland; and such have been his skill as an instructor, and his noble qualities of heart and mind in general, as evinced in his deportment towards them, that the persons just mentioned, and others of his scholars, have ever entertained for him not only feelings of deep respect, but those also of affection. Among other very pleasing instances of this is one found in the case of Mr. and Mrs. Briggs of Massachusetts, the former a son of Ex-Gov. Briggs of that State, and the latter a native of Cleveland, a lady of great refinement and general culture, who, up to the time of her marriage, was a pupil of Mr. Holland. This estimable couple, who formerly and semi-annually visited Cleveland, never failed at such times to pay their respects to Mrs. Briggs's former tutor, showing by this course that neither time nor space could obliterate the warm regard which had been created by previous pleasant associations.

The writer has thus far said but very little of Mr. Holland's abilities as a performer on, and teacher of, the flute and piano-forte. Let it suffice to say, briefly, that these abilities are such as to show, that, had he chosen to devote himself to either of these two instruments as much as he has devoted himself to the guitar, he might have attained to great distinction in the same. But, even as it is, he is regarded as a fine flutist and pianist. For the piano he has composed and arranged a number of pieces. He has played in public occasionally, of course always with the greatest acceptance. He has, however, never sought for nor made occasions to play in public; being always noticeable for a love of the quieter, and to him pleasanter, walks of musical life.

And now, if this were not intended as a book on musical history alone, the writer might occupy many more pages in narrating the many important events connected with the life of Mr. Holland as a distinguished member for years of the order of Free Masons. We may be allowed to mention incidentally, that his reputation as one of the "noble craft" is even greater than his reputation as a musician. It is more nearly worldwide; for we find that as a Mason he is well known in the South and West of this country, and in South America, Italy, Germany, and France. A sketch of his life, together with his portrait, was published at Vienna, Austria, in the illustrated monthly " Der Freimaurer " (" The Freemason "), in the number for February, 1877. From this journal I learn that Mr. Holland has been a most active and indispensable member of Excelsior Lodge No. 11 of Cleveland (which he assisted in forming in 1865), and of the Grand Lodge of Ohio. In the former he has held the offices of Secretary and Junior Warden; and in the latter he first served two terms (declining a third) as Worshipful Master, and afterwards was elected Senior Grand Deacon, Deputy Grand Master, Deputy Grand High Priest, of the Grand Chapter of Royal Arch Masons for Ohio, — serving three terms, — and Most Excellent Grand High Priest. In conducting the foreign correspondence of the Grand Lodge, Mr. Holland has for a number of years performed a most invaluable service. In this work, his familiar acquaintance with the French, Spanish, German, Italian, and Portuguese languages was put to uses the most important, as through the same, and his very intelligent and painstaking management, the colored Masons of Ohio have been fully recognized by, and brought into communication with, the Grand Lodges of France, Peru, Germany, Portugal, and Spain. Mr. Holland has also been appointed the representative in this country of the Grand Lodges of France and Peru, each appointment a very rare distinction. He has several times received complimentary mention in the addresses of the Grand Masters of the Ohio Lodge; and in 1866 he was the recipient from the members of the latter of a set of highly eulogistic resolutions, and of a valuable gold watch appropriately inscribed. All these honors were tendered as earnest tokens of the high estimation in which he was held by the brotherhood for the skill and zeal he had so often displayed in serving a cause founded on the noble principles of faith, hope, and charity.

What a busy, what a useful, honorable life, have we been following! It is hoped that the reader has been entertained and instructed by even this far from perfect unfolding of the same. As for the writer, he leaves its present consideration with feelings of affectionate regret; while he would fain remain to study again and again the valuable lessons that it teaches, and to watch with unabated interest the fortunes of its future. May the latter bring to our noble friend and artist as little of disappointment as may be! and when the end shall finally come, as come it must some day to all, may he have, as a crowning and sweet reward for the manly, the heroic past, a sleep like that of him who "lies down to pleasant dreams"!

THOMAS J. BOWERS.

IX.

THOMAS J. BOWERS,

TENOR-VOCALIST;

OFTEN STYLED

THE "AMERICAN MARIO."

"Sweet is every sound;
Sweeter thy voice."
TENNYSON.

THOMAS J. BOWERS, who, owing to his resembling in the magnificent quality of his voice that celebrated Italian singer, has been styled by the press the "American Mario," was born in Philadelphia in the year 1836.

When quite a lad he evinced a decided fondness for music, and much musical talent. His father, a man of considerable intelligence, and for twenty years the warden of St. Thomas's P. E. Church in Philadelphia, being desirous that his children should learn music, first procured a piano and an instructor for his eldest son, John C. Bowers; intending, after he became competent so to do, that he should teach the other children. This purpose was accomplished; and our subject was instructed by his brother to perform upon the piano-forte and organ. At eighteen he had become somewhat proficient in the playing of these instruments, and succeeded his brother as organist of St. Thomas's Church.

I must not fail to mention here, that the younger of his two sisters, Sarah Sedgwick Bowers, became a fine singer. In the rendering of classical and all operatic music she exhibited much talent, was of handsome appearance, and elicited very complimentary notices from the press. I shall have occasion to speak of this lady more at length hereafter.

The parents of the subject of this sketch, although highly pleased with the natural musical qualities and with the accomplishments displayed by their children, were such strict church people as not to wish them to become public performers. Recognizing the pleasing, refining influence of music, they desired its practice by their children in the home-circle, for the most part; but were not averse, however, to hearing its sweet and sacred strains issue from choir and organ in church-services, nor to having their children take part in the same.

The wishes of his much-loved parents Mr. Bowers respected. For this reason he refused to join the famous "Frank Johnson's band" of Philadelphia, although strongly urged by its director; and all offers made to him to join other public organizations were declined for a long time.

But his very rare powers as a tenor-vocalist were those which previous to the attainment of his majority had most attracted the attention and excited the admiration of many persons. Indeed, his voice was considered as something extraordinary in its power, mellowness, so to speak, and its sweetness.

Thus endowed, it was not possible, in the nature of things, that he should remain only a singer in private; and so, at Sansom-street Hall, Philadelphia, in 1854, he was induced to appear with the "Black Swan" as her pupil.

Although it was not at this concert that he made his first public "hit," as it is called, yet the press of Philadelphia spoke of his performances on that occasion in the most flattering terms, and called for a repetition of the concert. This was given, our subject meeting with still greater success. At this time, one of the critics, in commenting on the voice and style of singing of Mr. Bowers, called him the "colored Mario." Considering the almost if not quite peerless position then held in the musical world by the distinguished Italian tenor, Mario, this was a most strikingly favorable comparison. But our artist was so modest as to doubt that he merited such high praise. The press, however, generally persisted in styling him the "colored Mario," the "American Mario," &c.; and by these sobriquets he is most known to-day.

Col. Wood, once the manager of the Cincinnati Museum, hearing of the remarkable singing qualities of Mr. Bowers, came to Philadelphia to hear him. He was so much pleased, that he entered into an engagement with him to make a concert tour of New-York State and the Canadas. This was in company with Miss Sarah Taylor Greenfield, the famous songstress. The great vocal ability as well as the novelty formed by the complexions of this couple produced quite a sensation, and secured for them great success wherever they appeared.

During this tour Col. Wood wished Mr. Bowers to

appear under the title of the "*Indian* Mario," and again under that of the "*African* Mario." He withheld his consent to the use of either of these names, but adopted that of " Mareo." This he has since retained as his professional cognomen.

Mr. Bowers was induced to engage in public performances more for the purpose of demonstrating by them the capacity of colored persons to take rank in music with the most highly cultured of the fairer race than for that of making a mere personal display of his highly-rated musical abilities, and for the attainment of the enjoyment which they would naturally be supposed to afford him.

Writing to a friend, he thus speaks of the principle that governed him:—

" What induced me more than any thing else to appear in public was to give the lie to 'negro serenaders' (minstrels), and to show to the world that colored men and women could sing classical music as well as the members of the other race by whom they had been so terribly vilified."

Nor would he ever yield to that mean and vulgar prejudice, once so prevalent, but now happily disappearing, which either sought to prevent colored persons from entering at all the public-amusement hall, or else to force them to occupy seats near the entrance, or away up in the gallery. All must be treated alike, or he would not sing. As illustrating this characteristic, I give the following incident connected with the concert tour in Canada:—

In Hamilton, a Dr. Brown purchased for himself and some friends six reserved-seat tickets, at a cost of one dollar each. After he had done so, Mr. Bowers's agent was informed by the proprietor of the hall in which the concert was to be held that "colored people were not admitted to first-class seats in Canada." This created much excitement. Our artist espoused Dr. Brown's cause; informed Col. Wood that he would not sing, if he refused to admit the doctor's party on the terms implied by his tickets; that if, after entering, there should be any attempt to oust them, he would assist them; and that he did not leave his home to encourage such mean prejudice. This noble stand against unjust discrimination resulted in granting to Dr. Brown the seats for which he had purchased tickets; and, after this time, no attempt was made to exclude colored persons from the concerts of the troupe.

Mr. Bowers, during his career, has sung in most of the Eastern and Middle States; and at one time he even invaded the slavery-cursed regions of Maryland. He sang in Baltimore, the papers of which city were forced to accord to him high merit as a vocalist.

When we consider the high ideal cherished from the very commencement of his career by our subject, it is not surprising that his musical performances have never been marred by the singing of other than classical or the best music. He does sing, at times, songs in the ballad form; but these are always of the higher class, and such as would be adopted by any first-class singer. His *repertoire* is composed of most all the songs for the tenor voice in the standard operas and oratorios. He sings with fine effect such gems as "Spirito Gentil," from "La Favorita;" "Ah! I have sighed," from "Il Trovatore;" and "How so Fair," from "Martha."

Mr. Bowers resides at present in Philadelphia, and is a little past forty years of age. He sings as well now as ever; some think better than ever. He appears occasionally in public, but only in company with the first artists, as he firmly believes in maintaining always for himself and others a high musical standard. His voice ranges within a semitone of two octaves.

He is a man of decidedly handsome form, and of graceful, pleasing stage appearance; is, indeed, an ideal tenor, and a real artist.

I append, from among the many press-notices that have appeared during his career, the few that follow.

"The Daily Pennsylvanian" of Feb. 9, 1854, after describing the Sansom-street Hall concerts, and alluding to some defects in the manner of his gestures, thus speaks of the performances of our subject: —

"He has naturally a superior voice, far better than many of the principal tenors who have been engaged for star opera troupes. He has, besides, much musical taste."

"The Boston Journal" said, —

"The tenor of this troupe (Mr. Bowers) possesses a voice of wonderful power and beauty."

Another paper said, —

"As most of our citizens have heard the 'colored Mario,' it is unnecessary for us to speak of his singing, as it is generally admitted that his tenor is second to none of our celebrated opera-singers."

Another said, —

"The concert given by the Sedgwick Company was a great success. . . . 'Mario's' fine tenor voice was never more feelingly exercised, nor more rapturously encored."

Again he is thus highly praised: —

"The 'colored Mario's' voice is unequalled by any of the great operatic performers."

A Montreal paper said, —

"'Mario' is a very handsome specimen of his race, and has a fine tenor voice. . . . He, too, was repeatedly encored, both in his solo-pieces and in his duets with Miss Greenfield."

The true value of the foregoing comments from the press will be better understood when the reader calls to mind the fact, that, when they were made, Mr. Bowers had as contemporaries the wonderful Signor Mario, the eminent "Swedish Nightingale," Jenny Lind, the not much less charming songstress, Parodi, as well as several fine tenor-singers connected with the Italian opera companies then performing throughout this country. With such models as these to elevate their tastes and guide their judgments, the critics knew well the worth of all they said in praise of Mr. Bowers. Forming our judgments, then, from what they did say of him (only a very few of their highly favorable comments have here been given), we may safely say that Mr. Bowers is to be ranked with the very first tenor-vocalists of his time.

X.

JAMES GLOUCESTER DEMAREST,

GUITAR AND VIOLIN.

"Soft is the music that would charm forever."
WORDSWORTH.

THE guitar, although not of sufficient power for general orchestral purposes, is yet excellent for finished solo-playing, and as an accompaniment to a voice. It was much used by the ancient troubadours, its dulcet tones according well with their songs. In Italy and Spain, in other parts of Europe, as well as in some sections of this country, the guitar is much esteemed. It has always been the favorite instrument of the serenading gallant; and to perform upon it, previously to their more general adoption of the piano-forte, was considered as an almost necessary accomplishment for the gentler sex. Among the greatest of guitar-v rtuosos that have lived may be mentioned F. Sor, F)ssa, Aguado, Giuliani, Carulli, Holland, Douglass; and, as comparing favorably with these, I may mention Demarest, of whom I shall now briefly speak.

Mr. Demarest, for many years a resident teacher of Boston, was one of the finest guitar-performers in the

United States, and, I believe, had only a few equals in the world. With him the numerous guitar "pickers" of the country are not at all to be mentioned; for, thoroughly educated in music, with rich natural gifts all fully cultivated, giving to the instrument the closest, the most conscientious study, and of long practice, he was thus enabled to draw from it music of such richness and beauty, as few, before hearing his playing, imagined it capable. He but rarely indulged himself or his hearers in playing accompaniments to songs (the use, by the way, to which the guitar is often put); but with masterly skill he ever aimed to develop its fullest resources, and showed that, when in his hands at least, the guitar could be rendered a solo instrument of very noticeable power, as well as great sweetness of tone. At public and private performances in Boston and elsewhere, Mr. Demarest has often delighted audiences by fine interpretations of the best music published.

He was also a proficient arranger of music for the guitar, and, besides, composed some fine pieces for it. I do not know that any of his works were ever published: I think they were not; they being prepared simply to facilitate the progress of his pupils, and for his own amusement.

It is said that on one occasion a prominent guitarist, — a teacher of and writer for the guitar, — when asked to give his opinion of one of Demarest's compositions, remarked that it was "too difficult for the guitar." However this may have been, no one could say that it was too difficult for the composer to perform; and, that being true, it ought not to have been considered as beyond the possible reach of other skilful players. Still the critic referred to may only have meant by his remark that the piece was too difficult to become "popular." I only mention the incident to show that Demarest always aimed high.

As a teacher of the guitar he took high rank with those who believed in advancing its performance to the most elevated standards. He found but few pupils, however, that were willing to give the instrument that closeness of study, or who were possessed with that spirit of patience, so necessary to render them remarkable performers. At the almost marvellously skilful manipulations of the strings by their teacher, they listened with the utmost delight; but some of them, regarding him as one exceptionally endowed, despaired of ever being able to follow him into those higher and fuller forms of guitar-playing whither he ever earnestly strove to lead them. He always insisted on a conscientious study of the instrument, and the practice of only the best music, in order that his pupils might place themselves on a much higher level than that occupied by the many who contented themselves with merely "thumping" a simple, unvaried accompaniment to the popular love-songs of the day.

Mr. Demarest was also a violinist of fair ability. In his performances on the violin he evinced the same scholarly spirit as he did in his other studies. He, however, but seldom performed upon the violin in public, and but little in private, save for his own diversion. In 1874, while still a young man, bidding fair to rise to the highest distinction as a musician, he died, deeply regretted by many, not more on account of his high musical than his gentlemanly, genial qualities.

" Sweet Mercy! to the gates of heaven
This minstrel lead, his sins forgiven."

THOMAS GREENE BETHUNE.

XI.

THOMAS GREENE BETHUNE,

OTHERWISE KNOWN AS

"BLIND TOM," THE WONDERFUL PIANIST

> " Who ran
> Through each mode of the lyre, and was master
> Of all."
> MOORE.
>
> " Bright gem instinct with music."
> WORDSWORTH.

HE is unquestionably and conspicuously the most wonderful musician the world has ever known. No one has ever equalled him in quickness and depth of musical insight and feeling, nor in the constancy with which he bears within himself, in all its fulness, that mysterious power which can be called by no truer name than *musical inspiration*. He is an absolute master in the comprehension and retention of all sound (and in *all* sound *he* finds music); a being in whose sympathetic soul lies the ready, the perfect correlative of every note of melody in nature or in art that is caught by his marvellously sensitive ear. We often speak of those who have an " ear for music." Here is a musician who surpasses all others in all the world in the possession of this quality; for his is a *perfect* ear. You may sit down to the piano-forte, and strike any note or chord or discord, or a great number of them; and he will at once give their proper names, and, taking your place, reproduce them. Complete master of the pianoforte keyboard, he calls to his melodious uses, with most consummate ease, all of its resources that are known to skilful performers, as well as constantly discovers and applies those that are new. Under his magnetic touch, this instrument may become, at his will, a *music-box*, a *hand-organ*, a *harp* or a *bagpipe*, a "*Scotch fiddle*," a *church-organ*, a *guitar*, or a *banjo:* it may imitate the "stump speaker" as he delivers his glowing harangue; or, being brought back to its legitimate tones, it may be made to sing two melodies at once, while the performer with his voice delivers a third, all three in different time and keys, all in perfect tune and time, and each one easily distinguishable from the other! It would be vain to call such performances as these mere tricks. They are far, far more; since they show a musical intuition, and an orderly disposition and marshalling of the stores of the mind, quite beyond the powers of the performer of mere musical tricks. But, even were they such, this wonderful musician would not need to depend upon their performance for the greatness of his fame; for there is no work of the great masters too difficult for his easy comprehension and perfect rendering.

He remembers and plays full seven thousand pieces. In short, he plays every piece that he has ever heard. How almost godlike (it cannot be brought to human comparison) is this retentive, this *perfect* memory, as relating to all that is musical, or even unmusical, in sound!

Nor does he need to depend upon the music composed by others. His own soul is full of harmony, endless in variety, and most ravishing. Take from him, were it possible, all remembrance of the music written by others, and he would still be an object of delight and amazement on account of his matchless power in improvisation. Listen to his own "Rain Storm," and you shall hear, first, the thunder's reverberating peal, and anon the gentle patter of the rain-drops on the roof: soon they fall thick and fast, coming with a rushing sound. Again is heard the thunder's awful roar, while the angry winds mingle in the tempestuous fray, — all causing you to feel that a veritable storm rages without. After a while, the tempest gradually ceases; all is calmness; and you look with wonder upon this musical magician, and marvel that the piano-forte can be made to so closely imitate the sounds made by the angry elements.

No one lives, or, as far as we know, has ever lived, that can at all be compared with him. Only the musical heroes of mythology remind us of him; for he is

"As sweet and musical
As bright Apollo's lute strung with his hair:"

And Ariel, Shakspeare's child of fancy, who on Prospero's island constantly gave forth melodies of ever-varied, ever-enchanting sweetness, filling all the air with delicious harmony, — that musical spirit was but an anticipation of the coming of this actual wonder in music. Of him an eloquent writer has beautifully said, "There is music in all things; but 'Blind Tom' is the temple wherein music dwells. He is a sort of door-keeper besides; and, when he opens the portals, music seems to issue forth to wake the soul to ecstasy." The skilful metaphysician or the psychologist pauses before him, completely balked: they cannot classify this mind, human-like indeed in some respects, yet in many others surpassing all humanity, and closely approximating that which is godlike.

Some persons, it is true, judging from certain manifestations of his, or from certain lack of manifestations, have had the temerity to say that "Blind Tom" is an idiot. Out with the idea! Who ever heard of an idiot possessing such power of memory, such fineness of musical sensibility, such order, such method, as he displays? Let us call him the embodiment, the soul, of music, and there rest our investigations; for all else is futility, all else is vain speculation.

Thus have I alluded in a general way to the characteristics of this most wonderful pianist. A more particular but brief sketch of his life from infancy to manhood cannot but be interesting, not only to the student in music, but to all classes of readers.

"Thomas Greene Bethune" (I am quoting from his biography), "better known to the public as 'Blind Tom,' was born within a few miles of the city of Columbus, Ga., on the twenty-fifth day of May, 1849. He is of pure negro blood, and was born blind. His first manifestation of interest in any thing was his fondness for sounds; the first indication of capacity, his power for imitating them. Musical sounds exerted a controlling interest over him; but all sounds, from the soft breathings of the flute to the harsh grating of the corn-sheller, appeared to afford him exquisite enjoyment. His power of judging of the lapse of time was as remarkable as his power of remembering and imitating sounds. Those who are familiar with clocks that strike the hours, have observed, that, a few minutes before the clock strikes, there is a sharp sound different from and louder than the regular ticking. There was a clock in the house; and every hour in the day, just precisely when that sound was produced, Tom was certain to be there, and remain until the hour was struck.

"He exhibited his wonderful musical powers before he was two years old. When the young misses of the family sat on the steps of an evening, and sang, Tom would come around and sing with them. One of them one evening said to her father, —

"'Pa, Tom sings beautifully; and he don't have to learn any tunes: he knows them all; for, as soon as we begin to sing, he sings right along with us.'

"Very soon she said, —

"'He sings fine seconds to any thing we sing.'

"His voice was then strong, soft, and melodious. Just before he had completed his second year he had the whooping-cough, from the effects of which his voice underwent an entire change; it became and continued for years exceedingly rough and harsh, though it did not affect the taste or correctness of his singing.

"He was a little less than four years of age when a piano was brought to the house. The first note that was sounded, of course, brought him up. He was permitted to indulge his curiosity by running his fingers over and smelling the keys, and was then taken out of the parlor. As long as any one was playing, he was contented to stay in the yard, and dance and caper to the music; but the moment it ceased, having discovered whence the sounds proceeded, and how they were produced, he was anxious to get to the instrument to continue them. One night the parlor and the piano had been left open: his mother had neglected to fasten her door, and he had escaped without her knowledge. Before day the young ladies awoke, and, to their astonishment, heard Tom playing one of their pieces. He continued to play until the family at the usual time arose, and gathered around him to witness and wonder at his performance, which, though necessarily very imperfect, was marvellously strange; for, notwithstanding this was his first known effort at a tune, he played with both hands, and used the black as well as the white keys.

"After a while he was allowed free access to the piano, and commenced playing every thing he heard. He soon mastered all of that, and commenced composing for himself. He would sit at the piano for hours, playing over the pieces he had heard; then go out, and run and jump about the yard a little while, and come back and play something of his own. Asked what it was, he replied, 'It is what the wind said to me;' or, 'What the birds said to me;' or, 'What the trees said to me;' or what something else said to him. No doubt what he was playing was connected in his mind with some sound, or combination of sounds, proceeding from those things; and not unfrequently the representation was so good as to render the similarity clear to others.

"There was but one thing which seemed to give Tom as much pleasure as the sound of the piano. Between a wing and the body of the dwelling there is a hall, on the roof of which the rain falls from the roof of the dwelling, and runs thence down a gutter. There is, in the combination of sounds produced by the falling and running water, something so enchanting to Tom, that from his early childhood to the time he left home, whenever it rained, whether by day or night, he would go into that passage, and remain as long as the rain continued. When he was less than five years of age, having been there during a severe thunder-storm, he went to the piano and played what is now known as his 'Rain Storm,' and said it was what the rain, the wind, and the thunder said to him. The perfection of the representation can be fully appreciated by those only who have heard the sounds by the falling of the water upon the roofs, and its running off through the gutters.

"There was in the city of Columbus a German music-teacher who kept pianos and music for sale. The boys about the city, having heard much of Tom, sometimes asked the boys of the family to take him to town, that they might hear him. Upon these occasions they asked permission of this man to use one of his pianos; and, though he would grant the permission, he would not hear him. If he was engaged, he would send them to the back part of the store, which was a very deep one; if he had nothing to do, he would walk out into the street. When Tom was about eight years of age, a gentleman, having obtained permission to exhibit him, hired a piano of this man, and invited him to visit his concert. He indignantly rejected the invitation.

"The man, however, succeeded in awakening the curiosity of the wife of the musician sufficiently to induce her to attend; and she gave her husband such accounts, that he went the next night. After the performance was over, he approached the man, and said, —

"'Sir, I give it up: the world has never seen such a thing as that little blind negro, and will never see such another.'

Encouraged by this, the exhibiter the next day applied to him to undertake to teach Tom. His reply then was, —

"'No, sir; I can't teach him any thing: he knows more of music than we know, or can learn. We can learn all that great genius can reduce to rule and put in tangible form: he knows more than that. I do not even know what it is; but I see and feel it is something beyond my comprehension. All that can be done for him will be to let him hear fine playing: he will work it all out by himself after a while; but he will do it sooner by hearing fine music.'

"It has been stated that Tom was born blind. In his infancy and for years the pupils of his eyes were as white and apparently as inanimate as those of a dead fish. But nature pointed out to him a remedy which gradually relieved him from total darkness, and in process of time conferred upon him, to a limited extent, the blessings of vision.

"When he was three or four years of age, it was observed that he passed most of his time with his face upturned to the sun, as if gazing intently upon it, occasionally passing his hand back and forth with a rapid motion before his eyes. That was soon followed by thrusting his fingers into his eyes with a force which appeared to be almost sufficient to expel the eyeballs from their sockets. From this he proceeded to digging into one of them with sticks, until the blood would run down his face. All this must have been pleasant to him, or he would not have done it; and there is no doubt that he is indebted to the stimulus thus applied to his eyes for the measure of sight he now enjoys. When five or six years of age, a small, comparatively clear speck appeared in one of his eyes; and it was discovered that within a very small space he could see any bright object. That eye has continued to clear, until he is now able to see luminous bodies at a distance, and can distinguish small bodies by bringing them close to his eye. Persons that he knows well he can distinguish at the distance of a few feet; and it is hoped that in process of time his sight will so far improve as to relieve him from many of the difficulties to which he is subject.

"The mere technicalities of music Tom learns without difficulty. Its substance he seems to comprehend intuitively. To teach him the notes, it was necessary only to sound them, and tell him their names. With the elements and principles of music he seemed to be familiar long before he knew any of the names by which they were indicated ; as a man going into a strange country may be perfectly acquainted with the appearance and nature of the material objects which meet his view, without knowing the names applied to them by the people.

"Considering that in early life he learned nothing, and later but little from sight, that he is possessed by an overmastering passion, which so pervades his whole nature as to leave little room for interest in any thing else, and the gratification of which has been indulged to the largest extent, it is not surprising that to the outside world he should exhibit but few manifestations of intellect as applicable to any of the ordinary affairs of life, or that those who see him only under its influence should conclude that he is idiotic.

"The elegance, taste, and power of his performances, his wonderful power of imitation, his extraordinary memory, — not only of music, but of names, dates, and events, — his strict adherence to what he believes to be right, his uniform politeness, and his nice sense of propriety, afford, to those who know him well, ample refutation of this opinion.

"Tom sometimes indulges in some strange gymnastics upon the stage, which are considered by many a part of his stage training. So far from this being the case, it is but a slight outcropping of his us al exercises. If those who see him upon the stage could witness his performances in his room, and the enjoyment they affo d him, they would perhaps regret the necessity of his restraint in public. He never engaged in the plays of children, or manifested any interest in them. His amusements were all his own. With a physical organization of great power and vigor, and an exuberance of animal spirits, he naturally sought physical exercise. Compelled by want of sight to limit himself to a small space, he put himself in almost every conceivable posture, and resorted to those exercises which required the most violent physical exertion. They are now necessary certainly to his enjoyment, perhaps to his health.

"Tom has been seen probably by more people than any one living being. He has played in almost every important city in the United States and in a great many of the smaller towns, in Paris, and in most of the principal cities of England and Scotland. . . . Those who have observed him most closely, and attempted to investigate him, pronounce him a 'living miracle,' unparalleled, incomprehensible, such as has not been seen before, and probably will never be seen again."

I find, in reading his biography, that in Philadelphia and Pittsburg, in England and Scotland, scientists were asked to give an opinion as to "Blind Tom's" musical genius. I select only one from these opinions. The others (from Charles Halle, I. Moscheles, and Professor H. S. Oakley, all very eminent musicians) agree with this one, and need not be given.

PHILADELPHIA, Sept. 16, 1865.

DEAR SIR, — The undersigned desire to express to you their thanks for the opportunity afforded to them of hearing and seeing the wonderful performances of your *protégé*, the blind boy pianist, Tom. They find it impossible to account for these immense results upon any hypothesis growing out of the known laws of art and science.

In the numerous tests to which Tom was subjected in our presence, or by us, he invariably came off triumphant. Whether in deciding the pitch or component parts of chords the most difficult and dissonant; whether in repeating with correctness and precision any pieces, written or impromptu, played to him for the first and only time; whether in his improvisations, or performances of compositions by Thalberg, Gottschalk, Verdi, and others; in fact, under every form of musical examination, — and the experiments are too numerous to mention or enumerate, — he showed a power and capacity ranking him among the most wonderful phenomena recorded in musical history.

Accept, dear sir, the regards of your humble servants,.

B. C. Cross,   J. H. Redncr,
James M. Beck,   Carl Roese,
C. Blandner,   C. Blancgaur,
J. A. Stern,   J. A. Getza,
And several others.

Here are some clippings from American and English newspapers.

From "The Public Ledger," Philadelphia, Sept. 27, 1865: —

"Many professors of music of great eminence have been ready, after listening to him, to declare that they would never touch the piano again. What he has done in public in the way of playing the most difficult pieces after hearing them but once, and with a perfection that years of practice could not usually apply, is known to all the lovers of music in this city.

"The secret of this wonderful power is the most perfect ear for the harmonies of sound ever observed, — 'only this, and nothing more.' To him every thing is music. Discords do not seem to disturb him ; but his ear catches every harmony, and his whole being seems entranced and controlled by it. Let him stand with his back to a piano, and any number of chords be struck, and he will instantly tell every note sounded, showing that he has been able to discriminate, and his memory to retain distinctly and perfectly, each sound. The phrenologists say that memory is in proportion to clearness and strength of the impression produced at first; and this must be the case with him. From two years old this remarkable power of sound over him has been noticed. He has been blind from birth ; and it would seem here, as often observed before, that, by a compensative law of our being, in proportion as one sense is defective, the expenditure of vital energy thus saved is absorbed by some other sense. Probably all our sensations are the result of vibrations; and the pulsations of light that usually enter and give all their exquisite pleasure through the eye-ball are in his case compensated for by the pulsations of sound, which strike on an ear possessed of nerves of double delicacy and vital energy from the absorption and concentration of two senses in one.

"'Blind Tom' is not, however, the senseless being that most imagine him, but rather like one completely guided and governed by this one sense alone. As a lad, the song of a bird would lead him to wander off into the woods; and then the sound of the flute would bring him to those who went in search of him. . . .

"Perhaps a proper study of the case of this lad might show to what extent all (though in less degree) might be educated through music. It is certainly this alone that can be most easily developed. Probably the highest and best emotions might be thus permanently excited within him; while the desire for those pleasures leads him to put forth intellectual efforts that nothing else can. . . . But his performances in music show how the highest results of art and study are most easily reached by this lad in his one-sided culture and development, — that of the ear alone. It is with him a sort of inspiration. The science of music he will probably never be able to master; but we must remember that the art of it preceded the science in Egypt, in Palestine, in Greece, and in Rome, by long ages. Indeed, it was the music of the Hebrews, and then of the Christian Church, that gave birth to scientific music, and alone developed it, until that of the opera gave rise to a distinct branch of the culture. This re-acted powerfully on sacred music itself. 'Blind Tom' at present likes operatic music best."

"The Albany (N.Y.) Argus" of January, 1866, said, —

"Now test the power of analysis. Three pianos are opened: at two of them persons present hammer away, with the design of producing the most perfect discord imaginable; at the third piano, the professor makes a run of twenty notes. The confusion ceases, and Tom repeats in a moment each of the twenty notes sounded. Still another test. Tom takes the stool himself. With his right hand he plays ' Yankee Doodle ' in B flat. With his left hand he performs 'Fisher's Hornpipe' in C. At the same time he sings 'Tramp, tramp,' in another key, — maintaining three distinct processes in that discord, and apparently without any effort whatever. 'Most marvellous!' you say; 'but can he express as well as he perceives?' The gentlemanly director will let you see. He asks Tom to render 'Home, Sweet Home,' by Thalberg. You know, that, of all productions in the current *repertoire*, there are none which have finer or more difficult shades than this. 'Blind Tom' proceeds; and, were you to close your eyes, you could not tell but Thalberg himself was at the instrument, so perfect and so exquisite is the conception and the touch. Then you have renderings in imitation from Chopin, from Gottschalk, from Vieuxtemps, from anybody you will mention who has been deemed a master of the art; and you turn away convinced, surfeited with marvels, satisfied that you have witnessed one of the most incomprehensible facts of the time."

From " The Manchester (Eng.) Courier," Sept. 26: —

"'Prodigies' of all kinds are presented ever and anon to the public nowadays; but we have had nothing yet produced so truly marvellous as the negro phenomenon known as 'Blind Tom,' who appeared for the first time in Manchester, at the Theatre Royal, last night. In order to test 'Blind Tom's' powers of memory, Mr. Joule gave a short impromptu, avoiding any marked rhythm or subject, but which was imitated very cleverly. To test his powers of analyzing chords, Mr. Joule played him the following discordant combinations: the chord of B flat in the left hand, with the chord of A with the flat fifth and sharp sixth in right hand; the chord of E in the left hand, and the chord of D, two sharps, in the right; the chord of A, three flats, in the left hand, with that of A, three sharps, in the right. All these chords were at once correctly named by enumerating each note in succession from the lowest. Mr. Seymour subsequently was called upon, and gave a subject, which he reproduced upon the piano-forte with great success."

From " The Glasgow (Scotland) Daily Herald," Jan. 2, 1867: —

"'Blind Tom,' the wonderful negro-boy pianist, made his *début* in Glasgow yesterday, when he gave three of his entertainments, or rather musical exhibitions, in the Merchants' Hall, — two during the day, and one in the evening. He is, without doubt, an extraordinary lad; born blind, though he is now able to distinguish light from darkness; and having a defect in some of his mental faculties, though what that defect is it is very difficult to say. Nature seems to have made up for these deficiencies by endowing him with a marvellously acute ear and a retentive memory. It is not uncommon to find blind people with their other senses much more highly developed, and much more susceptible of impression, than in people possessing all their faculties; but in no case have we ever heard or known of one with auditory nerves so fine, or with memory so powerful, as 'Blind Tom.' Mozart, when a mere child, was noted for the delicacy of his ear, and for his ability to produce music on a first hearing; but Burney, in his 'History of Music,' records no instance at all coming up to this negro boy for his attainments in phonetics, and his power of retention and reproduction of sound. . . . He plays first a number of difficult passages from the best composers; and then any one is invited to come forward and perform any piece he likes, the more difficult the more acceptable, and, if original, still more preferable. Tom immediately sits down at the piano, and produces *verbatim et literatim* the whole of what he has just heard. To show that it is not at all necessary that he should be acquainted with any piece beforehand to reproduce it, he invites any one to strike a number of notes simultaneously with the hand, or with both hands; and immediately, as we heard him do yesterday, he repeats at length, and without the slightest hesitation, the whole of the letters, with all their inflections, representing the notes. Nor are his wondrous powers confined to the piano, on which he can produce imitations of various instruments, and play two different tunes — one in common time, and a second in triple — while he sings a third; but he can with the voice produce, with the utmost accuracy, any note which his audience may suggest. Yesterday afternoon, for instance, he was asked to sing B flat, F sharp, and the upper A, — a very difficult combination; and, beginning with the latter, he at once satisfied his auditors of his success. One very funny feat he executed, which, as much as any thing else, showed what he could do. When at Aberdeen, as Dr. Howard explained, Tom heard, in a large ante-room adjoining the hall where he was, a teacher of dancing tuning his fiddle, the strings of which apparently had been rather difficult to get tightened up to proper tune. Tom had but to listen, and he retained every sound which the dancing-master produced. Tom's imitation on the piano — first of the striking of the violin-strings with the fingers for some time, after the manner of violinists, then seeing if they chorded well, again touching up the strings, anon giving a little bit of a polka, and once more adjusting the strings, and so on, all exactly as he heard it — was as amusing as it was astonishing. No one with an ear for music should miss the opportunity of going to hear him ere he leaves."

From " The Edinburgh Scotsman : " —

" 'BLIND TOM.' — Last night this negro boy, of whose remarkable performances so much has been said and written of late, made his first appearance here in the Operetta House. There was a crowded audience, among whom were a number of the musical *cognoscenti* of Edinburgh, whose curiosity had been excited by the reputation he had gained in America, as well as by the favorable notices of the press in this country, and the testimony of such men as Moscheles and Halle. . . . It is only when he sits down to the instrument, that he becomes, as it were, inspired. He played several pieces on this occasion from memory, and displayed great execution, and a greater amount of feeling and expression than we were prepared to expect. One of the best of these was the fantasia on the Hundredth Psalm, which was brilliantly executed. One of his most extraordinary feats is the reproduction of any piece once played over to him. On this occasion, Mr. Laurie, who was present, at the invitation of the manager ascended the platform, and played a composition by R. Muller, which occupied nearly five minutes. He no sooner left the instrument than ' Blind Tom ' took his seat, and gave a correct imitation. His ability to name any combination of notes, no matter how disconnected and puzzling the intervals, was fully proved. The professional gentleman we have named struck simultaneously no less than twenty notes on the piano; and these ' Blind Tom ' named without a single mistake."

From " The Dundee Advertiser: " —

" 'BLIND TOM.' — This extraordinary musical prodigy gave two performances in Dundee yesterday, and on each occasion the powers displayed by him were so marvellous as to verge upon the miraculous. Our readers must not suppose that his proficiency is merely of an ordinary kind, or that his notoriety is another species

of Barnumism. The letter we published yesterday from a private
friend, in whose opinions we place the greatest confidence, shows
that it is not so ; and we believe the opinions of all who yesterday
heard him will be found to be those of astonishment and admiration.
History affords no parallel to 'Blind Tom.' His ability would be
marvellous, even if he had his eyesight ; but, as we have before
remarked, when it is considered that he is blind, it is beyond
measure strange. Unless one sees or hears him play, he is unable
properly to understand the extent of his ability. Test him how
you may, he never fails. His memory is as miraculous as his
musical powers ; and he plays over a piece he has never heard
before with almost infallible exactitude. Yesterday several gentlemen went to the platform, and played over pieces ; and, during the
time they were so occupied, it was amusing to witness Tom's contortions of his body, and his movements generally. He swayed
himself about, his eyeballs rolled, his fingers twitched involuntarily,
and he seemed like one possessed ; and, on being allowed to
seat himself at the piano, he repeated from memory the various
pieces which had been played to him. In the evening, Mr. Hirst
played over a number of pieces of the most difficult character, all
of which Tom produced with fidelity.

" On inquiry, we find that his proficiency is a natural gift. From
his earliest infancy he betrayed the utmost interest in musical
sounds of every kind, — the cries of animals, the moaning of the
wind, the rushing of waters, and the like ; and when he was allowed to go out in the fields, if he heard a bird sing, he rushed off
towards it with frantic delight. We publish a letter we received
the other day from an intimate friend in another town, — a gentleman of great musical taste, and no little executive ability, — who
is well qualified to give an opinion on such matters. He says, —

" ' I presume you have not heard " Blind Tom " play. If not,
you never heard a better performer. Like most people, of course, I
was inclined to regard this wonderful prodigy as a wonderful hum-
bug ; but I assure you, that so far from this being the case, or
any thing like it, Tom is as genuine an artist, and possesses as
much (and, for any thing I can tell, a great deal more) musical
talent or power, either as regards the execution of the compositions
of others or of his own, as either Thalberg, Halle, Madame God-
dard, or anybody else you ever listened to. I write merely to

disabuse your mind of the common impression which we are all apt to form of these singular geniuses ; and very strongly recommend you not only to *hear* him play, but privately test him (as I have done) in any way you like. Improvise to him as difficult or elaborate or out-of-the-way piece as you please, and he will instantly reproduce it. Now, this is no common gift ; and therefore you and I, and all who know any thing of music, should use our best efforts to let the public know, that, so far from there being any thing in the nature of clap-trap about Tom, he is, in fact, a musical gem of the first water. Of course I have nothing to do with him; but I have been so highly pleased with his performances, that I thought it might be as well to let you know beforehand (in case you have not already heard him) what my own real impression is of him.'

" He not only repeats every piece he hears from memory, but he improvises and composes ; and he last night sang a song of his own composition, — 'Mother, dear mother, I still think of thee,' — of great merit for its simple sweetness and pathos. As he cannot possibly remain longer in Dundee than to-night, we would earnestly urge upon all who can afford it the absolute duty of seeing and hearing this wonderful blind negro boy. He is only seventeen; but no man of any age could surpass him for executive ability, as his testimonials from such men as Moscheles, Halle, &c., prove. He performs two or three different melodies at the same time, and plays with his back to the piano with apparently as much ability as in the ordinary position. We would especially recommend all who are interested in anthropology, phrenology, and psychology, to see and hear him for themselves. His ability is a singular confutation of the theories of Hunt and Blake about the inferiority of the negro ; for we may challenge any white man to compete with him, in perfect safety. His parallel is not to be found the world over, nor in any time of which the records are known."

As previously stated, Bethune plays full seven thousand pieces. From the subjoined partial list, which I take from his biography, some idea can be gained of the character, the ever-varied character, of the music contained in his amazingly extensive *repertoire*.

BLIND TOM'S CONCERTS.

PROGRAMME.

Classical Selections.

1. Sonata "Pathétique"..............................*Beethoven*
2. "   "Pastorale," Opus 28........................   "
3. "   "Moonlight," 27............................   "
4. Andante..*Mendelssohn*
5. Fugue in A minor.................................*Bach*
6. "   in G minor..................................   "
7. "Songs without Words"............................*Mendelssohn*
8. "Wedding March"..................................   "
9. Concerto in G minor..............................   "
10. Gavotte in G minor...............................*Bach*
11. "Funeral March".................................*Chopin*
12. "Moses in Egypt"................................*Rossini*

Piano-Forte Solos.

13. "Trovatore," Chorus, Duet, and Anvil Chorus.........*Verdi*
14. "Lucrezia Borgia," Drinking Song (Fantasia).......*Donizetti*
15. "Lucia di Lammermoor"..............................   "
16. "Cinderella," Non Piu Meste.......................*Rossini*
17. "Sonnambula," Caprice.............................*Bellini*
18. "Norma," Varieties................................   "
19. "Faust," Tenor Solo, Old Men's Song, and Soldiers'
    Chorus..*Gounod*
20. "Le Prophète"....................................*Meyerbeer*
21. "Linda"...
22. "Dinora"...*Meyerbeer*
23. "Bords du Rhine".................................
24. "La Montagnarde".................................
25. "Shells of the Ocean"............................
26. "La Fille du Régiment"...........................*Donizetti*

Fantasias and Caprices.

27. Fantasia, "Home, Sweet Home"......................*Thalberg*
28. "   "Last Rose of Summer".......................   "

29. Fantasia, "Lily Dale," for left hand.................*Thalberg*
30.   "   "Ever of Thee," &c...................   "
31.   "   "Carnival de Venise"..................   "
32. Reverie. "Last Hope"..........................*Gottschalk*
33. La Fontaine......................................
34. "Whispering Winds"............................
35. "Caprice"..*Liszt*
36. Fantasia, "Old Hundredth Psalm"...................
37. "Auld Lang Syne," and "Listen to the Mocking-Bird" (Piano-Forte Imitations of the Bird)......*Hoffman*

Marches.

38. March, "Delta Kappa Epsilon".......................*Pease*
39. "Grand March de Concert".........................*Wallace*
40. "Gen. Ripley's March"............................
41. "Amazon March"..................................
42. "Masonic Grand March"..........................

Imitations.

43. Imitations of the Music-Box.
44.   "   "   Dutch Woman and Hand-Organ.
45.   "   "   Harp.
46.   "   "   Scotch Bagpipes.
47.   "   "   Scotch Fiddler.
48.   "   "   Church Organ.
49.   "   "   Guitar.
50.   "   "   Banjo.
51.   "   "   Douglas's Speech.
52.   "   "   Uncle Charlie.
53. Produces three melodies at the same time.

Descriptive Music.

54. "Cascade".......................................
55. The Rain Storm................................*Blind Tom*
56. The Battle of Manassas..........................   "

Songs.

57. "Rocked in the Cradle of the Deep"..............
58. "Mother, dear Mother, I still think of Thee".....
59. "The Old Sexton"................................
60. "The Ivy Green".................................
61. "Then you'll remember Me"......................

62. "Scenes that are Brightest"........................
63. "When the Swallows homeward fly"..............
64. "Oh! whisper what Thou feelest"................
65. "My Pretty Jane".................................
66. "Castles in the Air".............................
67. "Mary of Argyle"................................
68. "A Home by the Sea"............................
69. Byron's "Farewell to Tom Moore"...............

Parlor Selections.

70. Waltz in A flat...*Chopin*
71. Waltz in E flat... "
72. Waltz in D flat... "
73. Tarantelle in A flat............................*Stephen Heller*
74. "Josephine Mazurka"................................*Heller*
75. "Polonaise"..*Weber*
76. Nuit Blanche.................................*Stephen Heller*
77. Spring Dawn Mazurka........................*William Mason*
78. "Monastery Bells"............................
79. "California Polka"...*Herz*
80. "Alboni Waltzes"................................*Schuloff*
81. "L'Esplanade"..................................*Hoffman*
82. Anen Polka..

Programme for the evening to be selected from the **preceding.**

XII.

ANNA MADAH AND EMMA LOUISE HYERS,
VOCALISTS AND PIANISTS.

THE "HYERS SISTERS."— AN ACROSTIC.

"Hail, tuneful sisters of a Southern clime!
Your dulcet notes inspire my rhyme:
Each in your voice perfection seem, —
Rare, rich, melodious. We might deem
Some angel wandered from its sphere,
So sweet your notes strike on the ear.
In song or ballad, still we find
Some beauties new to charm the mind.
Trill on, sweet sisters from a golden shore;
Emma and Anna, sing for us once more;
Raise high your voices blending in accord:
So shall your fame be widely spread abroad."

M. E. H., *in Boston Daily News.*

ONE day, two little girls, the one aged seven and the other nine years, came gayly, gleefully tripping into the room where their parents sat quietly conversing, and soon began to sing some of the songs and to enact some of the scenes from operas, performances of which they had occasionally witnessed at the theatre. This they did, of course, in childlike, playful manner, yet not without a showing, considering their ages, of a surprising degree of correctness.

Their parents at first, however, only laughed at what

EMMA LOUISE HYERS.

ANNA MADAH HYERS.

they considered the gleesome antics of these embryo personators in opera. But, the little girls continuing in the presence of their relatives and playmates their performances, it was ere long discovered that they possessed no small degree of lyrical talent; that their voices, considering their tender years, were remarkably full and resonant; and that they exhibited much fondness for music, and a spirit of great earnestness in all they undertook.

With these manifestations their parents were of course highly pleased; and they at once resolved to give their children such instruction in the rudiments of music as lay within their power.

Thus, then, did those two gifted little girls, Anna Madah and Emma Louise Hyers, early show their devotion to art, and make that beginning, which, in a few years afterward, was to grow into a musical proficiency and a public success in the highest degree creditable to them.

After one year's instruction, it was found that the girls had advanced so rapidly as to have quite " caught up " with their teachers (their parents); and it was therefore found necessary to place them under the instruction of others more advanced in music. Professor Hugo Sank, a German of fine musical ability, became then their next tutor, giving them lessons in vocalization and on the piano-forte. With this gentleman they made much progress. Another change, however, being decided upon, our apt and ambitious pupils were next placed under the direction of Madame Josephine D'Ormy, — a lady of fine talents, an operatic celebrity, and distinguished as a skilful teacher. From this lady the sisters received thorough instruction in the Italian, and were taught some of the rudiments of the German language. It is, in fact, to the rare accomplishments and painstaking efforts of Madame D'Ormy that the Misses Hyers owe mostly their success of to-day. For she it was who taught them that purity of enunciation, and sweetness of intonation, that now are so noticeable in their singing of Italian and other music; while under her guidance, also, they acquired that graceful, winning stage appearance for which they have so often been praised.

Although, as was natural, quite proud of the rich natural gifts possessed by their children, and extremely delighted with the large degree of their acquirements in the art of music, their sensible parents were in no haste to rush them before the public; and it was therefore nearly two years after leaving the immediate musical tutelage of Madame D'Ormy when these young ladies made their *début*. This they did before an audience of eight hundred people at the Metropolitan Theatre in Sacramento, Cal., April 22, 1867. On this occasion, and on others afterwards in San Francisco and other places in California, their efforts were rewarded with grand success: the musical critics and the press awarded them unstinted praise, and even pronounced them "wonderful." As a sample of all these comments, I here append the following from "The San Francisco Chronicle:" —

"Their musical power is acknowledged; and those who heard them last evening were unanimous in their praises, saying that rare natural gifts would insure for them a leading position among the prime donne of the age.

"Miss Madah has a pure, sweet soprano voice, very true, even, and flexible, of remarkable compass and smoothness. Her rendition of 'Casta Diva,' and her soprano in the tower scene from 'Il

Trovatore,' and Verdi's 'Forse e' lui che l'anima,' as also in the ballad, 'The Rhine Maidens,' was almost faultless, and thoroughly established her claims to the universal commendation she has received from all the connoisseurs in melody who have heard her.

"Miss Louise is a natural wonder, being a fine alto-singer, and also the possessor of a pure tenor-voice. Her tenor is of wonderful range; and, in listening to her singing, it is difficult to believe that one is not hearing a talented young man instead of the voice of a young girl. Her character song was one of the greatest 'hits' ever made; and henceforth her position as a favorite with an audience is assured."

After these concerts they retired to severe study, preparatory to making a tour of the States. Finally, deciding to proceed towards the East, they sang to highly-appreciative and enthusiastic audiences in several of the Western towns and cities. At Salt-Lake City they were received with the very highest marks of favor. On the 12th of August, 1871, they gave a grand concert in Salt-Lake Theatre, offering some five operatic selections. At this concert, and for some time afterwards, the ladies were assisted by Mr. Le Count, a baritone singer of excellence. I append the following scientific analysis of the music used, and the manner of its rendition on the occasion just mentioned. It is from the pen of Professor John Tullidge, and is copied from "The Deseret News:"—

REMARKS ON THE HYERS SISTERS' CONCERT ON SATURDAY, AUG. 12, 1871.

BY PROFESSOR JOHN TULLIDGE.

"A portion of two scenes from the first and second acts of Donizetti's opera of 'Linda di Chamounix' occupied the whole of the first part of the concert.

"The first act opened with a *recitativo e cavatina*, selected from No. 4, on the words, 'Ah, tardai troppo eal nostro favorito.'

"The *recitativo* is in A flat major. But there are no flats or sharps in the signature: these are placed before the notes as required. When the transitions are rapid, — as they are in this piece, — it renders the reading very difficult in securing correct intonation. But notwithstanding these frequent changes, and intricate skipping intervals, Miss Anna accomplished the difficulty with ease, and perfectly in tune. The rapid cadence on the dominant was artistically rendered.

"The aria follows with an allegretto in three-four time, and the execution in this division is very rapid; but the vocalist was equal to the task, and performed it with ease and grace. But the most astonishing feat was the cadenza in the cavatina: the singer, instead of closing on D flat, — fourth line of staff, — took an improvising flight, catching in that flight an appoggiatura grace on the note E flat above the lines; and closed with the D flat, a note below on the pause.

"This was a dangerous flight for one so young: nevertheless, the note intoned was clear, distinct, and bell-like.

"Miss Emma sang the alto in the 'Caro Ballato' with Miss Anna, in a duetto on the words, 'Qui si pria della partenza.' The alto takes the notes a sixth below the soprano, and her deep mellow voice produced a fine effect. The next is a *recitativo* by soprano and alto. In this division the intervalic skippings are difficult; but they were correctly interpreted. The alto then takes up a larghetto in six-eight time, key D minor. This portion required much *con dolore* expression, which was delivered with much tremolo effect by Miss Emma; and her rich, pure contralto voice in the low register told well. The scene finished with a duet by the two sisters, who were warmly and deservedly applauded.

"The scene in act second contained much of the same forms of execution as the first, with the exception of a brilliant duetto in D major, which reminded me of that beautiful florid piece, 'Quest est homo,' from Rossini's 'Stabat Mater.'

"This duet not only requires fine voices, but rapid execution also, or the rendition would be imperfect; but the sisters gave a charming interpretation to the piece.

"Part third commenced with the 'Magic-wove Scarf,' from Barnett's opera of 'The Mountain Sylph.' Barnett is a fine composer, and was theoretically educated in Germany; and, on his return, he composed the above opera. The musicians in England were much surprised when this clever author left the field of composition, after he had received such popularity from his opera of 'The Mountain Sylph;' but the author was obstinate, and I believe he was offended with some remarks of the critics.

"The scene of the scarf is laid in Scotland. The mountain sylph is a fairy, and falls in love with the tenor, a young Scotchman. The baritone is a Scotch necromancer. The young lover, fearful of losing his fairy love, appeals to this demon for aid; and he, wishing to destroy the power of the fairy, gives the young man the 'Magic-wove Scarf' to throw around her. He told him that the scarf would secure her. He was enticed, and threw the scarf around; but, the moment it touched her, she became spell-bound, and is supposed to die, but is released by a fairy of superior power.

"The trio opens with a fine baritone solo; and, considering Mr. Hyers is not a professional singer, the part was creditably rendered.

"The tenor, Miss Emma, conveyed the author's meaning truly; and her imitation of that voice took her to the F sharp below the staff. This note was intoned with perfect ease.

"In Miss Anna's part there are some beautiful rouladial passages, which were delivered by the young lady smoothly and distinctly; and, when she became spell-bound by the scarf, her *espressivo* and *energico* were fine.

"The trio throughout was creditably performed, and was loudly applauded by the audience.

"'Brighter than stars soft gleaming,' from the opera 'Il Trovatore,' is a fine composition abounding in *espressivo* and *bravura* passages: the compass is also extensive, requiring great range for a baritone voice. The piece was rendered with credit by the young vocalist Le Count.

"A very choice selection from Donizetti's opera of 'Lucia di Lammermoor' followed, and was sung by Miss Anna Hyers. The first line of the English words is, 'See, 'tis the hour: how sinks the sun!' The whole of this movement is in the *affetturoso con amoroso* style; and in order to render such a theme effective, as love without hope, but still hoping, the singer must throw a vast amount of pathos into the subject to secure a fine interpretation; which rendition by the artist was all that could be required. The second movement is in D major. The words of the principal line are, 'Grow dark, yes, love's pure flame grow dark, like earthly fire.'

"The author has interpreted these words with rapid sextoles (groups of six notes) and triplets in difficult intervalic skips, and finishing with an intricate florid cadenza in seconds and thirds. Many passages of the same form may be found in Handel's 'Messiah.' The young lady not only glided over these difficulties with ease and grace, but also brought out the *espressivo* so necessary for the effective rendition of this division. The remaining portions of this fine composition are much varied with rapid executions; and the compass of voice required for effect is extensive, ranging from C above the staff to C below. Every point was delivered by the young vocalist with purity and force.

"I believe this young lady's compass of voice is from E flat above the lines to A below; having at her command the soprano register, the mezzo-soprano, and a portion of the alto.

"Both of the sisters sing in the Italian with fluency and with correct pronunciation.

"'Par Excellence,' sung by Miss Emma, was a complete triumph with the audience, and received a triple call. This was a great compliment after Lingard, the original. But it was the lady's pleasing manner that took the comic-loving patrons by storm: hence the third encore."

After the performance described by Professor Tullidge, the Misses Hyers were tendered by the leading citizens of Salt-Lake City a complimentary benefit. The following correspondence, taken from "The Deseret News," explains itself: —

SALT-LAKE CITY, Aug. 14, 1871.

TO THE HYERS SISTERS, — We the undersigned, residents of Salt-Lake City, having witnessed your performances during your recent engagement at the theatre, and being willing to acknowledge talent wherever found, as a slight testimonial of our esteem tender you our influence and assistance in making a remunerative benefit, to take place at the Salt-Lake Theatre at such time as may suit your convenience.

JOS. R. WALKER.
A. W. WHITE.
WELLS, FARGO, & CO.
(Per C. F. SMITH.)
JNO. CUNNINGTON.
J. B. MEADER.
M. H. WALKER,
A. M. MORTIMER.
JNO. MANN.
S. A. MANN.
A. BENZON.
D. CANDLAND.
J. C. LITTLE.
TILDEN & LAWRENCE.
B. G. RAYBOULD.
JAS. SMITH.
N. S. GOULD & SON.
SEIGEL BROTHERS.
TAYLOR & CUTLER.
H. O. PRATT.

HOOPER, ELDREDGE, & CO.
WILLIAM M. JOHNS.
ROBERT K. REED.
CALDER BROTHERS.
PROFESSOR THOMAS.
JOS. J. DAYNES.
HUGH W. McKEE.
R. ROSS.
THOMAS FITCH.
JNO. T. CAINE.
W. F. ANDERSON.
MARK CROXALL.
J. F. HAMILTON.
CAPT. SHAW.
G. W. LEIHY.
F. T. WISWELL.
TEASDEL & CO.
H. S. BEATTIE.
JNO. L. BURNS.

To this the following reply was returned: —

SALT-LAKE HOUSE, Aug. 15, 1871.
Messrs. WALKER, TILDEN, A. W. WHITE & CO.,
HOOPER, ELDRIDGE, & CO., AND OTHERS.

Gentlemen, — Your esteemed favor is before us; and, gratefully accepting your high compliment to our humble endeavors, we respectfully name Thursday, Aug. 17, as the time of the proposed benefit at the Salt-Lake Theatre.

Respectfully,   HYERS SISTERS.

While in St. Joseph, Mo., they elicited from "The Daily Herald" of that city the following encomium: —

"Whoever of our readers failed to visit the Academy of Music last evening missed a rare musical treat. The concert of the Hyers sisters was absolutely the best, furnished those in attendance with the choicest music, which has been in St. Joseph since we have resided here.

"The Hyers sisters are two colored ladies, or girls, aged respectively sixteen and seventeen years; but their singing is as mature and perfect as any we have ever listened to. We had read the most favorable reports of these sisters in the California papers, but confess that we were not prepared for such an exhibition of vocal powers as they gave us last night.

"Miss Anna Hyers, the eldest, is a musical phenomenon. When we tell musicians that she sings E flat above the staff as loud and clear as an organ, they will understand us when we say she is a prodigy. Jenny Lind was the recipient of world-wide fame and the most lavishly-bestowed encomiums from the most musical critics in the Old and New World simply because she sang that note in Vienna twenty years ago. Parepa Rosa, it is claimed, reached that vocal altitude last summer. But the sopranos who did it flit across this planet like angels. Several competent musicians listened to Anna Hyers last evening, and unanimously pronounced her perfectly wonderful. With the greatest ease in the world, as naturally and gracefully as she breathes, she runs the scale from the low notes in the middle register to the highest notes ever reached by mortal singers. Her trills are as sweet and bird-like as those with which the 'Swedish Nightingale' once entranced the world. In Verdi's famous 'Traviata' there was not a note or modulation wrong: her rendition was faultless, her voice the most sweet and musical we ever listened to.

"In the duet, 'There's a sigh in the heart,' her voice was exhibited in wonderful range; and, in the tower-scene from 'Il Trovatore,' its great power was singularly and very agreeably apparent.

"We do not remember to have been more completely and agreeably surprised than we were last evening in the matchless excellence of the singing of the Hyers sisters. They deserve a crowded house; and we predict that in Boston or New York, by the most severe critics, they will be pronounced musical prodigies."

In Chicago their success was none the less flattering. In this, styled by many the "Queen City of the West," the remarkable musical powers of these young ladies created intense excitement, especially among people of the highest musical culture. The extraordinarily high range of the voice of Anna Hyers quite astonished every one who heard her, and evoked the warmest praise of the critics. For the purpose of assuring those who had not heard her sing, or who, although present, failed to exactly locate in the scale her greatest altitude, as well as to more pointedly mark this rare achievement in vocalism, a number of the best musicians of Chicago published a card in " The Tribune," in which they declared that " Miss Anna Hyers sang at the concert last night the second G above the staff, — a note touched by no other singer since Jenny Lind."

Still proceeding towards the East, they next appeared in Cleveland, O., where their delightful vocal powers were thus alluded to by " The Daily Leader : " —

" On Saturday evening last, we had the pleasure of listening to the Hyers sisters, who have, since their appearance in public, been the recipients of the most flattering testimonials; and are warranted in saying, not without the best claim to them, the exhibition they gave of their ability was most satisfactory. The soprano (Miss Anna) has an exceptionally pure, sweet voice, with ample power for all the demands of the concert-room. Her execution was admirable. The contralto (Miss Emma) possesses a voice of remarkable quality; and we do not hesitate to say that a richer or more evenly-conditioned contralto voice is rarely heard. Her execution was all that could be desired."

Encouraged by the marked success which had thus far crowned their efforts, their father, with whom and under whose direction the Misses Hyers had travelled since leaving California, now determined to enlarge his troupe. This he did by engaging the services of Mr. Wallace King of Camden, N.J., a gifted and accomplished tenor-singer; Mr. John Luca, widely and favorably known from his connection formerly with the celebrated "Luca family," and who sang baritone; while as accompanist he engaged the fine pianist, Mr. A. C. Taylor of New York.

An intelligent idea of the composition of Mr. Hyers's troupe can be formed by a perusal of the following, which was the preface given to the programme of his concerts: —

THE GREATEST MUSICAL PHENOMENA OF THE AGE!

THE FAMOUS CALIFORNIA VOCALISTS,
THE
HYERS SISTERS!
(COLORED.)

MISS ANNA MADAH HYERS.........................*Soprano*
AND
MISS EMMA LOUISE HYERS..........*Contralto and Tenore*
ASSISTED BY
MR. WALLACE KING....................................*Tenor*
AND
MR. JOHN LUCA.......................................*Baritone*
AND THE GIFTED PIANIST,
A. C. TAYLOR.

These young ladies (as will be seen from criticisms annexed) have created a great sensation wherever they have appeared; and, it being the intention of their father (who accompanies them) to take them to Europe to perfect them in their art, he has been induced, at the request of numerous friends, to make a tour through the principal cities of America, to afford the musical public and those anxious to hear these truly wonderful artists of the colored race an opportunity of hearing them, and judging for themselves. The music they sing is always of the highest order, and their selections are from the most difficult and classical pieces that have been sung by the most accomplished artists.

Mr. WALLACE KING (tenor) possesses a fine voice of splendid quality and great compass, which he uses with marked skill, and is especially adapted to music of dramatic character.

Mr. JOHN LUCA (baritone) is also the possessor of a splendid voice, and sings in admirable style, both in songs and concerted music.

Mr. A. C. TAYLOR (pianist and accompanist). This gifted artist, besides being an excellent accompanist, is also a solo-player of great promise. He has had the honor of playing before the most critical audiences of New York and Boston; and it is predicted by our leading musicians he will rank with the first pianists of the day.

As will be seen by the comments drawn from the press, which have been already and which will be hereafter given, Mr. Hyers's statements of the artistic merits of his company were by no means exaggerated.

Their performances in the city of New York and in other parts of the State drew large, cultivated, and enthusiastic audiences, and were, to use the words of one writer, considered "a revelation."

Thus spoke " The New-York Evening Post : " —

"The Hyers sisters are colored, and, to the musical instincts of their race, have added careful musical training. Miss Anna Hyers possesses a flexible voice of great compass, clear and steady in the higher notes. Miss Emma, the contralto, has a voice of great power and depth; qualities which, in impassioned strains, give it a richness not often heard in chamber concerts.

"The gem of the evening was the 'Miserere' scene from 'Il Trovatore,' which was skilfully rendered by the sisters, Miss Emma singing the tenor part with very fine effect.

"A duet by Millard, sung by Miss Anna and Mr. J. Luca, was also remarkably well rendered; Miss Anna displaying the admirable qualities of her voice and her careful training to the greatest advantage.

"The audience was enthusiastic, and the encores were frequent."

Said "The New-York Tribune," —

"A concert was given last evening by the Hyers sisters at Steinway Hall. These are two young colored girls who have received a musical training in California, and who are by no means mere 'Jubilee' singers, as the programme of last evening clearly shows. It embraced several airs and duets from 'Martha' and 'Trovatore;' the last being the 'Miserere,' which called forth hearty applause."

"The Evening Telegram" alluded to them in the following complimentary terms: —

... "The selections last evening embraced a high order of music, operatic and otherwise ; and were rendered with a taste and grace that elicited frequent applause.

"One of the young girls possesses a very pure soprano, the other an equally excellent contralto voice; and, singly or together, their execution is marked by a refinement, culture, and attractiveness that deserve first-class audiences and first-class appreciation."

So great was the success of the talented troupe in the metropolis, that when they visited Brooklyn they were already fully advertised, and a general and very eager desire was manifested in that city to witness their performances. So great was this desire, that, said "The Brooklyn Daily Union,"

"Not only was every inch of standing-room in the Young Men's Christian Association Hall occupied, but the ante-room and even the stairway were completely jammed. In spite, however, of the uncomfortable crowding, every one was pleased to be present, and all were delighted with the concert.

"The young ladies are gifted with remarkable voices, and sing together with perfect harmony; displaying the full compass and beauty of their voices, which are clear and sweet.

"Mr. Wallace King's rendering of Tennyson's beautiful song, 'Come into the garden, Maud,' was really exquisite, and was followed by a vociferous encore. The concert was one of the finest of the series."

But notwithstanding the many critical tests to which these young ladies had been subjected all along from California to New York, and despite the fact that their journey had thus far been marked by a continual series of triumphs, — the thick walls of color-prejudice everywhere yielding before the force of their rare musical abilities, their almost marvellous sweetness of song, — they now approached with feelings somewhat akin to dread the "modern Athens," that acknowleged centre of musical and general æsthetic culture, Boston, whose critical audiences ever receive coldly, at first, all newcomers, and who, guided by their own judgments, and having their own standard of merit, never yield praise because it has been accorded in other sections.

The Misses Hyers, although fully recognizing all this, were not to be daunted by it; and they therefore chose an ambitious, but what proved to be a wise course: they at first appeared at Tremont Temple before a select circle of musical connoisseurs. At this test performance, Mr. Eben Tourjée, Mr. P. S. Gilmore, and others of the highest musical ability in Boston, were, by invitation, present. Before the Misses Hyers began to sing, Mr. Tourjée said that they would be judged by the same standards as would be Nilsson or Kellogg. Mr. Hyers, speaking for his daughters, readily assented to this: and the sequel proved that his confidence was well founded; for all became satisfied, after hearing them sing, that these young ladies had not been too highly praised by the press of other cities. Said Mr. Gilmore, "These ladies promise much that is great."

But the following, taken from one of the Boston papers appearing the day after the performance just referred to, best describes the effect of the same on those present: —

"We were invited with some fifty other persons this forenoon to hear the singing of two colored young ladies, named Anna and Emma Hyers, of San Francisco, at the Meionaon. They are aged respectively sixteen and fourteen years, and, after a casual inspection, may be called musical prodigies. They are, without doubt, destined to occupy a high position in the musical world.

"Anna sings not only alto, but tenor, and both with great excellence. They sang ' Ah forsetui ' from ' Traviata,' ' M'appari ' from

'Martha,' and the 'Miserere' from 'Trovatore,' each with remarkable clearness and accuracy, and surprised all with the general skill they displayed. Anna has also the faculty of reaching E flat above the staff. Judging from present data, they are on a par vocally with our better concert-singers; and a further hearing may place them in rank with more pretentious vocalists."

Having at this *musicale* satisfied the critics, they were spoken of in words of warmest praise by the public press; and their subsequent performances in Boston created, after all, the same enthusiasm as that awakened in the West and in New York. I copy from "The Boston Journal" the following: —

"The young California singers, Miss Anna and Emma Hyers, gave their last concert at Tremont Temple last evening. The audience was both large and enthusiastic; and a duet from 'I Masnadieri,' 'Home, Sweet Home,' by Miss Anna, a duet from 'La Traviata,' a cavatina from 'Lucia di Lammermoor,' and 'The Last Rose of Summer,' also by Miss Anna, appeared to give great satisfaction. The young ladies have made a very marked impression in their concerts here. . . . Mr. Wallace King has a pure, sweet tenor voice of remarkable compass, and sings with excellent taste."

In Boston they made many warm personal friends, receiving from many of its most cultured people very flattering attentions; and here, too, were pointed out to them, in a candid and friendly spirit, such slight defects in their voices, or manner of singing, as only those skilled in the highest *technique* of the musical art could detect. All such suggestions were readily received by the young ladies, who, acting upon the same, made much advancement in the technical requirements of the lyrical art. They lingered long in Boston, being loath to leave its congenial art-circles, and to leave behind its many facilities for improvement in their profession.

Finally deciding to start again on their travels, they visited many of the towns and cities of Massachusetts, and sang also in the principal cities of Rhode Island and Connecticut. Their singing everywhere gave the utmost satisfaction; and cultivated New England confirmed, in words of highest praise, the verdict of the West and of New York.

A writer in "The Springfield (Mass.) Republican" thus spoke of the troupe: —

"One of the largest, and certainly one of the best pleased audiences of the whole season, attended the concert of the Hyers sisters at the Opera House last evening. The voice of the soprano, Miss Anna Hyers, is beautifully pure and liquid in its higher range; and she sings notes far above the staff with the utmost ease, where most sopranos gasp and shriek. So easily, indeed, does she sing them, that few persons are aware of the dizzy vocal heights which she scales. Mr. King possesses that great rarity, a *real* tenor voice, pure and sweet, and of great compass. But the charm of the concert consisted not so much in individual excellence as in the combination of the voices in some wonderfully fine four-part singing. Nothing in this line so exquisite as the 'Greeting to Spring' (Strauss' 'Beautiful Blue Danube' waltz vocalized) has been heard in Springfield for many a year. The voices were as one; the shading was perfect; the modulations were absolutely pure and true; melody and harmony were alike beautiful."

At Worcester, Mass., the performances of the company created a decided excitement in musical circles and among the people generally. "The Daily Press" of that city referred to the performance of the troupe in the following complimentary manner: —

"A larger audience than that of last Saturday evening greeted the Hyers sisters at Mechanics' Hall last evening. The programme was a new one, with the exception of the 'Greeting to Spring,' which was repeated by request, and was enthusiastically received. The 'Excelsior' of Messrs. King and Luca, the 'Cavatina Linda of Miss Anna Hyers, the 'Sleep Well' of Mr. King, and the 'Non e'ver' of Miss Emma Hyers, were encored, as well as nearly all the quartets. The quartet-singing was unaccompanied, and was the finest that has been heard in this city for years. The voices blended beautifully, and were full of expression. Nor can too high praise be bestowed upon the soprano and tenor. They showed great cultivation, and a quality of voice rarely equalled."

While they were in Connecticut, "The Daily Union" of New Haven remarked, —

"New Haven has but rarely heard such extraordinary artists, or reaped so much benefit as from their concerts."

And "The Providence (R.I.) Journal" said, —

"Seldom in the history of our pleasure-seeking has it been our good fortune to enjoy an hour of such exquisite pleasure as we were blessed with on the occasion of our attending a concert given here, a short time since, by the Hyers sisters."

Our talented artists had now acquired throughout New England a fame so fair, that Mr. P. S. Gilmore felt warranted in inviting them to appear at the great Peace Jubilee concerts; and here, before an audience of fifty thousand people, and in the company of several of the great solo-vocalists of the world, surrounded by a chorus of twenty thousand voices and an orchestra of one thousand performers, these gifted girls occupied a proud position, reflecting upon themselves and all with whom they were identified additional honors.

During the winter of 1875, the Hyers troupe several times appeared (on Sunday evenings) on the Boston-Theatre stage in sacred concerts, supported by a select orchestra of forty performers, all under the management and conductorship of that fine musician and prince of gentlemen, Mr. Napier Lothian, leader of the

Boston-Theatre orchestra. At these concerts the music rendered was mostly classical; although the programmes contained also numbers of a popular character, — such as were suited to the tastes of the large, miscellaneous audiences in attendance, — which showed to the highest advantage the versatility of talent and extensive musical resources of the troupe. The writer recalls with much pleasure the delightful emotions which, on one of the evenings alluded to, were awakened in his breast by the very graceful stage appearance and the divine harmony produced by these accomplished musicians; for when not thrilled alone by their music, so faultlessly, so sweetly rendered, he could not repress the thoughts that came forcibly into his mind, of not only how much these noble artists were doing for the cause of pure music, but for that other righteous one, — the breaking-down of a terribly cruel prejudice, founded on the accident, so to speak, of the color of the face.

The concerts just alluded to, it is needless to say, brought out the warmest praises of the Boston journals. It is unnecessary, after the numerous comments, so highly eulogistic, already given, to quote what would only be a repetition of the same.

The Misses Hyers have, since the events heretofore mentioned, visited most of the cities and towns of the State of Maine. In that State they are great favorites, and sing always to large and delighted audiences. "In Lewiston," says "The Folio," "they received at a concert thirteen encores; and at Auburn a full house was gotten out on a half-day's notice."

It would be pleasant to follow the Misses Hyers into that other walk of art, the drama, which they have of late been pursuing so successfully, were such a course within the province of this book; but, as it is not, we will only briefly state, in concluding this sketch, that they have lately, with an enlarged company, been acting in a drama called "Out of Bondage," written expressly for them by Mr. Joseph B. Bradford of Boston. The drama is in four acts; comprehends four phases in the life of a freedman, beginning in slavery, and continuing through to his attainment of education and refinement; and is full of interesting incidents. Their success in this new field has already, in the smaller places in New England, been great; and it is the intention of the troupe to produce the drama ere long on the Boston stage, and in other of the large cities.

Mr. Hyers still holds to a resolve to take his talented daughters to Europe, in order to there perfect them in the higher requirements of their art, and to fit them for the operatic stage.

It is to be hoped that he will not relinquish this ambitious and creditable resolve ; for certainly his gifted children have already clearly shown such rare musical powers, and, incidentally, so much of dramatic talent, and have had so much stage experience, as to fully warrant him and all their friends in firmly believing that these versatile young ladies may, after a short course of training under the best masters of Europe, easily attain to the highest distinction on the operatic stage.

XIII.

FREDERICK ELLIOT LEWIS,

PIANIST, ORGANIST, VIOLINIST, ETC.

Like the honey-making bee,
Passing from flower to flower,
Tasting and gathering the sweets of each.

IN musical versatility, in capability for playing upon a great variety of musical instruments, there may be possibly, among the large number of talented artists of this country, a few who equal the subject of the following sketch: the writer, however, confesses, that, if there be such, he does not know of them. But, be this as it may, such an instance as I am about to present is one, which, in its showing of great musical talents and diversity of acquirements in instrumental performance, will be readily admitted as, to say the least, most extraordinary.

For Frederick E. Lewis performs with ease and with pleasing finish on the piano-forte and the organ, on the violin, viola, violoncello, double-bass, and the guitar, on the clarinet and flute, on the cornet, and on nearly every one of the wind-instruments. Indeed, you can scarcely bring to this remarkable musician an instrument

FREDERICK ELLIOT LEWIS.

upon which in tasteful and artistic manner he cannot perform.

It is not my purpose, however, to present him here as a musical "prodigy," nor as one of those rather abnormal, supernatural beings who astound their hearers by playing upon an instrument almost at sight, without previous study, or without observable method; playing, as it would seem, from a kind of instinct. I present him rather as he is, — an intelligent, a cultured gentleman; an artist so great in natural gifts as to often excite astonishment certainly; but yet one with intelligent method, and fully able to understand and explain all he so skilfully performs.

His extraordinary success in acquiring a good degree of proficiency in playing upon at least fifteen instruments — on two or three of which he excels as a performer, and most of which, too, he teaches — is due not alone to his great natural endowments, but is largely the result of an assiduous cultivation of the same, and of a severe, steady, and long-continued study and practice of each one of these instruments, in which occupation he has ever aimed at the classical, and avoided all that was coarse or commonplace, either in the compositions used, or in his execution of the same.

On choosing an instrument for study, Mr. Lewis's plan has been to first learn all about its structure, the theory concerning its qualities, its tone-producing capabilities; and then, choosing the best practical text-books procurable, to commence, without other teachers than the latter, its practice. He is acquainted, therefore, not only with the musical capacity of all the instruments he plays, but also knows so much in regard to their mechanism, that, when out of order, he can generally repair them; thus possessing in this latter respect an ability far from common among musicians. He has at his rooms quite a large family of stringed instruments, consisting of two or three violins, a viola, two 'cellos, a double-bass, and a guitar. These have all been carefully chosen for their beauty of form, and nicety and sweetness of tone, their owner being a decidedly good judge, a real connoisseur; and none of them are for sale.

His rooms are neatly but not expensively furnished. A few choice pictures hang on the walls: but here, there, and everywhere are to be found the emblems and accessories of the musical art, — a piano-forte, on the back part of which are great piles of music, and in which are the latest and choicest publications; a number of music-stands; several of the viol family hanging on the walls, or placed in their boxes on the floor; two or three varieties of the clarinet; a cornet, a guitar, a flute, &c. In fact, there is music, music everywhere, and enough instruments to form at any time an orchestra of at least a dozen performers; with a skilful instructor or conductor near at hand in the person of Professor Lewis, ready to wield an efficient *bâton*, to play the leading part, or with pleasing compliance to play in a subordinate capacity.

A visit to these rooms is always highly pleasing and instructive, not only to the practical musician, but to all lovers of good music. With the former Mr. Lewis is ready to join in a duet; allowing his visitor to choose from among his many instruments the one with which he is familiar, while he himself is prepared to take any other one necessary in forming the duet. To those who cannot play, or who, perhaps, choose to listen rather than to play, he is ever obliging, and acts as though he considers it a very pleasant duty to entertain his friends. At such times he will commence with his favorite, the piano, and go through successively a performance upon each one of his many instruments, giving his delighted listener a taste, so to speak, of the melodious sweets of each. He delights not only to play, but is also quite fond of conversing on general music; with which subject he is very familiar, and is ever interesting and instructive in discoursing upon the advantages and pleasures to be enjoyed by its study. Indeed, at such times one is in doubt whether to admire him most as a performer or as a theorist; for as the latter he is remarkably proficient, and in treatment delightfully eloquent. As may be inferred from the foregoing, Mr. Lewis is in his manners extremely affable and easy. He charms his visitor by his simplicity, modesty, and freedom from that conceit which might be perhaps expected from one so wonderfully skilled in his profession. Pope's expressive lines apply to but few persons so closely as they do to Mr. Lewis; for he is truly

> "Of manners gentle, of affections mild;
> In wit a man, simplicity a child."

In these times of charlatanry, when titles are so often assumed with a reckless disregard of truthfulness, I hesitate to apply even to one so fully qualified, so extra skilled in music, as Lewis, the prefix *professor;* for I wish, as I ought, to entirely disassociate him from the mere pretenders to whom, in general, I have just referred. But to him the title surely belongs; and there is no competent judge, who, when made aware of the great talents and acquisitions, theoretical and practical, of Mr Lewis in the science of music, will not cheerfully accord it to him. Mr. Lewis does not encourage a use of this title as applied to himself: it is, however, habitually given to him by those who enjoy his acquaintance, and who believe that it belongs of right to him.

Although depending for his support upon the profession of music, his intense love for the noble art is so pure, is so conscientious, as to lift him far above the exhibition at any time of a spirit of cupidity, and to cause him frequently to discourse the most exquisite music, when he can expect no other reward than the pleasure he feels in thus gratifying his auditors.

I have thus given a somewhat general outline of the characteristics and accomplishments of our subject. But what is his history in particular? What have been the beginnings, the circumstances, that have united to produce a character so pleasingly and so harmoniously formed? These questions I shall now endeavor to briefly answer.

Frederick Elliot Lewis was born in Boston in the year 1846. His parents, both natives of New England, were people of musical and general culture; his father being a performer on the flute, violin, violoncello, and piano, as well as a chorister; while his mother was a pianist, a leading soprano-singer in choirs, a lady of fine musical taste, appearing often in public, and taking always a leading part.

At the early age of six years, Frederick evinced a surprising fondness for music; but it was not until he was eleven years old that he began its real study. This he did under his mother's direction, taking lessons on the piano-forte. At this time he found the study of music difficult, and the acquirement of its scientific rudiments was to him dry work. In one year, however, its charming beauties began to open before his young mind; and after this he rapidly developed a talent for music, felt the inspiration of the beautiful art, and became ambitious to excel.

After studying for some time the piano, and becoming, for one of his years, quite proficient as a performer, he began to take lessons on the organ under the direction of Miss R. M. Washington, an accomplished teacher of that instrument, of the piano-forte, and of harmony. The organ for some time quite absorbed his attention. This grand and most comprehensive of instruments, with its great scope and capacity for the production of harmonic beauties, so delighted, indeed so charmed, our young enthusiast, — for such he had now become, — as to leave him with scarcely any inclination or time for other studies. He resolved then to learn all that it was possible to know about the organ, not only in awaking to life its tones of grandest harmony, but also, and in order to better accomplish the same, to study its wonderful mechanism.

With this latter purpose in view, he visited the extensive and celebrated organ manufactory of the Messrs. E. and G. G. Hook & Hastings, located at what was then called Roxbury, Mass., now a part of the city of Boston. These gentlemen were so pleased with his ambitious spirit, that they kindly gave him permission to visit at will their factory, and to examine into every thing connected with organ-making. After a while, this firm, discovering the ability of young Lewis as a performer, invited him, in the presence of, and at times in conjunction with, some of the most skilful organists of Boston, to test their organs before the same were offered for sale. Besides, he sometimes offered suggestions in regard to their construction before the organs were completed, some of which suggestions were adopted by the firm. It will thus be seen that our student was quite fortunate in having, in the first place, an excellent teacher, and afterwards such beneficial opportunities as those allowed him by the Messrs. Hook. No wonder, then, that with his natural abilities, his ambitious, art-loving spirit, industrious habits, and such facilities, he quite early became a proficient organist.

With his acquisition of skill as a performer on the piano-forte and organ already attained, as well as with his prospects for attaining to great distinction as a player of either of them, our artist might well have been content. But with these he was not satisfied: he longed to roam over the whole field of instrumental music, to evoke and to enjoy the harmonic beauties of the many other instruments. He had, in fine, become an enthusiast in music; and yearned to become a real connoisseur, theoretically and practically.

Mr. Lewis, therefore, next took up for study the violin, without other teachers than the best instruction-books treating on that instrument. Becoming enamoured of the tones of that sweet and soul-expressing instrument, using in his work only music of the highest kind (he never, indeed, had a taste for any other), choosing for his models — when not guided alone by his own ideas of fine expression — the most classical performers, he rapidly advanced as a pleasing and scholarly violinist, and made his first public appearance as a soloist at New Bedford, Mass., in 1861. About this time, having attained to a fine degree of general proficiency in music, and having overcome to some extent a certain shyness and timidity which had hitherto characterized him, he accepted invitations to appear in the best musical circles in Boston, and to take part occasionally in public performances there. This served to increase his desire to learn even other instruments, and caused him to study successively many of the pieces that are comprised in the formation of a large orchestra or a military band. He made, however, the cornet his principal study. Having at this time become quite partial to stringed instruments, he soon gave most of his time to the study and practice alternately of the viola, violoncello, double-bass, and the guitar. As a performer on all of these instruments, except perhaps the guitar (an instrument which he never much liked), he has on important public occasions appeared, eliciting at such times the favorable comments of the press.

Leaving for a while the instruments just mentioned, he turned his attention to the clarinet and flute. To the former he is at present much devoted, playing upon it with much taste and skill.

Being asked why he so much enlarged his field of instrumental performance, and why he did not confine his studies to not more than one or two instruments, he said that it was in order that he might be the better able to arrange and write music for an orchestra or military band; and in this ambitious endeavor he has attained to a fine degree of success.

I should have mentioned before this, that, at the age of fifteen, our subject was considered quite a competent performer on the piano-forte, the organ, and the violin; and that at that early age he began to teach the playing of these instruments.

Although his talent and acquirements are displayed more particularly as an instrumentalist, Mr. Lewis is also a fair vocalist, understands thoroughly its theory, and teaches singing. He is a valued member of several musical clubs of Boston and vicinity composed of artists of the highest culture, such as the Haydn and Mozart Clubs of Chelsea, Mass. He, besides, meets with a select few in Boston, in a circle of studious amateurs where none but the finest and most classical music is performed. He is a member of the "Boston Musicians' Union," which comprises in its membership most of the best musicians of the city; such as, for instance, Julius Eichberg, P. S. Gilmore, C. N. Allen, Messrs. Listemann, Lothian, &c.

In the Haydn and Mozart Clubs Mr. Lewis has played the part for first violin; and on several occasions, in the absence of the directors of those bodies, he has assumed acceptably the conductorship. His general musical accomplishments, and his acquaintance with each instrument used in these clubs, make him really the most useful and valued member; for, if a member fails to appear at a performance, he need not be much missed, since Mr. Lewis, if present, can take his instrument, whatever it may be, while his own regular place may be taken by the next first violinist in rank.

He has performed on several great occasions, notably at the World's Peace Jubilee, held in Boston in 1872, in an orchestra of nearly two thousand instrumentalists, all selected, and of fine skill. Before being accepted there, he was subjected to a most rigid examination by the superintendent of the orchestra, being required to play on the violin some of the most complicated and difficult compositions for that instrument. This test he stood so well, indeed, as to elicit from the super intendent, in the warmest manner, the comprehensive exclamation, "Lewis, you are a musician!" At the grand testimonial concert tendered P. S. Gilmore (the projector of the two great "Jubilees") at the Boston Theatre, prior to his going to New York to reside, Mr. Lewis appeared in a selected orchestra, and contributed not a little to the success of that interesting occasion.

He is constantly arranging and composing music for his classes, for orchestras and bands. At present he is engaged in composing for the piano what he will call "A Meditation," and in which he will include some of the finest ideas that constantly fill his musical mind. Some of these thoughts I have heard him play; and I have been so pleased by them, as to beg him not to relinquish his purpose to give them to the public, being convinced that in so doing he would afford delight to all lovers of good music, and add much to his already fine reputation.

Many complimentary notices touching the musical abilities of Mr. Lewis have from time to time appeared in the public journals. A few of the briefest are given below.

One of these journals, a good while ago, said, —

"Mr. Lewis is an amateur performer of marked ability."

"The Boston Journal," June 11, 1874, said, —

"Mr. Lewis gained much applause for his violin solos; and a duet and also a sonata by Mozart, for violin and piano, were well received."

"The Boston Globe," April 16, 1874, said, —

"Mr. F. E. Lewis, violin soloist, appeared once on the list, and was so demonstratively applauded, that he was a second time forced to come upon the platform. His first solo and the response were very artistically given."

In these driving days, when competition is so rife in all the trades and professions, and when, even among our best musicians, what begins as a spirit of honest rivalry often degenerates into that of detraction, it is pleasant to record instances in which it is shown that there are those who in their culture so strikingly unite the qualities of the skilful artist and the true gentleman, that their warmest admirers and friends are found among those of the same calling. Of Mr. Lewis, Mr. Alonzo Bond, director of Bond's Military Band, and a veteran musician of note, once said, " He is the finest accompanist (piano) in the United States." The writer has also in possession letters, highly commendatory of Mr. Lewis as a musician, from Mr. L. R. Goering, a skilful orchestra leader, member of that fine body of musicians, the Germania Band, and a teacher of great merit; from T. M. Carter, director of Carter's Band ; from J. O. Freeman, and J. H. Richardson, — all musicians of high rank, and gentlemen of excellent general culture. From the letter of one of these (Mr. J. O. Freeman) I quote the following reference to the subject of this sketch : —

"I look upon him as a person of remarkable musical ability. His performance on the violin, viola, violoncello, double-bass, clarinet, and also brass instruments, is really surprising. But where we see his real talent is in his conception and rendering of classical music on the piano-forte. Even in his own compositions he has shown much real talent. I regret that he could not have had the chances abroad that so many of our less-talented Americans have had. Besides the numerous instruments I have mentioned, there is still another (which, perhaps, in character ranks higher than any of the others): I mean the church-organ, upon which he also plays."

This writer, like all the others mentioned, could not refrain from closing his letter by a very handsome reference to Mr. Lewis's gentlemanly traits of character.

Slightly below the medium size, of graceful form, with regular, expressive features, and thoughtful cast of countenance; always neat in appearance; of gentlemanly, Christian deportment; genial in manners, — so amiable, as to be almost without an enemy; of very industrious habits; fully impressed with the beauty, the grandeur, and the great usefulness, of the divine art, as a potent means, when properly employed, for elevating the mind, adding to innocent enjoyment, and as an aid to polite culture; and with a soul absorbed in music, — all this can be truly said of Frederick E. Lewis. Not much more can or need be said to mark him, as he is, the Christian gentleman and the wonderfully talented musician, — one whose charming qualities fill the measure of our highest conception of **the true, the ideal artist.**

XIV.

NELLIE E. BROWN,

THE FAVORITE NEW-HAMPSHIRE VOCALIST.

> "The melody of every grace
> And music of her face."
> LOVELACE.

> " And thence flows all that charms or ear or sight;
> All melodies the echoes of that voice."
> COLERIDGE.

ALL musical tones please the ear, and affect to a greater or lesser degree the finer senses; for as beautifully and expressively sings Cowper, explaining this sensibility, —

> " There is in souls a sympathy with sounds:
> . . . .
> Some chord in unison with what we hear
> Is touched within us, and the heart replies."

The musical instrument, of itself lying cold and inanimate, may become, when touched by the hand of genius, seemingly a thing of life as the performer evolves from its board tones of melody so thrillingly sweet, so soulful, as to awaken in the listener's breast the holiest emotions. Even stout-hearted men have shed the tear of feeling when listening to the tenderly touching

NELLIE E. BROWN.

strains of the voiceful violin; while the musical moanings of the violoncello have caused them to experience feelings of a tender sadness.

I saw this exemplified, when, a short while ago, I listened with rapt attention to the marvellously sweet singing of the violin of that rare virtuoso, Ole Bull. The performer appeared like one inspired; and his noble instrument seemed sentient as under his magnetic hand its pure, melodic, and at times human-like voice, so replete with poetic, soulful expression, gave out tones of most exquisite beauty and grandeur, while every heart of his vast, enraptured audience throbbed in unison.

Still it is only once in a great while that one may witness the production of effects like those just described: and I think, that although the lines of Cowper, previously quoted, may refer to the effect of musical sounds in general, they yet are more particularly expressive of the impressions produced upon the ear and the heart by the melodious echoings of a *human voice* when heard in song; for then a real, a living soul, with aid of music's charm, breathes to soul its joys, its pathos, its inmost longings, — touching indeed the unseen,

"The electric chain wherewith we are darkly bound,"

while heart responds to heart.

Besides, we know that man, in his rudest, as well as in his most highly-civilized state, readily pays tribute to the power and beauty of song. In this form of musical expression the singer conveys to the listener's ear not only melodies that the latter naturally delights to hear, but utters also the words of sentiment, of instruction, that appeal to his mind, and touch his heart; thus doubly enchaining his interest, and enhancing his pleasure. Moreover, to the mere charm of resonant vocalization is added the one afforded by a warm, a living presence; the speaking eyes (so aptly called the "windows of the soul"), with their glowing, magnetic expression, and the effective gesture, forming together pleasure-giving elements that must ever be wanting in other forms of musical presentation.

And so easily are our musical sensibilities awakened, and so readily are we influenced by song-power, that these effects may be exerted upon us, to a very considerable extent, even by the singer of ordinary abilities. But by a beautiful cantatrice, gifted with a pure, resonant, sympathetic voice, its natural sweetness and power supplemented by careful artistic cultivation, possessing a pleasing, unaffected manner of appearance and expression, all these effects may be amplified, intensified. Such a one may often, nay, at will, call into life our most delightful emotions, and evoke the warmest admiration of those who see and hear her. Her sway is over all, and is absolute; the natural music of her voice merely serving as sufficient charm for those not highly cultured, while the embellishments of art which she so intelligently uses in her performance add to the pleasure of, as they satisfy, the æsthetic conceptions, the love of full, harmonious development, held by persons of the most critical tastes.

As prominent among those lyric artists of New England whose fine natural musical powers and many winning accomplishments have formed the theme of frequent praise, as they have been the source of constant delight for many persons in private circles and public audiences, I may confidently mention Nellie E.

Brown of Dover, N.H., — a lady who within a very few years has, by the great beauty of her voice, and the exhibition of many noble qualities of heart and mind, won a name of which she and all her many admiring friends may be justly proud.

At quite an early age Miss Brown evinced a fondness for music, the slightest sounds of which readily attracted her attention; and, long before she had acquired a knowledge of its rudiments, the natural sweetness of her voice, as she was heard merely humming a tune, often arrested the attention and called out the praises of those who heard her. Thus musically endowed, of an amiable disposition, with spirits ever as free as the mountain winds of her native State, she became the favorite of her school companions, and their leader.

A few years ago, while attending a private school in Dover, Miss Caroline Bracket, a teacher in the same, noticing that Miss Brown possessed a naturally superior voice, earnestly advised its fullest cultivation. This lady became her first music-teacher. Diligently pursuing her studies, she made rapid progress. Being induced to take part in occasional school and other concerts, our subject soon became quite prominent in Dover as a vocalist, and was engaged in 1865 to sing in the choir of the Free-will Baptist church of that city. Here she remained until November, 1872; at which time, having learned of Miss Brown's fine vocal powers, the members of Grace Church, Haverhill, Mass, earnestly invited her to become the leading soprano in their choir, offering her a liberal salary, besides the payment of her travelling-expenses twice each week between Dover and Haverhill. This very complimentary invitation she accepted; and for four years her fine singing and engaging manners rendered her deservedly popular with the members and attendants of the church mentioned, — people of fine Christian and general culture, — as well as of the citizens of Haverhill generally, before whom, in the public halls, she sang on several occasions.

She remained in Haverhill until November, 1876; when, on the completion of the new Methodist-Episcopal church at Dover, — the largest and finest church in the city, — she was induced to become a member of its choir. Not, however, until after a severe struggle did the Grace-church people relinquish their claims to the accomplished vocalist. They say that they will yet have her back with them. At present, Miss Brown is directress of the choir in Dover which I have just mentioned.

I have thus given a rapid sketch of our subject's career as a choir-singer; a career which, it is seen, has been a most gratifying one. But her musical achievements have not been made alone in the positions and places mentioned: in others, near and far, she has displayed such abilities as a songstress as to have won golden opinions of those composing her many large and cultivated audiences, while the press have awarded her the highest praise.

While a leading member of the choirs before alluded to, and while winning encomiums that perhaps would have turned the heads, so to say, of many, and caused them to have relaxed that assiduous and scientific study so necessary to the attainment of complete success, Miss Brown continued a zealous student of her much-loved art, being ever resolved to cultivate her voice to the highest point of excellence. *Apropos* of this, I may mention that she once wrote a friend as follows:

"My motto is 'Excelsior.' I am resolved to give myself up wholly to the study of music, and endeavor, in spite of obstacles, to become an accomplished artist." It may be observed, that none but those who are actuated by the most noble motives, and who give utterance to them in words of such inspiring earnestness as these, *do* become " accomplished artists."

Deciding, then, to secure the fullest development of her voice, and to gain those acquirements that belong to a technical education, living within a few hours' ride of Boston, she here became first a pupil of Mrs. J. Rametti, and afterwards entered one of the great conservatories, where she was placed under the guidance of Professor O'Neill, a gentleman highly esteemed as a teacher of voice-culture. She had not long been connected with the New-England Conservatory of Music, when its director requested her to appear at the quarterly concerts of that institution that were held in Music Hall. Here on two occasions, before large and highly-cultivated audiences, with beautiful voice, correct method of expression, and ease and grace of stage deportment, — singing, in Italian, music of a high order, — Miss Brown won the most enthusiastic applause. Predictions of her complete success as a brilliant lyric artist were freely made by many connoisseurs. But these have not been her only appearances in Boston. She has many times sung at concerts in the finest music-halls of the city, before many critical audiences; her charming rendition of the numerous English, Italian, French, Scotch, and Irish songs in her rich *repertoire* making her one of Boston's favorite cantatrices.

In order that the opinions heretofore given in regard to Miss Brown's vocal abilities and artistic accomplishments may be shown not to be exaggerated, I now desire to append some of the notices which her performances have elicited from the press of New England and other sections of the country. And here I am confronted by the first real difficulty that has appeared since I began this sketch; for I have before me nearly one hundred comments, all highly complimentary, only a very small number of which may here be reprinted. To properly arrange and give them *all* would be an easy and most pleasing task, since the collection forms an unbroken, a delightful series of musical descriptions, interspersed with high but always discreet praise of the artist whose performances, in the main, called them forth; but to be compelled, from want of space, to endeavor to select, from among these many encomiums, only those which, while they do justice to our subject, are yet brief and together varied and interesting, is a duty attended with some embarrassment. Before attempting to do this, I deem it proper to say, that, if printed together, the comments referred to would make a volume of considerable size; which, containing, as it undoubtedly would, the truthful, spontaneous tributes of lovers of art to one of its most faithful and accomplished devotees, might well be considered by herself and many admiring friends as of most inestimable value.

The following have reference to Miss Brown's appearances in Boston during the musical season of 1874: —

Said " The Boston Traveller," April 16, —

"Miss Nellie E. Brown has for some months been the leading soprano at Grace Church, Haverhill, Mass.; which position she has filled with eminent acceptance, and with marked exhibition of artistic powers."

And the same paper at another time said, —

"Miss Brown possesses a very fine voice under excellent culture, and gave with much taste several solos. Noticeably good was her rendering of Torrey's 'La Prima Vera.' In all her selections she exhibited excellent style and finish."

"The Globe," March 31, said, —

"Miss Nellie Brown showed a particularly well-modulated voice, trained study, and appreciative method, which served her well in the pleasant rendering given by her so gracefully and unaffectedly."

The same paper, after alluding to her rendition of "Del Criel Regina," said, —

"This lady is fortunate in her exceedingly sweet and well-trained voice, which, in conjunction with her fine personal appearance and stage manners, rendered her reception unusually enthusiastic."

Speaking of an entertainment given at Parker Memorial Hall. a musical writer said, —

"Miss Brown has a charming voice, and sings with intelligent expression and good taste. Two of her songs, 'Beautiful Erin' and 'Bonnie Dundee,' were rendered with great sweetness."

"The Boston Advertiser," March 31, said, —

"She has an exceptionally pure voice, which has been carefully trained."

"The Transcript," April 16, said, —

"A soprano of good voice and cultivation."

"The Journal," June 13, 1874, said, —

"A talented vocalist, with a well-cultivated voice of a remarkably fine quality. She pleased very greatly in several selections."

Said "The Post," Nov. 13, —

"An artist of exceptional merit, possessing a voice of rare compass, flexibility, and sweetness. In the solo, 'Land of my Birth,' by Operti, she received enthusiastic applause."

The public journals of her own city and state very early in her career chronicled Miss Brown's musical achievements, and even then felt warranted in awarding her strong but judicious praise. Latterly they have many times spoken in most enthusiastic terms of her added accomplishments. I shall quote only a few of the briefest of these.

"The Dover (N.H.) Daily Democrat," Dec. 19, 1873, said, —

"The concert given in the City Hall last evening by Miss Nellie Brown, assisted by Misses Gray and Bracket and the Amphion Glee Club of Haverhill, Mass., was a success. . . . Miss Brown was very warmly greeted, and surprised all with the ease and grace of her appearance, the richness of her voice, and the fine rendering of her music. She was enthusiastically encored."

"The Dover Enquirer," Sept. 7, 1876, said, —

"The organ and vocal concert at the new Methodist-Episcopal church on Tuesday evening was one of the finest ever given in Dover. . . . Dover's favorite, Miss Nellie E. Brown, was as warmly greeted as ever, sang most charmingly, and was loudly encored."

"The Dover Democrat," Sept. 6, 1876, said, —

"It [the concert] was a grand and complete success. . . . One little incident, or intended incident, was omitted at the concert. An elegant basket of flowers was sent by the friends of Miss Nellie Brown at Haverhill, for presentation to her at the close of her singing; but the express folks failed to deliver it in season. It was too bad; but Miss Brown and her numerous friends appreciate the good-will of the Haverhill people all the same. It was intended as a pretty tribute to one of the best singers in New England; and, so far as the act itself was concerned, it stands just as well as though the presentation had taken place."

Miss Brown has sung in quite a number of the larger towns and cities of Massachusetts, in which State she is scarcely less a favorite than in New Hampshire. She has appeared at concerts in company with some of the most eminent artists of the country (such as, for instance, Professor Eugene Thayer, J. F. Rudolphsen, Myron W. Whitney, Mrs. Julia Houston West, Mrs. H. M. Smith, and others), and always with fine success. In her own city and state she enjoys a popularity unequalled by any other cantatrice, her beautiful voice and many excellent traits of character winning her the warmest esteem of all. The people of Dover are very proud of her, and greatly delighted that one of their number is received with such marks of enthusiastic favor in other States. The Dover papers always readily record these triumphs, and proudly speak of her as "our prima donna."

In November, 1874, our subject sang in Steinway Hall, New York, and was highly complimented by several of the papers of that city.

"The Gazette," Nov. 4, 1874, said, —

"Miss Nellie Brown, born and bred among the hills of New Hampshire, possesses a voice of rare power and beauty, which she has diligently labored to cultivate and improve by close and unremitting study. She has also a rare charm of manner, which, united with her exquisite singing, won for her an enthusiastic reception."

Another paper thus referred to her: —

"Miss Brown is not a New-Yorker, but resides at Dover, N.H., where she is the leading soprano in the principal church. Her stage presence is quite prepossessing. She sang 'Salve Maria,' and

'Robert toi que j'aime,' with very good effect, besides assisting in several duets and quartets. She possesses a very good voice; and, although of light calibre, it is even now able to fill a hall like Steinway."

She has appeared at concerts in Washington, D.C., Portland, Me., Baltimore, Md., and St. John, N.B. In December, 1874, Miss Brown visited the national capital, where she sang in a series of concerts given in Lincoln Hall under the auspices of the Abt Society. Of the part taken by her in one of these " The National Republican " said, —

" 'La Prima Vera,' by Miss Nellie E. Brown, was beautifully and artistically rendered, the lady possessing a beautiful, full, round voice, which blended harmoniously with the perfect ease and faultless execution which graced her performance. It being her first appearance before a Washington audience, the expectation formed of her excellence in an artistic sense was more than realized. 'Nobody at Home but Me,' sung by the same lady in reply to an encore, more fully, if it were necessary, stamped her as an artist of the first class."

I believe I have already intimated that the very high esteem in which Miss Brown is held arises not alone from her possession of charming lyric qualities, but also from her obliging disposition and engaging manners. She has ever been the true artist; earnestly devoted to the fullest development of her own musical powers, but not envying those of others; loving music intensely, as something sacred, and always anxious to aid in extending its benign influence. The people of Dover, of Haverhill, of Boston, and other places, hold her in grateful remembrance for a frequent exercise of those generous impulses that have caused her to often sing without charge at concerts given for the benefit of many good objects.

As one among her many acts to benefit the young, to inspire them with a love of the beautiful in music, I may refer to the "Centennial Musical Festival" originated by her, and given under her direction in Boston on the evenings of May 16 and 17, 1876. For these occasions she had carefully instructed fifty young girls to perform the beautiful cantata of "Laila, the Fairy Queen," a juvenile operetta. This charming composition is admirably adapted to inspire a love of the beautiful in art, and to nurture sentiments of Christian kindness. The following is in brief the plot: —

"A band of mountain children are collected to spend the summer day in singing, gathering flowers, and feasting around their table spread beneath the shadowy branches of the trees. They are interrupted by the approach of a beggar-woman and her children. A part of the children at first repulse her, offended at having their joyous festival thus interrupted: but one of them, Laila, steps forth with a mild rebuke to her playmates for their unkindness: she welcomes the poor mother and children, and bids them make known their wants. The other children soon join with Laila in speaking kindly to the poor wanderers; and, after they have told them their tale of sorrow, they are invited to the feast which the children have prepared, and all together go out with a merry song to where the table is spread. But Laila, the favorite of all, wandering off alone to cull some wild flowers, in the ardor of her search loses her way, and wanders about until night approaches; and then, as weary and frightened she finds herself in a dark forest, she kneels to ask aid from her good angel, when suddenly a little band of fairies with their queen glide into her presence, glittering in their robes of beauty; and, after her surprise is over, at her entreaty they conduct her to her playmates.

"The mountain children soon miss Laila, and all the afternoon they spend in fruitless search for her; and, as night approaches, they collect in the grove where they first assembled, and are expressing their grief and terror at the loss of Laila, when she is led in by the fairies and their queen, who steps forth, and announces to the children that they are the same ones, who, disguised as wretched beggars, came in the morning to prove the generosity of their hearts; and tells them never in future to hesitate to give the needy, for virtue is sure to be rewarded. All unite in a joyous song, and Laila is crowned their queen."

The many persons who were so fortunate as to witness the performance of those charming misses will not soon forget the delights that were thus afforded them, nor will they fail to remember most gratefully the lady to whose painstaking and noble efforts they are so much indebted for what was a rare treat.

I would fain attempt a description of the scene of dazzling beauty upon which our eyes feasted, and the music of the fresh young voices that fell delightfully upon our ears, and touched with gladdening effect each heart; but I forbear, and give place to the musical critic of "The Boston Journal," who, on May 17, said, —

. . . "The occasion was the presentation of the cantata of 'Laila' by fifty young ladies, under the direction of Miss Nellie E. Brown. The misses, ranging from five to fifteen years, possess very sweet voices; and the music was given with much taste, and a degree of artistic excellence reflecting great credit on Miss Brown's efforts. . . . The audience were greatly pleased with the rendering of the music. . . . While the singing was good, there was exhibited considerable dramatic art by some of the young ladies. The dresses worn are neat and pretty, the fairy costumes being very striking and appropriate. The stage, too, was neatly set; and there was quite a good spectacular effort in the representation of the fairy grotto."

At Haverhill, Mass., Dec. 13, 1876, Miss Brown again gave this operetta, when the fifty young ladies appearing were chosen from the high school of that city.

"The Haverhill Bulletin," Dec. 14, 1876, said, —

" The presentation of the operetta of ' Laila ' at City Hall, on Wednesday evening, was a very gratifying success. . . . The whole affair was under the direction of Miss Nellie E. Brown, the popular soprano of Grace Methodist-Episcopal Church. She was assisted by some fifty young ladies of this city; and the promptness and harmony with which all the arrangements of the affair were carried out, as well as the musical and dramatic talent displayed by them, are certainly very creditable both to her superintendence and their co-operation."

In the month of July, 1876, Miss Brown was engaged to sing at the " Great Sunday-school Parliament " held on Wellesley, one of the famous Thousand Islands, in the River St. Lawrence. The now much-lamented Professor P. P. Bliss (who had become so eminent as a composer of popular sacred songs), his talented wife, and Miss Brown, were the leading singers and soloists on the occasion mentioned. The two former failing to arrive in time, the musical exercises, which were of a very fine order, were arranged, and for a while conducted, by Miss Brown. Mr. and Mrs. Bliss, however, arrived some time after the sessions had begun, and then participated in the singing. At this memorable gathering of Christian people from all parts of the United States and Canada, Miss Brown, in the display of fine musical powers, won new laurels; and her charming singing was made the subject of frequent and very complimentary allusion by newspaper correspondents writing from the island. In a handsome volume since published by the director of the " Parliament," and which is a record of its proceedings, she is several times creditably mentioned.

The following is one of many like notices which the musical exercises mentioned elicited : —

. . . " As to the singing of Professor Bliss and Miss Nellie Brown, it seems as though we are all in the third heaven at once, and that it is almost sacrilege to come down to meaner things."

Said Andrew Fletcher, "I knew a very wise man that believed, that, if a man were permitted to make all the ballads, he need not care who should make the laws, of the nation." This certainly was placing a very high, but perhaps not a much too high, estimate on the song-writing power. As coming next in greatness to the composers of meritorious popular ballads, we may mention those accomplished persons, who, possessing sweetly-toned, sympathetic voices, and evincing by their mode of expression a ready, a full conception of the author's meaning, have, in an eminent degree, the power to correctly, charmingly render them. In this form of musical expression Miss Brown delights her audiences not less than in her rendition of songs of a more pretentious character. In singing the former she exhibits a most winning *naïveté*, enters wholly into the spirit of the song, and with a full, pleasing voice, impresses deeply its melody and meaning upon the hearts of her hearers, thus exhibiting the highest kind of lyric eloquence. As a singer, then, of ballads alone, she would take high rank in the musical profession, even if she did not excel — it has been seen that she does — in the rendering of songs of a more technical character.

And now, in nearing the close of this sketch, if any reader shall ask to know the secret of the fine degree of success to which our subject has thus far attained (for, in considering great instances of individual achievement, we are ever prone to attribute the same to mysterious or fortuitous circumstances), let him be assured that there is really no "secret" about it. Miss Brown, no doubt, commenced her career with much musical talent, and Nature was otherwise kind to her: *but she has always been a diligent, persevering worker;* and to this cause, rather than to her possession of rich natural endowments, must be mostly attributed her praiseworthy achievements. Indeed, Nature's generous bestowment of talents, or even of genius, is of but little value when the favored one does not assiduously labor to cultivate and develop the same.

> "No good of worth sublime will Heaven permit
> To light on man as from the passing air:
> The lamp of genius, though by nature lit,
> If not protected, pruned, and fed with care,
> Soon dies, or runs to waste with fitful glare."

In her efforts to acquire an artistic acquaintance with music, and to reach her present high and enviable position as a vocalist, Miss Brown has had the warmest sympathy and active co-operation of loving parents and an accomplished brother.[1] Nor should I in this connection fail to advert to the helping, the inspiring influence of thousands of the noble people of New England, who, fond lovers and constant promoters of the beneficent art of music, are ever prompt in the recognition and encouragement of *all* its talented devotees. To the words of private cheer from many of these, and to the inspiriting effect of their upturned, delighted faces, and frequent plaudits, when listening to her beautiful voice in the crowded music-halls, she must often revert with

---

[1] Eugene L. Brown. He was possessed of very promising histrionic ability, had frequently taken a leading part in amateur theatricals at Dover and elsewhere in New Hampshire, and was the author of a drama which was highly spoken of by the press of Dover. Unfortunately, in 1875 he died.

feelings not less of justifiable pride than of the warmest gratitude. The writer is quite sure that he but echoes the sentiments of the admiring thousands just mentioned, when he predicts, that if Miss Brown shall continue to exhibit in the future, as in the past, the same conscientious, ambitious devotion to her chosen profession, she is destined to take rank with the world's greatest singers.

SAMUEL W. JAMIESON.

XV.

SAMUEL W. JAMIESON,
THE BRILLIANT YOUNG PIANIST.

"While a skilled artist's nimble fingers bound
O'er dancing keys, and wake celestial sound."
JULIAN.

"Nor Fame I slight, nor for her favors call:
She comes unlooked for, if she comes at all."
POPE.

"THE entertainments at Parker Memorial Hall on Sunday evenings in no wise lessen in interest and numbers. One evening, listening to Gounod's 'Ave Maria' by the famous Germania Orchestra, we felt that the worship of the Virgin, of which was born such heavenly strains, if for no other reason, was not without its use in the world even now. Another evening Mr. Jamieson awoke the echoes of the piano in a manner to do credit to a Liszt and Chopin."

Thus, a year or two ago, spoke one of Boston's first writers and musical critics, when, in an article published in "The Commonwealth," alluding to the accomplished pianist, Samuel W. Jamieson.

In the comparison here made, so highly complimentary to our subject, this writer does not stand alone; for the remarkably fine execution of Mr. Jamieson has often drawn from other piano-students praise none the less flattering; while his mastery of so many of the difficulties that are connected with piano-forte playing, and his fine general musical talents, entitle him to a prominent place in books far more pretentious than this one. He has, in fact, attained to such brilliant proficiency (although quite a young man) as to cause him to be already ranked with the first pianists of the country.

Mr. Jamieson was born in Washington, D.C., in the year 1855. He began the study of music, taking lessons on the piano-forte, when about eleven years of age. Since then he has been under the instruction of some of the best masters of Boston, such as James M. Tracy, and Fred. K. Boscovitz, the celebrated Hungarian pianist. He has been a pupil of the Boston Conservatory; from which classical institution he graduated in honor in 1876, receiving its valuable diploma.

While a student at the Boston Conservatory, he was nearly always chosen by the director, Mr. Julius Eichberg, to represent at the quarterly concerts the fine progress made by its pupils. At such times his performances of numbers, requiring rapidity of reading and execution, together with a good knowledge of piano *technique*, drew from the press the most favorable comments, and made him the favorite piano pupil at the institution mentioned. The following, as an instance of these comments, is taken from " The Boston Journal: " —

. . . " But the best thing in the piano line was the rendering of Chopin's ' Polonaise,' in E flat, by Mr. Samuel W. Jamieson. The ' Hungarian Rhapsodie,' No. 2, of Liszt, was most particularly characterized by a delicate touch, and a clear conception of the subject in hand.

"It is but just to say that this gentleman is an advanced scholar."

And this from "The Folio," referring to another like occasion: —

"Mr. Samuel Jamieson, pupil of the Boston Conservatory, but directly under the instruction of Mr. Tracy, carried off a good share of the honors of the recent *matinée* of that very successful school."

"The Boston Traveller," describing the performances of pupils of the Conservatory at Music Hall, after stating that all the performances were of a high order, makes special mention of Mr. Jamieson, saying that "his execution of a difficult number was worthy of the highest praise." Many other comments equally favorable could here be given, were it necessary.

His performances at these concerts soon made him widely known among the musical and general public of Boston and vicinity, and his services as a soloist became much in demand. As soon as he had attained to a fair degree of proficiency, he began to give lessons on the piano-forte; and by so doing, and by occasionally appearing at concerts, he secured the means to continue his studies at the Conservatory. His playing at one of these concerts was thus spoken of in a Boston paper: —

"The concert given on Tuesday evening at the Music Hall, though so little known as to be thinly attended, was a very satisfactory entertainment, and well deserved a large audience. Mr. Jamieson is a pupil of the Hungarian pianist Mr. F. Boscovitz, some prominent features of whose style he closely imitates. His playing shows him to be a careful, conscientious student, possessed of real musical sensibility, without any of the nauseous sentimentalism so common among young players. His best performance in every respect was Liszt's 'Rigoletto' fantasie, the mechanical difficulties of which he has well conquered, and the passionate meaning of which he interpreted very finely. In answer to an encore of this piece, he gave Mr. Boscovitz's exquisite little 'Chant du Matin,' Op. 68.

"He will make an excellent pianist if he prosecutes his study as faithfully as he has commenced it. Mr. Jamieson carries with him the good wishes and the highest expectations of those who heard him."

He early showed a singleness of devotion to his chosen work, and has always evinced a spirit of ambitious aim. Some particulars of the latter, while winning him the approval of the thoughtful, have caused him to be misunderstood and censured by others. With fine artistic taste, ever aiming high, fully in earnest, and with no more than (as the writer believes) a just estimate of his attainments and consequent rank as a musician, Mr. Jamieson has sometimes declined to appear at the "twopenny show" concerts given generally in the churches, and often by "artists" (?) of abilities so poor as to render them fit subjects for the training of a rudimentary music school rather than as objects of public view or favor. Still I do not believe that Mr. Jamieson has been unwilling to acknowledge the generally known fact, that much good has often been done by amateurs and others at church concerts, both by the aid thus afforded to meritorious causes, and by the musical practice and public acquaintance obtained for themselves. That he has not been without a ready sympathy for the persons or causes to be benefited by such entertainments is well evinced by the fact, that (notwithstanding he holds certain views mentioned in this connection) he has appeared at times at the same, at the better kind, making no charge for his services; and yet his occasional refusal to appear at certain of these concerts has been attributed — generally by ignorant persons, but sometimes also by others, who, as they knew better, must have been influenced alone by bad motives — to his possession of undue self-esteem, &c. But these unjust criticisms, although often causing him pain, could never swerve him from his chosen path. He would never lower his standard, and he always sought to enter the lists with those who contended for the highest prizes in art. The prominent position he holds to-day as an artist is proof that his course has been the right one, and the one which should serve as an example to all those young persons, who, endowed with musical talents, are yet neglecting to cultivate the same; who are, in fact, allowing them to gradually waste away by giving themselves to unmusical, injurious associations; and who quite too often spend the precious time that should be given under competent teachers to diligent, untiring study, in appearances before audiences whose applause, of doubtful value, is readily bestowed in unstinted quantities, and which serves, alas! but to dazzle, to deceive, and too often to permanently ruin, the young performer.

Mr. Jamieson's fine, ever-increasing musical abilities, his general intelligence and gentlemanly bearing, soon gained for him the *entrée* of the best musical circles of Boston and vicinity, and secured for him association at concerts with the most advanced artists. During the winters of 1875 and 1876 he several times appeared before large and enthusiastic audiences at a series of entertainments given at Parker Memorial Hall. A writer thus mentions his performances at one of these concerts: —

"Mr. Jamieson, the pianist, was before the public last season, and then gained strong praise. He is a promising young artist, and his performances on this occasion showed marked improvement. His selections embraced a fantasie on the 'Wedding March' of Liszt, a fantasie on themes from 'Rigoletto,' and variations on 'Home, Sweet Home;' and in all three he won deserved applause."

He has devoted himself solely to the piano-forte, and makes no pretensions to a knowledge of other instruments, considering the former as quite worthy of his undivided study, — especially in these days, when, in his own city and state at least, fine piano soloists are so numerous, and whose best performances he desires to equal, and, if possible, to excel.

From the first, Mr. Jamieson has given himself to the performance of only the higher class of music. So determined is he in this respect, that he will not play *dance-music*, not even that of the best order. The writer once asked him to play one of Strauss' most bewitching waltzes, — one full of those delicious, so to say, entrancing melodies, for which the productions of this gifted composer are so noticeable, and one which at the time had taken nearly every one completely captive. I refer to the "Beautiful Blue Danube" waltz. But he declined to play it. I again and again entreated him; for I not only delighted to hear as often as possible this charming selection, but, knowing Mr. Jamieson's rare powers as a pianist, I was especially anxious to hear *him* give life to its magic strains. No amount of persuasion could move him, however; and he finally ended the matter by telling me that he never, under any circumstances, played dance-music, as he deemed its practice an injury to one who wished to reach the highest positions as a pianist. So I was compelled to pocket my disappointment, and to go elsewhere for my "Beautiful Blue Danube."

Mr. Jamieson is an assiduous student, devoting several of the early morning hours of each day to practice on the piano-forte. Even during the heated term, when most artists neglect their instruments, and hie away to enjoy the refreshing breezes of the sea-shore or the mountains, he may much of the time be found at his rooms, undeterred by the hot atmosphere, diligently at work keeping up the nice degree of proficiency he has already attained, or bravely attacking whatever difficulties remain to be overcome. He does, it is true, go away every summer to a quiet nook in the country, remaining, however, only a short while, and during which he does not, to any great extent, lessen his hours of practice.

During the winter of 1874 he several times appeared at public concerts in Boston and in other parts of New England. His performances at a *soirée musicale* at the Meionaon, Tremont Temple, Boston, were alluded to in the following gratifying terms by "The Boston Globe:" —

"Mr. Jamieson exhibits much power and delicacy, and a certain confident but not obtrusive manner, which will go far, with his abilities, to place him in a high rank among our pianists. He gave much satisfaction; his performance of Liszt's fantasie on themes from Verdi's 'Rigoletto' showing great skill in mastering the difficult technicalities in the variations on the theme."

And in this manner by "The Boston Traveller:" —

"Mr. Jamieson has come into prominence in this city as a pianist, and the ability he has shown has won him the regard of musical people. His selections last evening were all of the highest order, and were uniformly well performed. Compositions of Chopin, Boscovitz, and Liszt, were given; and in each a clear appreciation of the character of the compositions was shown."

Referring to another occasion, "The Boston Globe" thus spoke of our artist: —

"The participant best known to the Boston public, perhaps, was Mr. S. Jamieson, who has appeared as pianist on several occasions in public and private with marked acceptability. He was on the programme for two solos, both of which were given with a skill and an artistic conception that sustained the favorable impression that he had previously made."

Mr. Jamieson has for some time cherished a hope of going to Europe, there to place himself for a while under the direction of one or more of the great masters of piano-forte playing; being firmly resolved to leave nothing undone the accomplishment of which will place him among the first pianists of the world. Those who know of his present abilities commend him for this desire, and feel warranted in predicting his complete success. Recently a few among the leading musical ladies and gentlemen of Boston tendered him a complimentary reception at the residence of one of the former, and at its close presented him a sum of money to aid him in carrying out the purpose just referred to. The occasion was thus alluded to by "The Daily Advertiser:" —

"A musical *soirée* was given last evening at the residence of Mrs. Jno. W. Perry in aid of Mr. S. W. Jamieson, the talented pianist of the Boston Conservatory, who contemplates a pursuance of his musical studies in Europe the coming summer. . . . The assemblage, which was one of the highest order of respectability, thoroughly enjoyed the choice music that was selected for their ears. Mrs. Kempton, Mrs. Perry, and Messrs. Jamieson, Jacobs, Tracy, Haggerty, Walker, Willard, and Sweetser, contributed in a programme made up of numbers from Rossini, Rubenstein, Schubert, Bendel, Mills, Campana, Chopin, Violetta, Liszt, and Gottschalk."

The writer of the above deemed it quite enough to merely mention the names of composers and artists, leaving to the musical reader to imagine (as easily he could) how rich and plenteous a feast of harmony must have been furnished to those fortunately present on this delightful occasion.

As may perhaps be inferred from the comments heretofore given, Mr. Jamieson, as a pianist, is noticeable for the clearness of his touch, the brilliancy of his style, and the thoroughness of his execution, — not failing to exhibit these pleasing qualities even when playing the most rapid passages, — while he ever shows a full and ready sympathy with the spirit and aims of the composer.

His remarkable proficiency as a pianist, and the private and public attention which the same has drawn to him, has secured him, from time to time, many pupils and as a teacher he has been quite successful.

If the doctrine of "heredity" be true, Mr. Jamieson may trace his possession of musical talent to his grandfather, who attracted much attention as a musician.

But there is no easy road to proficiency and eminence in the musical art; nor is there one in any other. Art is a right royal and exacting mistress; and he who would be numbered among the favored attendants at her court must fairly win the distinction by that devoted, undivided loyalty which is ever accompanied by the severest study, the most self-denying application. It cannot be denied, of course, that the possessor of genius or of talent may succeed far more easily than he who is without such powerful aid; but it is also true, that those who by their works present examples of great achievement in the science of music, and who cause us often to pause in utter amazement when reflecting upon the exceeding beauty, the magnitude and grandeur, of their creations, owed their brilliant success as much to indefatigable labor as to their great gifts of mind. Indeed, as has often been said, "*there is no excellence without great labor.*"

So our young artist — of course I speak of him in this connection in a comparative sense — owes his present high success not more to his possession of rich natural talents than to the tireless zeal with which he has cultivated the same.

Possessing naturally a loftiness of spirit, and with a just conception of his powers; having full faith in and trusting himself; not unmindful of, nor unduly elated by, the many commendations he has received from critical judges touching his musical abilities; wearing easily all the attentions and honors he so constantly wins, and quickly noting and acting upon any suggestions of errors in his performances; at all times a conscientious, a zealous student, impelled by a deep and enthusiastic love for the art of music, and never satisfied unless working amidst its higher forms, — possessing, as Mr. Jamieson does, these rare and valuable characteristics, and being withal still quite young, it is but reasonable to believe that he will ere long attain to the highest distinction, and be ranked with the very first pianists of the time in either the New or the Old World.

XVI.

THE VIOLIN.[1]

"Thou mystic thing, all-beautiful! What mind
Conceived thee, what intelligence began,
And out of chaos thy rare shape designed,
Thou delicate and perfect work of man?"
"*The Violin:*" *Harper's Magazine.*

THE violin, so often called the "king of instruments," is of great antiquity. As to just when it was invented is a point as yet unsettled, despite the indefatigable researches of historians of music and of general antiquaries. The instrument certainly existed, however, as early as the sixth century; this being proven generally by the figures of violins observable on very ancient and respectable monuments still existing, and particularly by a figure cut in the portico of the venerable Cathedral of Notre Dame in Paris, founded by Childebert in the sixth century, which figure represents King Chilperic with a violin in his hand.

It being thus used in a representative character shows, too, that it has for many hundreds of years been a

---

[1] The writer considers it proper to precede the sketch of the virtuoso, Joseph White, by a brief account of that wonderful instrument to which the latter has given his chief study, and in the playing of which he has become in at least four countries so deservedly famous.

favorite instrument. Of that ancient guild of musicians, the troubadours, — so long the principal devotees and custodians of the divine art, — those were most esteemed by royalty and the general public who were the best violists.

In the construction of most musical instruments, improvements have been constantly made up to the present time. This is particularly true of the pianoforte; the handsome form, and the purity and beauty of tone, observable in a lately-made "Chickering" or "Steinway," rendering them so much superior to a piano of the olden times, as to barely admit of the latter's being called by the same name. But this is not true of the violin, inasmuch as a long time has elapsed since any change has been made in its construction that would add to its delicate, graceful form, to its nicety, sweetness, and purity of tone, or general musical capacity. To-day a Cremona, or an Amati, as well as violins of other celebrated makers of the long past, commands almost fabulous prices. A Cremona very lately sold for four thousand dollars; while such instruments as I have mentioned, when in the possession of a soloist, are scarcely to be purchased at any price.

Up to the times of the celebrated violin-virtuoso, Paganini, there had not been, it would seem, much improvement made in performance upon this instrument. He startled and electrified the musical world, and in his wonderful playing developed and amplified such resources and effects, both as to instrument and performer, as were not, previously to his coming, thought possible. After him, and to be compared with him, have come Vieuxtemps, Ole Bull, Wieniawski, and Joseph White. The latter, although not as yet so well known as the others (he is only a little over thirty years of age), is considered by competent critics to be fully entitled to rank with them.

But these are "bright particular stars," men of genius. The instrument is so difficult of mastery, that few violin-students may hope to equal such marvellous players as those mentioned; although long-continued and severe application may make them good orchestral performers or fair soloists.

The violin is said to be the "king of instruments;" but, by this, reference is made to those powers and extensive resources of expression that are made manifest when the instrument is subject to the brain and hand of the very skilful performer.

At such a time it is made to sing a song, which, readily awakening the sympathies of the soul, causes the listener to recognize and feel the effects of the intonations of pathos, of passion, of deepest melancholy, or those of lightsomeness and wildest joy.

Indeed, this noble instrument, under the deft fingering and skilful bowing of a master-player, becomes almost sentient, and is shown to possess the superior and exclusive power of expressing nearly all the human voice can produce except the articulation of words. A music-teacher once wrote that "the art of playing on the violin requires the nicest perception and the most sense of any art in the known world;" and many there are who will agree with him.

The purity, the sweetness, of its tones, — to produce which calls into exercise the most delicate faculties of the mind, — and the power of these tones to awaken in the heart the most tender feelings, to lead the performer at times into delightful imaginations, into pleasing, restful reveries, — it is the possession of such charming qualities as these that has rendered the violin at all times the favorite companion of the leisure moments of men eminent in the walks of literature, of princes, and other persons of taste and refinement. Some among those first mentioned have excelled as violin-performers, notwithstanding their other occupations.

Girardini, when asked how long it would take to learn to play the violin, replied, " Twelve hours a day for twenty years." Another thus intimates how long and arduous must be the toil before its mastery can be acquired : —

" The difficulty of thoroughly mastering the violin — the difficulty, that is, of combining perfect execution with brilliancy of tone and perfect expression — is so vast, that nothing short of indomitable patience and perseverance, united with those indispensable faculties which all good players must possess, will succeed in overcoming them. ' Twelve years' practice,' says a musical critic, 'on the violin, will produce about as much proficiency as one year's practice on the piano.' If that is so, we may well imagine that a man, who by dint of perseverance has at length qualified himself to take his place in an orchestra, may content himself by merely maintaining his acquired skill, without attempting to rival the great heads of the profession.

" The time which some students will devote to fiddling is almost incredible. We have known a clever man to practise every waking hour in the day, rising early and sitting up late, and sparing hardly one hour in the twenty-four for meals, for two years together, in the hope of qualifying himself for the leadership in a provincial orchestra; which, after all, he failed in doing. We have known men who fiddled in bed when they could not sleep, rather than waste the time; and others who have carried a dumb finger-board in their pockets, in order to practise the fingering of difficult passages while walking abroad or travelling by coach."

It is, however, far from the purpose of the writer to

discourage those who may wish to become proficient as performers on this delightful instrument, or to do otherwise than attempt to increase the number of those, who, having carefully listened to master-players, and having thus learned of the wonderful intonations and of the great refinement of musical expression of which the violin is capable, have resolved to become far more than mere "fiddlers;" and are therefore conscientiously and patiently addressing themselves to an endeavor to overcome its difficulties, and to take rank as real violinists. To many of this number a good if not a perfect degree of success must come, as it ever surely comes to the earnest, persevering student of any art.

To all such, then, the writer tenders his best wishes; while he earnestly commends the above examples to all who may have a desire to learn to develop the beautiful harmonic mysteries of this expressive, soulful instrument.

XVII.

JOSEPH WHITE,

THE EMINENT VIOLINIST AND COMPOSER.

> "Across my hands thou liest mute and still:
> Thou wilt not breathe to me thy secret fine;
> Thy matchless tones the eager air shall thrill
> To no entreaty or command of mine.
>
> But comes thy master: lo! thou yieldest all, —
> Passion and pathos, rapture and despair:
> To the soul's needs thy searching voice doth call
> In language exquisite beyond compare."
>
> *"The Violin:" Harper's Magazine.*

MR. JOSEPH WHITE[1] is a child of the New World. He was born in Matanzas, Cuba. His first steps in art were made in his native town.

His father, an amateur in music, thought he had recognized from the early infancy of the great artist a more than ordinary taste for art. When the child heard the tones of a violin, he used to leave off play, and run in the direction where the instrument was singing, his eyes never losing sight of the virtuoso. Indeed, by

---

[1] By permission of Mr. White, I quote now, and to some extent shall do so hereafter, from his Biography, published in Paris in 1874 by Paul Dupont. For the excellent translation used I am much indebted to my friend Mr. Joseph W. Hendricks of Boston.

JOSEPH WHITE.

his actions at such times, he seemed not to belong to this world.

As soon as his hands were large enough to hold a violin, they gave him one; and were much astonished, when, at the end of a few months, he presented himself before a large audience, striking the same with amazement by the manner, entirely magisterial, in which he so early attacked the instrument.

He continued his studies until the year 1855, when, at the suggestion of the famous Gottschalk, who had noticed the signs of genius in the young man, he started for Paris, the city of wonders, and centre of attraction for all aspirations.

He came then, this young virtuoso, and presented himself at the Conservatoire, asking to enter as a pupil. After going through a brilliant examination, and after fighting against more than sixty rivals, he was received with unanimity.

In July, 1856, one year from the time of his entering the Conservatoire, White won all the "approbations," and wreaths and laurels were given him.

But we will let the newspapers of the time speak; for our own pen will be powerless to give an account of the successes of the eminent artist. The "Gazette Musicale" of the 3d of August, 1856, speaks thus:—

... "We will say as much of the pupil who has won the first prize for violin, and who came the last in the list of concurrents. The Viotti Concerto had already been played nineteen times; and, notwithstanding the great beauties of this classic work, the jury began to listen to it with but a dreamy ear. Mr. White appeared the twentieth. He belongs to a race whose complexion is more of a copper-color, with black and frizzled hair. He carries the head high, and his look is proud and intrepid. He approaches the eternal concerto, and it instantly becomes an entirely new creation

"The jury listened to it with as much pleasure as if they heard it for the first time; and scarcely had Mr. White finished this piece when the jury retired to vote, proclaiming him the victor.

"Mr. White is eighteen years and a few months old. Since a year ago he has been in the Conservatoire, and studies in Alard's class.

"But where has he taken his first lessons? How did this son of America become the equal of the greatest violinists known in Europe? That is what we do not know, and what we ask to know for the honor of the American school, of which Mr. White is a splendid example."

The paper, "Le Pays," of the 5th of August, 1856, expresses itself in terms none the less flattering: —

"The concourse of violinists has presented this year a beautiful sight. The fight has been one of the most brilliant. The first prize has been awarded to Mr. White, pupil of Mr. Alard.

. . . "As for Mr. White, he showed himself so much superior, that there ought to have been (so we think) created in his favor an exceptional prize. He has played with an extraordinary animation, not like a pupil, but like a master, — like a great artist who commands his auditory. The jury itself was electrified. In order to compete with that young man, there ought to have been masters there."

It was at this brilliant concourse that Rossini, the great composer, remarked of White, "Since the day he took an interest in him, and protected the young artist, there was no festivity at the maestro's without the violinist playing on his melodious instrument." Besides, this letter from Rossini, addressed to White at the time of his father's sickness, shows how much the master loved him: —

To Mr. White. *Sir*, — Allow me to express to you all the pleasure that I felt Sunday last at my friend Mr. David's. The warmth of your execution, the feeling, the elegance, the brilliancy of the school to which you belong, show qualities in you as an artist of which the French school may be proud. May it be, sir, that through my sympathetic wishes I may bring you good fortune by finding again in good health the one for whom you fear to-day! Accept my blessings. Sir, I wish you a happy journey, and a speedy return. G. ROSSINI.

In November, 1858, Mr. White was obliged to return to Havana, called back to his dying father. He then left France; accounts of his success in which, carried to the dying man, were a sweet consolation and happiness, — thus to see, before dying, his son who was called to such a brilliant career. After the death of his father, he started for France again; not, however, without having first obtained great success in different cities of Cuba, where he was received in triumph. Gottschalk, the celebrated pianist, who was one of the first who had advised White's family to send him to Paris, said that in all his life he had never seen such a beautiful success, and such a deserved one.

After his return to Paris, White gave a great concert. "L'Illustration" of the 4th of May, 1861, gives an account of that evening's entertainment in the following terms: —

"Mr. White, whom America sent to us a year ago, I think, through a courageous work, developed the talent which had caused him to receive the first prize at the Conservatoire. He played with equal success the concerto by Mendelssohn, and Paganini's fantasias: which is to say, that he is ready to play every thing you may wish; for there is a place for every thing between these two extremes. He played even his own music; and played at his concert a composition for violin and orchestra, very well instrumentated, full of happy melodies, and where the principal part contained features of a character as ingenious as piquant. He possesses an extreme dexterity in the use of the bow, and makes the staccato with as much audacity as perfection. He has the tone agreeable, the style elegant, and the expression just, and not affected. Here he is, then, placed in the first rank in that glorious phalanx of violinists which Europe envies us."

After having given a splendid description of this concert (which want of space forces us not to publish here), the "Patrie" of the 30th of April, 1861, speaks thus: —

"We have seen Mr. White begin. We have been present at the concourse at the Conservatoire, where he won successively all the prizes. Then it was but a scholar who gave brilliant hopes: it is a master that we congratulate to-day in him."

Some time after, he left for Spain, where he played at Mme. the Comtesse de Montijo's (mother of the Empress of France), and before the Queen of Spain. Her Spanish Majesty presented him, the brilliant virtuoso, with a magnificent set of diamond studs, and created him chevalier of the order of Isabella the Catholic. We reproduce some lines from "La France Musicale" of the 22d of November, 1863: —

"White, the violinist, has had the honor to be received on the 12th of this month by the Queen of Spain. Her Majesty has accepted the dedication of a piece composed by this eminent artist, and has told him that she would try and find an occasion for hearing him play it; and, in fact, our violinist played at the queen's on the 22d of December."[1]

After his return to France, he played at the Tuileries before their Majesties Napoleon the Third and the Empress Eugénie. These sovereigns congratulated the artist most fully. We reproduce an extract from the "Constitutionale:" —

"In the concert given at the Palace of the Tuileries on the 1st of March, Mr. White, violinist, and very distinguished, executed a

[1] For further accounts of his career in Spain, the reader is referred to La Correspondencia of 23d December, 1863; La Epoca, La Discusion, &c., of about the same date.

fantasie on Nabucco by Mr. Alard, in which he displayed all the qualities of a virtuoso. He knows how to make his instrument sing; and, when a difficulty presents itself, he carries it with a fascinating majesty. He is an artist who has succeeded in taking place among the best violinists of France and Italy."

This was going on in the year 1864.

This same year, Alard, White's old professor, was obliged to be absent, and leave his class in the care of others. After considering into whose care he should leave his class, Mr. Alard thought that White was more able to help him than any other, — White, his old first prize. Since that day, it was he, who, during the absence of the master, has had the directing of his class at the Conservatoire. In order to thank him for his services so well given, Alard presented White with a magnificent bow ornamented with gold and with tortoise-shells.

One reads in the "France Musicale" of the 24th of December, 1864, the following lines: —

"Our celebrated violinist Alard, who has been on a short tour in the country, has just returned to Paris. During his absence, one of his pupils, Mr. White the violinist, took the management of his class at the Conservatoire."

The "Art Musicale" of the 15th of January says, —

"Our celebrated violinist Alard is now in Nice, where he expects to spend a month. It is the violinist, Mr. White, who is charged with the direction of his class at the Conservatoire."

The "Presse Théâtrale" of the 26th of January, 1865, says, —

"In leaving Paris for a journey, the length of which is not fixed, Mr. Alard has confided the care of his violin class at the Conservatoire to Mr. White. This choice, there is no need to say, has been approved by the ministry of the emperor's house, and that of the Beautiful Arts. We need not say how much this honors the young artist who is the object of it."

After this new victory, our eminent violinist was heard at the Société de Concerts of the Conservatoire of Paris, where he was admitted as a member. He played the piece in F by Beethoven; and, when a second time they encored the artist, he distinguished himself in a classic work — the concerto by Mendelssohn — which masters alone dare to confront. The success was complete. One could have heard the buzzing of a fly in the hall. All eyes and hearts were in complete subjection to the bow of the young virtuoso.

Here is how the eminent musical critic of the paper "Le Siècle," Mr. Commettant, expresses himself on the date of the 13th May, 1872: —

"At the last concert of the Société de Concerts, Mr. White, violinist of our beautiful French school, a composer learned and inspired, executed the concerto by Mendelssohn, one of the most melodious and the best proportioned of this illustrious master. The virtuoso showed himself the worthy interpreter of the composer; and through his playing, full, correct, warm, and well-moderated, Mr. White has obtained a success which is akin to enthusiasm. They unanimously called back the artist; and he came to bow to the public, and then calmly went back to his place in the orchestra, from which he had just stepped forth. These are things which are only to be seen in this celebrated musical company of the Conservatoire, which, in spite of every thing, remains the first orchestra of the whole world."

The "Ménestrel" of the 12th of May, 1872, says, —

"Let us recognize the great success won last Sunday at the Conservatoire by the violinist White, in the concerto by Mendelssohn. He is an artist now complete, this young rival of the Sivoris and of Vieuxtemps. He is not only a virtuoso, but also a composer of note, having published several very remarkable pieces for the violin. We shall notice his six brilliant 'Studies for the Conservatoire.' He has composed one concerto with large orchestral accompaniment, a quatuor for strings, 'Songs without

Words,' several fantasies, and several pieces for one and two violins."

His concerto brought forth the following lines in the "France Musicale" of the 3d of March, 1867: —

"Mr. Joseph White is one of the most distinguished violinists of the French school. While yet very young, he jumped with one bound to the first rank ; and since then he has each day strengthened his reputation through new and incontestable successes. He has always distinguished himself as well by the manner, grand and magisterial, with which he renders the masters' works, as by his style, together elegant and sober, when he interprets music of our time. In order to be more than a virtuoso of note, there was only one thing wanting in him; and that was to cause himself to be appreciated as a composer.

"If virtuosity is acquired through obstinate work, guided by good studies, and helped by that indispensable element, natural aptitude, genius is a gift from Heaven, which neither treatise on harmony, nor the works on counterpoint, nor a given song, shall ever procure to those who have no sacred fire.

"Last Tuesday Mr. White gave a concert in the Herz Hall; and here he has had the good fortune to receive, from the delighted audience that surrounded him, a double wreath, given together to the violinist and to the composer. The concerto he played, and whose author he is, is one of the best modern conceptions we ever heard of the kind.

"The style of a concerto must be, at the same time, serious in thoughts and in their developments, graceful and brilliant, in order to bring forth the talent of execution of the virtuoso. Here is a double reef to avoid, and here many artists have been wrecked. Vieuxtemps and Leonard are the modern masters who have been the most successful in this difficult style; but how many have been less happy!

"Mr. White's concerto is very temperate, of unnecessary length. The fabric of it is very well cared for; the mother-thoughts are well separated from the very commencement; the harmonies are unmistakably elegant and fine; and the orchestration is written with a firm and sure hand, without fumblings or failings. The three episodes are naturally united by the *tuttis;* the third movement, '*rondo* à la turca,' is charming in cut and manner, its rhythms original and frank, and has won all approbations, and brought forth several times unanimous *bravos* from the whole assembly. This composition of a high value has been, in one word, the object of a true ovation for Mr. White, who was both author and composer."

The " Art Musicale " speaks thus of this concerto : —

" From the first measures one feels himself in presence of a nature strong and individual, and not in the presence of a *proletaire* of the large tribe of virtuoso composers.

" Not a single note in the composition has been given to *virtuosité*, though the difficulties of execution be enormous. ' With every true artist there is an eternally vibrating chord, which goes to the heart,' says Boileau; and that is why Mr. White asks only that his own emotion shall excite emotion, and, to the astonishment of charlatanry, renounces at once those means of success employed by coarse musicians."

Then follows an analysis of the work, which want of space prevents us from giving. No need to say that it is favorable to our violinist-composer.

We will mention only some of the papers which have spoken of the evening in question, — " La France," " La Liberté," " La Revue et Gazette des Théâtres," " La Presse Théâtrale," " La Ménestrel," " La Semaine Musicale," &c.

On the subject of the " Quatuor for Stringed Instruments " we will cite the article of the " Gazette Musicale " of the 12th of March, 1872 : —

" The old Schumann Society, all concerts of which are consecrated to the liberation of the territory, is not as exclusive in the composition of its programmes as its title would make you suppose.

" Thus is it that one has there very vivaciously applauded, Saturday, a ' Quatuor for Stringed Instruments,' by Mr. White. We signal this beautiful composition to the amateur's attention. This young master shows in it the most serious qualities united to a perfect clearness and purity of melody, with execution very remarkable, and which received one of the warmest receptions."

Here is the document we have before mentioned: —

IMPERIAL CONSERVATOIRE OF MUSIC AND DECLAMATION.
(*Extract of the Document of the Seating of the Committee on Musical Studies*, 16th *December*, 1868.)

The Committee on Musical Studies for Violin, of the Conservatoire, has read with interest the work which Mr. White has presented for its approbation.

The work is composed of six studies for violin, where the principal difficulties of execution which that instrument presents are confronted.

One remarks in these pages ingenious combinations proper to develop the mechanism of the left hand.

The committee approves these six studies, called to fortify the talent of a violinist.

(Signed)   AUBER,
Director of Conservatoire, and Pres. of Committee.

Then follow ten signatures of members of the committee.

As a token of his artistic value, four great masters have presented White with their likenesses, with the following dedications: —

"Remembrance, admiration, and thankfulness are offered to my young friend White, a violinist very distinguished.
"(Signed)   "G. ROSSINI."

"To Mr. White, whose talent is an honor to the Conservatoire.
"AUBER."

"To Mr. White. Friendly remembrance.
"AMBROSE THOMAS."

"To my young friend White.   "GOUNOD."

The numerous medals sent to him by the musical societies are homages rendered to his merit.

What remains to say after all these proofs of an incontestable talent?

There is nothing we might wish for Mr. White in

what touches his art: in it he unites every thing. He is certainly one of the most toasted and most appreciated professors of Paris, the soloist beloved by the public.

We repeat it, we can say nothing more, but that we wish to hear him as much as possible.

And here his biographer, after thus expressing, in terms the most affectionate and flattering, his inability to say more that would add to a fame so great, so nobly and so rapidly won throughout Cuba, France, and Spain, — here he closes the record.

With all these brilliant and remarkable achievements, with all these rare honors so enthusiastically awarded him by the most distinguished, the very *élite*, of the musical profession, both singly and combinedly, and by the sovereigns of France and Italy, White might well have rested, indulging himself in no further acquisitions.

But men of such transcendent powers, men within whose souls the fire of musical genius so brightly burns, *cannot* stop; for the essence, the very soul, of music, is the predominating, the all-absorbing quality that forms their natures; and therefore it is that their ever new, their ever charmingly beautiful revelations in divine harmony, cease only when the sacred flame is extinguished by death itself. Thus, then, it was with the subject of our sketch, who was to gain new laurels in still another country. To speak of the same briefly is the cause of this continuance of his history.

Although born so near the United States (in Cuba), White had never until the year 1876 visited this country. In that year, however, he came to New York. In keeping with that modesty of demeanor, which, despite the many and rare honors he had won in Europe, had ever characterized him, he came to our shores unpreceded by that blowing of trumpets (usually paid for) which generally heralds the approach of the foreign artist; and quietly, unostentatiously addressing himself to the *duties* that belonged to his beloved art, little was heard of him by the general public for some time. But such almost marvellous power as this artist, this master, possessed, could not long remain unrevealed. People of musical culture were ere long electrified by the sweet tones of wondrous melody which with perfect ease he drew from his violin. That terrible barrier so often, even at the present time, erected in this country, that shameful obstruction, *color prejudice*, could not long withstand the attacks of this quiet yet courageous musical genius; and people, at first indifferent because of his complexion, were won anon to his favor, not alone by his exceptional skill as a performer, but also by the polish, the ease and dignity, of his manners, so refreshingly free from ostentatious affectation on the one hand, or hesitating timidity on the other. They found that he was indeed the true, the conscientious artist, who loved music for its own sake, and was imbued with a spirit of truthful enthusiasm, in such pleasing contrast with the characteristics exhibited by many of the foreign artists who had preceded him, as to render the same decidedly charming. The possession of these rare traits of character served, of course, to add to the attractiveness of a form which was one of most pleasing symmetry.

A knowledge of his great abilities as a soloist spreading among musicians in New York, he was induced to appear in public. It is needless to say that his success was unequivocal. Of the impression he made in New York, a city that has so often been the scene of the success or failure of the foreign artist, I shall call another person — a purely disinterested and competent art critic — to testify in the following, written from New York to " The Musician and Artist" of Boston of March, 1876 : —

"Joseph White is in some respects the best violinist who has visited this country within my remembrance, *not* excepting Wieniawski. He and his companion Ignasio Cervantes, pianist, made their appearance in this city some few months since, very modestly advertised, and unheralded by any sensational newspaper paragraphs, and at their very first concert insured themselves undoubted future success. This success has been due entirely to White; for, although Cervantes is quite a nice pianist, he is nothing wonderful. But White was a *revelation*. His first New-York introduction to a large general audience was at a philharmonic concert (the date of which I cannot now recall), when he played the Mendelssohn concerto and the Bach chaconne. The Mendelssohn concerto was excellently played, especially the last movement; but it was in the Bach chaconne that he proved how really good he was. I have heard this composition by every violinist of eminence (except Vieuxtemps) who has visited our city; but I never heard so satisfactory a playing of it. The three voices flowed on so smoothly and evenly, never seeming to be in each other's way: there always seemed to be plenty of bow, and just in the right place for each individual voice to receive exactly its due prominence. The vociferous recall that followed this worthy performance was well earned. White is a Cuban mulatto, fine-looking, and extremely gentlemanly in appearance and conversation. A Brooklyn writer speaks of him as follows: 'His style is perfection itself; his bowing is superb, and his tone exquisite His execution is better than Ole Bull's; he possesses more feeling than Wieniawski; the volume of his tone is greater than that of Vieuxtemps.' All of which I indorse."

On March 12, 1876, he appeared in New York as soloist at a grand concert given by that justly celebrated and almost perfect body of musicians, the Theodore Thomas orchestra. His performances on this and several previous occasions elicited the most enthusiastic and unbounded praise from the critical "Arcadian" and the other New-York papers, nearly all of whom placed him beside the three or four great violin-artists of the world.

On the 26th of March, 1876, White appeared at a grand concert given in the Boston Theatre, in company with Levy the renowned cornetist. I shall long and delightfully remember the emotions of thrilling pleasure produced in my own breast by this virtuoso's magnetic execution, and the feelings of joyful pride that I experienced when witnessing, on this occasion, his great triumph. After he had played the first few bars of the "Ballade et Polonaise" by Vieuxtemps, the audience felt that he was a master; and his reception readily became a grand ovation. He received a double encore after the performance of each regular number on the programme. But of his grand success on this occasion I shall let the journals of Boston of March 27, 1876, speak.

"Daily Globe:" —

"The concert at the Boston Theatre last evening attracted one of the largest audiences of the season ; and it is seldom that any artist receives such an ovation as that which was given to Señor Joseph White, the Cuban violinist, who made his first appearance before a Boston audience. The numbers on the programme assigned to this gifted artist were a 'Ballade et Polonaise' by Vieuxtemps, and 'Chaconne' by J. S. Bach ; but a double encore to each of these was responded to by other selections, including the 'Carnival of Venice,' and a gavotte by Bach : all of which were rendered with a perfection rarely heard in violin performances, and recalled the best efforts of Ole Bull."

"Boston Journal:"—

"The chief feature of the concert at the Boston Theatre last evening was the appearance of a new violinist, Señor Joseph White, a Cuban, who has lately created quite a sensation. Rarely has any artist created so great a *furore* in a single hearing as Señor White. His really wonderful playing took the audience captive at once. His tone is remarkably true, pure, and firm, and his execution at all times clear and perfect. In short, he seems to have perfect command of the instrument."

"Herald:"—

"He handles the king of instruments with the utmost ease and confidence. He has no useless flourish in his manner, and none of the 'hifalutin' in his style. He draws and pushes his bow, and the instrument responds with delightful sweetness and passionate eloquence. He is probably entitled to a place in the catalogue of first-class violinists. Certainly those who heard him last night accorded him praises which would have perhaps ruined a less vain man."

"Daily Advertiser:"—

"But the success of the evening may be awarded to Joseph White. He plays in a style together firm and strong, and delicate and refined. His masterly rendition of Vieuxtemps' well-known 'Ballade et Polonaise' at once captivated the audience, and he was enthusiastically encored; and, the audience still calling for more, he played 'The Carnival of Venice.' This second selection was played without accompaniment; and he again was triply encored, the last time giving an air from 'Sonnambula.'"

I have reserved for the last a very excellent critical analysis of our artist's performances. It is taken from "The Daily Evening Transcript."

"The Sunday-night concert at the Boston Theatre last evening was made memorable by the introduction to the Boston public of Señor Joseph White, the Cuban violinist. . . . The musical fraternity, however, was very fully represented, the musicians knowing something of what was in store for the evening. But not even they were prepared for the wonderful and delightful playing of Señor White. . . . The first of his work last night was something of a disappointment. There appeared to be a deficiency of tone, owing, as it seemed, to the use of an instrument not loud enough for so large an auditorium. But it was soon evident that the selection of such an instrument was in accordance with the style and taste of the artist. Possessing the most perfect ease and freedom in his command of the resources of the violin, with a fine breadth of style, and an evidently strong and quick sensibility, yet he did not aim to produce his effects on a large scale of tone. He seemed to desire to confine his exhibition of the violin to the range where its fineness and sweetness, rather than its power, may be illustrated, and to check himself inside of the limit where a coarse, scratchy body of tone is obtained at the expense of purity and delicacy. His bow, though 'dividing the strings with fire,' seemed never to touch them. The direction or the position of its stroke, whether up or down, at the beginning or at the end of it, could never be told from any changes in the quality of the sound extracted. The tone flowed as though after the keen incisions of a knife-blade, not as if scraped out by the friction of horse-hair upon catgut. When to this delicious quality of tone was added an exhibition of the most perfect *technique*, the triumph of the virtuoso was complete. The mysterious flowing softness and smoothness of tone was carried with unflagging facility through the most rapid and difficult chord and harmonic playing; and this, with other wonderful feats of bowing, added new and bewitching charms to the *diablerie* of violin variations. The reception of the artist was cordial at the outset; but at the close of the first performance, a 'Ballade et Polonaise' by Vieuxtemps, the enthusiasm was overwhelming. In response to the encore, Señor White played a 'Styrienne' of his own arrangement; and this was followed by two more stormy recalls, the audience refusing to be quieted until he had again gratified them, this time with the 'Carnival of Venice,' arranged by himself in an elegant transcription of the familiar commonplace variations. At the conclusion of his second number, Bach's 'Chaconne,' a famous and difficult violin solo, which was played, and *interpreted* as well, in a most masterly manner, the applause was again equally enthusiastic, notwithstanding the character of the selection; and for an encore the scholarly artist responded with a finely intelligent and daintily clean-cut rendering of a gavotte by Bach. The tumultuous recalls that followed this would be satisfied with nothing less than another performance; and Señor White gave a rich and pleasing arrangement of his own upon a popular air from 'Sonnambula.' With these two 'double encores,' amid such excitement as is rarely witnessed at a concert, Señor White may well add Boston to the other American cities that have 'adopted' him."

And here, for the present, we will take leave of our great violinist.

It is not probable that he obtained, while in this country, a very great pecuniary success; and, from what has been heretofore stated in regard to his characteristics, this will not seem strange. White was not a *showman*. He has ever been too purely, too entirely devoted to his chosen art to admit of his using the means generally employed by the mere money-seeking musician, — means which seem so out of keeping with those finer aspirations which a contemplation and practice of the noble art of music are expected to promote, and the use of which, detracting as it does from his dignity, lessens the respect, the admiration, which people of culture would fain feel for the gifted performer.

A few months ago our artist sailed for Paris, the scene of his earliest triumphs. He has gone from our shores with his brow laden with new laurels, all honestly won; and he leaves behind an admiring multitude of musical people who will ever watch with deepest interest his future career, and fondly wish for his speedy return. Therefore we do not say to him "*Adieu!*" but "*Au revoir!*"

XVIII.

THE COLORED AMERICAN OPERA COMPANY.

"Who, as they sang, would take the prisoned soul,
And lap it in Elysium."
                                MILTON.

"For, wheresoe'er I turn my ravished eyes,
  Gay gilded scenes and shining prospects rise;
  Poetic fields encompass me around,
  And still I seem to tread on classic ground."
                                ADDISON.

THE opera, or music drama, in which, in lieu of the ordinary forms of speech, music and song are used to give elevated expression to thought, is the most extensive, and, to nearly all lovers of melody, the most charming, of musical compositions. In its construction several of the other forms of music are most pleasingly united.

In the opera, with the language of poetry, music is associated, giving increased ornamentation; and it is used also to bridge over, so to speak, the places where mere language, either common or poetical, could never pass. That is to say, there are some phases of feeling of such fineness and depth, that only the soulful tones of music can call them into exercise, or give them expression.

The requirements for operatic construction are of course very great, — so great, that none may hope to succeed in the same save those endowed, if not with genius, at least with very superior talents. They must possess both marked originality, and power for continuity of thought; in fact, must form in their capabilities a very "Ariel," a fountain-head of music, from which must constantly flow melody after melody, harmony after harmony, ever new, ever pleasing, the whole presenting an artistically-woven story of the vicissitudes of human life. In the composition of an opera, two persons are usually associated; the one creating the words of the drama (the song), and the other composing its music.

In this field of musical creation, men of great genius find a more varied, a wider scope for the employment of their powers; and but a few of the world's most eminent composers of music have failed to avail themselves of its opportunities for grand achievements, success in it being generally considered as necessary for a rounding-out of their inventive harmonic capacities; while, for the establishment of their titles to greatness, they have sought to make some grand opera the *chef-d'œuvre* of their life-work.

I would not imply, however, that all the great composers of opera worked simply for fame. To assert that they did, would, no doubt, be unjust, as it would be denying that they possessed the "sacred fire of genius," and that deep and pure affection for art, which, judging from the noble beauty, the grandeur, of their works, they must have possessed. It does not seem allowable, for instance, to believe that Beethoven created the charming and exalted beauties found in the opera of "Fidelio" while inspired by no higher feelings than those which fill the breast of him who labors mainly for renown. No: we think of Beethoven, and of others like him, as those, who, while they were favored with extraordinary native powers, were also imbued with a pure love for music, — a love of such strength, that it formed a part of their very natures. To such minds and hearts elevated artistic work was as natural as life itself; in truth, we might almost say, was necessary to life.

But, if great powers are required by the composer of an opera, so also is it necessary that those who are to make known its meanings fully — especially those who are to interpret its leading parts — should possess, as singers and actors, more, to say the least, than ordinary abilities; and those who, in their capability for complete, soulful sympathy with the author's aims, who form, in fine, the very embodiment of the latter's ideals, certainly deserve to stand next to him in greatness.

Generally the brightest vocal stars have shed their effulgence upon the operatic stage: here these singers have found the widest range for their extensive powers of voice and dramatic action. The part of a performer in opera (and here I refer not alone to one who acts the leading *rôle*) is a most exacting one; for the artist must unite in himself the qualities of both the singer and the actor. While called upon to demonstrate with proper melody of voice and expression the meaning of the music of the opera, he is also required to portray by suitable dramatic movements its corresponding meaning as found in the libretto. These remarks apply more particularly to those who constitute the *dramatis per-*

sonæ in operatic presentation. Of course we do not forget the very important aid afforded by those who are included in the pleasing chorus, nor those who by instrumental accompaniment add to the charm of — in fact, give indispensable support to — the whole performance.

It would perhaps be superfluous to here dwell, at least more than incidentally, upon the deep pleasure enjoyed by the lovers of music and of dramatic art when witnessing the performance of a good opera. At such a time their truly musical souls enjoy a delicious, a sumptuous feast of melody; while the kaleidoscopic prospect, formed by richly-costumed actors, and appropriate, beautiful scenery, fills them with delight. The harsh realities of every-day life are so much relieved by the poetic charms of the ideal, that they live amidst a scene of fairy-like enchantment. Nor does all that belongs to the bewitching occasion end with the regretted close of the performance; for

> " Music, when soft voices die,
> Vibrates in the memory;"

And for days and days, nay, often throughout life, do the best melodies, the " gems of the opera," delightfully " haunt the memory," and awaken in the heart the most pleasing emotions. In all this, no more than a just tribute is paid to the noble genius of the composer, and the fascinating power of his faithful coadjutor, the lyric actor.

These few thoughts, which, it may be, present nothing new to the student of the various forms of musical expression, fall very short of doing justice to a subject of most delightful interest, and one which, for its proper treatment, requires far more of elaboration than can here be given. They are among such as come to me while reflecting upon an achievement, that, although not in a general way extraordinary, was nevertheless, in some important respects, exceedingly remarkable and noteworthy. I refer to a series of performances given at Washington and Philadelphia in the month of February, 1873, by an organization called " *The Colored American Opera Company.*"

This troupe, formed in Washington, was composed of some of the most talented amateur musical people residing in that city. The following-named ladies and gentlemen were the principal members and performers : —

MR. JOHN ESPUTA	*Musical Director.*
MRS. AGNES GRAY SMALLWOOD . .	*Soprano.*
MISS LENA MILLER	*Contralto.*
MISS MARY A. C. COAKLEY. . . .	*Contralto.*
MR. HENRY F. GRANT	*Tenor.*
MR. RICHARD TOMPKINS	*Tenor.*
MR. WILLIAM T. BENJAMIN . . .	*Baritone.*
MR. GEORGE JACKSON	*Baritone.*
MR. THOMAS H. WILLIAMS	*Basso profundo.*

Mr. Henry Donohoe acted as business manager.

Around these, the central figures, were grouped a large, well-balanced chorus, and a fine orchestra; nor was appropriate *mise en scène*, nor were any of the various accessories of a well-equipped opera, wanting in the presentation.

The opera chosen for these performances was Julius Eichberg's excellent " Doctor of Alcantara."

The first performances were given in Lincoln Hall, Washington, on the evenings of Feb. 3 and 4, 1873; the next at Philadelphia, in Agricultural Hall, Feb. 21, 22, and 23. Returning to Washington, the two last performances of the series were given in Ford's Theatre.

246 *Music and Some Highly Musical People.*

Of the highly meritorious character of these presentations of opera there exists abundant evidence, emanating from disinterested, trustworthy sources, from which I quote the following.

From "The Daily Washington Chronicle," Feb. 4, 1873: —

"THE AMERICAN OPERA-COMPANY.

"The first colored opera-troupe of any merit ever organized in this country appeared at Lincoln Hall last night in Eichberg's opera, 'The Doctor of Alcantara.'

"Lincoln Hall was literally packed. Of course the majority of the audience was colored, and included a host of the personal friends of the singers. Glancing over the house, the full opera-dresses scattered liberally through the audience reminded one not a little of the scene at a concert by Carlotti Patti or the Theodore Thomas orchestra. Quite a third of the audience was composed of white ladies and gentlemen, largely attracted, perhaps, by the novelty of the affair; and among them were many representatives of the musical circles of the city, somewhat curious to hear and compare the performance with those they have been accustomed to hear.

"The criticisms, as a whole, were favorable. It was evident that the voices of two or three of the singers will be bettered by cultivation. The choruses were effective. In dramatic ability there was little lacking, and the singers were quite as natural as many who appear in German and French opera."

From "The Daily National Republican," Washington, Feb. 5, 1873: —

"The second representation of 'The Doctor of Alcantara' at Lincoln Hall last night was an improvement upon the first. The natural nervousness of the singers was better overcome, and they made a better use of their fine voices.

"For the sake of making some just reflections and comparisons, we select the name of Miss Lena Miller, who sang the *rôle* of 'Isabella.' Here is a young lady, really pretty in form and features, graceful in stage-presence, modest in manner, and imbued with true affection and spirit for art. At present she is not a great singer; but her voice is sweet and clear, and at times sympathetic. In this simple statement high but judicious praise is included; and here we might stop. But Miss Miller's presence in opera has a significance and a promise infinitely pleasing to all candid and well-judging minds concerning the race to which she belongs.

"Neither Miss Miller nor Mrs. Smallwood, nor any of the company, have had the advantage of musical training in European or American conservatories. They have to depend alone upon their natural gifts and personal acquirements. This fact is one which makes vastly in their favor, and protects them from the standard by which Adeline Patti or Louise Kellogg would be judged as artists. Under all the circumstances, they sing and perform extraordinarily well; and as for the chorus, it is superior to that of any German or Italian opera heard in this city for years.

"Mr. Benjamin's impersonation of 'Dr. Paracelsus' was really a good bit of acting, and Mr. Grant's 'Carlos' won for him deserved applause.

"The *rôle* of 'Don Pomposa' by Mr. Williams, the *basso profundo*, was finely rendered. His acting was good, and his voice full of richest melody.

"The opera last evening was largely patronized by distinguished people, among them being Senator and Mrs. Sprague, Gen. Holt, and many others.

"The experiment, doubtful at first, has proved a genuine success."

From "The All-Day City Item," Philadelphia, Feb. 22, 1873: —

"'The Doctor of Alcantara' has at last attracted a number of colored amateurs of Washington; and they have lately appeared in that city, with such success that they are induced to present it in Philadelphia.

"It must be remembered that this troupe is composed entirely of amateurs, and is the first colored opera-troupe in existence. We have had the 'Colored Mario' [Thomas J. Bowers], the 'Black Swan' [Miss Greenfield], &c.; but never until now have we had a complete organization trained for *ensembles*.

"The audience attracted to Horticultural Hall last evening was therefore prepared to make all sorts of allowances for the shortcomings of the amateurs; but it was hardly necessary, as the troupe — really excellent, well trained — possesses agreeable voices, sings intelligently, and with experience will, we are confident, attract a great deal of attention, and receive high praise.

"The principal success was achieved by Mrs. A. G. Smallwood, who sang the music of 'Lucrezia' remarkably well. Her voice is full and pleasing. Miss Lena Miller, however, sang 'Isabella' very prettily; her romance, 'He still was there,' being rendered with excellent taste. Miss Mary A. C. Coakley, as 'Inez,' acted and sang with considerable spirit. Her arietta, 'When a lover is poor,' was quite neatly sung.

"Mr. W. T. Benjamin, as the 'Doctor,' acted and sang with spirit; so did Mr. T. H. Williams as 'Don Pomposo.' Mr. H. F. Grant, the tenor, has a powerful voice, which, with cultivation, will become excellent. He sang 'Love's cruel dart' judiciously, and was effective in the opening serenade with chorus, 'Wake, lady, wake.' Mr. Grant is not yet at home on the stage, but acted and sang the duet, 'I love, I love,' with 'Lucrezia,' remarkably well.

"The chorus, numbering nearly forty, was worthy of warm praise. The serenade that opens the opera was charmingly sung by the male voices; and the finale to Act 3 was so spirited and effective, that it was encored. We do not exaggerate when we say that this is one of the best choruses we have heard for some time."

From "The Philadelphia Inquirer," Feb. 22, 1873: —

"THE COLORED OPERA-COMPANY.

"This opera-company made its first appearance in this city last evening at Horticultural Hall, and was most favorably received. The performance, which was given to quite a large and intelligent audience, was Julius Eichberg's opera entitled 'The Doctor of Alcantara,' which was excellently rendered.

"Miss Lena Miller, who sang the *rôle* of 'Isabella,' is young and graceful, with a pleasing voice; and her part was well given. Mrs. A. G. Smallwood was cast as 'Donna Lucrezia,' and had considerable to do. She sings well, and her acting far exceeds that of any other member of the company. 'Inez,' a maid represented by Miss Coakley, and a difficult part, was given with great accuracy. 'Carlos,' by Mr. H. F. Grant, was fairly rendered. . . . W. T. Benjamin as 'Dr. Paracelsus,' although a little stiff, fairly performed his part.

"The chorus, composed of probably thirty voices, male and female, was a feature; and their singing is really unsurpassed by the finest chorus in the best companies."

From "The Philadelphia Evening Star," Feb. 22, 1873: —

"COLORED AMERICAN OPERA-COMPANY.

"This company made its first appearance last evening at Horticultural Hall to an audience, which, though not large, was attentive and sympathetic. The attendance would, no doubt, have been larger, but for an unfortunate mistake. . . . As it was, the performance was an agreeable surprise to all who were present; not only being a decided success, but in the matter of choruses surpassing any performances of the same opera ever given in this city by any of the foreign or 'grand English' opera-troupes.[1] The cast of the colored troupe included Mrs. Smallwood, who has a beautiful ringing soprano-voice, a very easy lyric and dramatic method, and a carriage of unusual grace; Miss Lena Miller, whose voice, though less powerful, is very pleasant, and whose acting was notable for its unaffected style; Miss M. A. C. Coakley, a mezzo-soprano of very fair capacities; Mr. H. F. Grant, whose tenor-voice has good power, range, and quality; Mr. T. H. Williams, who possesses a deep bass-voice, controlled with a fair degree of culture; and Messrs. W. T. Benjamin and Smallwood, who filled their parts not unacceptably."

From "The Age," Philadelphia, Feb. 22, 1873: —

"The colored opera-troupe gave their first performance in Philadelphia last night in Horticultural Hall. The selection for their *début* was 'The Doctor of Alcantara,' by Julius Eichberg, which has frequently been given previously by various English companies, but, we venture to say, never so perfectly in its *ensemble* as by this company.

[1] The same opera was performed here a few days before with the following cast: Miss Howson, Mrs. Seguin, and Miss Phillips, and Messrs Seguin and Chatterson.

"There was a great deal of enthusiasm; and several numbers of the opera were vociferously re-demanded, including the *finale* of the first act, which revealed to us a choral effect which has never been heard upon the operatic stage in our country since the palmy days of Ullman's management. The chorus was large and efficient, every member doing his and her part; and, to all appearances, there was no 'dead wood' among them. It must be understood, besides, that *all* the music was sung; every part in harmony being taken with exactness and precision, whether as to time or intonation.

"Indeed, so admirably did the chorus sing, that we hope to hear them in a mass or an oratorio at some future time, being satisfied that they will make a most favorable impression."

From "The Philadelphia Evening Bulletin," Feb. 22, 1873:—

"A company of colored persons appeared at Horticultural Hall last night in Eichberg's opera, 'The Doctor of Alcantara.' The opera was given in a really admirable manner by singers who understand their business, and have vocal gifts of no mean description. The leading soprano, Mrs. Smallwood, has a full, round, clear, resonant voice of remarkable power; and she uses it with very great effect. She sang the music with correctness and precision, and played her part capitally.

"The tenor and bass are both excellent; but, while they display fine voices, they show a want of high training. This is also the single defect of the two subordinate female voices of the company.

"The chorus was very fine indeed; and its performance, like that of the principal singers, proceeded without a flaw or blunder from first to last."

From the Washington correspondent of "The Vineland (N. J.) Weekly," February, 1873:—

"On Tuesday evening it was the good fortune of your correspondent to attend the opera rendered by the 'Colored American Opera Company,' of which I spoke in my last.

"To say that every thing passed off well, simply, would be but faint praise. We all know that the colored race are *natural* musicians; and that they are susceptible of a high degree of cultivation is evinced by their rendition of the opera on the occasion of which I speak.

"As for the chorus, it is not saying any thing extravagant when I make the assertion, that it has never been excelled by that of any of the professional opera-troupes which have visited this city."

The comments just given, taken, as it may be seen they are, from the principal journals of Washington and Philadelphia, without regard to party bias, would be of little value here, were it not for the vein of candor that runs through them all. In them the writers have tempered very high praise with the faithful pointing-out of such defects as to them appeared in the performances. This is the spirit of true criticism, which, while it ever eagerly seeks to discover all the merits of a performance, fails not also to note, in the interest of true progress, all its errors. Praise, then, from such a source, is praise indeed. Moreover, it is not pretended that our little troupe of amateurs presented a *perfect* performance. Others of longer experience and of far more pretentious character had not done this. Nor was or is such a thing possible; for, as Pope says in his "Essay on Criticism,"

> "Whoever thinks a faultless piece to see
> Thinks what ne'er was, nor is, nor e'er shall be."

But, allowing for such errors as caught the sharp eye and ear of the critic (it is seen that these errors were but trifling in number and character), the series of operatic representations under consideration was a fine, a brilliant success.

For the happy conception and successful carrying-out of the idea of presenting to the public a rendition of opera by musicians of the colored race, words too high in praise of these ambitious *pioneers* of Washington cannot be spoken. Never before had there been an attempt by persons of their race to enter, as the equals of others, the exacting domain of the music drama. The performances, although few in number, were of such a highly-pleasing description, and the movement was withal so entirely novel, as to render it a somewhat startling and a most delightful *revelation*.

Mingled with the feelings of just pride that many persons experience when reflecting upon the grand musical and dramatic success achieved by these artists, ever and anon arise those of regret, — regret that they did not longer continue their charming performances, extending the same to other cities besides those mentioned. It is therefore earnestly hoped that ere long they will again appear. It is hoped that even now they are devoting themselves to rigid study, and to the arrangement of matters of detail; and that, guided by past valuable experience, they will soon give representations of opera in a style even exceeding in finish that which characterized those which they formerly gave.

As the *avants-courrières* in art of those of their race, whom, let us hope, a fast-approaching day of better opportunities shall make plentiful enough; holding as they do their torches in the remaining darkness, to light the pathway of those that shall follow them into the bright, the delightful realms of the operatic Muse, — theirs is therefore a beneficent, a noble mission, the continuance of which promises the happiest results for all concerned.

XIX.

THE FAMOUS JUBILEE SINGERS

OF

FISK UNIVERSITY.

"The air he chose was wild and sad:
. . . .
Now one shrill voice the notes prolong;
Now a wild chorus swells the song.
Oft have I listened and stood still
As it came softened up the hill."
Sir Walter Scott.

"If, in brief, we might give a faint idea of what it is utterly impossible to depict, we would adopt three words, — *soft, sweet, simple.*"
" *The Jubilee Singers:* " London Rock.

THE dark cloud of human slavery, which for over two hundred weary years had hung, incubus-like, over the American nation, had happily passed away. The bright sunshine of emancipation's glorious day shone over a race at last providentially rescued from the worst fate recorded in all the world's dark history. Up out of the house of bondage, where had reigned the most terrible wrongs, where had been stifled the higher aspirations of manhood, where genius had been crushed, nay, more, where attempts had been made to annihilate even all human instincts, — from this accursing region, this charnel-house of human woe, came the latter-day children of Israel, the American freedmen.

How much like the ancient story was their history! The American nation, Pharaoh-like, had long and steadily refused to obey the voice of Him who said, between every returning plague, "Let my people go;" and, after long waiting, he sent the avenging scourge of civil strife to *compel* obedience. The great war of the Rebellion (it should be called the war of retribution), with its stream of human blood, became the Red Sea through which these long-suffering ones, with aching, trembling limbs, with hearts possessed half with fear and half with hope hitherto so long deferred, passed into the "promised land" of blessed liberty.

Slavery, then, ended, the first duty was to repair as far as possible its immense devastations made upon the minds of those who had so long been its victims. The freedmen were to be educated, and fitted for the enjoyment of their new positions.

In this place I may not do more than merely touch upon the beneficent work of those noble men and women who at the close of the late war quickly sped to the South, and there, as teachers of the freedmen, suffered the greatest hardships, and risked imminent death from the hands of those who opposed the new order of things; nay, many of them actually met violent death while carrying through that long-benighted land the torch of learning. Not now can we more than half appreciate the grandeur of their Heaven-inspired work. In after-times the historian, the orator, and the poet shall find in their heroic deeds themes for the most elevated discourse, while the then generally cultured survivors of a race for whose elevation these true-hearted educators did so much will gratefully hallow their memories.

Among the organizations (I cannot mention individual names: their number is too great) that early sought to build up the waste places of the South, and to carry there a higher religion and a much-needed education, was the American Missionary Association. This society has led all others in this greatly benevolent work, having reared no less than seven colleges and normal schools in various centres of the South. The work of education to be done there is vast, certainly; but what a very flood of light will these institutions throw over that land so long involved in moral and intellectual darkness!

The principal one of these schools is Fisk University, located at Nashville, Tenn.; the mention of which brings us to the immediate consideration of the famous "*Jubilee Singers*," and to perhaps the most picturesque achievement in all our history since the war. Indeed, I do not believe that anywhere in the history of the world can there be found an achievement like that made by these singers; for the institution just named, which has cost thus far nearly a hundred thousand dollars, has been built by the money which these former bond-people have earned since 1871 in an American and European campaign of song.

But what was the germ from which grew this remarkable concert-tour, and its splendid sequence, the noble Fisk University?

Shortly after the close of the war, a number of philanthropic persons from the North gathered into an old government-building that had been used for storage purposes, a number of freed children and some grown persons living in and near Nashville, and formed a school. This school, at first under the direction of Professor Ogden, was ere long taken under the care of the American Missionary Association. The number of pupils rapidly increasing, it was soon found that better facilities for instruction were required. It was therefore decided to take steps to erect a better, a more permanent building than the one then occupied. Just how this was to be done, was, for a while, quite a knotty problem with this enterprising little band of teachers. Its solution was attempted finally by one of their number, Mr. George L. White, in this wise: He had often been struck with the charming melody of the "slave songs" that he had heard sung by the children of the school; had, moreover, been the director of several concerts given by them with much musical and financial success at Nashville and vicinity. Believing that these songs, so peculiarly beautiful and heart-touching, sung as they were by these scholars with such naturalness of manner and sweetness of voice, would fall with delightful novelty upon Northern ears, Mr. White conceived the idea of taking a company of the students on a concert-tour over the country, in order to thus obtain sufficient funds to build a college. This was a bold idea, seemingly visionary; but the sequel proved that it was a most practical one.

All arrangements were completed; and the Jubilee Singers, as they were called, left Nashville in the fall of 1871 for a concert-tour of the Northern States, to accomplish the worthy object just mentioned. Professor White, who was an educated and skilful musician, accompanied them as musical director. Mr. Theodore

F. Seward, also of fine musical ability, was, after a while, associated in like capacity with the singers. The following are the names of those who at one time and another, since the date of organization, have been members of the Jubilee choir: —

Miss ELLA SHEPARD, Pianist.
Mr. THOMAS RUTLING,   Miss MAGGIE PORTER,
Mr. H. ALEXANDER,   Miss JENNIE JACKSON,
Mr. F. J. LOUDIN,   Miss GEORGIE GORDON,
Mr. G. H. OUSLEY,   Miss MAGGIE CARNES,
Mr. BENJAMIN M. HOLMES,   Miss JULIA JACKSON,
Mr. ISAAC P. DICKERSON,   Miss ELIZA WALKER,
Mr. GREENE EVANS,   Miss MINNIE TATE,
Mr. EDMUND WATKINS,   Miss JOSEPHINE MOORE,
Miss MABEL LEWIS, and Miss A. W. ROBINSON.

This list might well be called the *Roll of Honor*.

I have not space to follow in detail this ambitious band of singers in their remarkable career throughout this country and in Great Britain. The wonderful story of their journey of song is fully and graphically told in a book (which I advise all to read) written by Mr. G. D. Pike, and published in 1873. A brief survey of this journey must here suffice.

The songs they sang were generally of a religious character, — "slave *spirituals*," — and such as have been sung by the American bondmen in the cruel days of the past. These had originated with the slave; had sprung spontaneously, so to speak, from souls naturally musical; and formed, as one eminent writer puts it, "*the only native American music.*"

The strange, weird melody of these songs, which burst upon the Northern States, and parts of Europe, as a revelation in vocal music, as a music most thrillingly sweet and soul-touching, sprang then, strange to say, from a state of slavery; and the habitually minor character of its tones may well be ascribed to the depression of feeling, the anguish, that must ever fill the hearts of those who are forced to lead a life so fraught with woe. This is clearly exemplified, and the sad story of this musical race is comprehensively told, in Ps. cxxxvii.: —

" By the rivers of Babylon, there we sat down, yea, we wept, when we remembered Zion.
" We hanged our harps upon the willows in the midst thereof.
" For there they that carried us away captive required of us a song; and they that wasted us required of us mirth, saying, Sing us one of the songs of Zion.
" How shall we sing the Lord's song in a strange land? "

And yet, ever patient, ever hopeful of final deliverance, they did sing on and on, until at last the joyful day of freedom dawned upon them.

To render these songs essentially as they had been rendered in slave-land came the Jubilee Singers. They visited most of the cities and large towns of the North, everywhere drawing large and often overwhelming audiences, creating an enthusiasm among the people rarely ever before equalled. The cultured and the uncultured were alike charmed and melted to tears as they listened with a new enthusiasm to what was a wonderfully new exhibition of the greatness of song-power. Many persons, it is true, were at first attracted to the concert-hall by motives of mere curiosity, hardly believing, as they went, that there could be much to enjoy. These, however, once under the influence of the singers, soon found themselves yielding fully to the enchanting beauty of the music; and they would come away saying the half had not been told. The musical critics, like all others in the audiences, were so lost in admiration, that they forgot to criticise; and, after recovering from what seemed a trance of delight, they could only say that this "music of the heart" was beyond the touch of criticism.

I have spoken of the origin and the character of these songs. Those who so charmingly interpreted them deserve most particular notice. The rendering of the Jubilee Singers, it is true, was not always strictly in accordance with artistic forms. The songs did not require this; for they possessed in themselves a peculiar power, a plaintive, emotional beauty, and other characteristics which seemed entirely independent of artistic embellishment. These characteristics were, with a most refreshing originality, naturalness, and soulfulness of voice and method, fully developed by the singers, who sang with all their might, yet with most pleasing sweetness of tone.

But, as regards the judgment passed upon this "Jubilee melody" from a high musical stand-point, I quote from a very good authority; viz., Theo. F. Seward of Orange, N. J.: —

"It is certain that the critic stands completely disarmed in their presence. He must not only recognize their immense power over audiences which include many people of the highest culture, but, if he be not entirely incased in prejudice, he must yield a tribute of admiration on his own part, and acknowledge that these songs touch a chord which the most consummate art fails to reach. Something of this result is doubtless due to the singers as well as to their melodies. The excellent rendering of the Jubilee Band is made more effective, and the interest is intensified, by the comparison of their former state of slavery and degradation with the present prospects and hopes of their race, which crowd upon every listener's mind during the singing of their songs; yet the power is chiefly in the songs themselves."

It would not do, of course, to assume that to the almost matchless beauty of the songs and their rendering was due alone the intense interest that centred in these singers. They were on a *noble mission*. They sang to build up education in the blighted land in which they themselves and millions more had so long drearily plodded in ignorance; and it was a most striking and yet pleasing exhibition of poetic justice, when many of those who really, in a certain sense, had been parties to their enslavement, were forced to pay tribute to the signs of genius found in this native music, and to contribute money for the cause represented by these delightful musicians.

But I must not give only my own opinion of these singers, as I am supposed to be a partial witness. Many, many others, among whom are the most talented and cultured of this country and England, have spoken of them in terms the most laudatory. Some of these shall now more than confirm my words of praise.

The Rev. Theodore L. Cuyler of Brooklyn, writing in January, 1872, to "The New-York Tribune," thus spoke of them: —

"When the Rev. Mr. Chalmers (the younger) visited this country as the delegate of the Scotch Presbyterian General Assembly, he went home and reported to his countrymen that he had 'found the ideal church in America: it was made up of Methodist praying, Presbyterian preaching, and Southern negro-singing.' The Scotchman would have been confirmed in his opinion if he had been in Lafayette-avenue Church last night, and heard the Jubilee Singers, — a company of colored students, male and female, from Fisk University of Freedmen, Nashville, Tenn. In Mr. Beecher's church they delighted a vast throng of auditors, and another equally packed audience greeted them last evening.

"I never saw a cultivated Brooklyn assemblage so moved and melted under the magnetism of music before. The wild melodies of these emancipated slaves touched the fount of tears, and gray-haired men wept like children. . . .

"The harmony of these children of nature, and their musical execution, were beyond the reach of art. Their wonderful skill was put to the severest test when they attempted 'Home, Sweet Home,' before auditors who had heard these same household words from the lips of Jenny Lind and Parepa; yet these emancipated bond-women, now that they knew what the word 'home' signifies, rendered that dear old song with a power and pathos never surpassed.

"Allow me to bespeak through your journal . . . a universal welcome through the North for these living representatives of the only true native school of American music. We have long enough had its coarse caricature in corked faces: our people can now listen to the genuine soul-music of the slave-cabins before the Lord led his 'children out of the land of Egypt, out of the house of bondage.'"

The welcome thus eloquently bespoken for the singers was enthusiastically extended to them all over the North. The journals of the day fairly teemed with praises of them; and often, in the larger cities, hundreds of persons were turned away from the concert-hall, unable to obtain admittance, so great was the rush.

After a while they visited England, where they sang before the Queen and others of the nobility, everywhere repeating the triumphs that had been theirs in this country. In fact, it was proved that their power as singers held sway wherever they sang; wherever was found a soul in unison with melodious sound, a heart capable of human emotion. It was not so much the words of their songs — these, it is true, were not without merit in a religious sense — as the strangely pathetic and delightful melody of their music, and the freshness and heartiness of the rendering, that gave them their greatest charm. This has since been most pointedly demonstrated in Holland and Switzerland, where these singers have drawn crowded and delighted audiences that neither speak nor understand a word of English: such is the beautiful, far-reaching power of this, in the truest sense, "music of the heart."

I now present a few of the many tributes of admiration which their performances drew from cultured English people. Thus spoke Mr. Colin Brown, Ewing Lecturer on Music, Andersonian University, Glasgow: —

"As to the manner of their singing, it must be heard before it can be realized. Like the Swedish melodies of Jenny Lind, it gives a new musical idea. It has been well remarked, that in some respects it disarms criticism; in others it may be truly said that it almost defies it. It was beautifully described by a simple Highland girl: 'It filled my whole heart.'

"Such singing (in which the artistic is lost in the natural) can only be the result of the most careful training. The richness and purity of tone both in melody and harmony, the contrast of light and shade, the varieties and grandeur in expression, and the exquisite refinement of the *piano* as contrasted with the power of the *forte*, fill us with delight, and at the same time make us feel how strange it is that these unpretending singers should come over here to teach us what is the true refinement of music; make us feel its moral and religious power."

Others spoke as follows: —

"I never so enjoyed music." — REV. C. H. SPURGEON.
"They have beautiful voices." — *London Graphic*.
"Their voices are clear, rich, and highly cultivated." — *London Daily News*.
"This troupe sing with a pathos, a harmony, and an expression, which are quite touching." — *London Journal*.
"There is something inexpressibly touching in their wonderfully sweet, round, bell voices." — REV. GEORGE MACDONALD.

Mr. Gladstone, while prime-minister of England, honored them with a complimentary breakfast, and listened to their songs, as Newman Hall writes, "with rapt, enthusiastic attention, saying, 'Isn't it wonderful? I never heard any thing like it.'"

"We never saw an audience more riveted, nor a more thorough heart entertainment. Men of hoary hairs, as well as those younger in the assembly, were moved even to tears as they listened with rapt attention to some of the identical slave-songs which these emancipated ones rendered with a power and pathos perfectly indescribable." — *London Rock.*

I might now, if it were necessary, fill many pages with the comments made upon these charming singers by the American press both before and after their trip to England; but these would only be repetitions of the laudatory notices just given. The following is quoted because it is descriptive of the improvement made by the singers. Said "The Boston Journal," —

"THE JUBILEE SINGERS. — The students of Fisk University, Nashville, Tenn., whose sweet voices made such a popularity for the Jubilee Singers in this city two or three years ago, and won royal favor on the other side of the Atlantic, gave their first concert since their return at Tremont Temple last evening. The audience numbered some two thousand persons, and manifested an enthusiasm seldom witnessed at a concert in this city. From the initial to the finale of the programme the singers were applauded and encored, and now and then the enthusiasm broke forth in the interludes. So many thousands have listened with delight to the full, rich voices of the 'Jubilees,' and the sweet undertone which disarms criticism while it charms the popular ear, that it is needless to speak of them at length. The simple purity of the rendering of the Lord's Prayer, which initiated the programme, gave evidence that they had lost none of their natural grace and simplicity of expression by their tour across the water; and this was confirmed by the peculiar and plaintive melodies of the South-land in the days of slavery, which made up the major part of the programme. A few selections of more artistic composition were introduced, for the purpose of demonstrating, as they did most fully, that the students have been educated to an appreciation of the higher grades of vocalization. The great charm of these singers will, however, remain in the reproduction of the melodies of an era that has gone, happily never to return, — melodies which were the natural expression of the fancies and sympathies of an emotional race, and which no musical culture or refinement can ever render with the sweet simplicity and charming grace that flow from the lips of those to whom they are the native music."

"In the summer of 1874 they returned to Nashville, having given two seasons of concerts in this country, and one in Great Britian. The best evidence of the appreciative and enthusiastic welcome given them in both countries is the fact that the net result for Fisk University was over $90,000." The "problem" of the little band of faithful teachers had been nobly, gloriously solved. The old government-building in which they began their labors was soon discarded. To-day, on a beautiful, commanding site of twenty-five acres, with all the appliances of the best modern colleges, stands a noble building, forever dedicated to learning and to Christianity.

Since the events whose record is just closed, it has been determined by the faculty of Fisk University to raise by other concert tours $100,000 as an endowment fund. At the present writing (June, 1877) the Jubilee Singers are making a tour of the Continent. They are now in Holland. Thus far their success continues unabated; and undoubtedly they will succeed in amply endowing the institution which, in a manner so praiseworthy and remarkable, they have erected. The following extract from a letter affords a pleasant glimpse at the European life of the singers: —

. . . "I will tell you something of our summer's experience. The company had passed through a hard year's work, and were

FISK UNIVERSITY, NASHVILLE, TENN.

greatly in need of rest. A charming country-seat was rented in the suburbs of Geneva at a very reasonable rate, and the months of July and August were spent there with great benefit to all. The citizens were evidently astonished at this introduction of a new shade of humanity; and the singers seldom passed along the streets without hearing some remark about '*les nègres*,' or '*les noirs*.' But they were invariably treated with the greatest respect, and, in fact, were never once annoyed by a rabble in the streets, as they frequently are elsewhere, gathering around with a rude and impertinent curiosity.

"Among other pleasant experiences, there was an afternoon spent with Père Hyacinthe. We found him very genial and agreeable, and his American wife no less so. He speaks no English at all, but Madame acted as interpreter; and there was none of the stiffness or awkwardness that might have been expected under the circumstances.

". . . The most notable event of our stay at Geneva was a concert given, just before leaving, in the Salle de la Réformation. It had been a question of much interest, as to whether the slave-songs would retain any thing of their power where the words were not understood. The result was a new triumph for those mysterious melodies, showing that the language of nature is universal, and that emotion is capable of expressing itself without the intervention of words. The hall was packed to its utmost capacity, and the enthusiasm at fever-heat. When asked how they could enjoy the songs so much when they knew nothing of the sentiment that was conveyed, the reply was, 'We cannot *understand* them; but we can *feel* them.' Père Hyacinthe presided at the concert as chairman, and evidently enjoyed it as keenly as the rest of the vast audience."

And now to discriminate; for the writer, while disclaiming all censorious or pretentious aim, yet, for reasons which may be readily understood and fully appreciated by the reader, intends this volume to inculcate the lessons of advancement by always attempting to honestly distinguish between that which is progressive in music and that which is the reverse. Have, then, these famous Jubilee Singers, who everywhere thrilled the hearts of their hearers, and whose charming melody of voice, and style of rendition, "disarmed the critic,"—have they established by all this a model for the present and the future? In some respects they have; in others they have not. And is there to be no aim beyond the singing of "Jubilee songs"? Professors White and Seward and all these talented singers will say, I am quite sure, that there is to be a higher aim. The songs they sang were for the present, forming a delightful novelty, and serving a noble purpose. Still it must be sadly remembered that these Jubilee songs sprang from a former life of enforced degradation; and that, notwithstanding their great beauty of melody, and occasional words of elevated religious character, there was often in both melody and words what forcibly reminded the hearer of the unfortunate state just mentioned; and to the cultured, sensitive members of the race represented, these reminders were always of the most painful nature. And yet such persons could not have the heart to utter words of discouragement to an enterprise having an object so noble. They, like all others, could not but enjoy the rich melody and harmony of the wonderful Jubilee voices. They, too, often listened spell-bound; and when inclined, as at times they were, to murmur, the inspiriting voice of hope was heard bidding them to turn from a view of the dark and receding past to that of a rapidly-dawning day, whose coming should bring for these singers, and all others of their race, increase of opportunities, and therefore increase of culture.

On the foregoing pages but little has been said of the secular songs with which at times the troupe indulged their audiences. Even in music of this kind they were exceedingly pleasing; and it is very gratifying to reflect that the members of the company constantly aimed to obtain a scientific knowledge of general music. No fears need be entertained that the students of Fisk University will ever lack for instruction in music of the highest order, as ample provision is there made for the same. Of course the model of slave "spirituals" will in a short while give place to such music as befits the new order of things. The students themselves will wish to aim higher, as the spirit of true progress will demand it. Nevertheless, some of the characteristics displayed by the great Jubilee choir it will be well for them to ever retain, and for all other singers to imitate: I mean the heartiness, the soulfulness, of their style of rendition. Indeed, in their striking exhibitions of these latter qualities, I think they may justly claim the honor of standing quite peerless and alone, and of having presented a model for the present and the future, — a model founded on that power of the singer, which enables him to melt, to stir to its innermost recesses, the human heart; that power that enables him to sing as one inspired.

And here let me conclude by venturing a brief prediction. My mind goes a few years into the future. I attend a concert given by students or by graduates of Fisk University; I listen to music of the most classical order rendered in a manner that would satisfy the most exacting critic of the art; and at the same time I am pleasantly reminded of the famous "Jubilee Singers" of days in the past by the peculiarly thrilling sweetness of voice, and the charming simplicity and soulfulness of manner, that distinguish and add to the beauty of the rendering.

XX.

THE GEORGIA MINSTRELS.

> "All the minstrel art I know,
> I the viol well can play;
> I the pipe and syrinx blow;
> Harp and geige my hand obey;
> Psaltery, symphony, and rote
> Help to charm the listening throng;
> And Armonia lends its note
> While I warble forth my song."
> *The Lay of the Minstrel.*

THE origin of troubadours, or minstrels, dates back to the year 1100 (A.D.) at least. There are accounts, somewhat vague, however, which make them still more ancient. They were at one time almost the sole producers of poetry and music, always composing the songs they sang, accompanying the same generally, at first, with the music of the dulcet-toned harp, and, at a later period, with that of the guitar.

Their accomplishments, especially in music, secured for them the ready *entrée* of the most refined society, particularly that of elegant ladies, of whom they were great favorites; while the most polished princes always extended them a warm welcome.

At one time in their history, the fate of letters was in the sole keeping of the troubadours. Had it not been for the frequent presentations and allusions made to literature in their songs, its chain, connecting past and present, would have been broken.

An elegant French writer, speaking of the ancient troubadours, observes, " They banished scholastic quarrels and ill-breeding, polished the manners, established rules of politeness, enlivened conversation, and purified gallantry. That urbanity that distinguishes us (the French) from other peoples is the fruit of their songs; and, if it is not from them that we derive our virtues, they at least taught us how to render them amiable."

I have thus briefly alluded to the early history and characteristics of the minstrel, because I consider such a course as just towards the present profession, and in order to show how sadly (in this country certainly) have its members deviated from the refined, the brilliant practices of their predecessors. Besides, in doing this, I am not without a hope that I may be contributing in some slight degree towards elevating a profession, the archetypes of which discoursed the finest music of their times, and whose courtliness of demeanor and varied acquirements were such as to render them the fit associates of persons of the highest culture. For, in this instance, why may not what has been be again?

It is unnecessary to dwell at length upon the fact so sadly apparent, that the American minstrel has had for his principal " stock in trade " the coarse, the often vulgar, jest and song; a disgusting (to the refined) buffoonery, attended with painfully displeasing contortions of the body; and, worst of all, the often malicious caricaturing of an unfortunate race.

It is, however, cause for gratulation, that American minstrelsy has of late been divested of much of its former coarseness; that its entertainments have become so much diversified and elevated in character — the musical portions of which at times so nearly approach the classical — as to render the same entirely different from the minstrel performances so common a few years ago. It is found that a public rapidly becoming enlightened, and freed from the influences of an unreasoning and cruel race-hatred, no longer enjoys with its former relish the "plantation act," so called, with all its extravagant and offensive accompaniments. Compelled to recognize this change of sentiment and taste, the best troupes now frequently give, instead of the "act" just mentioned, some other one, which, while comical enough, is yet free from features distasteful to people of refinement.

In view of all this, may we not ask, Is the minstrel guild going back to the standards of its ancient and more noble days? Let us hope that it is.

And to the attention of those who have regarded with aversion (often with good cause too) the modern race of "troubadours" I commend the cheering tendencies just noted, since these may be held as indicating the dawn of a brighter day for all concerned.

I next invite the reader to the perusal of a sketch of the famous "Georgia Minstrels," who not only in this country, but in some parts of Europe, have become justly celebrated as the finest troupe of minstrels extant. Being all *real* colored men, and therefore not dependent upon "burnt cork," — being, as some have put it, "the genuine article," — they in this respect possess an advantage over their naturally fairer-skinned brethren in the profession. Still, as will be seen hereafter, this complexional advantage (?) is not by any means the most important cause of their unprecedented success.

But the reader is first requested to pardon what may be thought a digression: the writer considers it a necessary one.

He is aware, that, in presenting in this book the following account of the Georgia Minstrels, — an account which, on the whole, must be regarded as highly complimentary to the latter, — he may be incurring the displeasure of some very excellent people who belong to the same race as that of the members of the troupe mentioned. This he very much regrets; for although he considers these persons as perhaps unnecessarily sensitive, and certainly mistaken in some of the opinions which they hold regarding *this* company of minstrels (whose performances, by the way, most of said persons have never witnessed), he yet entertains the fullest respect for the honorable *motives* that inspire their disfavor.

The main grounds of their opposition to minstrel performances in general, and to those of the Georgia Minstrels in particular, may be stated briefly, but fairly, as follows: That these performances consist, for the most part, in a disgusting caricaturing ostensibly of the speech and action of the more unfortunate members of the colored race, but which are really made to reflect against the whole; that these public performances do much to belittle their race generally, arouse and keep alive in the breasts of other races a feeling of contempt for it; and that these effects are greatly enhanced when colored men themselves engage in such performances, as they thus give "aid and comfort to the enemy." I shall not attempt to refute these statements. They may be true; but, whether they are or not, it is not within the province of this book to discuss. They are placed here in order that both sides may be heard. Against their severe and somewhat sweeping character I place the fine *musical* achievements of the subjects of this sketch. Of these, assuredly, we can *all* be proud; and therefore the recounting of these shall serve as a full justification of the course I have taken in presenting the sketch.

The author well remembers, that, when only a boy of fourteen years, he was so much opposed to seeing colored men appear as minstrels, that he indignantly refused to comply when requested to post and otherwise distribute play-bills for a company of colored minstrels who were to appear in the town in which he lived; for he considered it alike disgraceful for them to thus appear, and himself to give aid to such appearance. He fully retained this feeling of aversion up to a year or two ago, when, contemplating the preparation of this book (which, by the way, was for the sake of consistency, as a work on music, to trace the footsteps of the remarkable colored musician wherever they might lead), he had to force himself, so to say, into the hall, to witness the performances of the Georgia Minstrels. He resolved as he entered, however, that he would give his particular attention to the *musical* part of the programme, and try to discover in that such evidences of talent and fine attainments as would justify him in sketching the troupe. He was not pleased, of course, with that portion of the performance (a part of which he was compelled to witness) devoted to burlesque. Nevertheless, he found in the vocal and instrumental part much that was in the highest degree gratifying; for during the evening he listened to some of the most pleasing music of the time, sung and played in a manner evincing on the part of the troupe not only fine natural talent, but much of high musical culture. And so he came away, thinking, on the whole, that there were, to say the least, two sides to the minstrel question; feeling that the Georgia Minstrels had presented so much that was really charming in a musical way as to almost compensate the sensitive auditor for what he was ready to confess he suffered while witnessing that part of the performance devoted to caricature.

Commencing about twelve years ago, composed of men some of whom had been slaves in Georgia, all possessed of much natural musical talent, without (except in one or two instances) scientific training, the Georgia Minstrels began their career under the leadership of Mr. George B. Hicks. Although from the first attracting by their performances no little attention, their fortune was for some time only a varying one; nor did they attain to a firm position before the public until after Mr. George B. Callender assumed the directorship. By studious application, most of the original "Georgias" became fairly versed in music. The places of those who left were from time to time filled by adding to the company educated musicians and performers of high merit; the skilful director "pressing into the service," so to speak, as he passed through the country, the best talent obtainable. At present, only two or three of the original members are with the company.

The troupe is now composed of twenty-one performers; and each possesses either rare vocal or instrumental (most of them both) natural talents and acquirements; and, when these qualities are combined, a performance of such delightful beauty and finish is presented, as to elicit from their audiences the most enthusiastic applause. From the instrumentalists of this company either a fine orchestra or brass band can at any time, as occasion requires, be formed; while they present solo, single and double quartet, and *ensemble* singing, of most charming power and sweetness. At least four of their number have been in the past accomplished teachers of music; one has played in some of the best orchestras of England; one is a superior performer upon at least four instruments, while he is a fair player of twelve; several are excellent performers on two or three instruments; and three of the troupe arrange and write music.

The following-named persons are members of the troupe at this writing (May, 1877): —

GEORGE B. CALLENDER.	*Manager.*
GEORGE A. SKILLINGS.	*Musical Director.*
RICHARD G. LITTLE	*Stage Manager.*
WILLIAM W. MORRIS	*Interlocutor.*

F. E. LEWIS,	DAVID SCUDDER,
SAMUEL JONES,	JNO. T. DOUGLASS,
WILLIAM ELMER LYLE,	JAS. GRACE,
WILLIAM KERSANDS,	OCT. MOORE,
JAS. EMIDY,	R. EMIDY,
PETER DEVONEAR,	ROBERT HIGHT,
GEORGE COOPER,	CHARLES ANDERSON,
ROBERT MACK,	JAS. FERNAND,

AND MESSRS. THOMPSON AND GAINES.

As showing the estimation in which the vocalism of their quartet is held by persons of culture, I may state, that a year or two ago, while the company remained over Sunday in a Western city in which they had performed during the previous week, this quartet was invited to sing (as its choir) in one of the most fashionable churches there. The invitation was accepted; and it may be remarked, that although these fine singers did full justice to the proprieties of the occasion, and thus justified the bestowment of a marked honor upon them, — it may be remarked, I say, that they thus enjoyed a distinction rarely if ever before conferred upon members of a minstrel troupe.

While in Boston in 1876, the company were invited to a "camp-fire" of Grand Army Post 115, composed for the most part of ex-officers of high rank, and all gentlemen of education and good social position. On this occasion, their own classical quartet and that of the "Georgias" united in presenting some of the most exquisite music, while other pleasing incidents of the evening rendered it one long to be remembered. In the same city, at another time, they were entertained at the residence of one of the most accomplished of its musicians. I mention these pleasant occurrences simply to show the character and extent of the popularity which this excellent troupe everywhere wins: for to please a miscellaneous throng in public halls and theatres, and, after the curtain falls at the close of the performance, to be almost forgotten by the same, is the experience of most all minstrel companies; but to be sought after when off the stage by people of the best character, and invited to contribute with their fine musical attainments and social qualities to the enjoyments of select private circles, is a distinction, in the constant winning of which the Georgia Minstrels stand almost if not entirely alone.

And now, as proofs of the great popularity of this company on the stage, I shall present a few from among the many press notices, regarding their performances, in my possession. These, while fully in harmony with

what I have said respecting the merits of these famous performers, add some points of interesting description.
Says "The New-York Sun," —

"Every song was encored some two or three times."

"The New-York Herald," —

"The new melodies find in them the fittest interpretations."

"The Memphis Appeal," —

"We might write a column of praise, and even then there would be something unsaid of their merit. They are good in every thing they attempt."

"The Indianapolis Journal," —

"We doubt if a more successful entertainment of this kind has ever been given in this city. We no longer wonder that Boston sent forty thousand to hear them at the Hub."

"The Petersburg (Va.) Index," —

"We do not hesitate to pronounce Callender's Minstrels the superiors in this line to any we have ever seen. They far outreach the usual small range of excellence, and leave their rivals far behind."

"The Philadelphia Inquirer," —

"So great was the rush to see them, that the sale of tickets at the box-office had to be stopped half an hour before the performance. They are unquestionably excellent."

"The Philadelphia Record," —

"It is estimated that at least one thousand people were turned away from the box-office last night, unable to obtain tickets or entrance, so great was the rush."

"The Cincinnati Commercial" says, —

"They have drawn better houses in Cincinnati than any white troupe."

"The Brooklyn Eagle" says, —

"From first to last, all are absorbed in admiration."

"The Cincinnati Inquirer" says, —

"It is an unusually fine company, and superior to any that visit here."

"The Baltimore News" says, —

"There is no approach to vulgarity. Their audiences are the most fashionable. No minstrel company can compare with Callender's."

"The Brooklyn Union" says, —

"They are superlatively excellent."

"The Memphis Appeal" says, —

"They are masters of minstrelsy."

"The Baltimore American" says, —

"All other companies are tame in comparison with these."

William Lloyd Garrison writes, —

"It is gratifying to see that no imputation is brought against them of presenting any thing offensive to the eye or ear."

Mr. P. T. Barnum says, —

"They are extraordinary, and the best I ever saw. They fully deserve their large patronage."

Said Dexter Smith, the eminent song-writer, —

"Boston has unconditionally yielded to the Georgia Minstrels. If you wish to see the brains, beauty, and fashion of the musical metropolis, a peep into Beethoven Hall will give you an insight of it. Never has a minstrel troupe created such enthusiasm in any American city as the Georgia Minstrels have done in Boston."

And the Boston "Folio," that excellent journal of music, —

"The Georgia Minstrels, who are nightly appearing before crowded houses at Beethoven Hall, deserve more than a passing notice, on account of their excellence, and the utter absence of aught that could offend the most fastidious. 'The Traveller' expresses our sentiments so exactly, that we cannot indorse them better than by quoting : —

"'There is a freshness and a completeness about the whole performance which entitle it to the fullest praise. As for the whole evening's enjoyment, it may be characterized as novel from the fact that it is native and not imitative, commendable because it is wholly refined, and most pleasant because it is always artistic. The comedians are very numerous, and all unite in giving a perfection to the rendering of the whole bill.'"

"The Boston Herald" said, —

"Beethoven Hall was well filled last evening by admirers of Ethiopian delineations, assembled to see and hear the original Georgia Minstrels, who have returned from a very successful tour in Europe, and are now located at the above-named hall for a short season. The company is a novelty from the fact that all the members are colored, and their performances possess a genuineness which no burnt-cork artists can fully imitate. Their music, both vocal and instrumental, is excellent. Each performer seems to be not only a natural, but a cultured artist; and all have the faculty of being exceedingly mirthful, without overstepping the bounds of refinement. In fact, each performer seems perfect in his *rôle;* and all appear to be masters of minstrelsy."

Again the same paper said, —

"The Georgia Minstrels have burst upon us like an avalanche. All the reserved seats were sold last evening before the performance commenced; and the house was filled by a fashionable audience, — one rarely seen at a minstrel entertainment. The troupe have made a decided hit, and their performances last night were received with great enthusiasm. Their songs and choruses are excellent; their puns, jokes, and stories, fresh and laughable; and their special acts new, and of a superior order. The performances of the troupe have happily filled a void which existed in the amusement field.

"This troupe of native artists has won the very highest praise from every one wherever it has appeared. In England and America over three thousand performances have been given. The troupe has appeared before the Queen of England, and bears the highest testimonials of the press from across the water."

" The Boston Advertiser " said, —

" They (the Georgia Minstrels) are at the head of the minstrel business in this country."

The " Chicago Post," —

" The company merits all the praise which has been bestowed upon them."

I need only further mention, in conclusion, that several members of this troupe possess musical and histrionic abilities of an order so high as to fit them to grace stages of a more elevated character than the one upon which they now perform. Indeed, one formerly attached to it is now a valuable member of the " Hyers Opera Company." On the minstrel boards his talents as a singer and actor were developed. It is to be hoped (and here I crave the pardon of Mr. Callender, their gentlemanly director, who is requested to try to appreciate the good *motive*, at least, that prompts a suggestion which seems to aim at the disintegration of his famous company) that others of the " Georgias " will follow his example. Their motto should constantly be, " Excelsior ! "

I have been informed that in the city of Boston, at a certain time, not many years ago, the then directors of the three principal theatre orchestras were persons who had previously been members of minstrel troupes. It is also known that several of the finest operatic singers in this country learned their first lessons at this same school, — the minstrel stage. In their new, higher, and of course far more desirable positions, these persons have achieved artistic results which reflect upon them the highest credit, and which show also that the minstrel profession has some beneficial, elevating uses, notwithstanding all that may be truly said against it.

PART SECOND.

OTHER REMARKABLE MUSICIANS,

AND

THE MUSIC-LOVING SPIRIT OF VARIOUS LOCALITIES.

I.

"They are the abstracts and brief chronicles of the time."
SHAKSPEARE.

ON the following pages I shall make mention in collective form, and somewhat briefly, of a number of artists whose histories, although not less important than those by which they are preceded, could not, owing to various causes, be placed in the first part of this book.

The true value of musical proficiency does not consist alone in the power it gives one to win the applause of great audiences, and thereby to attain to celebrity: it consists also in its being a source of refinement and pleasure to the possessor himself, and by which he may add to the tranquillity, the joys, of his own and the home life of his neighbors and friends. And here will be found, therefore, a brief mention of those, who, although they are not public performers, are yet sincere devotees of the art of music, who possess decided talent, and who in their attainments present instances of a character so noticeable as to render the same well worthy of record.

It is considered proper to say, also, — a caution which perhaps may not be necessary, — that I shall here make mention by name of none but persons of scientific musical culture; of none but those who read the printed music page, and can give its contents life and expression, generally, too, with a fine degree of excellence, either with voice or instrument; and who evince by their studies and performances the true artistic spirit. The singer or player " by ear " merely, however well favored by nature, will not be mentioned. This course will be followed, not because persons of the latter class are regarded contemptuously, — not by any means; but because it is intended that the list here given shall be, as far as it goes, a true record of what pertains to the higher reach and progress of a race, which, always considered as *naturally* musical, has yet, owing to the blighting influences of the foul system of slavery, been hitherto prevented from obtaining, as generally as might be, a *scientific* knowledge of music.

Nor must the list of names furnished be understood as an exhaustive one. Had the author the time in which to collect more names, or had he here the space for printing the same, he assures the reader of this only partial chronicle that one could be furnished which would be many times larger. And moreover, if any meritorious musician shall complain because his name does not here appear, I ask him to pardon the omission, made not from choice, nor with the purpose of giving personal offence.

If the first edition of this book shall be received with such favor as to warrant the issuing of a second one, I shall, if it be found necessary, take the time and pains to supply in it such omissions as appear to be made in this one. If it be found necessary, I say; for I am inclined to opine that ere long, — judging from a "view of the field" that I have lately taken, and after witnessing there the many delightful evidences of musical love and culture, — that ere long neither such lists as this, nor just such books as this, will be considered as necessary.

Nevertheless, the writer requests all who are interested in the more general cultivation of music by the people to send him such names as have been here left out, together with all facts that may additionally illustrate the subject treated in these pages; all names and statements to be accompanied by as strong confirmation as can possibly be procured. These will be published in case other editions of the book are issued.

It is hoped that the persons here mentioned, on seeing that their present achievements in art are regarded as of so much value in indicating the æsthetic taste and musical capacity of their race, may be impelled thereby to put forth even greater efforts, and to thus attain to that still higher state of usefulness and distinction, which, it is believed, their talents and present accomplishments show is quite possible.

In the city of Boston, which is the acknowledged great art centre of this country, the amplest facilities for the study of music are afforded. There the doors of conservatories and other music schools, among the finest of any in the world, are thrown open to *all;* the cost of admission being, considering the many advantages afforded, quite moderate. A love of the "divine art" pervades all classes in Boston; and there the earnest student and the skilful in music, of whatever race he may be, receives ready recognition and full encouragement. It is, in fact, almost impossible for one to live in that city of melody, and not become either a practical musician, or at least a lover of music.

It need not, then, be a matter of surprise that so many of the most finely-educated artists mentioned in this book are found to have been residents of the city mentioned. Affected by its all-pervading, its infectious, so to say, musical spirit, they eagerly embraced the many opportunities offered for culture; and their noble achievements are only such as would have been made by others of the same race residing in other sections of the country, had the latter enjoyed there (as, alas! mostly on account of the depressing, the vile spirit of caste that prevailed, they did not) the same advantages as the former.

Commencing with Boston, then, I first mention *Miss Rachel M. Washington*, a lady of fine artistic qualities, thoroughly educated in music, performing in finished, classical style on the piano-forte and organ, and who is a most accomplished teacher of those instruments and of harmony. In the last-mentioned department of music she a few years ago graduated, receiving the valuable diploma of the New-England Conservatory at Boston. Many of the most pleasing amateurs of Boston and vicinity received their first instructions in music from Miss Washington. Hers is a musical family, as her two sisters and brother are each possessed of nice musical taste and education. The subject of this notice early awakened their interest, and directed their studies. It is gratefully acknowledged, too, that to Miss Washington's earnest efforts, more than to those of any other person in Boston, is due that love for and proficiency in musical art so noticeable in certain circles of that city. From what I have learned of this artist's history from my own observation and otherwise, I am convinced that its full recital here would add much to the interest and value of this book. But I am prevented from doing this by her own earnest request, conveyed in language which, although, as I think, a trifle too gloomy, yet shows that she is animated by the most elevated ideas concerning the beautiful art of which she is so noble an exponent. I cannot forbear quoting a part of her excellent letter, in which she says, —

"Now a word about my own musical life. . . . Perhaps I have had much success, and, like many others, many failures. My life has been one of persevering struggle to attain to a high degree of musical knowledge, and, through this, to assist in the elevation of my race. If I have been successful in any degree in helping to lay the foundation of future or present success, in awakening a love for the beautiful in musical art, or in kindling an ardent desire and aspiration for that which elevates and ennobles, removes the harshness of and dignifies our natures, then I am glad that I have not sown in vain, though another shall reap the harvest.

"A part of the reward for all these years of arduous toil has been the recognition of talent by those of the more favored race, as well as the appreciation and kindness shown me by those with whom I am identified. . . .

"As I read the lives of the great composers, and think of their sacred devotion to the art dearer to them than their own lives, I feel anxious for the time to come in our history when a child like Mozart shall be born with soul full of bright melodies; or a Beethoven, with his depth and tenderness of feeling; or a Handel, lifting us above this earth until we shall hear the multitude of voices joining in one vast song, — 'Alleluia! for the Lord God omnipotent reigneth.' *Nor is this impossible.* Our history, it seems to me, has but just begun. All the past is but sorrow and gloom, with here and there a bright ray to bid us hope. . . . I hope they [the colored youth of the country] will early develop a love and taste for the beautiful in musical art; that soon we shall be proud to mention those whose names through their works shall be immortal."

Miss Washington has long been the organist of the Twelfth Baptist Church, Boston, as well as the directress of its choir. She is a lady of fine general culture and Christian character, and has many times been the recipient of public testimonials, and of complimentary notices from the New-England press.

Mrs. Dr. C. N. Miller (*née* Ariana Cooley) was for a long time the leading soprano-singer of Rev. L. A. Grimes's church. She has been long and favorably known in Boston musical circles as a very pleasing vocalist, possessing a pure, rich voice of great range, and highly cultivated. She renders with fine expression the best music. Her *repertoire* of songs is quite extensive, and she has often been complimented by the press. "The Boston Globe" of March 31, 1876, alluding to her singing at a public concert, said, "She is the possessor of a well-cultivated voice of natural sweetness." Mrs. Miller was until recently a valued member of the Tremont-Temple choir, so noticeable for excellent singing. She is now a member of the Berkeley-street Church quartet.

Mrs. P. A. Glover and *Mrs. Hester Jeffreys*, who will be better known by their maiden names, — Phebe A. and Hester Whitehouse, — possess voices of rare natural beauty considerably cultivated. These sisters, had they so chosen, could have long since become public singers of much prominence; since their rich vocal gifts are supplemented by a fine knowledge of music, to which are added also very graceful, winning manners.

As it is, they have often delighted their hearers in private circles by their rendering of some of the choicest music of the day. They have occasionally appeared in public, always to the acceptance of large audiences. These ladies inherit their musical talents from their mother, who possessed a voice of more than ordinary range and sweetness.

Mrs. Dr. G. F. Grant (*née* Georgina Smith), formerly the efficient organist of the North Russell-street Church, has been regarded as a most pleasing vocalist, possessing a very pure, sweet soprano-voice. She was for some time a pupil of the New-England Conservatory of Music; and on more than one occasion was chosen to represent at its quarterly concerts, before large and cultivated audiences in Music Hall, the system taught and fine progress made by the attendants of that institution. On such occasions, her *naïveté*, her graceful, handsome stage-appearance, and expressive rendering, with voice of bird-like purity, of some of the best *cavatina* music, always elicited the most enthusiastic plaudits and recalls. The writer was fortunately present on one of these occasions, and remembers with much satisfaction the delight he felt, not only in hearing this lady's melodious voice himself, but in witnessing its charming effect on an audience of nearly four thousand people, representing generally Boston's best culture. Her reception really amounted to an ovation. The event was a most remarkable one, and, exhibiting as it so fully did the power of art to scatter all the prejudices of race or caste, was most instructive and re-assuring.

Of her appearance at one of the concerts just mentioned "The Boston Globe" thus spoke:—

... "Miss Smith, a fine-looking young lady, achieved a like success in all her numbers and in fine presence on the stage, and in her simple, unobtrusive manner, winning the sympathies of the audience."

And "The Boston Journal" said, —

"An immense audience, in spite of the storm and the wretched condition of the streets, assembled in Music Hall yesterday evening to listen to the quarterly concert of the New-England Conservatory of Music. The spacious hall was packed in every part. The most marked success during the evening was that won by Miss Georgina Smith, who has a fine soprano-voice, and who sang in a manner which could but receive the warmest plaudits."

Miss Smith was a member of the chorus, composed of selected singers, that sang at the memorable "International Peace Jubilee Concert," and, although still quite young, has had an experience as a vocalist of which she may well be proud.

Miss Louisa Brown, now deceased, was a pianist of ambitious aim and much promise. She had been instructed by some of the best teachers of Boston; but never appeared as a performer in public, being of a retired disposition. She, however, often by her musical performances, as well as by her general acquirements and knowledge in art-matters, afforded pleasing entertainment and instruction for the members of her family and their visitors. In her piano-studies she evinced a taste for only the highest kind of compositions, and, in her rendition of the same, exhibited evidence of most faithful application, and no little proficiency. She was a graduate of the Girls' High and Normal School of Boston, was fairly skilled in drawing, and had added much to her store of general knowledge by a visit to Europe. While in almost the flower of youth, and a state of highest usefulness, she was stricken down by death. All that has here been said, and much more, was expressed in some of the public journals by admiring friends shortly after her decease.

Among those whose musical abilities have thus far attracted much attention, and given promise that their possessor will attain to still higher distinction in the future, I mention *Mr. B. J. Janey*, whose fine tenor-voice has often won for him the praises of private and public audiences. He has studied privately under one of the professors at the New-England Conservatory of Music; is a pleasing performer on the flute; and, as a singer, has more than once been favorably mentioned by the press.

Miss Fannie A. Washington has for some time afforded much pleasure to public audiences as a contralto-singer. She was for a while a pupil of the Conservatory previously mentioned. She has been complimented by the press.

Miss Ellen Sawyer possesses a soprano-voice which is quite elastic, of great range, and strong and clear in the upper register. She has been favorably received on several occasions by public audiences.

Mr. W. H. Copeland and *Mr. E. M. Allen* deserve mention for their fine rendering of choice music; the former singing tenor, and the latter bass. They are conscientious lovers and students of music, ever seeking to attain to the highest positions as artists. Mr. Copeland's studies are directed at the New-England Conservatory. The ambitious spirit displayed by Mr. Allen is very praiseworthy, he having contended very perseveringly and with much success against great obstacles. He sang in the bass division at one of the great Jubilee concerts.

Mrs. Cecelia Boston, who will be better known by her maiden name, — Cecelia Thompson, — has long been much remarked for clever abilities as organist, pianist, and contralto-vocalist.

Miss Rachel Thompson is a ready reader of music, and a good soprano-singer.

Mrs. Phebe Reddick, possessing a clear, ringing soprano-voice, adds much to the singing of the Twelfth Baptist Church choir.

Mr. Francis P. Cleary, *Mr. James L. Edwards*, and *Mr. George W. Sharper*, all band-directors, deserve mention here for their efforts while connected with such organizations.

Of the musical bodies who play upon instruments of

"Sonorous metal, blowing martial sounds,"

I mention the "*Excelsior Brass Band;*" an ambitious title, it is true, but one which the future may show to be well taken. This band contains a number of young men who seem to be in earnest, and studious; and some of them possess noticeable talent. Their leader, Mr. George W. Sharper, is painstaking, and ambitious to have the band succeed.

Whenever in filling engagements it is necessary to add to the regular force of the "Excelsiors," no difficulty is experienced in securing the services of a number of fine musicians of the other race, — a fact which shows the power of music to destroy the distinctions of caste.

Mr. Joseph W. Hendricks has exhibited a commendable ambition in his efforts to acquire a knowledge of music, devoting several hours each day to practice on the piano-forte.

Mr. Joseph Thompson is an assiduous student of, and

fair performer on, the B♭-tenor and the flute. He is a member of the "Excelsior Brass Band."

I have thus mentioned briefly the best-known artists of Boston. As I have indicated, most of them have musical abilities of a high order, entitling them to a much fuller notice than can here be given. There are, of course, others of fine musical attainments who adorn private circles.

Boston contains two or three musical societies, and several vocal quartets. *The Auber Quartet* have attracted much attention by their very pleasing rendering of some of the best popular music of the day. The names of its members appear hereafter.

The Progressive Musical Union is the name of one of the societies above mentioned. It is well organized. Elijah W. Smith, the poet, is president. The noble purposes of this society are eloquently stated in the following lines, composed by the gentleman just mentioned, and which prefaced the programme of the first public concert given by this society, March 9, 1875: —

> "Progressive: ay, we hope to climb
> With patient steps fair Music's height,
> And at her altar's sacred flame
> Our care-extinguished torches light;
> And, while their soft and cheering rays
> Life's rugged path with joys illume,
> May Harmony's enchanted wand
> Bring sunshine where before was gloom!
>
> And though we may not walk apace
> With Mendelssohn or Haydn grand,
> Nor view with undimmed eyes the mount
> Where Mozart's shining angels stand;

> Yet in the outer courts we wait
>   Till Knowledge shall the curtain draw,
> And to our wondering eyes disclose
>   The mysteries the masters saw."

The following are the numbers performed on the occasion mentioned: —

PROGRAMME.

Part First.

1. TRIO FOR TWO VIOLINS AND PIANO.....................*Rhizia*
   DAVID OSWELL, MADALINE TALBOT, AND MRS. WILSON.
2. QUARTET. — "Sighing for Thee."
   AUBER QUARTET, — MESSRS. SMITH, HILL, RUFFIN, AND HENRY.
3. SONG. — "Down by the Sea" (Bass).................*Knowlton*
   JAMES HENRY, Jun.
4. DUET. — "On Mossy Banks"..........................*Gilbert*
   MISS P. E. ALLEN AND E. M. PINKNEY.
5. SONG. — "Thou everywhere"..........................*Lachner*
   MRS. WILSON.
6. ROMANCE. — "Alice, where art Thou?"................*Ascher*
   JAMES M. SCOTTRON.
7. QUINTET. — "The Image of the Rose"..............*Reichardt*
   MISS P. E. ALLEN AND QUARTET.

Part Second.

1. THEMA WITH VARIATIONS. — Violin and Piano..........*Rode*
   DAVID T. OSWELL.
2. DUET. — "Take now this Ring"...............*La Sonnambula*
   MRS. WILSON AND JAMES M. SCOTTRON.
3. QUARTET. — "Soldier's Farewell".....................*Kinkel*
   MESSRS. SMITH, HILL, RUFFIN, AND HENRY.
4. SONG. — "Waiting," with Violin Obligato.............*Millard*
   MISS P. E. ALLEN, MRS. D. WILSON, AND DAVID T. OSWELL.
5. MARCH. — Vocal ....*Becker*
   MESSRS. SMITH, PINKNEY, RUFFIN, AND HENRY.
6. QUARTET. — "Man the Life-Boat" (by request).
7. CHORUS. — "Angel of Peace".........................*Keller*
   WITH ORGAN AND PIANO ACCOMPANIMENT.

This concert gave delight to a large audience, and was very much praised by the public journals.

I close the list of Boston musical people by presenting the following programme of a hastily-arranged concert given by a number of artists on the evening of April 15, 1874. It is given simply as a specimen of the numbers often performed at concerts by those whose names appear, and by others mentioned heretofore, with but little rehearsal. Although the music is of a fine order, it is by no means as difficult as that frequently rendered by these persons at other concerts, the programmes of which I have not now at hand.

PROGRAMME.

Part First.

1. QUARTET. — "Alpine Echoes."
   MISS BROWN, MISS F. WASHINGTON, MR. JANEY, MR. FISHER.
2. PIANO SOLO. — "Fantasia Impromptu"................Chopin
   MR. S. JAMIESON.
3. SOLO. — "La Primavera"...............................Torry
   MISS BROWN.
4. DUET. — "Vien Mio Edgardo".........................Millard
   MISS F. WASHINGTON, MR. JANEY.
5. ARIA. — "Infélice"..................................."Ernani"
   MR. FISHER.
6. DUET. — "While thus around".................."La Favorita"
   MISS BROWN, MR. JANEY.
7. SOLO with Cello Obligato. — "Peacefully Slumber".Randegger
   MISS F. WASHINGTON.
8. SONG. — "Didst Thou but know".......................Balfe
   MR. JANEY.

Part Second.

1. QUARTET. — "Sweet and Low".........................Barnby
   MISS BROWN, MISS WASHINGTON, MR. JANEY, MR. FISHER.
2. PIANO SOLO. — "Le Courrier"..........................Ritter
   MR. S. JAMIESON.
3. SONG. — "Queen of the Night".......................Thomas
   MISS BROWN.
4. SONG. — "To the Storm Wind".........................Evers
   MR. FISHER.
5. DUET. — "Land of the Swallows".....................Massini
   MISS BROWN, MISS WASHINGTON.
6. SOLO. — For Violin.
   MR. F. E. LEWIS.
7. SONG.
   MISS F. WASHINGTON.
8. SONG. — "Love's Delight"..............................Abt
   MR. B. J. JANEY.
9. DUET. — "I Pescatori"...............................Gabusi
   MISS BROWN, MR. FISHER.
10. QUARTET. — "What Phrase Sad and Soft"............Bishop
    MISS BROWN, MISS WASHINGTON, MR. JANEY, MR. FISHER.

Mr. David T. Oswald, residing at Worcester, Mass., is an artistic violinist, performing in a finished style the most classical and difficult music for the violin. He has, besides, become deservedly popular as an organizer of musical entertainments, and as a promoter of a regard for good music by the people. He is quite well known in St. John, N.B., Portland, Me., and in Boston, in which places he has frequently appeared at public concerts; and has been often complimented by the press.

James Caseras, who was for a long time the organist of a Catholic church in Springfield, Mass., deserves, on account of his great skill as a performer on the organ and piano-forte, particular mention here. He came to this country some years ago from England, where he had attracted much notice for his fine musical qualities. In Scotland he had frequently played before the nobility. A few years ago, shortly after his arrival in this country, he was tendered a reception by some of the first musicians of Boston. This occurred at Mercantile Hall. Here he rendered with most remarkable skill, on the piano-forte, some of the more difficult music of the great masters, receiving the warmest praises of the best judges of art.

Mr. T. M. Fisher of Portland, Me., is noticeable as a fairly good baritone-singer. He has appeared occasionally at concerts in his own city and in Boston, and has been favorably mentioned by the press.

In another place the violin has been recommended as a proper instrument for study and practice by ladies. Among the latter who have given attention to it, I am pleased to mention *Madam Adaline Talbot* of Portland, Me. She has not yet become a great player, but now shows sufficient proficiency to warrant the belief, that, if she continues her studies of this delightful instrument, she may in time become an excellent performer.

The city of New York has some very excellent musicians.

John T. Douglass is very justly ranked with the best musicians of this country. His fame is by no means confined to New-York City or State, as he has travelled quite extensively, and has been engaged in many musical enterprises. He is a skilful, artistic performer on several instruments, chief of which are the violin and guitar. As a performer on the last-mentioned instrument he has few equals, while for it he has arranged and composed a great deal of music. He has also composed many fine pieces for orchestras and for the piano. When only about twenty years of age, he composed a grand overture called "The Pilgrim." He enjoys an enviable reputation in New York as a teacher of music, and is very remarkable for the enthusiastic, devoted attention he gives to the study of the art. As Mr. Douglass is but thirty years old, — having been born in New York in 1847, — it will be seen that he has made most wonderful progress, and that he has before him a very brilliant future.

Mr. David S. Scudder has fine natural talents, and has made very commendable progress in music. He is a fair performer on the flute, piano, and double-bass; playing quite well Mendelssohn's music, of which he is very fond. He deserves special mention for his successful endeavors to promote a love of good music among his acquaintances.

Mr. Walter F. Craig, although quite young, has already attracted much attention, and received the praises of the critics, as a performer on the violin. He is a close student, very ambitious and enthusiastic, and without doubt will ere long be ranked with the first violinists of the day. He has lately composed a march.

William Appo is a veteran musician, having had a long and varied experience, beginning his career when there were but very few persons of his race in this country that could compare with him in scientific acquaintance with music. He was for a long time one of the principal performers in the once famous " Frank Johnson's Band " of Philadelphia. He taught music for several years in New York. Quite advanced in years that have been filled with incidents well worth recording for the instruction of those who follow him, he now leads a retired life on his farm in New-York State.

These pioneer musicians of ours should ever be gratefully remembered. But few, if any, of the large number of musical students of these better times, can realize the vast difficulties that on every hand met the colored musician at the time when Mr. Appo and some others elsewhere mentioned began their ambitious, toilsome careers.

> First in loving art with all their might,
> They steadily strove in the unequal fight,
> Till Prejudice, convinced at last,
> Retired, ashamed of the cruel past.
> Now *all* who prize fair Music's ways
> Pursue their journey with far brighter days.
> The laurel crown, then, give the *pioneer*,
> Whom ever in our memories hold we dear.

Mr. William Brady, although numbered with those who have passed away, should not be forgotten whenever the noble deeds of colored men are to be mentioned. He was an artist of the finest natural talent, and of varied musical acquirements of a high order of excellence. Mr. Brady was very much esteemed as a composer, being the author of many fine pieces of music, such as quadrilles, polkas, waltzes, marches, and songs. He also essayed more elevated work with fine success, having been the composer of a musical service for the Episcopal Church, and a beautiful Christmas anthem. He died in March, 1854.

Among those of the gentler sex in New York who have won much praise for their fine rendering of vocal music are *Miss Mary Williams* and *Miss Blanche D. Washington*. They have occasionally sung in other cities at concerts, and have been favorably mentioned by the public journals.

Mrs. V. A. Montgomery and *Miss Emma B. Magnon* should have prominent mention here on account of their fine abilities displayed in piano-forte and organ performance. They both read music readily, — or "at sight," as we say, — and at present are engaged as organists in New-York churches.

Miss J. Imogene Howard, formerly of Boston, but now an esteemed teacher in one of the public schools of New-York City, deserves to be mentioned in this list. When in Boston this lady exhibited commendable zeal in the study of music, and at an early age was quite noticeable for good piano-forte performance. Miss Howard is a graduate of the Girls' High and Normal School of the city last mentioned.

A most encouraging indication of musical progress in the metropolis is the existence there of the *Philharmonic Society*, which was organized somewhat over two years ago. Two or three of its members are fine soloists, while others possess fair abilities. The music practised is instrumental, and all of a high order. The society is divided into two classes, called the one junior, and the other senior. The juniors are the newer and less skilful members: these are required to take lessons of a competent teacher, and are not allowed to play with the senior class until they attain to a certain degree of proficiency. At public performances, of course, only the seniors represent the society. The conductor (who is also president) is *Mr. P. H. Loveridge;* first violin, *Walter F. Craig;* solo cornet, *Elmore Bartelle;* flute, *Ph. Williams; William Lewis*, violoncello. At present the society numbers about twenty members, all young men of intelligence and moral character; and it has an excellent library of music, and a fund in bank.

It is entirely unnecessary for the writer to say a word in praise of this enterprise, for its present and prospective good results will be readily perceived by all; nor need he, it is hoped, for the same reason, urge upon the young men of other cities the great importance of organizing similar societies.

Miss Celestine O. Browne of Jamestown, N.Y., possesses fine ability as a pianist. She is thus mentioned by "The Folio" of Boston, in the number for December, 1876: "She is a fine pianist, very brilliant and showy as soloist and accompanist." Again: the same journal, in the number for February, 1877, said of Miss Browne, "A pianist of great merit. Her natural abilities have been well trained. She has a clear touch, and plays with a great deal of expression." This lady has for more than a year been a valued member of the Hyers Sisters concert-troupe.

Mr. Peter P. O'Fake is considered one of the most

noticeable of the musicians of Newark, N. J.; which is no slight distinction, since in that city are to be found some of the first musicians of the country. He was born there in 1820. His parents were also natives of Newark. Mr. O'Fake is what is termed "self-taught," and has cultivated most industriously, against many disadvantages, the talents with which he was naturally endowed. He is a skilful, expressive performer on the violin (his specialty) and the flute. He has, of course, often performed in public. In 1847 he took a prominent part at a concert given by the notable Jullien Society of New York, playing on the violin *De Beriot's Sixth and Seventh Airs with Variations.* In 1848 he took position on one occasion as leader in the Newark-Theatre orchestra, — a rare distinction for one of his race, on account of the prevailing color-prejudice. In 1850 he performed in Connor's Band at Saratoga, playing at times the cornet and flute. These are some of the most notable of his public appearances. He is occasionally called upon to take part in concerts given by the various musical organizations of Newark, the accident of complexional difference but seldom serving to counteract the effects produced by his well-known musical abilities. He often furnishes the music for receptions given at the homes of the *élite* of Newark. Mr. O'Fake has composed, and his orchestra often performs to the great delight of all who hear it, a most bewitching piece of quadrille-music called "The Sleigh-Ride," in which he most ingeniously and naturally introduces the crack of the whip and the merry jingle of the sleigh-bells. At such times the dancers are excited to a high state of joyousness by the bewitching music, the latter being of a character so suggestive as to cause them to almost imagine themselves in the enjoyment of a veritable sleigh-ride. This composition has greatly added to the fame of the author.

Mr. O'Fake is also a fair vocalist, — singing baritone, — and has been director of the choir of one of the Episcopal churches in Newark since 1856. This choir frequently renders Dudley Buck's music, and that of others among the best composers, eliciting most favorable comments from the press.

Misses Rosa and Malvina D. Sears are musical people of Newark, N. J., who deserve mention here.

Philadelphia has, of course, many fine musicians. The most prominent vocalists are *Madam Brown*, *Mr. John Mills*, and *Mrs. Lucy Adger;* and the most prominent instrumentalists are *Miss M. Inez Cassey*, pianist, *F. J. R. Jones*, violinist, and *Edward Johnson*, violinist.

This city enjoys the honor of having been the home of *Mr. Frank Johnson*, and the place of organization of the celebrated brass band that bore his name. It has been the intention of the writer to give a somewhat extended sketch in this book of this famous impressario and his talented body of performers; but as yet he has not succeeded in obtaining the necessary materials. He will mention, however, briefly, that Mr. Johnson was a well-educated musician, very talented and enthusiastic, with fine powers for organization and leadership. He was exceedingly skilful as a performer on the bugle. In his hand this instrument

> "Became a trumpet, whence he blew
> Soul-animating strains: alas! too few."

Besides, he played well several other instruments. He was very much esteemed, and was foremost in promoting in many ways the musical spirit: he was, in fact, the P. S. Gilmore of his day. His band attracted much attention all over the country for fine martial music.

Some time between the years 1839 and 1841 Mr. Johnson organized a select orchestra, with which he visited several of the principal cities of the country, "astonishing the natives" by a fine rendering of the best music in vogue at that time. Indeed, the novelty formed by such an organization, — all colored men, — its excellent playing, and the boldness of the enterprise, all combined to create a decided sensation wherever these sable troubadours appeared. It is said that sometimes, while the band was on this tour, many persons would doubt the ability of its members to read the music they were playing, believing that they performed "by ear," as it is called; nor could such persons be convinced of their error until a new piece of music — a piece not previously seen by them — was placed before the band, and by the same readily rendered from the printed page.

Mr. Johnson at one time visited England with his band, and gave concerts in all the principal cities, being received everywhere with the most demonstrative marks of favor. They were invited to play before Queen Victoria and her court. This noble-hearted sovereign was so highly pleased with the musical ability displayed by Mr. Johnson and the other members of the band, that she caused a handsome silver bugle to be presented to him in her name. Returning to this country with such a nobly-won mark of honor, he became the centre of attraction, and thereafter, as a musician, easily maintained before the country a position of great popularity. At his funeral, which occurred in 1846, the bugle just alluded to was placed upon the coffin, and so borne to the grave, as a fitting emblem of one of the important victories he had won, as well as of the music-loving life he had led.

The memory of this gifted musician and indefatigable worker should long be kept green in the hearts of all the members of his race, and in those of his countrymen in general. For the former he of course performed a specially noble service in demonstrating so powerfully its capability for musical comprehension and for the scientific performance of music, — points which, strange to say, were much in dispute when he began his career; while in his well-nigh matchless ability as a musician, displayed in no selfish manner, but in a way that promoted in a high degree a general love for the elevating art of music, Frank Johnson proved himself an honor to the whole country, and one who should be long and gratefully remembered by all.

The band continued in existence, and was much in demand, for many years after the great leader died, retaining its old and honorable name, "Frank Johnson's Band." *Mr. Joseph G. Anderson* next became director. This gentleman was a musician of most remarkable powers, both natural and acquired. He performed in a very skilful manner upon almost every instrument that was in use, reading music like one reads a book. In short, it has been said of him, that "what he did not know of music was not worth knowing." He, too, was a great organizer; and he showed himself, in many important respects, a fit successor of Johnson.

When, during the late war, the State of Pennsylvania was forming regiments, Mr. Anderson was kept busily employed for a long period organizing and instructing brass bands for many of these regiments. With his great musical skill and experience, he proved to be indispensable at this time to the State, and won the brightest of laurels.

Under Mr. Anderson's leadership, the band was occasionally engaged to go to distant parts of the country to play for gatherings of one kind and another. The writer well remembers when in 1852, on "St. John's Day," this fine corps of musicians came to Cincinnati. With ranks so deployed as to almost extend across Broadway Street, they moved in most soldierly manner up the same at the head of a Masonic order, playing indeed most "soul-animating strains," and winning the while the warm admiration of a vast throng of people that lined the sidewalks. Ah! we were very, very proud of them; so elated with their triumphal entry, and so inspirited by the noble music, that it seemed as though we could have followed them for days without yielding to fatigue.

Mr. Anderson died at Philadelphia in 1874.

The successor of "Frank Johnson's Band" is called "The Excelsior." I am informed that the latter consists of a number of superior musicians.

"Madam Brown" was long regarded as the finest vocalist of her race in this country, while only a few of the other race could equal her. Although now no longer young, she still sings artistically and beautifully. Her *repertoire* comprises the gems of the standard operas; and these she has sung, and does now sing, in a style that would reflect honor on those far more pretentious than herself.

The other day, while looking over the "scrap-book"

of a friend, I met with another of those pleasant surprises that have occasionally cheered me since I began this volume. In this "scrap-book" I found a large number of cuttings from Philadelphia, New York, and other papers, that related to the concerts given in the year 1856, and later, by *Miss Sarah Sedgewick Bowers* By these comments, I find that this lady possessed a voice of most charming power and sweetness, and that in her interpretations of operatic and music of a classical character she was well-nigh, if not quite, equal to the finest cantatrices then before the public. These papers styled Miss Sedgewick — this was her professional name — the "Colored Nightingale."

It would perhaps be interesting to here append a number of these very complimentary comments. A single and representative one must, however, suffice. It is from "The Daily Pennsylvanian" of May 3, 1856.

"We have never been called upon to record a more brilliant and instantaneous success than has thus far attended this talented young aspirant to musical honors. From obscurity she has risen to popularity. She has not been through the regular routine of advancement; but, as it were in a moment, endowed by nature with the wonderful power of song, she delighted the circle in which she moved, and is now enchanting the public. Last evening the hall was thronged at an early hour. In every song she was unanimously encored."

Miss Bowers now lives quietly at her home in Philadelphia, singing in public only on special occasions She is, of course, still a devoted lover of the art of which she has been so fine an exponent; while she yet possesses, through voice and method, the power to charm an audience.

The name of *Mr. John Moore* should be mentioned

here. He was a born musician, so to speak, and was ever "full of music." I remember him as the leader of the band of the Fifty-fifth Massachusetts Regiment during the late war. Although in this position he generally played upon the E♭-cornet, he could also play most of the other instruments used in the band; and was, besides, a good performer on the violin and flute. Very pleasant recollections of " our band," as we soldiers fondly termed it, remain, I am quite sure, with all the surviving members of the Fifty-fifth Regiment. In camp-life it often enlivened the dull hours, and gave, by sweetest music, a certain refinement to what would have been without it but a life of much coarseness; while upon the wearisome march we often forgot our fatigue as we briskly marched, keeping step to the animating music. To Mr. Moore, the leader, much praise is due for the great benefits afforded the members of the regiment by good music; nor do we forget the skill displayed by the other members of the band, which enjoyed the reputation of being the best in the Department of the South. Mr. Moore died at Philadelphia in 1871.

Professor Lott of Pittsburg, Penn., has attracted attention as one of the very first violoncellists of the country. He has travelled quite extensively in the United States with a concert-troupe.

Mr. Z. A. Coleman is a good singer of bass.

Mr. E. Minor Holland of Cleveland, O., is a good performer on the B♭-cornet, violin, and double-bass. He is quite a young man, and, possessing much talent, may become a musician of great merit if he continues his studies.

Miss Mary F. Morris performs upon the piano-forte with fine skill and taste, and is a vocalist of excellent powers. She has pursued her musical studies in the Cleveland Convent, the teachers of which enjoy a high reputation; and also under Professor Alfred Arthur, one of the finest instructors of Cleveland.

I. A. D. Mitchell, playing the E♭-cornet, is the very efficient leader of a band.

Miss Annie Henderson is a very pleasing vocalist. She also studied at the convent previously mentioned, and under Professor Arthur.

Miss Clara Monteith Holland, a young daughter of Justin Holland, the celebrated guitar virtuoso, gives much promise of becoming a brilliant pianist.

Washington, O., enjoys the honor of being the home of *Mr. Samuel Lucas*, a fine baritone character-singer, the author of a book of songs. He, besides, has but few equals as an actor in comedy; has travelled throughout the country as a performer, receiving everywhere the warmest praises of the press.

While on a visit to his home last summer, Mr. Lucas was the recipient of a complimentary benefit tendered by the admiring citizens. The offer of this flattering testimonial was signed by over fifty of his most respectable townsmen, and the affair was in all respects a successful one. Mr. Lucas was assisted in the performances by the following young ladies: Misses S. Logan, Dora Chester, Laura Reed, Delia Lamon, S. Melvin, and Fannie Chester. Mr. Lucas is at present a valued member of the Hyers Sisters opera-troupe, who are performing in "Out of Bondage" throughout the West.

"The Milwaukee Sentinel" of a late date thus alludes to his performances with this troupe: —

"As an actor he takes high rank; but it was in his singing that he made an already-delighted audience more pleased than ever

His rendition of 'Grandfather's Clock,' with distant chorus and refrain, was the sweetest music we ever listened to. The audience was breathless; the lowest whisper could be heard distinctly all over the house; and, as the last tones died away in the seeming distance, a hush as of death came over the audience, followed by thunders of applause."

The writer would be very remiss did he fail to mention here the very remarkable music-loving spirit which has been exhibited by the colored people of Chillicothe, O. This very forcibly arrested his attention, when, several years ago, he visited that somewhat ancient city, once the capital of the State. It was then found that among the class of persons just mentioned — who formed, by the way, only a small portion of the city's entire population — there existed two or three singing societies, two brass bands (the latter the only organizations of the kind then in existence there), and two church-choirs, one of the same being composed of very good vocalists indeed.

In 1857 *Rev. John R. Bowles* organized in Chillicothe a choir for his church, under the leadership of *Jas. D. Hackley.* This choir was considered one of the very best in Southern Ohio. Its leader possessed a tenor-voice of rare sweetness and power, and was quite proficient in rendering church-music, and in directing the singing of the same by his choir. But a few persons in the State equalled Mr. Hackley in the possession of these qualities. Of the two bands, the one called the "*Scioto-Valley Brass Band*" was organized in 1855 under the leadership of *Richard Chancellor* and *John Jones.* The other was called the "*Roberts Band,*" and was organized in 1857, the directors being *Thomas Harris* and *William Davis.* In 1859 these two organizations were united under the name of the "Union-Valley Brass Band," *Thomas Harris* and *A. J. Vaughn* leaders. This consolidation, composed of the best musicians of the two bands previously in existence, made a corps of performers that was unequalled in Ross and the adjacent counties, while it was one of the finest in the State. They owned a handsome band-wagon, and furnished the music for all such gatherings — irrespective of the color of the attendants — as county fairs, picnics, celebrations, political meetings, &c., throughout Ross County. This band contained several performers of such excellent natural and acquired abilities as would render them prominent among the best musicians of any section of the country.

Besides those already mentioned as leaders, I would now refer to *Mr. William H. Starr*, one of the finest musicians of Ohio. He has been for a long time the leading spirit in all matters musical among the people. A good reader of all kinds of music, Mr. Starr easily gives it beautiful expression on any one of the many instruments used in a brass band of ordinary size. On several of these he is a pleasing soloist. His favorite is the E♭-alto, while he is also a skilful arranger of music for them all. Mr. Starr has also composed a number of pieces for his own and other bands; besides others, a quickstep, a march, and a polka. As a teacher Mr. Starr has been quite successful. One of his former pupils is now the leader of a band.

Mr. Thomas Harris should also have special mention here. He was a superior E♭-cornet player, a good bugler, and a very good performer on the clarinet; a good reader of music for each of these important instruments.

Mr. William H. Dupree, at one time the very efficient manager of the Union-Valley Brass Band, in which he was also a performer on the B♭-baritone, is a gentleman whose history is such as to warrant particular mention here, not only on account of his having always possessed an ardent music-loving spirit, but also from his general intelligence, and the fine progress he has made in attaining to several high stations of honor and usefulness. Mr. Dupree remained a member of the band in Chillicothe until 1863, when, on the first call for colored troops for the late war, he went to Massachusetts, and enlisted in the Fifty-fifth Regiment. He became first sergeant of Company H; in which position he won golden opinions from those in command for his strict attention to duty, his steady and rapid acquirement of military knowledge (becoming one of the very best drill-masters and disciplinarians of his regiment), and for his generally fine, officer-like bearing. At one time Sergeant Dupree was manager of the regimental band, in which position he rendered important service. In 1864 he was promoted to the grade of a commissioned officer, — a rare distinction for one of his race, owing to causes so well understood that they need not be mentioned here. In this new place of honor he so discharged his duties as to prove the wisdom of those who tendered the appointment; for he was always distinguished for an increased display, if possible, of those excellent qualities, the possession of which caused his promotion.

Mr. Dupree is now the very capable and popular superintendent of Station A Post Office in Boston, Mass. This office is situated in a district that comprises nearly forty thousand inhabitants, composed, for the greater part, of those among Boston's most intelligent and wealthy citizens. He was formerly connected with a musical organization in Boston. Although prevented by his other occupations from devoting much attention to music, Mr. Dupree has lost none of his old-time love for it; nor has he forgotten the pleasant days of yore when he was connected with the brass band at Chillicothe, of whose members he now speaks in terms of the most friendly regard.

Cincinnati now claims to be (very justly too) a decidedly musical city; and Boston and other older places, which have all along enjoyed the reputation of leading in matters pertaining to general art-culture, have been warned to look well to their laurels if they would not lose them through the advancement made by this their younger sister, so long considered the "Queen of the West." It is true that this distinguishing title has within a few years been claimed by Chicago, and even St. Louis. These latter, however, base their right to the name mostly on the results of the census-returns. In all that relates to the substantial greatness of a city, — viz., the general intelligence, solidity of character, and proportionate wealth of its inhabitants, — Cincinnati, I think, may still be considered as approaching nearer to the Eastern cities than either of the others mentioned. This is certainly true as regards the musical devotion of its people; and this characteristic is the one, perhaps, which most threatens the supremacy so long held in the East.

Having said this much of Cincinnati's residents in general, it will of course be expected that a very promising and brilliant addition is now to be made to these records. The reader, however, must be reasonable, and not expect *too* much; for the same depressing causes (these have already been sufficiently particularized in other parts of this book) which have operated in other sections of the country against the subjects of these sketches have been also always fully in force in Cincinnati. It is thought that all candid observers will agree with the writer when he confidently avows his belief, that no other people, while laboring under so many disadvantages, would have or could have done better than these have done. But, judging from the facts at hand, there is really no need to beg the question; and therefore, without offering further excuses, I shall proceed with the record.

The colored children attending the public schools of Cincinnati are regularly taught to read music. They are frequently complimented for their good singing by their music-teachers.

The mention of the Cincinnati schools, by the way, brings to the writer's mind very pleasant recollections of his boyhood's home, and of the times when he attended school there. Twenty-five years ago, the colored school-children of Cincinnati were much remarked for excellent singing. They were not then, as they are now, taught to read music in the schools, but readily "caught" the pieces to be sung from the teacher, who sang them over a few times. I remember that at one time our favorite school-song was one called "The Captive." But only detached portions of it come to me now. It was a piece descriptive of the fortunes of war. A soldier of the defeated army is left behind a prisoner. The song describes his longings for freedom, and desire to rejoin his now-distant comrades.

I think the chorus ran in this wise: —

> "Sound again, clarion, — clarion loud and shrill!
> Sound! Let them hear the captive's voice.
> Be still, be still!"

No answer being made to this signal, the prisoner thus laments his cruel fate: —

> "They have gone; they have all passed by, —
> They in whose wars I have borne my part,
> They whom I loved with a brother's heart:
> They have left me here to die."

The melody was quite pretty, and the solo of the captive was of music so appropriate and pathetic as to bring tears to the eyes of both singer and auditory. Some of my former schoolmates, now grown to womanhood and manhood, will probably remember better than myself this song and others that with "glad hearts and free" we used to sing so earnestly in the schoolroom and at our school-exhibitions. From what I learn from credible sources, it may be stated, that a visit now to the schoolrooms of Cincinnati would reveal a scientific acquaintance with music so great as to almost prevent the making of a comparison between the two periods under consideration.

The Mozart Circle, under the direction of *Mr. William H. Parham*, is a vocal organization of twenty-five members, established about three years ago. In July, 1875, this society gave a public performance, in costume, of the cantata of "Daniel." No attempt was made to notify the press that the cantata was to be rendered; but a gentleman of fine taste, and one who is generally on the lookout for all signs of art-advancement made by the colored people, was present on the occasion referred to. His impressions of the performance were recorded the next day in the Cincinnati "Gazette" and "Commercial," and were as follows: —

CONCEALED MUSICAL TALENT.

Mr. Editor, — Permit me the use of a small space in your next issue to speak in deserved praise of a musical entertainment enjoyed by a portion of our citizens last Monday night.

It was the cantata of "Daniel," rendered in full costume by the recently organized Mozart Circle, which, embracing about twenty members, has in the short space of six months developed a capacity which gave them success in this enterprise. It is a pity that their excessive modesty prevented their seeking the service of the press; for they have thereby kept themselves in an obscurity which it is my hope that this article will serve to draw them from. The preparation made for this entertainment should not have its service limited to a single occasion. It deserves repetition, and an appreciative public deserves the opportunity to enjoy it.

Louisville, Columbus, Toledo, Cleveland, and other cities more or less remote, would give themselves a treat, could they prevail on the Circle to render the cantata in their midst. Not having consulted any one connected with it, it is a voluntary suggestion from me, that parties craving the enjoyment of a refined musical entertainment open communication with Mr. William H. Parham, its musical director. W. P. W.

Cincinnati, July 7, 1875.

The *Rev. Thomas H. Jackson*, pastor of Allen Temple, himself an excellent singer, a few weeks ago organized a select choir for the purpose of rendering the cantata just mentioned. *Mr. William H. Morgan*, who sings in the principal *rôle*, is a young gentleman quite worthy of the high praise which his performances have elicited. All the members of the choir sing well; but among them no one gives more marked promise than does a young schoolgirl of only thirteen years, named *Elnora Johnson*. The compass and sweetness of her voice are considered marvellous. This society promises to give the cantata "Esther."

From the foregoing it will be seen that much attention is being given to a study of some of the higher forms of composition, — a very encouraging sign indeed.

Another vocal society is called the Arion Quartet Club. *Messrs. Andrew D. Hart* and *John Lewis* are two of its members: the names of the others I have not learned.

There are at present no instrumental societies except one or two very good quadrille bands.

Mrs. Ann S. Baltimore is an accomplished pianist, and possesses, besides, a melodious voice. She has been favorably noticed by the press.

Professor Moore plays skilfully the parlor-organ and piano-forte. He teaches the playing of these instruments, and also teaches vocal music.

Mr. D. W. Hamilton is the very popular leader of a string-orchestra.

The private circles of Cincinnati are ornamented by several classical singers of both sexes.

First among the ladies is *Miss Fannie Adams*. She is welcomed as a member of the Cincinnati Choral Society; and is a skilled pianist, giving lessons on that instrument.

Misses Ernestine and Consuelo, daughters of Peter H. Clark, Esq., are sweet and scientific singers. They are pianists also.

Misses Mary and Fannie Cole, members of the Mozart Circle, are distinguished for the beauty of their voices, the last-mentioned particularly.

Miss Sarah Werles has a voice which is much appreciated, and under her fingers the cabinet-organ itself seems to sing.

Misses Ella Smith and *Ella Buckner* must not be forgotten as valuable aids on public musical occasions.

Among the males, *James P. Ferguson* is distinguished as a bass, and *Thomas Monroe* as a tenor singer.

Joseph Henson's voice always has in it music of an inspiring character.

Fountain Lewis, jun., was diligently prepared during his boyhood for an organist, and in that direction is proving quite worthy of his father's care.

By reference to a programme of a combined dramatic and musical entertainment given in Cincinnati in May, 1876, under the direction of the popular elocutionist, Powhatan Beaty, I find the names of the following musical people not previously mentioned: —

Mr. Charles Hawkins performed "Streamlets" and "A Summer's Reverie" on the piano; Mrs. Emma E. Clark sang the solo, "Brightest Eyes;" Mr. Charles Singer sang a baritone solo; Mr. Edwin de Leon sang "Poor Old Joe;" and Mr. William H. Jones sang "My Soul is Dark."

I am not informed as to the extent of proficiency displayed on this occasion by these performers; but relying, as I ought, upon the good judgment of Mr. Beaty, presume that he called none to his aid except those at least fairly skilled in the rendering of music. The above names are, therefore, recorded here.

The city of Chicago contains quite a large number of very excellent musicians belonging to the race whose acquirements are here recorded. Besides several very fine church-choirs, there is a large organization of well-trained vocalists, the performances of which have been highly spoken of by the journals of Chicago and those of other cities in the State of Illinois.

Mrs. Frances A. Powell, the founder and directress of this society, is also the leading soprano of the Olivet Baptist Church choir. She was educated at Buffalo, N.Y.; and her superior powers as a vocalist have been made the occasion of very flattering testimonials by the press of Chicago and of the States of Illinois and Wisconsin.

Mrs. Harriett E. Freeman, an excellent mezzo-soprano, leading the singing of Quinn-Chapel choir, has been complimented by the press. She was educated at New Bedford, Mass.

Mrs. Charlotte M. Alexander, leading soprano of Bethel-Church choir, was educated at Cincinnati.

Mrs. Bessie Warwick, soprano and brilliant pianist, was formerly a pupil of Professor Baumback of Chicago.

Mrs. Hettie Reed possesses a contralto-voice of remarkable purity and sweetness. She is one of the principal singers of the society first mentioned, and has been highly complimented by the critics of Illinois and Wisconsin.

Miss Eliza J. Cowan, educated at Chicago, a member of the Olivet-Church choir, is a very promising contralto-singer.

Miss Flora Cooper has a voice of such great depth, that it really may be styled baritone. She was educated in Chicago, and is a teacher in one of the public schools of that city.

Mrs. Esther Washington (neé Miss E. Fry) is a finished performer on the organ and piano-forte. This lady is a graduate in thorough-bass and harmony from Warren's Conservatory of Chicago.

Miss Frankie Buckner, an accomplished organist and pianist, received her training at Detroit. She has been praised by the papers of Madison, Wis.; was at one time pianist to a large singing society; and is a contralto vocalist.

Mr. William D. Berry is a finely-cultured tenor, a ready reader of music, and excellent in oratorio performance. Mr. Berry formerly lived in Hamilton, Ont.

Miss Ida Platt is a brilliant pianist.

Mr. Elias Perry is a young tenor-singer with a very pleasing voice. He is a member of Olivet-Church choir.

Mr. John F. Ransom, baritone and organist, is a musician of excellent culture, possessing one of the finest male voices in Chicago. He was educated at Columbus, O. Is organist of Olivet Church.

Mr. George W. Mead is leading basso of the singing society heretofore mentioned, and of Olivet-Church choir. Mr. Mead renders his music with correct and very pleasing expression. He has been favorably mentioned, in connection with others with whom he has performed, by the papers of Chicago.

All of the persons whose names are included in the list just closed read music at sight, and are entitled to be ranked as artists.

II.

SOME MUSICAL PEOPLE OF THE SOUTH.

"Songs from the sunny South-land." — A. K. SPENCE.

THE colored people of the South are proverbially musical. They might well be called, in that section of the country, a race of troubadours, so great has ever been their devotion to and skill in the delightful art of music. Besides, it is now seen, and generally acknowledged, that in certain of their forms of melodic expression is to be found our only distinctively *American* music; all other kinds in use being merely the echo, more or less perfect, of music that originated in the Old World. All who have listened to the beautiful melody and harmony of the songs sung by those wonderful minstrels, the "Jubilee Singers," will readily admit that scarcely ever before the coming of the latter had they been so melted, so swayed, so entirely held captive, by a rendering of music; nor will they fail to admit that in these "slave-songs" of the South was to be found a new musical idea, forming, as some are wont to term it, a "*revelation.*"

And if it were necessary to prove that music is a language by which, in an elevated manner, is expressed our thoughts and emotions, what stronger evidence is needed than that found in this same native music of the South? for surely by its tones of alternate moaning and joyousness — tones always weird, but always full of a ravishing sweetness, and ever replete with the expression of deepest pathos — may be plainly read the story of a race once generally languishing in bondage, yet hoping at times for the coming of freedom.

Of the character of this music, and of its effect upon those who hear it, no one speaks more clearly than does Longfellow in the following lines from his poem, "The Slave singing at Midnight:" —

> "And the voice of his devotion
> Filled my soul with strange emotion;
> For its tones by turns were glad,
> Sweetly solemn, wildly sad."

Mrs. Kemble, in writing of life on a Southern plantation, tells how on many an occasion she listened as one entranced to the strangely-pleasing songs of the bond-people. Often she wished that some great musician might be present to catch the bewitching melodies, and weave them into a beautiful opera; for she thought them well worthy of such treatment.

It is often said that the colored race is naturally musical. Certainly it is as much so as other races. More than this need not be, nor do I think can be, claimed. It is, however, very remarkable, that a people who have for more than two hundred years been subjected, as they have, to a system of bondage so well calculated, as it would seem, to utterly quench the fire of musical genius, and to debase the mind generally, should yet have originated and practised continually certain forms of melody which those skilled in the science consider the very soul of music. Moreover, one is made to wonder how a race subjected to such cruelties could have had the heart to sing at all; much more that they could have sung so sweetly throughout all the dark and dismal night of slavery. Here is seen, it must be admitted, what appears very much like genius in the melody-making power. Something it is, undoubtedly, that shows an innate comprehension, power in expression, and love of harmony, in a degree that is simply intense. The history of the colored race in this country establishes the fact, too, that no system of cruelty, however great or long inflicted, can destroy that sympathy with musical sounds that is born with the soul. Only death itself can end it here on earth, while we are taught that for ever and ever heaven shall be rich in harmony formed by the songs of the redeemed. Perhaps other races, under the same terribly trying circumstances, would have shown a power to resist the mind-destroying influences of those circumstances equal to that which has been so fully shown by the colored race. But, be that as it may, the latter has actually been subjected to the awful test; and the sequel has proved, that, to say the least, it may be considered as the equal naturally of any of the other " musical " races composing the human family.

But the music of which I have been speaking was never cradled, so to say, in the lap of science; although, in its strangely-fascinating sweetness, soulfulness, and perfect rhythmic flow, it has often quite disarmed the scientific critic. It is a kind of natural music. Until quite recently no attempt was made to write it out, and place its melodies upon the printed music-page. Slavery, of course, prevented that. And this vile system, although it could not stamp out the "vocal spark," the germ of great musical ideas, could still prevent such growth of the same, such elaboration, as would have been secured by education in a state of freedom. Yet, since the war, many of the religious slave-songs of the South, words and music, have been printed. It has been found that they are as subject to the laws of science as are others; that they were not, as many persons have supposed, merely a barbarous confusion of sounds, each warring, as it were, against the other. For a proof of this (if there be those who doubt), the reader is referred to the "History of the Jubilee Singers of Fisk University," in which he will find printed the music of many songs like those to which I have alluded.

Thus have we considered, in part, the native minstrelsy of the South.

Notwithstanding their lack of a scientific knowledge of music, colored men, as instrumentalists, have long furnished most of the best music that has been produced in nearly all of the Southern States. At the watering-places, orchestras composed of colored musicians were always to be found; in fact, at such places their services were considered indispensable. Many of them could not read music; but they seemed naturally full of it, and possessed a most remarkable faculty for "catching" a tune from those of their associates who learned it from the written or printed notes: in truth, the facility of all in executing some of the most pleasing music in vogue was so great, that, when these little orchestras played, it was almost impossible to discover the slightest variation from the music as found on the printed page.

"A good many years ago," writes a correspondent from the White Sulphur Springs of Virginia, "the statesman Henry Clay was here, enjoying a respite from his arduous government duties. Being present at a grand reception where dancing was in progress, Mr. Clay wished to have played the music for a 'Virginia Reel;' but, to his great surprise, he learned that the colored musicians present did not know the necessary tune. Not to be cheated out of an indulgence in this, his favorite dance, Mr. Clay took the band over to a corner of the room, and *whistled* the music to them. In a very few minutes they 'caught' it perfectly; and, returning to their places, the enterprising statesman and his friends enjoyed themselves in dancing the 'Virginia Reel' just as though nothing unusual had occurred." At levees, at other public festive gatherings, and at the receptions given in the homes of the wealthy, these orchestras were nearly always present, adding to the enjoyments of the hour by discoursing the most delightful music. In short, they were to be found everywhere, always receiving that warm welcome with which a music-loving people ever greet the talented musician.

But, besides the associations of which I have just been speaking, — associations composed in part of those who understood music as a science, and in part of those who did not, — there has always been a goodly number of other persons of the same race, who, in spite of obstacles that would seem to be insurmountable, have obtained a fair musical education, and who have exhibited an artistic skill and general æsthetic love and taste that would be creditable to many of those who have enjoyed far greater advantages for culture.

I shall now proceed to mention the names of only a few of such persons residing in some of the principal towns and cities of the South. The list could be largely extended did time and space permit.

Baltimore, Md., has quite a number of musical people well worthy of mention in this connection. The following are members of the choir of St. Mary's Episcopal Church, of which the Rev. C. B. Perry is rector: —

Mr. H. C. Bishop, general director; *Mr. W. H. Bishop*, precentor; *J. Hopkins Johns* (who has a very pleasing voice); *Mr. J. Taylor* (a fine basso, who has been a member of a meritorious concert-troupe); *Mr. C. A. Johnson*, organist; and *Mr. George Barrett*, tenor. Mr. Johnson has on several occasions been the director of excellent public concerts in Baltimore and its vicinity, and is deserving of much praise for his activity in promoting the music-loving spirit. The same may be said of Mr. George Barrett.

Mr. Joseph Ockmey is organist of the Bethel (Methodist) Church.

The following are members of the Sharp-street Church choir: —

Mr. Simpson, leader; *Mr. Dongee*, organist; *Miss Mary F. Kelly*, soprano; *Miss Emma Burgess*, soprano.

Baltimore has an association of musicians called "The Monumental Cornet Band," of which Mr. C. A. Johnson is the efficient leader.

Some time ago I found in the musical column of "The Boston Herald" of Sunday, July 9, 1876, the following notice of another "Blind Tom:" —

"A rival of 'Blind Tom' has been found at Blount Springs, Ala., in the person of James Harden, a colored boy from Baltimore. He plays the guitar, and sings the most difficult music, exceptionally well; and is also something of a composer. He has received no instruction, but is most emphatically a natural-born musician."

Louisville, Ky., shows its appreciation of music by organizing a society devoted to the latter, numbering over a hundred persons. This fact has attracted the attention of Brainard's " Musical World," which journal, in the number for October, 1877, alludes to it as a bright evidence of the dawn of better times in the South.

In St. Louis [1] live *Mrs. Georgetta Cox* and *Miss Nellie Banks*, — two ladies who have won golden opinions for their exhibition of fine musical qualities. They are both excellent vocalists and pianists.

Mr. L. W. Henderson as a vocalist, *Mr. Alfred White* and *Mr. Samuel Butler* as vocalists and instrumentalists, all possess artistic abilities of a fine order.

Miss Johnson has attracted the attention and won the high praise of competent judges for her proficiency in piano-forte performance.

Mr. James P. Thomas is a finished violinist.

With such artists as the above mentioned, and others whose names I have not learned, it will be seen that the city of St. Louis is not behind in musical culture.

Helena, Ark., is fortunate in numbering among its citizens *George H. W. Stewart*, — a gentleman of rare musical and general culture. He was, I think, educated in Indiana, and received a diploma as a graduate from a college of music located at Indianapolis. Mr. Stewart's specialty as a performer is the piano, with which instrument he finely interprets the best music of the masters.

---

[1] St. Louis is placed in this section of the record because the latter is devoted to such localities as before the war were within slave territory.

He has also a soft yet powerful baritone-voice; and, as a singer, he has often delighted private and public audiences.

Miss Annie S. Wright of Memphis, Tenn., has few equals in that State as a ready reader of music, or in the feeling and expression with which she awakes the echoes of the piano-forte.

In Memphis there are several others possessing good ability as instrumentalists.

No fears need be entertained that Nashville, Tenn., will not keep pace with the advance of other cities in musical culture. The famous Jubilee Singers of Fisk University, located near Nashville, may well be mentioned here as noble representatives of that city, and as those whose splendid example and achievements as singers will always serve as a stimulus to the cultivation of music by their towns-people.

I mention here with much pleasure the *Lord family* of Charleston, S.C. The father was a musician of good ability, a pleasing performer on the cornet and (I think) one or two other instruments, and was leader of an orchestra. He early gave his two daughters instruction in music.

I recall with much interest a visit I made this accomplished family early in 1865, when the regiment with which I was connected lay encamped near Charleston. On this occasion, after our indulgence in conversation touching the war, &c., I begged that I might be favored with some music. The request was readily complied with, the father and daughters uniting in a performance of several very pleasing selections.

Other members of my regiment, I know, also retain very pleasant recollections of the Lord family, not only on account of the charming musical qualities of the latter, but also on account of their winning courtesy to the Union soldiers. One of these was so far captivated (it could not have been by the music alone) by the elder daughter, as to invite her to adorn as his bride a home of his own. Our gallant Sergeant White was accepted; and the lady has since shared with him the enjoyment of many honors which his fine abilities have won for him in the "sunny South."

Mr. Lord died a few years ago. His example in inculcating in his children a love for the elevating art of music cannot be too strongly recommended for the imitation of all heads of families who desire to form at their firesides such sources of interest, refinement, and pleasure, as will cause their children to prefer them, as they ever should, to all places not comprised in the sacred name of "home."

In making this brief survey, another locality of the South is now approached, which is so rich in musical culture as to occasion (at least to the writer) delightful surprise, and warrant special mention of the circumstances connected with the same. I refer to the city of New Orleans, which will be treated in the next chapter.

III.

NEW ORLEANS.

THE MUSICAL AND GENERAL CULTURE OF ITS COLORED CITIZENS.

"Though last, not least."
SHAKSPEARE.

BEFORE the late war, the city of New Orleans was often styled "the Paris of America." The Province of Louisiana, originally settled by the French, and until 1812, when it became a State of the American Union, contained a population naturally distinguished by the same general characteristics as those which marked the people of France. The Frenchman has for a long time been proverbially a devotee of the fine arts; and of these that gay and brilliant city Paris — which has ever been to its enamoured citizens not only all France, but all the world — became for France the centre.

Here, then, a love of that beautiful art, music, since the days, hundreds of years ago, of the courtly *menestrels*, has been a conspicuous trait in the character of the people. Of course, in leaving Paris and France, and crossing the seas, — first to Canada, and then to

Louisiana, — the Frenchman carried with him that same love of the arts, particularly that of music, that he felt in fatherland. And so New Orleans, which in time grew to be the metropolis of Louisiana, became also to these French settlers the new Paris. In fact, even for years after the State was admitted into the Union, and although meanwhile immigration had set in from other parts of the country, New Orleans remained of the French "Frenchy." The great wealth of many of its citizens, their gayety, their elegant and luxurious mode of living, their quick susceptibility to the charms of music, their generous patronage of general art, together with certain forms of divine worship observed by a large number of them, — all this served for a long time to remind one of the magnificent capital of France.

The opera, with its ravishing music, its romance of sentiment and incident, its resplendent scenery, and the rich costumes and brilliant delineations of its actors, — all so well calculated to charm a people of luxurious tastes, — has always been generously patronized in New Orleans; and so, too, have been the other forms of musical presentation. Amateur musicians have never been scarce there: such persons, pursuing their studies, not with a pecuniary view (being in easy circumstances), but simply from a love of music, have ever found congenial association in the city's many cultured circles; while many others, who, although ardently loving music for its own sake, were yet forced by less fortunate circumstances to seek support in discoursing it to others, — these have always found ready and substantial recognition in this music-loving city.

But does all I have been saying apply to the colored people of New Orleans as well, almost, as to the others?

Strange to say, it does. Natural lovers of the "art divine," and naturally capable of musical expression, — they too, although with far less of advantages for culture than the others, have with voice and instrument, and even as composers, helped to form the throng of harmonists, playing no mean part in the same. The colored people of New Orleans have long been remarked for their love of and proficiency in music and other of the elegant arts. Forty years ago " The New-Orleans Picayune" testified to their superior taste for and appreciation of the drama, especially Shakspeare's plays. A certain portion of these people, never having been subjected to the depressing cruelties of *abject* servitude, although, of course, suffering much from the caste spirit that followed and presented great obstacles to even such as they, were *allowed* to acquire the means for defraying the expenses of private instruction, or for sending their children to Northern or European schools. Indeed, as regards the exhibition of this ambitious musical spirit, this yearning for a higher education and a higher life, these people often exceeded those of fairer complexions; many of their sons and daughters attaining to a surpassing degree of proficiency in music, while they became noticeable for that ease and polish of manners, and that real refinement of living, which ever mark the true lady or gentleman.

Again: there was another portion of this same race, who, in the circumstances of their situation, were far less fortunate than even those of whom I have just been speaking: I mean those who were directly under the "iron heel of oppression." Nevertheless, many of these were so moved by a spirit of art-love, and were so ardent and determined, as to have acquired a scientific knowledge of music, and to have even excelled, strange to say, in its creation and performance, in spite of all difficulties. As to just how a thing so remarkable, nay, I may say wonderful, was accomplished, would form many a story of most intense and romantic interest. But with present limits I may not narrate the many instances of heroic struggle against the foul spirit of caste prejudice, and the many noble triumphs over the same, that belong to the lives of nearly if not quite all of the artists of whom I shall presently briefly speak.

And here it is utterly impossible to resist the depressing effects of that deep feeling of gloom which settles upon one as thoughts like the following crowd into the mind. How much, how very much, has been lost to art in this country through that fell spirit which for more than two hundred years has animated the majority of its people against a struggling and an unoffending minority, — a spirit which ever sought to crush out talent, to quench the sacred fire of genius, and to crowd down all noble aspirations, whenever these evidences of a high manhood were shown by those whose skins were black! Ah! we may never know how much of grandeur of achievement, the results of which the country might now be enjoying, had not those restless, aspiring minds been fettered by all that was the echo of a terrible voice, which, putting to an ignoble use the holy words of Divinity, cried up and down the land unceasingly, "*Hitherto shalt thou come, but no farther!*" For to judge as to what "might have been," and what yet may be, despite the cruelties of the past (since, even in this instance, "the best prophet of the future is the past"), we have only to look at what is. But from those bitter days of a barbarous time, when hearts were oft bowed in anguish, when tears of blood were wept, and when often attempts were made to dwarf yearning intellect to a beastly level, — let us turn quickly our weeping eyes from those terrible days, now gone, we hope never again to return, towards that brighter prospect which opens before our delighted vision: let us joyfully look upon what is, and think of what may be. For

> "The world is cold to him who pleads;
> The world bows low to knightly deeds."

Returning, then, directly to the subject in hand (viz., the colored musical artists of New Orleans), I first quote from a paper prepared by a cultured gentleman of that city, himself a fine musician, the following retrospective comment on some of the former residents there:—

"For want of avenues in which to work their way in life, and for many reasons which are easily understood, our best artists [colored] removed to other countries in search of their rights, and of proper channels in which to achieve success in the world. Among these were Eugène Warburg, since distinguished in Italy as a sculptor; Victor Séjour, in Paris, as a poet, and composer of tragedy; Caraby, in France, as a lawyer; Dubuclet, in Bordeaux, as a physician and musician; and many others." All these were forced to leave New Orleans, their native city, because of the prejudice that prevailed against them on account of their color. In other countries, which Americans have been wont to style, forsooth, "despotic," these aspiring men found ready recognition, and arose, as has been seen, to high distinction in their chosen callings.

Of a few others who for these same reasons left their

native city and went abroad, as well as of a large number of talented, educated musical people who remained in New Orleans, I shall now speak.

The Lambert family, consisting of seven persons, presents the remarkable instance of each of its members possessing great musical talent, supplemented by most careful cultivation.

Richard Lambert, the father, has long been highly esteemed as a teacher of music. Many of his pupils have attained to a fine degree of proficiency as performers of music, and some of them are to-day composers.

Lucien Lambert, very early in life, attracted attention by his ardent devotion to the study of music. He used to give six hours of each day to practice, and became a pianist of rare ability. With a style of performance really exquisite, he has always excited the admiration, and sometimes the wonder, of his auditors, by easy triumphs over all piano difficulties. But his genius and ambition were such, that mere performance of the music of others did not long satisfy him. He became a composer of great merit. A man of high soul, he also, ere long, grew restive under the restraints, that, on account of his complexion, were thrown around him in New Orleans. He longed to breathe the air of a free country, where he might have an equal chance with all others to develop his powers: and so, after a while, he went to France; and, continuing his studies in Paris under the best masters of the art, he rapidly attained to great skill in performance and in composition. He finally went to Brazil, where he now resides, being engaged in the manufacture of pianos. He is about fifty years of age, a gentleman of imposing appearance.

Lucien Lambert has written much music. Below is given the titles of only a very small number of his compositions: —

"La Juive;" "Le Départ du Conscrit" (fantasie march); "Les Ombres Aimées;" "La Brésiliana;" "Paris Vienne;" "Le Niagara;" "Au Clair de la Lune," with variations; "Ah! vous disais-je, Maman;" "L'Américaine;" "La Rose et le Bengali;" "Pluie de Corails;" "Cloches et Clochettes;" "Étude Mazurka."[1]

Sidney Lambert, stimulated by the instruction and good fame of his father and the high reputation gained by his brother Lucien, and himself possessing rich natural powers, soon became conspicuous for brilliant execution on the piano-forte, and as a composer of music for that and other instruments. He has also written a method for the piano, the merits of which are such as to cause him to be lately decorated for the same by the King of Portugal. He is now a professor of music in Paris, France. Here is a partial list of pieces composed and arranged by him: —

"Si j'étais Roi;" "Murmures du Soir;" "L'Afri-

---

[1] Only to those who have not read the introduction to these sketches will it seem strange that the titles of these, and of the works hereafter mentioned, although they are the creations of Americans, are yet given in the French language. For the information of such persons, I repeat in substance what has already been said, that these authors, in adopting the course just referred to, have only followed a custom which is most generally observed in the highest art-circles of New Orleans, "the Paris of America," — a custom, too, which, no doubt, is in harmony with the tastes, as it is with the acquirements, of the authors themselves, all of whom speak and write the French language quite perfectly. It may be well to here say also, that all of the above-mentioned works, and all others (not otherwise specified) mentioned hereafter, bear the imprint of some one of the principal music-publishers of the day, from whom, of course, copies may be ordered, if desired.

caine;" "Anna Bolena;" "La Sonnambula;" "L'Élisire;" "Transports Joyeux;" "Les Cloches."

Mr. E. Lambert is the very efficient leader and instructor of the St. Bernard Brass Band. He is a fine musician, performing with much skill on several instruments.

John Lambert, only sixteen years of age, is already regarded as an excellent musical artist. He was educated in St. Joseph School, New Orleans. He seems almost a master of his principal instrument, the cornet, playing with ease the most difficult music written for the same. He is a member of the St. Bernard Band, — a very valuable member too, since he can play a variety of instruments.

The two Misses Lambert are accomplished pianists. One of them is an excellent teacher.

Edmund Dédé was born in New Orleans in the year 1829. He learned first the clarinet, and became a good player. He afterwards took up the violin for study, under the direction of C. Deburque, a colored gentleman. After a while he took lessons of Mr. L. Gabici, who was at one time chief of the orchestra of the St. Charles Theatre. Dédé was a cigar-maker by trade. Being of very good habits, and economical, he accumulated enough money after a while to pay for a passage to France, where, on his arrival in 1857, he received a welcome worthy of a great people and of so fine an artist. He is very popular, not only as a violinist, but as a man, being of fine appearance, of amiable disposition, and very polite and agreeable in his manners. While a student in New Orleans, many were they who seemed never to grow tired in listening to his peculiarly fine playing of the studies of Kreutzer and the ' Seventh Air Varié de Beriot." He is considered alike remarkable in his perfect making of the staccato and the legato; is very ardent in his play, throwing his whole soul into it; and meets with no difficulties that he does not easily overcome. Mr. Dédé is now director of the orchestra of "L'Alcazar," in Bordeaux, France. He is of unmixed negro blood, and is married to a beautiful and accomplished French lady.

The titles of only a very few of the works composed by Edmund Dédé can now be given. They are as follows: "Le Sement de l'Arabe," "Vaillant Belle Rose Quadrille" (this it was called originally; but I believe the piece has been published under another name), "Le Palmier Overture."

Basile Barés was born in New Orleans Jan. 2, 1846, and is what may be called a self-made man. He to-day enjoys a fine reputation as a pianist and composer. His studies on the piano were begun under Eugène Prévost, who was, in years gone by, director of the Orleans Theatre and the opera-house orchestras. Barés studied harmony and composition under Master Pedigram. In 1867 he visited the Paris Exposition, at which he remained four months, giving many performances upon the piano-forte. Mr. Barés resides in New Orleans. I append this partial list of his works: "La Capricieuse Valse," "Delphine Valse Brillante," "Les Variétés du Carnaval," "Les Violettes Valse," "La Créole" (march), "Élodia" (polka mazurka), "Merry Fifty Lancers," "Basile's Galop," "Les Cents Gardes" (valse), and "Minuit Polka de Salon."

Professor Samuel Snaer, a native of New Orleans, is in his forty-fourth year, and is a musician of remarkably fine powers. He is a brilliant pianist, and a most skilful performer on the violin and violoncello. As a violoncellist he has but few equals anywhere. He is an esteemed teacher of violin and piano, and is organist at St. Mary's (Catholic) Church.

But Professor Snaer's musical abilities do not end with the accomplishments just mentioned. He is, besides, a ready composer, and has produced much music of a varied and very meritorious character. Extreme modesty, however, has prevented him from publishing many of his pieces. Generally his habit has been to sit down and compose a piece, and then allow the manuscript to go the rounds among his acquaintances. As he would make no request for its return, nor express solicitude regarding its fate, the music rarely returned to the composer; so that to-day the most unlikely place to find copies of his works is at the professor's own residence.

Professor Snaer has a memory of most wonderful power. When he was eighteen years old (that was twenty-six years ago), he composed his "Sous sa Fenêtre." Without having seen this music for many years, he can to-day write it out note for note. He remembers equally well each one of his many compositions, some of which have been of an elaborate and difficult character. He has lately rewritten from memory, for a gentleman in Boston, a great solemn mass which he composed several years ago. Those who are familiar with the original draught of this mass say that the present one is its exact counterpart.

The following comprises in part a list of the works of Professor Snaer: —

"Sous sa Fenêtre," published by Louis Grunewald, New Orleans.

"Le Chant du Départ," published by Louis Grunewald, New Orleans. (Two editions issued.)

"Rappelle-toi," published by Louis Grunewald, New Orleans. (Two editions issued.)

" Grand Scène Lyrique" (solo and duetto).

" Graziella" (overture for full orchestra).

"Le Vampire" (vocal and instrumental).

" Le Bohémien" (vocal and instrumental).

"Le Chant des Canotiers" (trio); and a large number of Polkas, Mazurkas, Quadrilles, and Waltzes.

Professor Snaer is also a man of letters, a *littérateur;* and in such matters, as well as those of music, much deference is paid to his judgment by his contemporaries.

Mr. Henry Staes is a youth quite ardent in his study of the piano-forte.

Mr. Lanoix Parent, formerly a member of the Philharmonic Society, is a performer on the violin, viola, and some other instruments.

Professor A. P. Williams, born in Norwich, Conn., in 1840, is highly esteemed as a vocalist and pianist. He is an efficient teacher of vocal and instrumental music. He received his musical training from his father, Mr. P. M. Williams, who, a native of Massachusetts, was a proficient vocalist and organist. Professor Williams is a man of decided intellectual merit, and is principal instructor in a grammar-school in New Orleans.

Mr. E. V. Macarty, a native of New Orleans, was born in 1821. He began lessons on the piano under Professor J. Norres. In 1840 he was sent to Paris, where, through the intervention of Hon. Pierre Soulé and the French ambassador to the United States, he was admitted to the Imperial Conservatoire, although he was then over the age prescribed for admission. At the Conservatoire he studied vocal music, harmony, and composition. He has composed some pieces that have been published, the names of which, however, are not known to the writer. Mr. Macarty is especially distinguished as a vocalist: as a singer he is full of sentiment, and very impressive; is a fine pianist; and much admired, too, as an amateur actor. In the *rôle* of Antony, in the play of that name, by Alexandre Dumas, as well as in that of Buridan in "La Tour de Nesle," by the same author, Mr. Macarty has won high honors. He also has held several positions of trust under the State government.

Mr. F. C. Viccus is a gentleman of fine musical abilities, a performer on the violin, cornet, and even other instruments.

McDonald Repanti, before going to Mexico, became one of the most remarkable pianists of New Orleans. His trade in early life was that of a worker in marble; and being very fond of music, and desirous to study the piano, he used to work very hard at his trade during six months of the year, and then devote the other six to severe study of music, and practice on his favorite instrument. This he did under the instruction of his brother, Fierville Repanti, who was formerly a teacher of marked ability, and a composer of music. Fierville removed to Paris, where he died some years ago.

Maurice J. B. Doublet was born in New Orleans in the year 1831. In that city he takes rank with the best violinists, and is highly rated as a general musician. Modesty has kept him away from the public but too often, since he possesses powers that would cause him always to be the recipient of much applause from large and cultivated audiences. He studied under L. Gabici. Mr. Doublet, as a violinist, is most remarkable for the purity of the tones produced, and the faithfulness he exhibits in giving expression to the composer's thoughts. These qualities, which it seems were given him by nature, are also noticeable in all of his pupils. Mr. Doublet is also a composer, but is so modest as to hide from the general public all that he has done in that line.

Dennis Auguste was born in New Orleans in 1850, and is therefore twenty-seven years of age. Although so young, he is regarded as a fine musician. He grew to manhood in the family of Col. Félix Labatut, by whom and his wife Dennis was treated as a son. Mr. and Mrs. Labatut, who were a noble and high-minded couple, of well-known liberal ideas, spared no pains to give their charge a thorough education. Teachers were employed to instruct him in many branches of learning. Mr. Ludger Boquille, a colored gentleman, became his teacher in French; Prof. Richard Lambert gave the youth his first lessons in music and on the piano; Prof. Rolling, a well-known artist, directed him in the same studies afterward; while in vocal music, harmony, and composition, he became proficient under Mr. Eugène Prévost. Mr. Auguste has proved himself worthy of the care that was given to his training by his Christian-like guardians and faithful teachers. As a performer he is held in high esteem, and is often employed by the best families of both races in his native city.

Henry Corbin, for several years a resident in New Orleans, was born in Cincinnati, O., in the year 1845. He learned the violin under a German teacher and under Professor Bonnivard. He has played as an amateur on many occasions at concerts, and always with marked acceptance to his audiences. Mr. Corbin's musical achievements are very fine, considering the great amount of time he has given to employments connected with state and city government. He was at one time private secretary to Gov. Pinchback; at another, secretary of the Board of Directors of the Public Schools of New Orleans; and is now tax-collector for the Sixth District in that city.

J. M. Doublet is only eighteen years of age, but is considered already a violinist of excellent ability. He has studied music under the direction of his father, J. B. M. Doublet.

Adolphe Liantaud is one of the best performers on the cornet in New Orleans: indeed, for purity and smoothness of tone, as well as power, he is regarded as most remarkable.

Mr. Henry Berrot is considered an excellent player on the contra-bass, although beginning its practice only a few years ago, and at an age when most persons would despair of acquiring a knowledge of that or any other instrument.

Mrs. P. Casnave is a brilliant pianist.

Miss Macarty has on several occasions appeared at public concerts, and has always been received with marked favor. She is quite studious, and renders difficult and classical compositions for the piano in a most creditable manner.

As may be readily supposed of a community like that of New Orleans, where there is a large colored population composed of so many people of culture, the gentler sex are only behind the other, in possessing a knowledge of music, to that extent which has been caused by those unreasonable, unwritten, yet inexorable rules of society, that have hitherto forbidden women to do more than learn to perform upon the piano-forte and guitar, and to sing. But among the ladies of New Orleans there are many who may be called excellent pianists, and those who, possessing good voices, sing the choicest music of the day with a fine degree of taste and expression. Most of these (only a few of them are performers in public), by their musical culture, and the possession of those general graces of a beautiful womanhood, — graces the possession of which

"Show us how divine a thing
A woman may become," —

add to the adornments and refining pleasures of many private circles, and thus keep pace with their male relatives and friends in demonstrating the intellectual equality of their race. It would, however, take up far too much of space to here present a larger number of the names of these accomplished ladies than has already been given; and it is therefore hoped that the latter, — fair representatives of many others that might be given, — and the general mention just made, may suffice.

Returning to the other sex, I first refer to *Constantin Deberque*, who is a musician of fine ability, a teacher of great skill, and a gentleman of good general culture. Mr. Deberque will again be mentioned on a succeeding page.

Dr. E. Dubuclet is a finished violinist. He is a brother of Dr. Dubuclet, heretofore mentioned as having removed to Bordeaux, France.

The Dupré family are remarkable for their excellent musical qualities. Each of the brothers, Ciel, Lucien, and Esebe, play upon several instruments; while their two sisters are also well versed in music.

Mr. Raymond Auguste, as a cornetist, is quite noticeable for the purity, strength, and fine expression of the tones he produces.

Eugène Convertie is a classical student; wins golden opinions for his piano performances; and has been highly esteemed as a teacher of that instrument. He is now succeeding as a dry-goods merchant in New Orleans.

Mr. Kelly, band-director, is very effective as a performer on the cornet.

Mr. Émile Ricard is regarded as a good pianist and teacher.

Joseph A. Moret is a violin-player, to whom all listen with pleasure. He was first a pupil under Professor Snaer, and afterwards studied under Professor Bonnivard. Mr. Moret, having been instructed by such good teachers, possessing much natural talent, and being withal so young, has before him a brilliant future.

Joseph Mansion is an amateur violinist, and a gentleman of much intelligence. He was formerly a member of the Louisiana House of Representatives, and is now State-tax assessor.

Joseph Bazanac was an excellent performer on the flute and bassoon, and a teacher of music. He was, besides, acknowledged as a skilful instructor in the French and English languages. He died a few months ago.

Charles Martinez, who died in 1874, was most remarkable for proficiency in performance upon a great number of instruments, — being an artistic guitarist and violinist, a player upon the contra-bass, — and was also a good singer. Being of an ambitious turn of mind, Mr. Martinez studied, without a teacher, to become a notary-public, and was appointed as such.

Professor Thomas Martin was at a time one of the first musicians of New Orleans and of Louisiana, being without an equal as a guitarist, was a great performer on the violin and piano-forte, and played even other instruments. He was also a fine vocalist, a ready and good composer, and was much celebrated for abilities in teaching music. A fine-looking man, very agreeable and gentlemanly in his manners, Professor Martin soon won his way against all obstacles, and became the favorite musical instructor not only of those of his own race, but also of many persons connected with the most aristocratic white families of New Orleans and its vicinity. This once talented musician is now no more; he having died some years ago in Europe, as I am informed.

Octave Piron was once very prominent as an excellent vocalist and guitarist. He devotes his attention now more to the contra-bass, upon which instrument he is regarded as a good performer.

J. M. Holland is a young man who gives much promise of becoming an excellent pianist.

And thus I might go on and on, mentioning name after name, and achievement after achievement; but warned by the great number of pages already devoted to these praiseworthy musical people of New Orleans, and believing that enough has been presented to serve the object had in view when these notices were begun, I will shortly close this record.

As a sample of the concerts frequently given in New Orleans by *amateur* musicians of the colored race, I append this programme of one lately given:—

GRAND
Vocal and Instrumental Concert,
ON OCTOBER 14, 1877,
IN

Masonic Hall, cor. of St. Peter and Claude Streets,

UNDER THE DIRECTION OF

LOUIS MARTIN, ASSISTED BY HIS AMATEUR FRIENDS.

PROGRAMME.

Part First.

1. OVERTURE. — "La Muette de Portici"........ORCHESTRA.
2. THE FAVORITE. — "Prière." — *Donizetti*.... Miss Mc——.
3. LE BOHÉMIEN. — *Samuel Snaer* [1] ....Mr. O. P.
4. SYMPHONY. — For Two Violins and Piano, { L. M., J. M., and Miss A. F.
5. MY SUNDAY DRESS. — Song................Jos. L., Jun.

Intermission. — Part Second.

6. OVERTURE. — "Sémiramis"..................ORCHESTRA.
7. JUDITH. — *Concone*...........................Miss R. F.
8. THE ENCHANTRESS. — Fantasie for Violin..........L. M.
9. L'EXTASE. —Valse brillante. — *L'Arditi*............Miss F.
10. FORTUNIO'S SONG. — "Alsacian Dream"....Jos. L., Jun.

Intermission. — Part Third.

11. OVERTURE. — "La Dame Blanche"............ORCHESTRA.
12. CONSTANTINOPLE. — *A. Loyd*.................Miss R. F.
13. UNE DRÔLE DE SOIRÉE. — Scène Humoristique,
J. A. COLLIN.

Miss A. F. will preside at the Piano.
The Orchestra under direction of Mr. LOUIS MARTIN.

DOORS OPEN AT 6. - - - - CONCERT TO BEGIN AT 7 PRECISELY.

[1] This composer has been previously mentioned in these sketches, "Le Bohémien" is one of several of Professor Snaer's pieces that show him to be a writer of fine abilities.

From the notes of a musical critic of New Orleans I learn that this concert was in all respects a fine success. The different overtures were well executed by an *ensemble* of twenty instrumentalists, all colored men; while all the numbers on the programme were rendered, generally, in a manner that would have been creditable, even had the performers been, as they were not, professionals.

The audience was a large and brilliant one, composed of members of both races, and was quite demonstrative in the bestowment of applause and in floral offerings. As at first remarked, concerts like the one just described are frequently given in New Orleans.

New Orleans has several fine brass bands among its colored population. "Kelly's Band" and the "St. Bernard Brass Band" deserve particular mention here. The "St. Bernard" is composed of a very intelligent class of young men, studious, and of excellent moral character; in fact, they form a splendid corps of musicians, equalled by but few others, and excelled by none. With these two bands and some others, the names of which I have not now at hand, the people of New Orleans are always well supplied with the best of martial music.

Before the late war, the city had an association of colored men called the "Philharmonic Society." Several liberal-minded native and foreign gentlemen of the other race were always glad to come and play with the "Philharmonics" overtures and other music of a classical character. This was really a scholarly body of musicians, with whom the very best artists of any race might well be proud to associate. Constantin Deberque and Richard Lambert were among those who at times directed the orchestra. Eugène Rudanez, Camille Camp, Adolph Angelaine, T. Delassize, Lucien and Victor Pessou, J. A. Bazanac, Charles Martinez, and over one hundred other amateur musicians, added a lustre to the good name of the colored men of New Orleans, even during the gloomy days of oppression. These men with all their souls loved music and the drama; but were kept away from the grand opera, from concerts and theatrical performances, because they would not submit to the degradation of sitting in a marked place designated "for colored persons." Nevertheless, they were not to be deterred from following that bent of their minds which a love of art directed; and so, thrown entirely upon their own resources, these high-minded men formed the "Philharmonic Society" and other musical associations, finding in the same much to compensate them for what they lost by being debarred from entering those circles of culture and amusement, the conditions of entrance to which were, not a love of and proficiency in art, but that ignoble and foolish one, the mere possession of a white face.

And thus has been briefly and (as the writer fears) imperfectly told the story of these highly musical people of New Orleans. Bearing in mind the great and manifold difficulties against which they ever had to struggle, — not only such difficulties as all must encounter who study the science of music, but also those far, far greater ones that are caused by color-prejudice, the extent of whose terrible, blighting power none can ever imagine that do not actually meet it, — bearing in mind, I say, all these obstacles, and their triumphs over the same, it will be seen that much has been accomplished that may be considered realy wonderful. As better opportunities for culture, and that fulness of recognition and appreciation without which even genius must languish and in many cases die, — as these come to them, as come they surely will in this new era of freedom, — then will such earnest votaries as have here been mentioned, with

> " No fears to beat away, no strife to heal,
> The past unsighed for, and the future sure," —

attain to even greater degrees of proficiency and eminence in that noble art of which Pope thus beautifully sings : —

> " By Music, minds an equal temper know,
> Nor swell too high, nor sink too low.
> If in the breast tumultuous joys arise,
> Music her soft, assuasive voice applies,
> Or, when the soul is pressed with cares,
> Exalts her in enlivening airs;
> Warriors she fires with animated sounds ;
> Pours balm into the bleeding lover's wounds·
> Melancholy lifts her head ;
> Morpheus rouses from his bed ;
> Sloth unfolds her arms, and wakes;
> Listening Envy drops her snakes ;
> Intestine war no more our passions wage ;
> And giddy factions bear away their rage.
>   .   .   .   .
> Music the fiercest grief can charm,
> And Fate's severest rage disarm ;
> Music can soften pain to ease,
> And make despair and madness please;
> Our joys below it can improve,
> And antedate the bliss above."

APPENDIX.

MUSIC.

PREFACE TO THE MUSIC.

IT is deemed necessary to offer a few words of explanation touching the music printed on the following pages.

The collection is given in order to complete the author's purpose, which is not only to show the proficiency of the subjects of the foregoing sketches as interpreters of the music of others, but, further, to illustrate the ability of quite a number of them (and, relatively, that of their race) to originate and scientifically arrange good music.

For want of space, only a few selections have been made from the many compositions in the writer's possession; and, for the same reason, only parts of several works, somewhat elaborate in character, have been given; the latter curtailment having been made in the cases of the following: "The Pilgrim" (a grand overture, originally occupying about twenty pages, sheet-music size), only one-third of which appears in this collection; of an elegant arrangement of the air of "Au Clair de la Lune" (containing Introduction, Theme, First, Second, and Third Variations, and Finale), only the "Theme" and Third Variation are given; of the Parisian Waltzes (a set of five), only the introduction, coda, and Waltz No. 3 are given; of "Les Clochettes,"— fantaisie mazurka,— only a part appears; and so of "La Capricieuse;" while, of the "Mass," only two movements appear, the "Gloria" and "Agnus Dei." The attention of all who shall examine the music is particularly called to the above statements, in order that there may be no surprises, and no injustice done the composers.

In two instances only have very long compositions been reprinted in full. The first (the "Anthem for Christmas") is so given as a mark of respect to the memory of a pioneer musician, now deceased; and the second ("Scenes of Youth"), because a different treatment would seriously interrupt a continuous description which has been so vividly given by a young and talented composer.

The author of "Welcome to the Era March" is less than eighteen years old. The author of "Rays of Hope" has just attained to his majority.

But none of the foregoing statements are made as excuses; nor, on the other hand, is there any intention on the writer's part to present them in a boasting way. The collection of music is submitted to the candid consideration of all music-loving people, with the hope that it may add to their enjoyment, and help to serve the purposes for which this book was prepared.

CONTENTS TO THE MUSIC.

	PAGE
ANTHEM FOR CHRISTMAS (*William Brady*)	4
WELCOME TO THE ERA MARCH (*Jacob Sawyer*)	22
ANDANTE (*Guitar*) (*Justin Holland*)	26
THE PILGRIM (*Overture*) (*J. T. Douglass*)	30
PARISIAN WALTZES (*H. F. Williams*)	44
LE SERMENT DE L'ARABE (*Dramatic Chant*) (*Edmund Dédé*)	53
LA CAPRICIEUSE WALTZ (*Basil Barés*)	60
AU CLAIR DE LA LUNE (*Lucien Lambert*)	69
LAURIETT (*Ballad*) (*H. F. Williams*)	81
LES CLOCHETTES (*Fantaisie Mazurka*) (*Sidney Lambert*)	86
RAYS OF HOPE MARCH (*W. F. Craig*)	96
SCENES OF YOUTH (*Descriptive*) (*F. E. Lewis*)	101
MASS FOR THREE VOICES ("*Gloria*" and "*Agnus Dei*") (*S. Snaer*),	127

ANTHEM FOR CHRISTMAS.

Composed and Arranged by **WM. BRADY. N. Y. 1851.**

ANTHEM FOR CHRISTMAS. Continued.

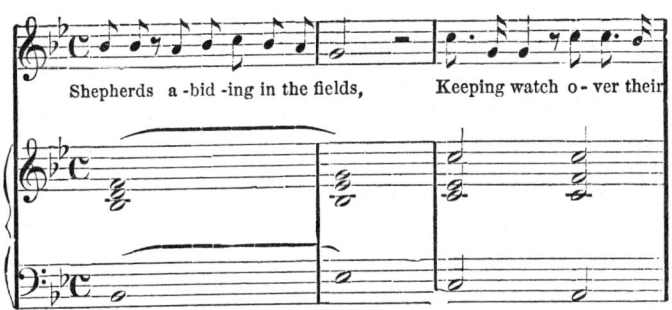

ANTHEM FOR CHRISTMAS. Continued.

ANTHEM FOR CHRISTMAS. Continued. 7

ANTHEM FOR CHRISTMAS. Continued.

ANTHEM FOR CHRISTMAS. Continued,

ANTHEM FOR CHRISTMAS. Continued. 11

12 ANTHEM FOR CHRISTMAS. Continued.

ANTHEM FOR CHRISTMAS. Continued. 13

CHORUS. *Allegretto.*

14 ANTHEM FOR CHRISTMAS. Continued.

ANTHEM FOR CHRISTMAS. Continued. 15

16 ANTHEM FOR CHRISTMAS. Continued.

ANTHEM FOR CHRISTMAS. Continued. 17

ANTHEM FOR CHRISTMAS. Continued. 19

ANTHEM FOR CHRISTMAS. Concluded.

To Miss Florinda J. Ruffin, Boston.

WELCOME TO THE ERA.
MARCH.

J. SAWYER.

Copyright, 1877 by John F. Perry, & Co.   Used by per.

AN ANDANTE.

For the Guitar, by *JUSTIN HOLLAND.*

AN ANDANTE. Continued.

AN ANDANTE. Continued.

Variation.

AN ANDANTE. Concluded.

THE PILGRIM.

GRAND OVERTURE.

Composed by JOHN T. DOUGLASS.

THE PILGRIM. Continued.

THE PILGRIM. Continued.

THE PILGRIM. Continued.

THE PILGRIM. Continued.

THE PILGRIM. Continued.

35

THE PILGRIM. Continued.

THE PILGRIM. Continued.

THE PILGRIM. Continued.

THE PILGRIM. Continued. 39

THE PILGRIM. Continued

THE PILGRIM. Continued. 41

THE PILGRIM. Continued.

cres.

THE PILGRIM. Concluded.

THE PARISIAN WALTZES.

Composed by **H. F. WILLIAMS.**

Copyright, 1867 by Oliver Ditson, & Co.   Used by permission.

46 THE PARISIAN WALTZES. Continued.

No. 3. *Tempo di Valse*

THE PARISIAN WALTZES. Continued.

THE PARISIAN WALTZES. Continued.

THE PARISIAN WALTZES. Continued.

50 THE PARISIAN WALTZES. Continued

THE PARISIAN WALTZES. Continued.

THE PARISIAN WALTZES. Concluded.

LE SERMENT DE L'ARABE.

CHANT DRAMATIQUE.

Paroles de A. DEMARTON.   Musique d' Em. DÉDÉ.

58 LE SERMENT DE L'ARABE. Continued.

LA CAPRICIEUSE.

VALSE.

BASILE BARÈS. Op. 7.

Copyright, 1869, by A. E. Blackmar.   Used by permission.

LA CAPRICIEUSE. Continued. 61

LA CAPRICIEUSE. Continued.

LA CAPRICIEUSE. Continued

LA CAPRICIEUSE. Continued.

LA CAPRICIEUSE. Continued.

Con franchezza.

LA CAPRICIEUSE. Continued.

LA CAPRICIEUSE. Continued.

LA CAPRICIEUSE. Concluded.

AU CLAIR DE LA LUNE.

(VARIATIONS ET FINAL SUR L'AIR.)

LUCIEN LAMBERT. Op. 30.

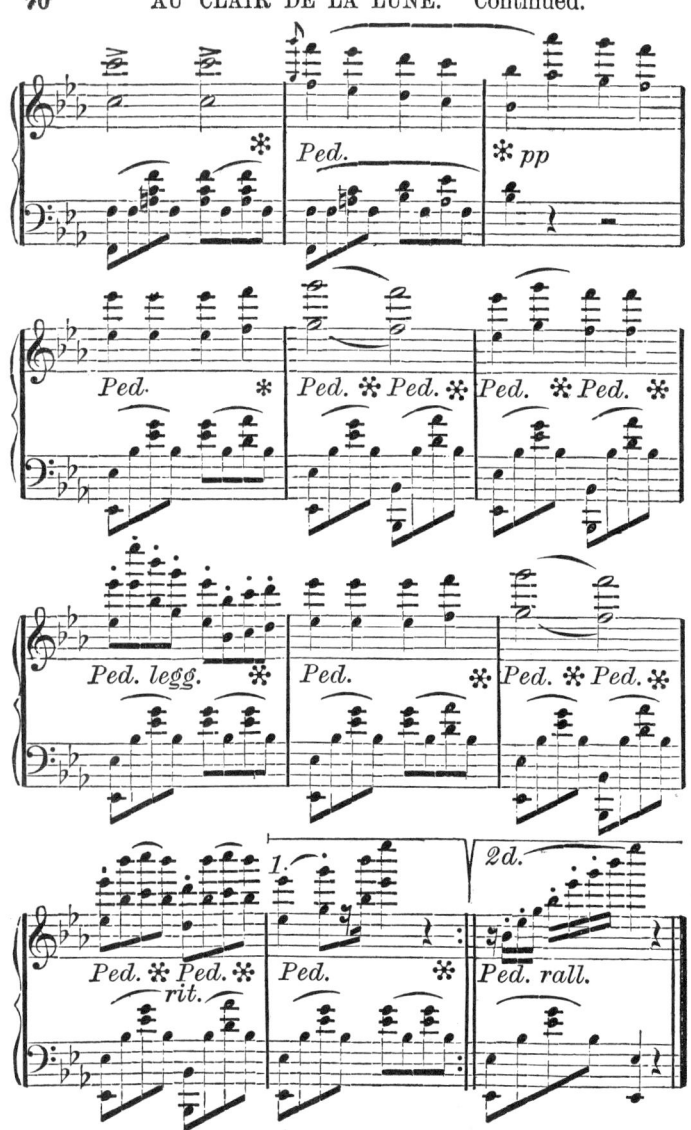

AU CLAIR DE LA LUNE. Continued.

3d Variation

Andante religioso.

AU CLAIR DE LA LUNE. Continued.

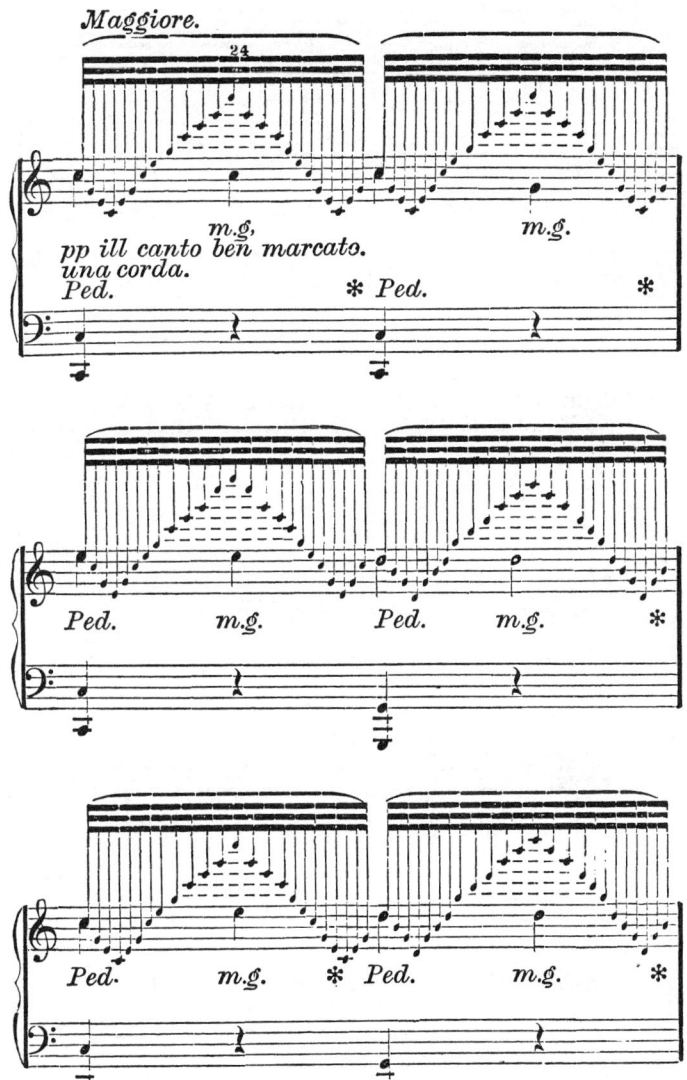

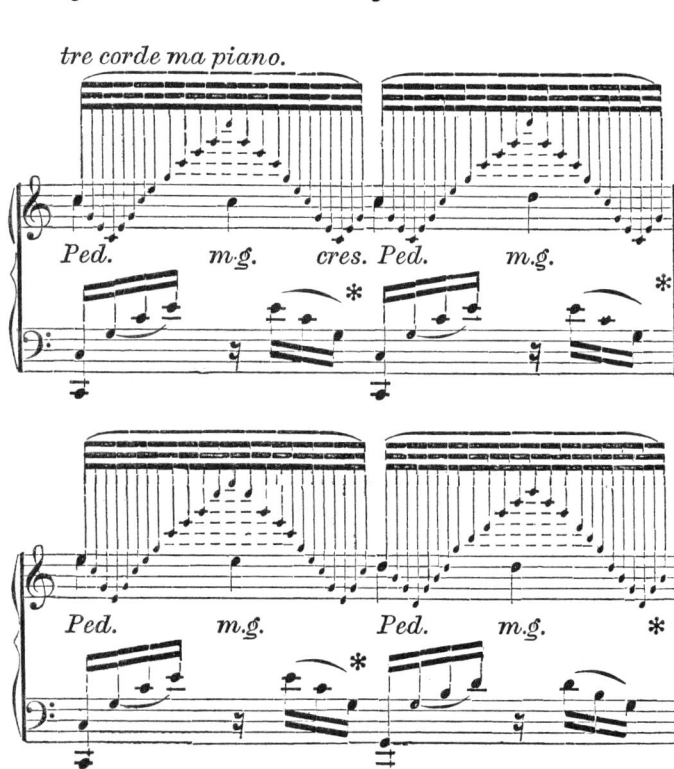

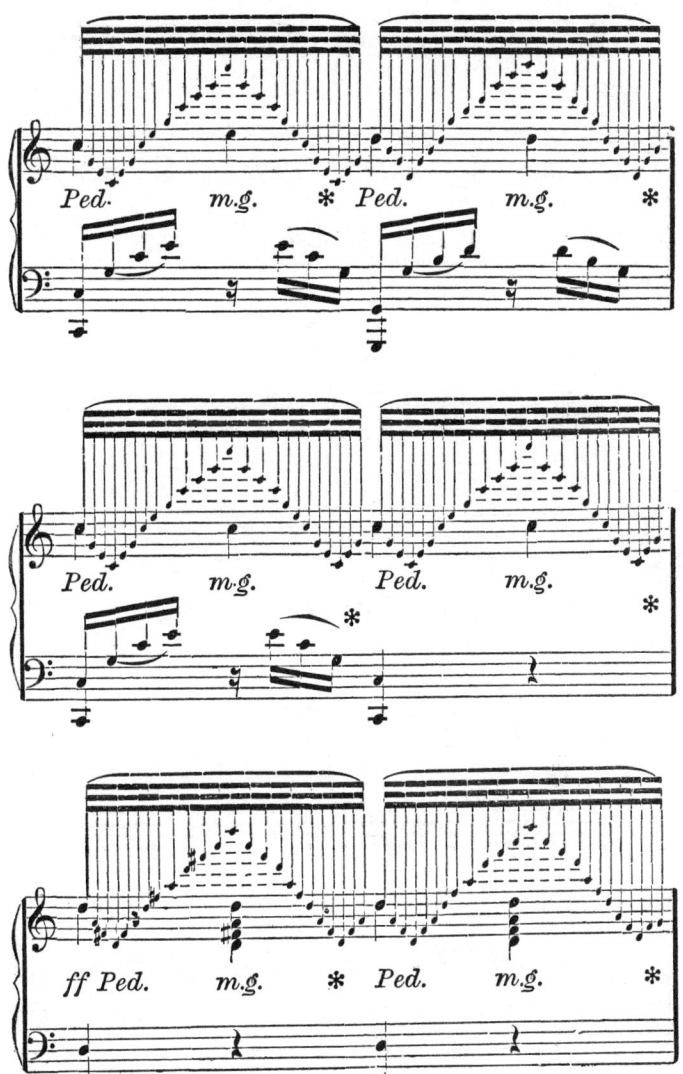

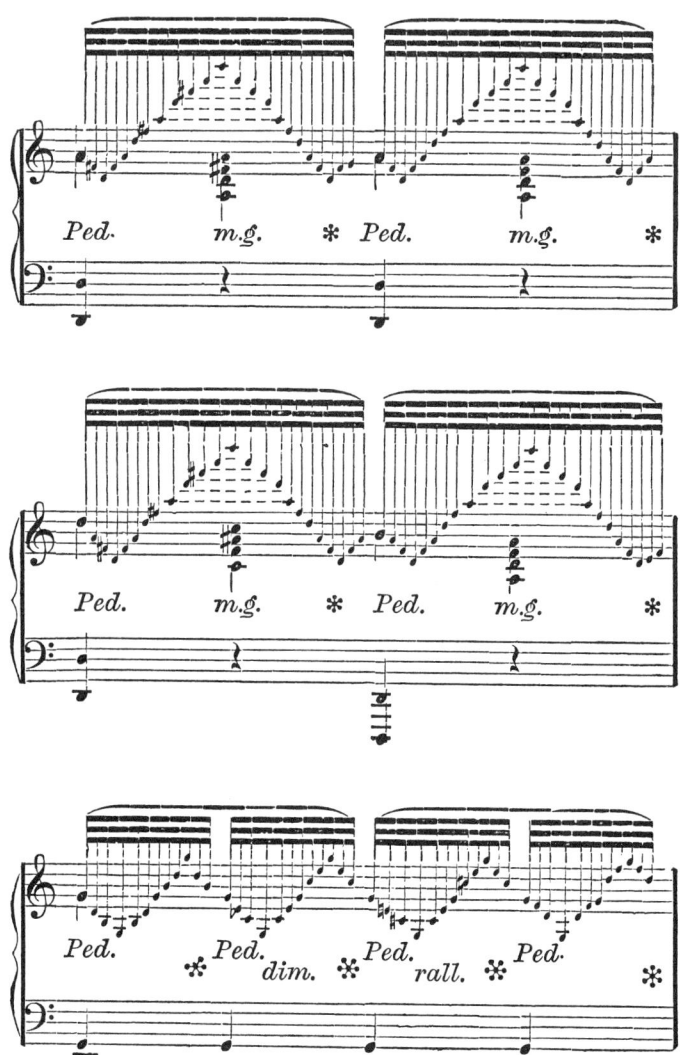

AU CLAIR DE LA LUNE. Continued.

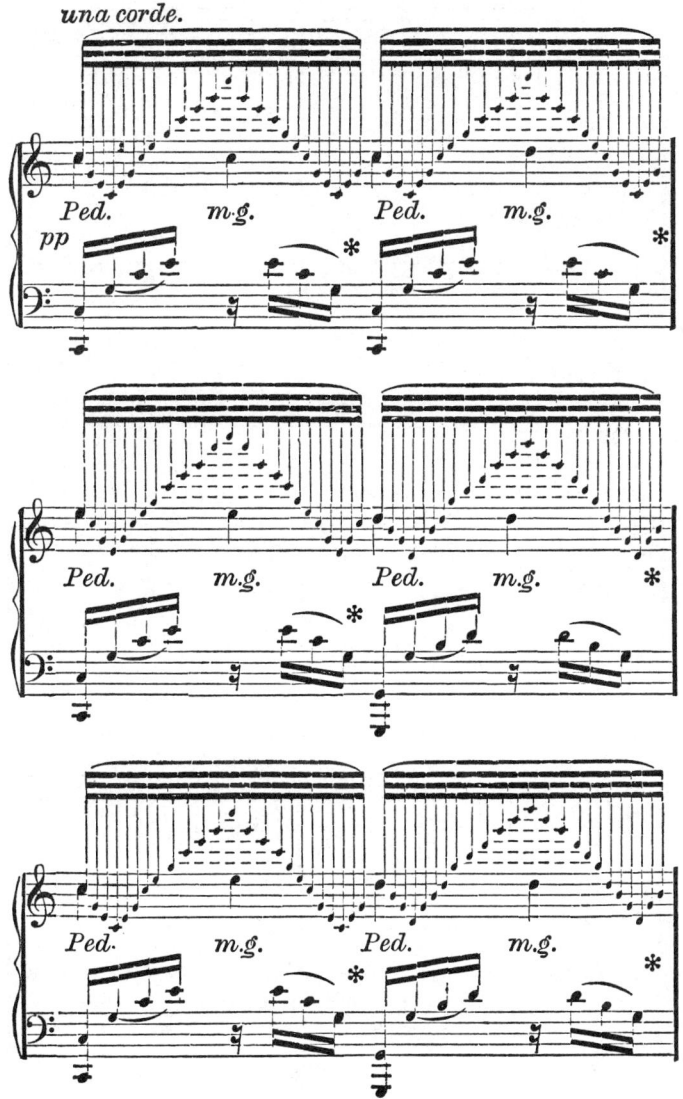

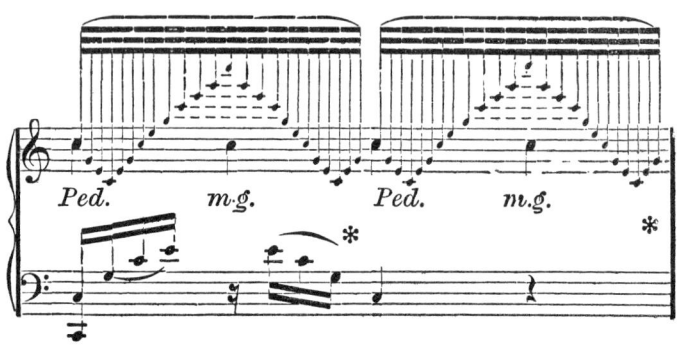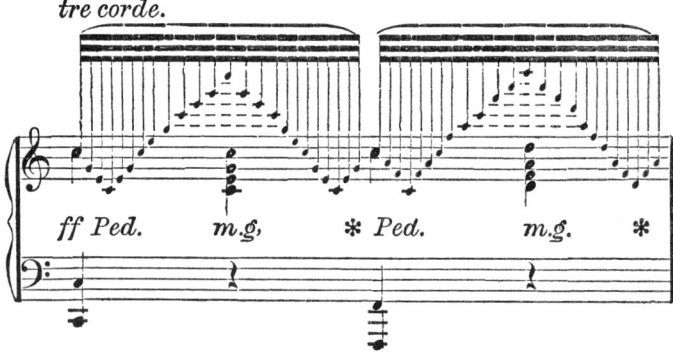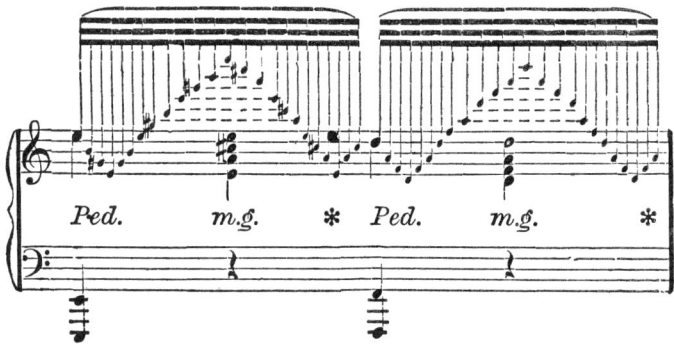

AU CLAIR DE LA LUNE. Continued.

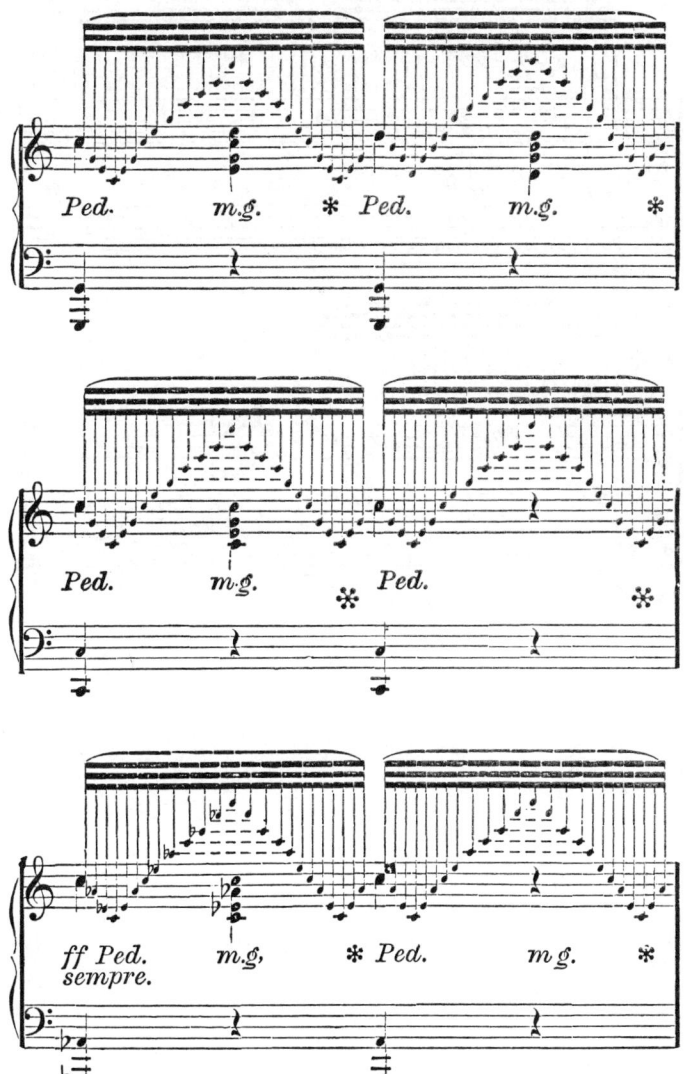

AU CLAIR DE LA LUNE. Continued.

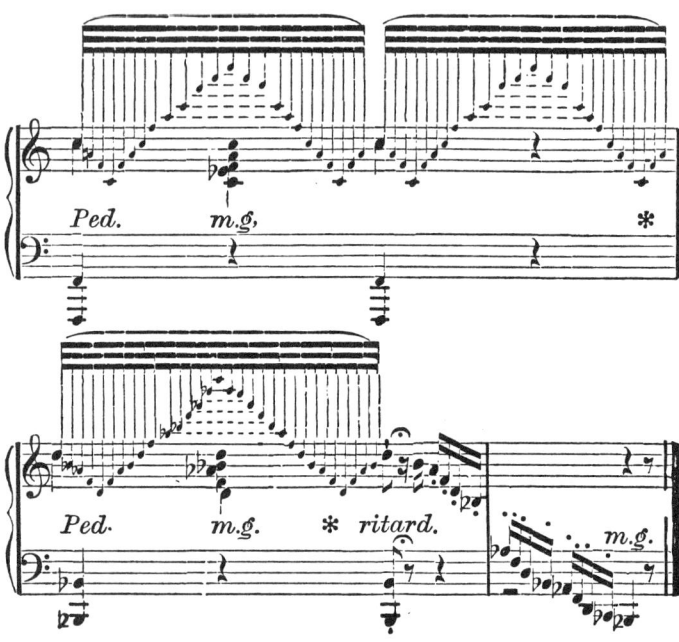

LAURIETT. Continued.

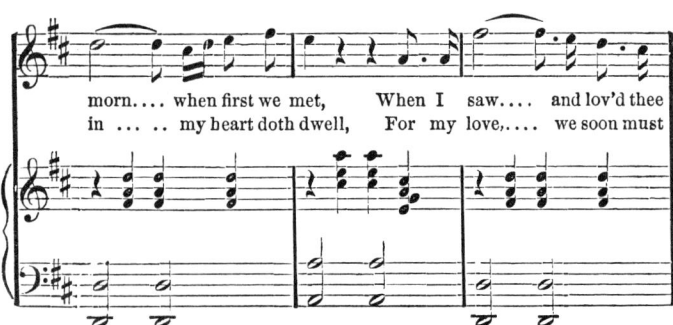

LAURIETT. Continued.

LAURIETT. Continued.

LES CLOCHETTES.

FANTAISIE MAZURKA.

SYDNEY LAMBERT. Op. 9.

Alphonse Leduc. Paris.

LES CLOCHETTES. Continued.

LES CLOCHETTES. Continued.

LES CLOCHETTES. Continued.

LES CLOCHETTES. Continued.

LES CLOCHETTES. Continued.

LES CLOCHETTES. Continued.

LES CLOCHETTES. Concluded.

"RAYS OF HOPE."
MARCH.

Composed by **WALTER F. CRAIG.** Op. 1.

RAYS OF HOPE. Continued.

SCENES OF YOUTH.

FANTAISIA for PIANO

By F. E. LEWIS. Op. 3.

SCENES OF YOUTH. Continued.

104   SCENES OF YOUTH.   Continued.

SCENES OF YOUTH. Continued.

SCENES OF YOUTH. Continued.

SCENES OF YOUTH. Continued.

SCENES OF YOUTH. Continued. 109

SCENES OF YOUTH. Continued.

SCENES OF YOUTH. Continued.

112 SCENES OF YOUTH. Continued.

SCENES OF YOUTH. Continued.

SCENES OF YOUTH. Continued.

SCENES OF YOUTH, Continued. 119

120 SCENES OF YOUTH. Continued.

SCENES OF YOUTH. Continued.

SCENES OF YOUTH. Continued.

SCENES OF YOUTH. Continued.

126 SCENES OF YOUTH. Concluded.

MASS
FOR THREE VOICES.
GLORIA.

By SAMUEL SNAER, New Orleans.

GLORIA. Continued.

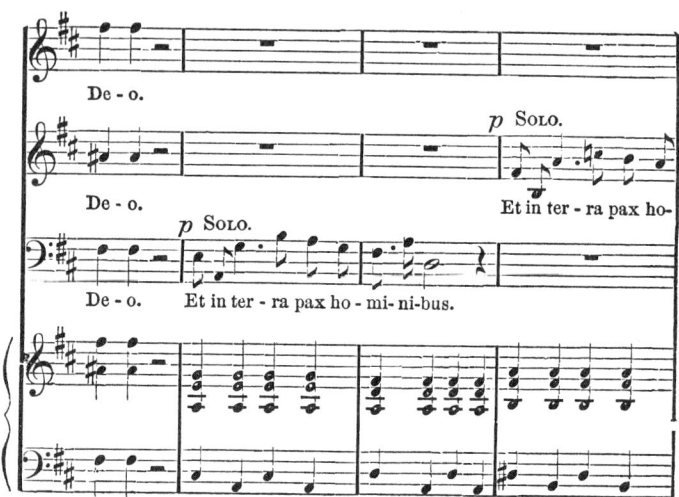

GLORIA. Continued. 129

130 GLORIA. Continued.

GLORIA. Continued.

132 GLORIA. Continued.

GLORIA. Continued.

GLORIA. Continued.

GLORIA. Continued.

136 GLORIA. Continued.

GLORIA. Continued.

GLORIA. Continued.

GLORIA. Concluded.

AGNUS DEI.

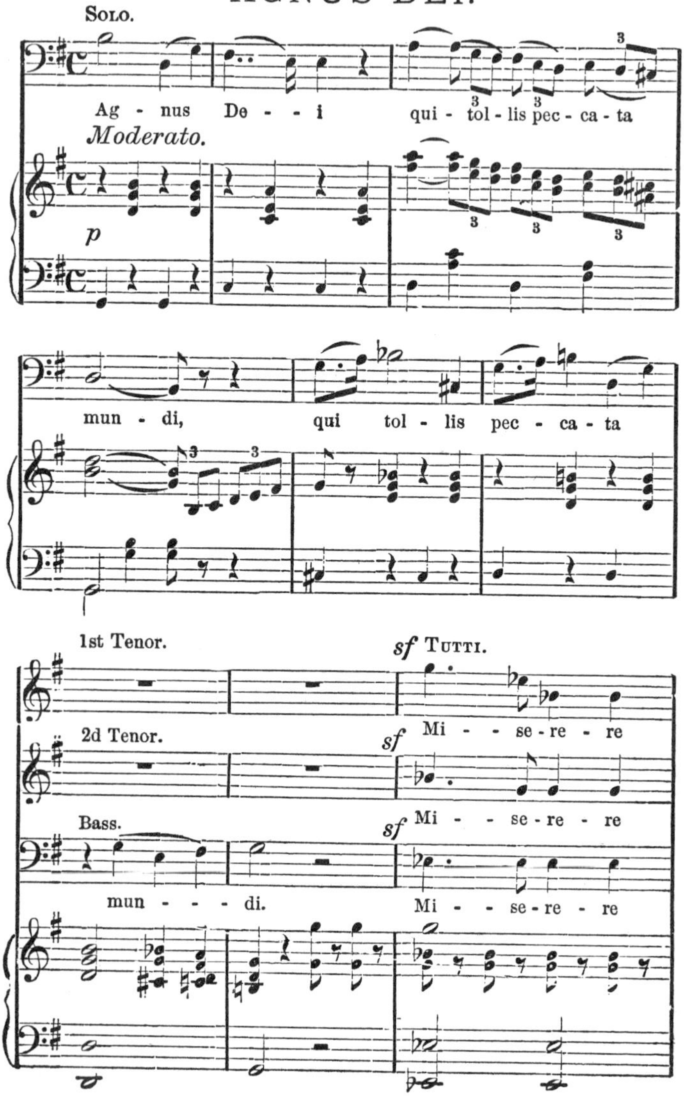
Solo.
Ag - nus De - - i qui - tol - lis pec - ca - ta
Moderato.
p
mun - di, qui tol - lis pec - ca - ta
1st Tenor.
sf Tutti.
Mi - - se - re - re
2d Tenor.
sf Mi - - se - re - re
Bass.
sf Mi - - se - re - re
mun - - - di.

AGNUS DEI. Continued.

143

144 AGNUS DEI. Continued.

AGNUS DEI. Continued.

146　　AGNUS DEI. Continued.

AGNUS DEI. Continued.

AGNUS DEI. Continued.

AGNUS DEI. Continued.

AGNUS DEI. Continued.

AGNUS DEI. Continued.

152 AGNUS DEI. Concluded.

Date Due

CAT. NO. 23 233   PRINTED IN U.S.A.